Ellis Peters has gained universal acclaim for her crime novels, and in particular for *The Chronicles of Brother Cadfael*, now into their eighteenth volume.

'Elegantly spellbinding' *The Sunday Times*

'Ellis Peters writes as well as ever and her many fans are in for another treat' *Today*

Holiday With Violence

Ellis Peters

HEADLINE

First published in 1952
by William Heinemann Ltd

First published in paperback in 1992
by HEADLINE BOOK PUBLISHING PLC

10 9 8 7 6 5 4 3 2 1

ISBN 0 7472 3923 1

Printed and bound in Great Britain by
HarperCollins Manufacturing, Glasgow

HEADLINE BOOK PUBLISHING PLC
Headline House
79 Great Titchfield Street
London W1P 7FN

Holiday With Violence

CHAPTER ONE

INTERESTING JOURNEY OF THE
FIRST-CLASS PASSENGER TO TURIN

(1)

THE train came round the curve of the line just as the long, wavering fingers of the morning reached out from behind the eastern rocks. A reflected light flowed hesitantly over the upper edges of the great ridge which climbed, somewhere to the south, into the spear-guarded bowl of the Aiguilles d'Arves; and the blue of the highest faces of rock flushed suddenly into iris, into rose, into liquid gold, one distant peak grasped firmly in the palm of the Midas-hand, and turned into a chrysolite, a coruscation of flame.

Peter, who had stumbled down the road to this early departure more asleep than awake, now became entirely and enthusiastically wakeful, and when he should have been scouting along the train for a vacant spot in the corridor, clawed out his camera and turned his back squarely on Italy in favour of the dawn on the Grande Chible. The other three, with rucksacks already hoisted on one shoulder, were snuffling along the track like hounds, even before the train had slowed. It looked worse than they had expected. Rows and rows of people standing in the corridors, heads nodding out like large, pale, heavy flowers in window-boxes, every doorway, as it opened, bulging and heaving softly with released humanity; but from all this convulsion of escape only one or two people descended.

'We'll have to shove in anywhere,' said Punch recklessly, and selected what he considered the least congested doorway, and heartily shoved. A babel of excited and inimical French broke over his head, but he was getting used to that; likewise, he no longer expected anyone to budge so much as an inch to let him in. They stood four-square, and one shoved. In this operation, and more particularly in hauling the girls aboard after him, a full-size ex-Commando rucksack was the best ally in the world. Where it passed painfully, Phyllida's slenderness could easily slither after, and Mab was only pocket size, and could practically wriggle in under the elbows of the enemy.

Punch hauled himself between the two plump women who stood in his way, and found a little more breathing space than he had expected. Ample for the four of them. He reached back for Phyllida's brown wrist, and pulled her up after him, and then leaned out for Mab; but she hung back at the last moment to look for Peter. She was always the one who did that, and it always infuriated the other two, who could never get ahead from one place to another fast enough to suit them, and resented having their progress checked by the brake of Peter's incalculable mental aberrations. Punch craned out from the doorway to look where Mab was looking, and there was the irresponsible child, straddling a luggage-trolley far up the long platform, with his camera glued to his eye, and far more interested in the jewelled mountain-tops than in the train to Turin.

Mab shouted, but she was not equipped for shouting against the formidable opposition of a French railway station, and her voice did not reach Peter. He completed his picture, turned his film, appeared to be considering more shots.

2

'Come *on!*' bellowed Punch, observing with misgivings a purposeful human tide which was sliding along the crowded train still questing for space, and washing every moment nearer to their coach.

'He heard you,' said Mab, rather reluctantly suffering herself to be drawn aboard. 'He waved!'

'Well, you get in, at any rate. He can take his chance.'

'He'll be all right,' said Phyllida peacefully. 'He always is. Never knew anybody fall on his feet like Peter does, considering he never looks where he's going.' She heaved a relaxing sigh, and eased her rucksack carefully down from her shoulder, smiling in brilliant but wordless apology upon a large Frenchwoman in a white hat, whose ample hip thrust back against the passing pressure viciously. 'Well, anyhow, we're in!'

Peter arrived on the run, too late by some thirty seconds to find even a toehold beside them. The tide, thinning as it came, had lipped at their doorway just ahead of him, and all they saw of him was a sudden eruption of bright blond hair and an unabashed grin, visible momentarily beyond the heaving shoulders of an entire French family. He gestured forward, shouted something which was lost in the general din, and padded on up the line.

Mab was upset. After all, he was the youngest of the party, and it seemed unkind to let him pile in somewhere on his own. She wriggled arduously towards the doorway.

'I'll go with him, and keep him company.' She meant it sincerely, as she always meant everything she said, but it was quite beyond her power to carry it out, for a strong current was running against her, and the doorway was occupied by two square French sons hoisting their enormous mother aboard.

3

'Like hell you will!' said Punch, holding her back by the arm. 'Don't be such an ass! Once you got out of here you'd never get in again. You stay where you are.'

'But Peter—! And he doesn't even speak French!'

'He doesn't need to,' said Phyllida, without a trace of sisterly anxiety. 'I keep telling you – the luck always sticks to him like jam. Anyhow, when we stop at Modane there'll probably be a long wait, and we shall find him all right then.'

It was reasonable to suppose that Phyllida knew her brother's capabilities, after observing them for seventeen years; but Mab was still uneasy. However, it was too late to do anything about it, for she felt the train already beginning to move again. The doors slammed. The station buildings, fawn and cement-grey as if for protective colouring among the bewildering planes of fawn and grey rocks which rose beyond, slipped slowly by, and dwindled into a single railing. The steel-blue roofs, the hard cream walls, the garden fences heavy with vines, the tall, slender, Italianate church tower, all the precarious Alpine artery of St. Michel-de-Maurienne narrowed and slid away behind.

Now all they could see from the window was a gaunt and stony river valley coiling alongside the track, its small flow of ice-blue mountain water strangled among piled rocks; and beyond it, the great, gaunt, sterile shelves of mountain climbing one beyond another out of sight, lightening from blue to paler blue in the distance, until they reached the direct transmuting sunlight, and became golden. Bonily beautiful, the Alps of Savoy folded themselves into the Alps of the frontier, straining towards Italy and the sun.

It grew warm very quickly in the crowded corridor, and everyone began to shed garments, stuffing the discarded wind-jackets and pullovers under the

4

straps of rucksacks, since there was no elbow-room for packing and unpacking. Periodically, brave and impervious people made an infinitely slow way down the corridor to the end of the coach, stepping over children and luggage, undulating in and out of open doors, squeezing past fat women and emerging beyond them with almost audible pops. Inside the compartments French and Italian family parties had already begun to pack up the portable homes they had brought with them from Paris, the rolls of rugs, the little pillows, the baby's small string hammock for slinging between the luggage racks, the baskets of food and bottles of cider and wine. Mab could just see into the first carriage. The people there looked as if they had lived in it for three weeks rather than merely overnight, and had brought with them everything except the four-poster.

By the time they reached Modane the sun was well up, the sky brilliantly blue, and no cloud in sight. They drew rather suddenly alongside a very long white platform, heavily built over with official-looking sheds and offices, and already extremely populous. Small vociferous men in uniform dashed along the platform shouting unintelligibly, and as soon as the train stopped, every door was flung open, and hundreds of people began to pour out and add themselves to the hundreds already darting uneasily about on the concrete.

'Going to be an empty train,' said Phyllida, flattening herself into a doorway to let the whole population of the corridor flow by her. But her optimism was followed by a shadow of doubt. 'These people can't *all* live on the border. Punch, we don't have to change, do we? You said—'

'Not until Turin,' said Punch very firmly. 'Besides, the people in the compartments aren't budging. But

5

there's something fishy going on, all the same. Can you tell what he's shouting?'

They all listened, but the peculiar shorthand of railway stations was too difficult for them to decipher, in French or in Italian. Punch leaned out of the window, and clutched at a passing porter; and having listened arduously and with a scowl of intense concentration, offered rather damp thanks, and turned glumly to hoist his rucksack.

'Come on, we've got to get out.'

'What, we have got to change, after all?'

'No, we have to find places in this train again afterwards – if there are any by then,' he said dubiously. 'It's the Customs and passport control examination. All those who haven't got seats on the train have to clear the corridor, and go through the Customs sheds on the platform. The lucky devils with seats stay right where they are, and the blokes come to them.'

Disgustedly but hastily they picked up their rucksacks and jumped down, to race along the platform and join the crowd already circling about the sheds. Phyllida, thrusting her wind-jacket under the straps, had almost dislodged the rolled-up fawn raincoat already buckled there, and when she began to run it uncoiled itself, and tried to trip her up. She tugged it clear, and continued to race after the others with the coat draped over her shoulder.

'I bet Peter's right up in front of the queue,' she cried as she ran.

But Peter wasn't. He was leaning out of a window in the train, placidly watching them run, and grinning over his calmly folded arms as they recognised him and pulled up to stare.

'Catching a train?' he asked sweetly.

'You can get out of there,' said Punch, not without

satisfaction, 'and bring your things with you. And better make it nippy, or we shan't even get a toe in the door next time. All those who haven't got seats have got to go through the Customs sheds, and leave the corridors clear.'

'I know,' said Peter, 'but I have got a seat.'

'You have?'

'I've had one all the way. And there are four more in the same carriage. Come on in!'

'What did I tell you?' said Phyllida, beginning to giggle.

Punch had already turned to make a dive at the door of the coach, but at sight of it he halted again suddenly, and frowned up at Peter's bland smile. 'It's a first!'

'So what?' said Peter. 'I didn't notice. And I don't understand French.'

Punch had an arrogant conscience which disdained compromise, even where no rights were concerned except those which he did not acknowledge; but he had also, or conceived that he had, two girls on his hands, and they had been up since five o'clock, and it was a long journey to Turin, and even there they would only have begun the strenuous travels of the day.

'Anybody else in there?' he asked, hesitating.

'One old gentleman. *He's* all right, you don't have to worry about him.'

It was, in fact, too late to hesitate, for Phyllida was already on the train, and Mab was following her loyally. Women, of course, hadn't any consciences at all, and these two had been in league ever since they first went to the same high-school at eleven years old. So Punch hoisted his rucksack after them, and followed resignedly past four full compartments, and into the fifth, whither Peter beckoned them royally.

Two large hide suitcases were piled in the rack over

the corner seat facing the engine, and under them, just looking up at the doorway with some surprise but no displeasure, sat a middle-aged gentleman, nursing a large brief-case against his side. He had a well-kept head of bright, short grey hair, and an innocently interested face, as smooth and pink-and-white as a child's; and his eyes, which wandered with a quick, welcoming intelligence over Phyllida, over Mab, over Punch in turn, were as blue as the sky over Italy.

(2)

Signor Arturo Galassi had been in the train since about eight o'clock the previous evening, and though the weekend journey between Paris and Turin was a mere matter of routine to him, he had never yet learned to sleep through it, and required, as a rule, some amusement beyond books or magazines to get him through it without boredom. Accordingly he had made it his habit to travel third-class when he was not carrying goods for his firm, and to involve himself in the affairs of the people who travelled with him. He liked people. It was an incurable weakness of his to like them, and no amount of disillusionments could teach him sense. In the third-class the company was almost invariably first-class, whereas in the first he had often found it either completely missing on the night train, or regrettably third-class. But this time he carried back from Paris merchandise too precious to be risked; he might even have reserved a whole compartment, and so secured complete privacy and absolute boredom, but for the consideration that such a step would only call attention to the nature of his charge. The risk among the poor, voluble and gay in the cheap coaches was, mark you, one in which he himself did not believe, and he would have taken his own valuables among them without a qualm; but the firm were nervous about their property, and in protecting it he punctiliously observed their standards, not his own.

At six-thirty in the morning, therefore, after ten hours on the train, Signor Galassi was feeling the want of human companionship; when suddenly the door of his compartment was opened by an insinuating hand, and the hand followed by a long, slim brown arm, and then a very young and demure face, several shades darker gold from the sun than the tow-coloured hair above it. The boy looked at him, not so directly as to catch his eye, which was willing to be avoided lest it should scare him away, but sufficiently sharply to find him harmless; and then came in jauntily but gently, very circumspect and adult in defiance of his attire, which was not calculated to add any years to his appearance or sophistication to his bearing, consisting as it did of a short-sleeved plaid shirt open at the neck, a pair of very short corduroy shorts, and a pair of sandals composed of the minimum of straps possible.

With grave deliberation he deposited in the rack an ex-Army rucksack, studded with badges, and dangling a pair of formidable climbing boots which bristled with triple hobs and grinned with clinkers; laid beside it a very new-looking camera in a leather case, and his khaki wind-jacket; and went neatly to sleep in the corner seat beneath them, with the aplomb of a bored puppy. Or perhaps this was strategy rather than sleep, at least for the first five minutes; but after that it was certainly genuine, for after that the soft, light snores began.

Signor Galassi let him sleep. Now at least he had

9

someone on whom to exercise his mind after the stale-ness of the night; and there was surely no need to take defensive action against a stray English boy of about seventeen. Many Italians would have said American, being used to the idea that all who spoke English belonged to the dominant race; but Signor Galassi was not deceived. The rucksack, for one thing, was ex-English-Army, the climbing boots were something the Americans seldom sported, or at any rate seldom used, and these had been used a good deal, for the hobs were worn flat in the middle of the sole, and the uppers very much scratched. But the small material evidences were hardly needed. It was an English face, an English manner of intruding, not without grace for all its impudence; and besides, if he had been American he would probably, indeed almost certainly, have had a first-class ticket, whereas his dignified and austere entrance had made it quite clear that he possessed no such thing.

Signor Galassi liked having someone young and per-sonable on whom to exercise his imagination. This boy would be still at school, he judged. Some student spend-ing his summer holiday wandering about the mountains of Savoy and Italy; and what could be better? His own son was just turned seventeen, at much the same stage as this; and his daughters were in the early twenties; and if he had a decided preference for one kind of human creature rather than another, it was the young he liked best.

The boy slept firmly and placidly until Modane, and then awoke as promptly as he had fallen asleep, and got up and went out into the corridor to lean forth from the window. Presently there were several young voices exclaiming together; one of the newcomers had scruples about making use of a first-class coach, the tow-headed sprig had none. Signor Galassi smoothed out the smile from his face as they trooped in. He spoke excellent English, but there was no need to advertise the fact that he had also excellent hearing.

Four of them altogether. The first, a tall, slender, lively girl, shaped like the blond boy and not unlike him in features, but with darker eyes, and masses of dark hair. Maybe a year or two his elder. She heaved her rucksack into the rack beside Signor Galassi's cases, tossed her raincoat carelessly in between, so that it dangled a foot or so of its skirts from the rack, and sat down with a sigh of relief, and stretched all her spare but graceful body with a sensuous delight. Then she yawned; she was tired, too, maybe they had had to get up very early and come down by bus out of the mountains to catch the train at St. Michel. He wondered to what part of Italy they were bound now.

The second was a very slight little girl of much the same age, a dainty, grave person as fair as a primrose. Her features were extremely serious and rather irregular, her eyes heavily lashed, and of the deep colour of wood violets. But for her colouring, and the beautifully neat shape of the head which her short, soft cap of smooth hair set off so severely, he supposed she was really quite plain; but it did not matter. One would look at her a second time to sense the texture of the fine, pale hair, and a third time to remark that her mouth was set slightly on one side, and after that one would go on looking simply because by that time it would have become a pleasure.

And the last member of the party was the young man with the conscience, and probably, though not by more than a year or two, the eldest of them. That did not make him very old, say nearly twenty, Francesca's age. He was a big, brown young thing, with russet forehead

11

and emphatic nose, and his brown hair was cropped rather severely short, probably because it showed an over-exuberant tendency to curl when given its head. At the end of his muscular brown legs stuck out deep-cut rubber climbing boots, compared with which the blond boy's clinkered ones looked almost diminutive. Signor Galassi's blue eyes lingered on them with fascinated delight, for he had never had time to be a climbing man himself; but the young man, observing the hypnotised gaze, unexpectedly blushed, and tucked his impressive feet as far as possible under the seat. To tuck them completely out of sight was quite impossible. No doubt he was wishing he had draped those boots through the straps of his rucksack, like his friend, and worn his sandals for travelling.

Signor Galassi was annoyed with himself for allowing his interest to embarrass the boy, and shifted his gaze hastily; but he could not resist stealing a glance up at the rack, to see what kind of footgear the girls carried. Their side pockets bulged with knobbly shoes – they would not have held boots – but he could not see more of them than their shape through the canvas. Regarding the two pairs of small, sandalled feet, a little dusty already with travel, he saw that even with a liberal allowance of nails thrown in, their walking shoes would not look very daunting.

They settled themselves firmly back in the deep cushions, and looked at one another with guilty but gleeful looks, thinking of the suffering, sweating mob round the Customs sheds. And at that moment fortune assisted Signor Galassi to the tune of a long and distorted stream of French over the loudspeaker system of the station. The four invaders started and pricked their ears like nervous colts, trying to distinguish words, and failing.

'What did he say?' asked the dark girl, turning with

12

ardent confidence towards the elder boy, who seemed, so far as the party owned a leader, to be in charge of the expedition.

'I couldn't tell, the amplifier's dinning like mad.'

'Do you suppose it was anything to do with us?'

Signor Galassi said, in very gentle, exact English: 'Another train comes, that is all. It is not for us. Now we must only wait, and have ready our passports.'

They all turned to gaze at him with round, pleased eyes, as if he had said something brilliant. He blushed modestly, looking under his lowered eyelashes at them, like a complimented child.

'Oh, thank you!' said the dark girl, delighted with him. She was not, like her brother, an insinuating diplomat, but as direct and wild as a young filly, and every bit as friendly and inquisitive, gazing at him with large, clear eyes of a purplish brown, like a certain kind of pansy. 'You speak English!' she said; as if he had worked a minor miracle.

'Not well,' said Signor Galassi deprecatingly, 'but I speak it.' His innocent eyes, absolved of too offensive a curiosity, went over her with candid friendliness, over them all as warmly, took in their scanty luggage and sunburned foreheads and legs. 'You come to spend your holiday in my country?' he asked, settling hopefully half-round in his corner seat, to make a more exact segment in their circle.

'Yes,' said the dark girl, glowing. 'At least, we've had one week of it already, in Savoy, but we're coming to Italy for another eight days. Then Punch – that's Punch, because of his nose, you know—!' Her hand indicated the elder boy and his most striking feature in one airy wave. '—Punch has to go back. He's an architect, or going to be one, and he only has a fortnight holiday. But in any case, I don't suppose any of us will have

13

any money left by then, not more than enough to take us home.' She settled her hands in her lap, in the folds of her grey flannel skirt, with a sudden resigned, confessional grace, and said disarmingly: 'Of course, you realised from the first moment we haven't any right to crash into your carriage. We've only got third-class tickets. But it seemed such a fag going through the Customs on the station – there are so many people, and we're not so frightfully good at French, and we don't speak a word of Italian. It must seem frightful cheek of us, butting in like this. But if we're annoying you, we'll go away as soon as the passport men have been through – really!'

'Oh, please!' protested Signor Galassi, releasing his large brief-case for a moment to wave away the suggestion with both ageing white hands. 'Am I looking annoyed? Please, you shall stay here, and rest. The train is too crowded in the third class. And here is room to spare. The thing could not be simpler. If you travel through the day you will be very tired. Sit, then, while it is possible.'

Of course, she had never been worried for a moment about his answer; he knew that, and she was aware of his knowledge, and smiled without shame. 'You're very kind! We are a bit sleepy, because we had to start off very early this morning, and walk down to St. Michel from le Vigny.'

'And in Savoy you have climbed mountains?' His eyes were on the magnetic boots again, respectfully, but not enviously, admiring their air of weathered accomplishment. And now that he had accepted the whole company with such reckless generosity, they were all turning a little towards him, and settling back comfortably into the cushions, and opening their elusive and inscrutable young faces to him like buds under the

14

sunshine, laying aside their reserve as they had laid aside their wind-jackets.

'Well, yes – at least, we did some fairly tough scrambles, but nothing you could really call climbing. We've never tried any rock-climbing yet. We've been about three thousand metres, that's the highest.'

To Signor Galassi it sounded quite high enough to justify the note of pride, almost of astonishment, in her voice. 'And you enjoyed that?' he asked earnestly; not doubting it, merely zealous to understand fully the allure of those grey, bony and inhospitable places to which the twentieth-century young seemed to elevate themselves with so much effort and so little reward.

'Oh, *yes!* We were above the snow two or three times – only patches of snow over the streams in the gullies there, but quite a lot of it. And then one day we actually walked into a snow-storm up on the Grande Chible. It was terrific!'

'In Italy,' said Signor Galassi regretfully, 'we shall have no snow to offer you, unless you will go very far north in the Tyrol. I am sorry!'

'Oh, but we're looking for the sun, too. It's all the same. The snow was just thrown in, to make it more interesting. We're just trying to get as much into our holiday as possible, while it lasts,' she explained for them all.

'You are, perhaps, students? In those days, of course,' he said punctiliously, 'when you are not mountaineers!'

'Yes, more or less,' she agreed, acknowledging his small joke with a flashing grin. 'My name's Phyllida Thorne, I'm a librarian, so is Mab – Mab Isherwood! We room together. Punch I've told you about already; his other name's Hazlitt. And Peter is my brother. He's just on his last year of school, and then he's going to study to be a veterinary surgeon.'

'You are, then, in flight from books for a little while,' he said comprehendingly, and smiled his bright, confederate smile, at once indulgent and wistful. 'I do not climb, but to look at some new place, that I like, that is good. And you will like Italy. Do you go to the high mountains here, also? To the Dolomites, perhaps?'

'Not exactly,' said Punch. 'We're going more to the south, to a tiny little place in the Trentino, up north of Lake Garda. It's called Rocca della Sera. I was there once with a school party, and I always wanted to go back. There's nothing there, it's just a village, but there are some grand walks, and if we get very energetic we can go up into the Brenta Group, and have a go at Cima Tosa, or something. Then maybe we'll come down into Verona, or Padua, or even as far as Venice, if the money holds out.'

'Ah!' said Signor Galassi, beaming, 'the Trentino I know, though your village I do not know. There north of Garda you will get good wine very cheap. And fruit – very good peaches, not so large as in the south, but a better flavour. There is also very beautiful country, you will like it.'

'Oh, yes!' agreed Phyllida, with shining eyes. 'Punch has done nothing but talk about it ever since he was there last time. It was his idea that we should come back for part of our holiday. You should see the maps he's collected for the job! A military expedition couldn't be better equipped. Show him, Punch!'

Punch, a shade pinker than normal, but complacent, hauled them out of his map pocket, and spread them obligingly over his knees, underlining Rocca della Sera with a blunt brown finger. All five eager heads bent devotionally over the magic pictures, conjuring out of the contours and curves a delightful future. All their tongues were going nineteen to the dozen when the guard came down the corridor almost unnoticed, and hung in at the open door of the compartment to gaze at them with some astonishment and more misgiving. Punch, who was nearest as well as most susceptible of the four, felt the pervasive presence suddenly chilling him, and grew guiltily silent. Signor Galassi, observing the guard's experienced eye roving knowledgeably over their hobnails and rucksacks, looked at him appealingly over the urgently preoccupied heads, and frowned, and shook his head with an almost imperceptible gesture of deprecation. The guard took the hint, and as inscrutably as his gaze had moved over them, it now moved away; and so did he, towards the rear of the train.

They were drawing breath after his departure, and all competing to meet Signor Galassi's bright, pleased eyes, when a warning voice gave tongue in slurred French along the corridor.

'Ah, the passport control!' said Signor Galassi, evading thanks and pretending that he was not a conspirator. 'You have ready your passports? Here will be new stamps for you, the exit from France, and then the entrance into Italy at Bardonecchia. Now we progress! Are you not already bored that nothing happens, when in the Trentino you have so much to do?'

They folded away the maps, and fished out their passports, which were presently collected in the doorway by an abrupt little official of the French Customs service, who matched up each face with the accompanying photograph in one swooping glance, and thereupon turned down the whole bundle, ready opened, over the window-rail; whence a second, younger and gayer official in Italian uniform, with a roving eye for the two girls, but no time to indulge it, presently retrieved them, stamped them, and handed them in to Punch to distribute to their owners. It was all over in a few minutes. Of Customs examination proper there was no sign, except a nod to Signor Galassi, who was known on this line, and a casual disdainful glance along the row of rucksacks in the rack.

'They always do that,' explained Phyllida, when the voices and footsteps had both been cut off short by the closing of the door at the end of the coach. 'You get used to it. They all take it for granted that people who carry rucksacks and walk can't possibly have anything on them worth examining.'

'How can they?' said Punch reasonably. 'No money!'

'No, but it might not be beyond the brains of smugglers to see the possibilities of an automatic reaction like that. For all they know,' said Phyllida, waving an airy hand towards her rucksack, 'that might be bulging with heroin, or cocaine, or diamonds – whatever the stock line is, these days.'

'I think perhaps,' said Signor Galassi, with an indulgent smile, 'they look also at faces, when they regard so disdainfully those little knapsacks.'

'And I don't look the kind of person to have a bag full of contraband diamonds about me?' she asked wistfully.

'No, you have not that look. But of course,' he admitted, the nice smile crinkling the corners of his eyes, 'there is no rule, how to be sure of that.'

Punch, still seeking to improve the occasion while opportunity offered, said seriously: 'You know, there's only one snag about this village of ours. It's well off the tourist track, and there won't be anybody there – at least, there won't be many – who can speak English. And we've got a few words from grand opera, and two rather dated phrase-books between us.'

'But you have already managed there once,' said Signor Galassi.

18

'Oh, no, not really. We were a gang of kids, we had someone in charge of us, and didn't have to worry about any of the practical part of it. He was an awful dope, really,' said Punch, with the relentless judgment of youth, 'but he was *there*. This time we've got to fend for ourselves. Oh, we'll do it all right, I know that. But I wondered – if you wouldn't mind – could you tell us the words for some of the things the phrase-books forget to put in?'

Signor Galassi lay back in his corner and laughed with such goodwill that it was obvious he did not mind in the least; and in a moment they were all fishing out envelopes, diaries, the fly-leaves of their despised phrase-books, to write down carefully the words he dictated to their orders. Mab, the small, serious, silent one, suddenly leaned forward eagerly to speak for the first time, and her voice was equally diminutive, definite and solemn as she said: 'Would you believe it, neither of them tells you how to ask for a cup of tea?'

They all laughed immoderately, for it was rather as if she had gone out of her way to hang a label upon her Englishness. As if the fineness of her bones, the fair hair and immense gravity were not enough to identify her in any country! But Signor Galassi told her gently and carefully what she wanted to know, and she wrote down in the back of her diary, unabashed: *Una tazza di tè*, and furrowed her brow after the next query.

The lesson was in full spate, and all the pencils at work, and all the young tongues protruding, when the train began to move. Everybody had been too busy to notice the scurrying return of the passengers from the Customs sheds, since they passed by to invade the third-class coaches, and made little stir in this privileged place. But now Peter suddenly raised his head to see the long grey station sliding by and melting into tall,

19

dark-green slopes of trees and white faces of rock. The fingers of the mountains, closing again gently after the relaxed half-hour at Modane, stroked the train as it passed, as if an amused giant played with it and wished it no harm.

'We're away!' said Peter, tilting his cheek against the window to see the sky, which was receding almost from sight, a narrow ceiling to the lofty green corridor.

It was at that precise moment that the guard re-appeared in the doorway, looking a little wooden, a little severe. He avoided Signor Galassi's eye, and said firmly: 'Tickets, please!' Everyone recognised the purpose of the request, but, after all, they had had their rest and escaped the scramble outside, and had no complaints to make. Punch fished out the tickets resignedly, and listened to the polite gambit, which was phrased in French he had no difficulty in understanding: 'These tickets are for the *second-class, monsieur*—'

Peter made a face at Signor Galassi, and said: 'Here it comes!' in the undertone used by schoolboys in order to be heard, but not distinctly, by sensitive and suspicious pedagogues.

'I know!' said Punch. 'We haven't any right here, but we wanted to sit through the Customs inspection, and this gentleman was very kind, and let us. OK, it's all right, we'll go now.' He stood up, and hooked a hand through the straps of his rucksack; but not hurrying the process too much, in case the passenger could again raise one eyebrow and effectively remove the qualms of officials. And Signor Galassi, with a hurt and astonished air, was already trying. The young people were guests in the country, their first visit; he had no objection whatever to their presence, indeed he liked it, and desired that it should continue; and surely, when there was room to spare, and the third-class already crowded—

The guard shrugged, repeatedly, helplessly, and talked double as fast as before, so that he might as well have been talking Greek for all Punch understood of it.

'I am sorry!' said Signor Galassi, spreading his hands in distress. 'It is not his fault, he does only his duty. There is some passenger has observed you and made a complaint, so he cannot help it, he *must* take some action. He does not wish to do it. He says that he regrets, but it is his occupation, you see.'

'Oh, it doesn't matter,' Punch said, heaving the rucksack down. 'Of course we'll go. That's all right. Don't worry about us, we've had a good rest, and got out of that shindy, and learned something, too. You've been very kind. Thanks for everything!'

'But I am very sorry! I also regret it. I would have been happy if you could have stayed with me, to travel to Turin in comfort. I am desolated!' And he actually looked it. Phyllida was quite touched by his disappointment, and felt warmly towards herself for being even a fourth part of the reason for it. She gave him her nicest smile as she hauled down her rucksack and wind-jacket, and hoisted them on to one shoulder.

'Don't bother a bit about us, we shall be OK. *Addio, e mille grazie!*'

He looked surprised and pleased at that, and they all echoed it loyally as they lugged their packs out into the corridor, to divert his mind for a moment at any rate from the frustration of his good intentions, and fix it gratefully upon the excellence of his teaching. They were already fond of him, and didn't like him to be hurt. Mab looked back through the window to catch the last glimpse of him, and saw him sitting back resignedly in his corner, drawing the curtain across the window against the slanting light of the sun, and closing his eyes.

'Well, anyhow,' she thought, looking on the brighter side of things with her usual determination, 'he wouldn't have been able to get any sleep with us pestering him. Now it will be quiet for him.'

She followed the others stumbling and swaying along the corridor, and through the roaring junction of the coaches into the hot, resilient mass of humanity in the third-class; and at that moment the train rushed into the mouth of the Mont Cenis tunnel, and the daylight dwindled abruptly into so many dim pinpoints of light. Just enough light to see the darkness by.

Back in the first-class compartment, Signor Galassi sighed, got up, and turned out the lights, so that only the faintest gleam came in from the corridor. Since he was deprived of his young and disarming company, he might as well sleep until the train reached Turin, and here was his opportunity to begin. He sat back, felt out with his left hand for the brief-case which nestled against his side, and then, satisfied with the close touch of it, folded his plump but shapely hands over his stomach, and composed himself for rest. Seven and a half miles through the tunnel; at the end of that timely darkness it would take more than a stray shaft of sunlight between the blinds to wake him.

(3)

When they steamed out into the bright sunlight again on the other side of the divide, they were in a different world. Savoy, with its harsh outlines, its neutral colours, and wild, mobile, subtle shadows, was gone like a dream. In the station at Bardonecchia, Punch craned between his fellow-passengers to flatten his cheek against the window and gaze upward at

22

a flaunting slope of conifers, brilliant in a hundred different greens. Sunlight gilded even the stones. The grass dazzled. The sky was blue as delphiniums. All the austere, dissolving monochromes of the French Alps were burned out in a single astonishing explosion of colour.

All the way down the fabulous Valley of Susa, while the train coiled downhill by its shelf along one slope, they dodged and twisted hungrily among their neighbours to stare at Italy. The great valley, embracing villages, small towns, viaducts, rivers, waterfalls, with a beautiful, frank delight in its own lavish exuberant loveliness, spread itself before them in a thousand prodigal colours, plunging downhill by many half-seen terraces, rising beyond by as many more, through planes of trees and cliffs of rosy rock, to distant creamy summits on the skyline, cool against the bright, excited blue. Deep in the green valley, little towns made punctuation points with their hot reds and gay whites, lifting the slender tapered towers and spires of their churches joyously high into the air. The mountains hung enormous over these tiny communities, and they were not in the least abashed. They spread their red roofs to the sun, and were as unconcerned with their ant-like smallness as are the ants.

The train stopped at a few larger stations, and more people got in. Fat priests and thin priests – there never seemed to be any in between the two extremes – in shovel hats, and cassocks so long that even their feet were obscured; sometimes accompanied by stringy little Boy Scouts in shorts so abbreviated that they made even Peter's look like Army issue; old countrywomen with draped heads and rush baskets; middle-aged country-women bare-legged and bare-headed, in printed silk dresses strained tightly over opulent breasts; young

23

girls in elegant cottons of cunningly simple cut, walking resplendently. They all wedged themselves smilingly, good-humouredly, into the already crowded corridors, and Punch and his companions, flattening themselves with indrawn breath to allow the newcomers to get aboard, were nevertheless washed gradually from their holds into the quaking darkness between the coaches; until the tide flooded in from the sun-drenched platforms in a higher wave, and swept them clean through into the corridor of the first-class coach.

Peter, drawing breath passionately, lugged himself through into a sunny emptiness, squared his elbows along the edge of the open window, and applied his camera firmly to his eye; he had been angling in vain for a clear view of the Valley of Susa for half an hour, and had no intention of being dislodged from it again. Punch followed gratefully into the light, the girls after him. The bright, vacant corridor rocked in front of their eyes, washed with sun as far as the closed door at the other end, close beside the compartment where Signor Galassi slumbered. They looked in that direction, and smiled to think of him.

With the door shut behind them, it grew cool and quiet there. No one stirred about the coach, except a square-built, black-moustached man in the dark grey uniform of the Customs service, who was sitting on a small bracket seat at the end of the coach, beside the door which had just swung to from Phyllida's hand. He looked them all over with quick, surprised black eyes, and then got up from his place, and went to lean upon the window-rail at Phyllida's elbow.

They were passing along a high shelf in the side of the valley, which widened steadily away from under them with a small town in its green, bright heart, and the forested slope beyond as remote and gaily coloured as a backcloth, soaring into a single rounded peak against the sky. In the valley the pattern of fields was exact and crowded as a new patchwork quilt, varicoloured and of many textures. Even far up the slopes, to the rim of the cliffs where only trees could cling, every acre of land which could be induced to bear a crop was triumphantly bearing one, terraced into small contoured fields of rippling shapes, tufted with corn, tasselled with maize, coloured in vivid fresh greens. Beyond the field level went the vineyards, flattened against the slope in the full gold of the climbing sun, built into narrow, irregular segments within grey drystone walls; and beyond these the perpendicular but persistent forests, and the faces of sheer rock, drier and whiter than in France, and the sky above all, the eye plunging into blue from the summit of the rock, like a swimmer into a pool.

Phyllida, staring in delight across this fairy-tale landscape, felt a touch upon her hand, and looked down in some surprise to find a strong, square-nailed fingertip resting there. Having arrested her attention, it indicated the little town with a gentle gesture, and the Customs officer said in her ear: 'Chiomonte!'

The word could have meant anything, but she understood that he was telling her what the town was called, and was childishly pleased to find that it bore a name as charming as its appearance. She turned to smile at him, nodding her vehement comprehension and thanks. He was not the same man who had stamped their passports at Modane, but one of the black, square, thick-set Italians, of whom she had seen so many in this one morning that as yet they all looked alike to her. Rather a dapper person, who valued himself upon his appearance; his black hair was immaculately flattened, his hands well-kept, and the bold moustache he cultivated would have been much admired in the

25

R.A.F. He looked upon Phyllida, as young and even not so young men frequently did, with candid pleasure, and went on earning her attention by giving the rosy-white cone on the skyline a name in its turn. The Rocca something-or-other! She promptly forgot it again, but did not forget to thank him for it with a dazzling smile. Phyllida was not averse to being admired.

They began a conversation which afterwards turned out to be almost invariable in the first stages of Phyllida's acquaintance with the Italian male. He said something about the scenery – so much she recognised – in slow and coaxing tones, unsure how far she could follow him. She shook her head regretfully, and treated him to her most accomplished sentence: '*Siamo inglesi – non so parlare Italiano.*' It slid from her tongue so lightly, from constant rehearsal, that it was not easy to believe it, and he thereupon smiled on her with a great flash of white teeth from ambush, and made what she easily understood to be the polite rejoinder: 'But the signorina speaks Italian very well!'

Peter, deflecting his gaze for a moment from the lavish glories of the Valle di Susa, reached out a foot to kick Punch on the ankle, and call his attention to the international idyll proceeding a couple of yards away from them. He had seen much the same gambit already many times in English.

Aloud he said, as brazenly as if he had been merely remarking upon the spectacle outside the window, and with much the same intonation: 'Doesn't our Phyl shoot a nice line? She'll have him kissing her hand before we get to Turin.'

Punch, scandalised, muttered: 'Shut up, you ass!'

'Oh, it's all right,' said Peter airily. 'If he could speak it, he'd be speaking it. He won't be any the wiser. And as for her, don't you worry, it takes more than this to

26

cramp her style, once she's got going. You don't know yet what you've taken on!'

She had, indeed, observed his diversionary tactics, and found no difficulty in ignoring them. She went on memorising the names of places and mountains, and trying to use the instructions of Signor Galassi. The Customs man, obviously, travelled back and forth to the frontier on these trains, and had now nothing left to do but amuse himself until they entered Turin, and if she could enliven the already fascinating time still more with his help, she was not going to be put off by her whipper-snapper of a brother. She turned a placid shoulder on Peter and an animated face on the Customs man, and went on trying to say: 'We are in Italy for the first time,' with special emphasis on the bits where she had to relapse into English.

Peter, standing back from the window as if to get a different angle and a steadier stance for his sixth picture, slyly turned the lens on the engrossed couple leaning on the rail. He had to pass them and move down to the next open window to get them into focus, almost within sight of Signor Galassi in his corner, and for a moment he considered looking in to exchange a greeting with him; but when he bent his head to peep in at the window he saw that the compartment was still shaded by drawn blinds, and the elegant grey head still reposed against the cushions. So he turned softly away again and made his exposure; quite a good shot, too, a double intent profile, Phyl passionately serious, concentrating for all she was worth, with that over-generosity of flattery which made the males go wild, and the Customs man leaning over her shoulder, his cheek close to her hair, his right hand expounding wonders in the valley, his left arm stretched possessively round her with the hand clasping the rail.

Phyllida almost upset his aim, clamouring at him at the crucial moment to turn his camera on a new vision in the valley, a small white monastery toy-like against a wall of black cypresses, on a high shelf under the opposite cliffs.

'Quick, we must have that! He says it's a Franciscan house, and very old. Look how the water-pipes go up to it over the rock, right from the valley. Don't miss it!'

Peter took it, as soon as he could turn his film. 'But don't make such a shindy. The old man's sound asleep, just like a baby. We'll wake him if we make too much noise.'

He wound the monastery away, and finished his film with a second stealthy snap of them from the opposite side, hiding his design behind Punch's lean shoulder. He said imperturbably: 'She's all set until Turin now, and even there we'll have to keep an eye on her, or she'll go off in the wrong direction.' But Phyllida, hearing perfectly, merely made him a quick, grimacing smile while her cavalier was not looking, and went on enjoying herself.

The sun was now high in the sky, the valley widening steadily, the mountains slowly condescending, all their arrogant lines smoothing themselves out into the softer undulations of the plateau of Piedmont. The world grew bigger, and instead of being shut between two enormous walls of trees and rocks, embraced a wide plain full of sunlight, of white buildings, of suddenly expanded fields of maize. Instead of the small, cramped roads tightrope-walking over the rocks, broad white arterials lined with towns and factories, and presently smoke staining the gilded air, and a quiver of heat between the smoke. And then the gaps in the white walls, like missing teeth, the gaps where the bombs had fallen. Then they knew they were nearing Turin.

The Customs man said something apologetic about his duty, or so Phyllida understood it, made her a precise little bow, nodded and smiled at the others, and went off up the train, thrusting a way ruefully through the perspiring third-class passengers in the corridor. The fields of maize gave way to great open spaces of tangled railway lines, factories, sidings, wayside platforms, some of them bombed and abandoned, and busily growing rosebay willow-herb like any forsaken station at home. In fact, this was something like any big industrial town at home, only whiter and sunnier. A few passengers came yawning and stretching out of the first-class compartments to stand in the corridor and assemble themselves ready for alighting. The train slowed, drew breath heavily, and pulled in slowly alongside very long, low white platforms, from the open sun to the shade of awnings, and the noise of many voices clamouring, many feet running, and many doors swinging open.

They hoisted their rucksacks, and climbed down into a splendid noonday heat and a formidable bustle of people. And just as they were running critical eyes over one another's appearance to make sure nothing had been left behind, Mab suddenly said:

'Phyl, what have you done with your raincoat?'

(4)

Phyllida clutched the straps of her rucksack, which confined only a light-blue wind-jacket. 'Oh, damn, I left it in the old chap's carriage! Good thing you noticed, I shouldn't have been any the wiser until it rained. Half a minute, I'll go and fetch it.' And she turned back to the train at a run, evaded an elderly lady who was just majestically descending, and flashed down the corridor to the end compartment.

The blinds were still drawn, and for a moment she checked in the doorway in sheer surprise to see the old man still lying back in his corner, with his head lolling a little towards the obscured window, and his plump white hands folded patiently in his lap. The sun was filtering between the curtains, and made a stabbing advance obliquely across the floor and the seat; and to shut it out from his eyes he had draped the white linen antimacassar over his head, where it dangled just to the end of his nose, and quivered faintly at every snoring breath. Phyllida felt maternally fond of him, so childlike he was in his profound sleep, and so innocent and vulnerable. It was high time for him to awaken, yet she entered the compartment almost on tiptoe, and reached for her raincoat as gingerly as if in fear of startling a slumbering baby. She thought how nice it was that she could say goodbye to him, after all, on behalf of all of them, for such a gentle contact, however brief, should be gently rounded at the close.

'*Signore!*' she said, as she crushed the old raincoat carelessly together, and rolled it up tightly. 'Signore, è Torino!'

He didn't move; and indeed the small, coaxing voice she had thought proper to the occasion could hardly have been expected to penetrate so deep a sleep. She smiled, buckling the raincoat bundle heedlessly into the straps of her rucksack; and when her hands were free of it she went and touched him gently, shaking his arm. The folded hands rolled apart on his thighs, and slipped back to rest emptily on the cushions beside him. The arm she had disturbed lay helplessly across the fat brief-case. But otherwise Signor Galassi did not move.

Phyllida stood quite still for what seemed to her a long time, bending over him with stopped breath, while her senses, which were unaccustomed to encountering fear suddenly out of a sunlit morning, adjusted themselves to the abrupt need. Actually it was not fully a second before she reached out her hand, and turned back the linen from his face.

There wasn't any blood. As far as she could see without disturbing him, the scalp wasn't broken. She wished she could be as sure about the skull. The fallen jaw, the snorting breath, so long in the drawing, so painful to hear, these ought to have warned her. But it was not until she saw his eyes, half-open and staring, with shocking glimpses of their clear, childlike blue between the stiff lids, that she understood. Her comprehension was marvellously limited, but covered the essentials, and there was no time for more. She turned, and ran for the corridor and the window, and leaning out, shouted for Punch in a voice which fetched him at the double. He gaped up at her, the other two drawing in quickly at his heels. Her eyes flared down at him, enormous with shock.

'What's the matter? What's happened?'

'Find the guard!' said Phyllida, wasting no words. 'If you see a policeman first, get him here, and quick. Tell him we need a doctor. I don't know the word, but make him understand. It's the old man! He's hurt – maybe badly! It could be a fractured skull, I don't know – but he's been hit on the head, and he's *bad*— Get somebody, quick!'

Peter shed his rucksack on the platform, and span on his heel, and went off up the platform like a hare from its form. The glimpse she had of his face showed it as quite comically blank with astonishment, as if his wits had not kept up with his ears, but by the time he laid hands on someone in a uniform he would know what to say, and find some way of saying it. Punch stayed only to ask, with sudden incredulous fear: 'He's alive, isn't he?'

'Oh, yes, he is yet.' She caught back a hard breath. 'But I don't like his breathing. I think – he might *not* live. Oh, do find a doctor, quickly!'

Punch pushed Mab wordlessly towards the door of the coach, and followed Peter at a resounding run towards the populous part of the station, forsaking the emptying platform on which only a few slow starters now drifted. Mab, climbing into the corridor, soon stood beside Phyllida, staring great-eyed at the inert body of Signor Galassi, whose every rending breath tore their senses.

'He was like this when I came in,' said Phyllida. 'I tried to wake him. I thought he'd only fallen rather fast asleep. But you can see he's unconscious. And it sounds like pretty bad head injuries, doesn't it? That awful snoring—'

'But he's sitting here,' said Mab, utterly bewildered, her violet eyes incredulously hurt, 'just as we left him. Nothing's fallen, or anything like that, to injure him. How *could* he get head injuries, simply sitting here in a train, quite alone?'

She went nearer, and very gently lifted the stiffly drooping hand, and felt with her fingertips for a pulse which was just perceptible. The slight disarrangement of his cuff uncovered an empty buttonhole in the wrist of his shirt. Mab sat staring at it while her fingers dredged for the faint, collapsing beats of his blood. She remembered that two hours before it had not been empty. Small accidental things catch the eye and stick in the mind, and usually for no purpose, but this time something significant had lodged itself.

In a careful small voice she said: 'Phyllida! He was wearing small pearl cuff-links. Little gold ovals with a row of seed pearls, quite plain.'

'I didn't notice,' said Phyllida, 'but if he was, they're gone now.'

'Maybe they're not the only things that are gone. Don't you think his coat's a bit sort of untidy, too? He was so very neat, and look, his shirt's pulled all loose and crossways in front. As if someone had been feeling in his inside pockets, in a hurry.'

'I haven't thought,' said Phyllida. 'I haven't had time. I don't care about his cuff-links, I don't care about his wallet or anything else, only that I think he's dying. I think somebody left him for dead, and was in too much of a hurry to stay and make sure. And he was such a darling,' she said hotly, drumming her fist into the cushions, from which a faint dust arose and clouded the air. 'And I don't even know what to *do* for him! Oh, I wish Punch would hurry up!'

He came on the word, his boots clumping dully on the concrete of the platform, the guard in tow, and a lean grey gentleman striding behind. And after them Peter hotfoot with two policemen. And suddenly, after the bright expectant dawn and the glittering journey, Rocca della Sera and Garda and the whole gaiety of holiday had receded into an immeasurable distance, and there they were, shut into a first-class compartment at Turin, with a doctor and an almost-dead body, and the darkly opening bud of a police investigation for murder.

CHAPTER TWO

INNOCENTS AMONG
THE ITALIAN TRAINS

(1)

EVERYONE was very kind, the doctor, the policemen, the interpreter who took them under his wing in a more than professional way, saw to it that they were fed, and found them rooms for the night; yet the spoiled day ebbed into a twilight which was more of nightmare than of evening. In a bleak and dangerous world which had not even existed when they had set out from St Michel-de-Maurienne that morning, they sat in a small room with three intent police officers and the interpreter, patiently going over and over and over every detail of the journey to Turin. Singly and collectively, they dredged up minutiae which might or might not mean something to minds more accustomed to this kind of jigsaw puzzle than were theirs.

Certainly Signor Galassi had been in perfectly good health when they left him, at the guard's request, at the beginning of the Mont Cenis tunnel. Equally certainly no one had entered his compartment from the time when they were washed back into the coach at Susa, until Phyllida's discovery at Turin. Peter had even looked in at the window, and seen him, as he thought, sleeping. If, as the doctor said, someone had struck him three blows on the head with something short, blunt and heavy, and left him for dead or dying – if, as the police

35

said, someone had been through his luggage in great haste, and rifled it of studs and other small valuables, and his body of watch and links and wallet – if this was what had happened, it had certainly happened between the beginning of the tunnel and the re-invasion at Susa. Privately, everyone thought: 'Somewhere in the seven and a half miles of the tunnel!' But it could not be taken for granted.

A sordid, ordinary little robbery with violence, that was all. And that kind, candid, gracious, charming old man was in a hospital operating theatre, having the weight of a fractured skull lifted from his brain, and only precariously emerging from the operation still breathing. And his wife and family, fresh from the pleasant excitement of coming to the station to meet him, had followed the ambulance to the hospital and were sitting by his bed waiting for a sign whether he was going to live or die; of which alternatives the latter seemed at the moment considerably the more probable. All for a few notes, and a few pieces of modest personal jewellery! There was no proportion in it!

And who could possibly have done it? Who had had even the opportunity to do it? All the other passengers in the first-class coach would have to account for themselves or their fellow-travellers, since any one of them, wanting some other voice to guarantee him, could conceivably have slipped into the compartment during the passage of the tunnel. Who else? The door at the far end of the coach was locked, had been locked ever since Modane, and only the guard and the Customs officers had passed through it. And though a few people had certainly clawed their way back and forth in the half-dark past Punch and his companions, in the aimless fashion of restless travellers on crowded trains everywhere, they could give only a dubious account of any of them, and had remarked none in particular.

It was not such a helpful story they had to tell, and being a little stupefied with shock, as well as totally inexperienced in this sort of thing, they were uneasily aware that they did not even tell it well. Who would have thought it could be so difficult to remember? They disagreed on details, they contradicted one another on times, they even wondered if they were not a little suspect themselves, so implausible did they sound, with their many hesitations.

The police, however, had no reservations in the matter. They looked with indulgence, out of the strung circle of their own preoccupations, upon four shocked, tired, large-eyed innocents, drooping and sweating with the effort to remember accurately, their holiday appearance suddenly grotesque and pathetic, their faces bewildered, incredulous and angry by turns. Their innocence was obvious and absolute. They had forgotten all about their holiday, letting the fine plans they had made go out unnoticed with the train for Venice; but there was no reason why they should not realise them, after all. What more could they do here for Arturo Galassi? A distracted wife and two dazed young daughters were quite enough to sit holding their breath over his motionless suspension between life and death.

Punch was a little taken aback, even a little indignant, to be told that they could go on to Rocca della Sera next day. Leave an address, said the police, and notify us of any subsequent change of address, so that in case of need we can always find you at short notice; and then forget a business you can't help, and go off and enjoy yourselves. It was like being told to run away and play, because the adults wanted to discuss serious topics. But when he thought it over, he saw that they were right.

There was no point in merely sitting here waiting for news, when their presence would alter nothing. He turned to look at their shelved plans again, and was astonished to find that the colours soon came back into the Trentino landscape, and that with only eight days more of holiday, it needed only one look over his shoulder at these charming remembered places to renew his eagerness for them. He felt a monster, but he was too honest to pretend that his appetite was anything but normal.

So here they were, back on the wide platforms of the station, hunting along the small palmy gardens of flame-red flowers for the Milan-Desenzano train. They found the indicator board: 'Milano – Desenzano – Venezia', but Punch, with his usual over-caution, must pause with his hand already on the rail of the coach to ask a passing guard for confirmation. He had infuriating habits which did not leave him even when, as now, he was more or less walking in his sleep. The guard grinned, and tossed the name back to him good-naturedly, wafting them aboard with a gesture of both hands: '*Si, Milano, Milano!*'

And there they were again, sitting in an Italian train, a good half-hour before its time of departure because of Punch's scruples, on their way to the mountains of the Trentino just as if nothing had happened. Except, of course, that none of it was quite real any more. Maybe it would be, when they actually arrived, when several hundred miles separated them from the cool, void corridors of the hospital in Turin, and the two slender, dark girls sitting there with great stunned eyes and tight-shut hands, waiting for their father to regain consciousness. Antonia, aged twenty-two, Francesca, aged twenty. The little one was exactly like her father. They were both in a stupor of suspense, and leaving them like that seemed terrible, like abandoning two children in a slowly sinking boat. And yet, go or stay, there was absolutely nothing four insignificant strangers from England could do. Better to go away quietly, and not presume on a chance encounter. They could ask for news of Signor Galassi from the police, without bothering his family any more. But they were almost sure what the news would be. He hadn't moved, he hadn't stirred or murmured; he was still just alive, and that was all.

Up to then they had scarcely discussed it at all; the circumstances had simply taken hold of them and put them through certain mechanical paces at the bidding of other people, and in the hotel at night they had had no heart for conversation, but had sat each immured in a little bubble of astonishment and shock. Now, in the bright noon sun, in the slatted seats of the second-class coach among congestions of baskets and children and cheap suitcases, they sat two and two staring at one another and the astonishment became one and shared. Sooner or later they had to talk about it, or for ever give up the attempt to fit it into this bright, matter-of-fact world in which, after all, it had most certainly happened.

Phyllida said suddenly, as the train began to move out from the noon dazzle, quivering with heat: 'I still can't believe in it. Why should anyone take such a risk, just for so little? It isn't *sane!* Not even *sane!*'

'We don't know,' said Punch sombrely. 'We don't know how much he had on him. It might be a lot to some people here. When you've got almost nothing—'

'Yes, but the risk! There were a lot of people in the coach, even if he was the only one in that carriage. Imagine just walking in on him and deliberately knocking him out, like that, with dozens of people almost within hearing of a whisper, let alone a scream! And without even knowing how much you were going to get out of it! Oh, it doesn't make sense. Professional thieves don't behave like that, surely, the odds are impossible.'

The hot air in the coach stirred lazily in a faint breath from the open window. The broken white buildings arched along the track began to slide by, one by one.

'We don't know that it was a professional job,' argued Peter. 'And besides, he was asleep. Maybe whoever it was didn't really mean to injure him at all. Maybe he was just going through his cases – and his pockets – and hoping to get away with it quietly, without disturbing him. And then he woke up, and this fellow panicked, and hit him. It could have happened like that. It's more credible. An ordinary small-time pickpocket caught like that might easily lose his head and lash out, and then run for it.'

'But where would he run to?' asked Punch.

'Well, a few people did pass us, both ways, while we were in the tunnel. Or it could have been someone who was already in one of the first-class compartments. Anyhow, a man in a panic would be much more likely to attack him like that – it surely can't have been planned.'

'It may not have been in the tunnel,' said Mab. 'We can't even be sure of that. We can't be sure of anything.'

'Not even what we saw or didn't see,' admitted Punch bitterly. 'If only you could *know* how important it was going to be to notice things clearly. I don't even know how many people pushed past us into the next coach in the dark, let alone what any of 'em looked like. I've driven myself silly trying to remember, and the only one I can be sure about was a big hefty fellow who came along elbowing everybody right and left, and tried the door of the lavatory, and then shoved through into the first-class, because it was occupied. And I can't even be sure whether he ever came back. If only we'd known it was going to matter so much.'

'But why *him*, out of all the first-class passengers on the train?' wondered Peter.

'Because he happened to be alone in the carriage. And because he went to sleep. It may all have been done on the spur of the moment, just because someone looked in, and there he was, fast asleep and looking rather prosperous. It may have been done by someone who'd never done any such thing before. How do we know? It may easily have been like that, and then he would really panic easily, when the poor old boy showed signs of waking up.'

'And what did he hit him with?' asked Punch helplessly. 'And what did he do with it afterwards, whatever it was? You see, we simply don't know anything, not the first thing. A hell of a lot of use we were!'

'I wouldn't mind so much,' said Mab, 'if only we knew he was going to get better. I can't care what's been stolen. It doesn't seem to matter. I wouldn't even care whether the thief's ever caught, if only I could be sure he was going to live.'

But Mab hadn't any real moral sense, of course; nothing existed for her except persons, and they existed in such peculiarly simple and yet subtle ways that she could use them as erasers to rub out all the surrounding circumstances. Punch cared that a near-murderer – terrible thought, perhaps quite a murderer by now! – should be brought to account. He cared that an untidy mystery should be reduced to a proper pattern, and a wrong balance restored to decent equilibrium. And until he could get the incident of Signor Galassi into true focus with a summer holiday and a trainload of gay, noisy, friendly, quarrelsome Italian people on their lawful occasions, he would never be satisfied.

Now that they had become voluble at last, and talked themselves out of the paralysis of shock which had frozen them since the discovery, they could not stop talking about it until they had exhausted every approach. Slowly warming out of their trance, slowly drawing closer together, they talked themselves and the train out of Turin, and away into the hot gold and green plain among the maize-fields of the mountains; across the southward-flowing tributaries of the Po one by one, trickles of depleted, dull water in wide beds of stones, all their summer life drawn off into the irrigation system of Lombardy. The air quaked with heat, making every distant outline tremulous; but in all the golden grainfields men, women and children worked through the blazing zenith of the day to make the harvest secure. The train became like an oven, and everyone sweated and suffered. And talk as long as they would, they were no nearer understanding what had happened in the Mont Cenis tunnel.

'What's the use?' sighed Peter, wiping the beads of sweat from his upper lip. 'It doesn't make any sort of sense, however you look at it. I suppose the fact is, those things just don't make sense to ordinary, honest people. For all the good we're doing we might as well do as we were told, and forget it. Lord, I'm thirsty!' he said limply. 'What time do we reach Desenzano, Punch? Do you suppose there'll be a chance of a drink somewhere along the way? I'm not sure I can hold out until then.'

'About six, I think. Well, we can hope for something at Milan, maybe. But it was you who finished the lemonade.'

They were drawing near Milan already, running among many sidings and conglomerations of grey-white factory buildings, while away beyond distant roofs the spiky pinnacles of the cathedral bristled at the blue sky like the quills of a giant porcupine. Punch was craning to see it more clearly when a tall young man in an immaculately tailored suit leaned over from the gangway of the coach, cushioned upon the ample shoulders of a middle-aged woman hung with bags and baskets, and said in hesitant English:

'Excuse! I hear Desenzano. You go there, to Desenzano?'

Surprised, visibly wondering 'What now?', they said in anxious chorus that they did.

'But this coach – this part of train – goes only here to Milano. Then finish! – no more! For Desenzano you must go in other part of train.' He waved them, two-handed, towards the rear of the train, but no obliging miracle happened. 'Three coaches back – three! Then is all right.'

'Oh, well!' said Punch, relieved. 'That's just a matter of changing coaches, then. That's not so bad. I thought, for one awful minute—Thanks awfully for telling us! We'd have been in a mess if you hadn't spoken. And I *asked*, too!'

'You asked for the Milan train,' said Peter, clawing down his rucksack in haste, for the train was drawing in towards the station in a long, sweeping curve. 'I heard you. When are you going to get sense, and ask for one station past your destination, instead of one on the near side of it?'

'Well, what's the odds? It's the right train, anyhow, isn't it? Are you too tired to climb out and walk a hundred yards along the platform?'

The young man who spoke English, gently gathering his own baggage, watched them preparing cheerfully for flight, and his eyes were helplessly sympathetic. He had

43

been a prisoner of war in England just long enough to have command of the words needed to explain their mistake, but his vocabulary was quite inadequate to the task of preparing them for the ordeal ahead. He tried. He began deprecatingly: 'Will be many people—' but that sounded so weak that he stopped again, and felt for another opening. And by that time the train was running alongside the long concrete platform in the canopied shade of the station, like sudden evening. Like, in fact, a sudden evening in hell, full of rushing bodies and howling voices and vicious explosions of steam. And then there was no more need for any description of what beggared description; they hung gaping out of the window, dragging wits and strength together for the fight ahead, bereft of words themselves, though Peter managed a long, shrill whistle of dismay.

The solid mass of humanity arrayed along the platform broke into platoons before the train had stopped, attached themselves leech-like to the doors of the coaches, and clung there until it came to a halt. By which time it was humanly impossible for a newcomer to get within ten yeards of any doorway in that part of the train which went on to Desenzano and Venice. It was a time either for despair or for extreme measures, and Punch rose to it with all the more determination because he felt to blame for the necessity.

'Come on!' he yelled, and hoisted a powerful shoulder into the strap of his rucksack, and charged.

(2)

There was this to be said for Peter, that he knew when to stop arguing and follow in blind faith. It looked senseless to him, but he picked up his heels and ran, sparing only a moment to reach back a hand for Phyllida, and steady her on her feet, as she leaped down the three tall steps after him. In fact he had believed that it was Mab who was close behind him, or he would have left her to fend for herself, partly because one simply does not make a fuss of a sister, partly because in the case of Phyllida it had never yet proved necessary. He caught one glimpse of Mab, tangled in the corridor with a tall man in a light-grey suit, whose suitcase was just being politely manoeuvred out of the way to permit her rucksack to pass. 'Better get one aboard!' thought Peter, weighing up probabilities in a hurry, and streaked head-down after Punch.

To approach the doorway was out of the question, for at least forty people, in a gently heaving but immovable mass, were attempting to get through it at the same time, and not one of them was succeeding. Punch had made squarely for the middle of the coach, as if he meant to emulate Popeye the Sailor and plunge clean through it; but under the open corridor windows, from which half a dozen interested Italian heads leaned out to watch, he suddenly shed his pack, dropped on his knee against the side of the coach, and waved Peter peremptorily upward.

'Get in!' he roared, in the battle voice which came so oddly in emergencies from his ordinarily mild, reserved and conscientious throat.

Peter, reacting automatically, was on his shoulder before the gallery in the corridor had realised what was about to happen. He was a lightweight, he went up with beautiful ease, and though a dozen excited voices immediately began to yell in his face what he could only assume to be violent imprecations, double as many gesticulating hands promptly reached out to haul him in. It wasn't as simple inside the window

45

as it had looked from the outside. They pulled him through head first, and he rode for a moment buoyed up upon a heaving sea of tangled human creatures, bundles, cases, bags and bottles, helplessly struggling to get a foot to the floor. Then he found toe-space, and wriggled his precarious claim large enough to turn and face the window, where Punch was already heaving up the rucksacks, and the indignant denizens of the corridor, still volubly protesting against this invasion, were busily receiving them and adding them haphazardly to the chaos already present.

Phyllida was scrambling up with hers still slung on her shoulder, but Peter carefully counted the other three, and then gave up worrying. They would be somewhere around, salvable once the train was in motion, somehow reclaimable at any rate before they reached Desenzano. He reached down for Phyllida's hand as she walked up Punch by thigh and shoulder, and pulled her through into the lap of a stout lady who was sitting half-buried among the luggage. When he looked for her again she was three yards away beyond a mound of miscellaneous packages and people, clinging valiantly to the window-rail and trying to disentangle her other leg from among a welter of children. She was laughing, and so were most of her neighbours; Phyllida mercifully had that effect on people.

Mab, so light that Punch practically threw her aboard, had not enough ballast to come easily to ground once she was through the window, and an inconsequent tide of movement caught her in the opposite direction and swept her away towards the end of the coach. Peter saw her receding like a cork on a stream, all timid violet eyes of astonishment and ruffled blonde hair. But at least she was in. Now for Punch, who came up with a horrid scraping of boot-toes and a dogged-does-it expression.

The still-protesting passengers gave him a hoist as soon as they could get their hands to the nearest portions of his anatomy, and fetched him aboard head-down and half-undressed, just as the train began to move. It took him several minutes to get his formidable boots safely to the floor, and when he managed it at last they became immovable for the next half-hour. But they were all in, and that was in itself a triumph.

Borne to the remote edges of the flood before she could come to rest, Mab was finally brought up breathless and dazed in the forward corner of the coach, darkly immured from window and door. She thought, almost crossly: 'This is getting monotonous.' But hope is irrationally durable, and when she had recovered her breath, and grown very tired of the view of the lavatory door, she began to wonder incorrigibly if there might not be a little more room in the next coach. She squeezed apologetically past a resigned old man who had no such hopes to buoy him, and groped through into the light of the next corridor; and at once she saw, through the glass panel of the intervening door, that it was practically empty, only one man standing negligently gazing out on the green plain of maize. A moment later, as she turned the handle, she understood why. All her travels in Italy were running true to pattern. The next coach was a first-class, and the door between was very firmly locked against invasion.

Mab made a face at the solitary first-class passenger's oblivious back, a large, shapely, light-grey back, very elegantly tailored; maybe a thought flattered at the shoulders, for very few men could in reality be so beautifully straight and wide and flat in outline, but still, he was a fine sight. A suave hat of light-grey felt curved its slightly exaggerated, slightly disdainful brim above well-cropped black hair. He stood a moment longer with

47

one hand on the door of his compartment, the other on the window-rail; and then, with a flick of large, decisive fingers, slid open the door and went into the carriage, and clashed the door to again after his going. She caught a glimpse of his face as he turned, long and gentle and inexpressive, one of those faces which have no age, but stay exactly the same perhaps from twenty years old to fifty or more, and through the whole of that time don't give much away. Behind a face like that you could juggle with stocks and shares, army surplus supplies, or for the matter of that armies, and nobody would be much the wiser until he found himself considerably the poorer, and you another million to the good; or perhaps that was an over-estimate, and he was only the minor version of the same thing – say something in the middle ranks of the diplomatic service.

It wasn't until she had turned her back upon him, and gone back into her hot, dark corner of the second-class corridor, that she began to wonder where she had seen him before. Maybe, after all, she was particularising from only a vague recollection of the type, but certainly she had that eerie sense of familiarity which gives you no peace until you can put a finger on its source. And she couldn't. The more clearly she tried to examine the memory of him, the less probable did it seem that she had ever set eyes on him before; but the moment she turned a resolute shoulder on the attempt, intuition nudged her again, and said positively: 'You have, you know!'

The other three appeared to be enjoying themselves, in spite of a certain degree of discomfort. Cushioned among their sweating fellow-victims, the two boys were making fairly good going, in a mixture of English, French, Italian and sign-language, with the fat lady and her leggy children; most particularly, Mab noticed, with the eldest child, who was feminine, about seventeen, and somewhere very close to the discovery of beauty. Phyllida was making a big hit with a scarred young man who spoke tolerable English. She had found a precarious perch on top of an up-ended case, with her knees under her chin, and her rucksack still wedged tightly under her left arm against the window, for having come aboard with it slung on one shoulder she had now no room even to get rid of it. The fat woman covered one side of her like a feather-bed, the youngest child sat on the pile of luggage against her thighs, and retained its position by a tight grip of two hot little hands in the folds of her skirt; and her feet were mixed up inextricably with bags, bundles and rucksacks, among which sat a short, square man, half-submerged. He had no English, apparently, but a fine rotund flow of Italian and a gale of high spirits compensated for the lack. He was teasing the young man by trying to cut him out with Phyllida, and he had everyone within earshot laughing at his jokes, so that it seemed rather a pity that no one was capable of translating them.

He could, Mab thought, have sat for any conventional portrait of a brigand, being exceedingly dark and weathered of face, with a large, ragged moustache, an incandescent grin perforated with a few broken and decayed teeth, and small, thin gold rings in his ears. He was in his shirt-sleeves, with his greasy coat slung on one shoulder; and his hands and forearms, like the rest of his visible person, were extremely dirty. He had, however, a certain generosity of gesture which he wore as a grace; and Phyllida rather liked him, and accepted his wickered bottle of Chianti with goodwill when he offered it. His left hand, full in the sunlight as he accepted it from her again, summed him up pretty well, thought Mab, watching with interest from her corner: dirty knuckles, blackened and scored nails, but a rough silver ring on the little finger, and a ring of some character, too. When you have no inhibitions it is difficult to be entirely commonplace, at any rate.

But with all the goodwill in the world, and the best of company, it could not be said that the journey from Milan to Desenzano was a comfortable one. Cramps afflicted them, and the heat grew really daunting, so that they even lost interest in looking out of the windows, and limply awaited their arrival. Conversation helped, but even this flagged by the end of the afternoon; and it was like a sudden breath of wind when one of the children suddenly pointed ahead, and shrilled: '*Il lago, il lago!*'

They were drawing into the soft rim of the hills again, tumbled rolling country of villages and cypresses and olives, and white, cool walls, beautiful in the first still of the evening. The distant mountains were only iris-coloured shapes of mist, and against them, among clustering villages like a shower of pale flowers, Lake Garda opened vastly, incredibly blue, a blue into which the senses plunged and could find no bottom. And in a few moments more they were running into the station at Desenzano, among the flowering pallor of buildings, and the corridor was a grand chaos of heaving, struggling people, from which they disentangled themselves laboriously, and emerged scarecrows. Punch leaped down from the window with an enormous thudding of his rubber-soled boots, and received the rucksacks into his arms, and after them Phyllida; but the other two made a more decorous exit via the doorway.

A great many people were also alighting here. Their friend with the Chianti bottle saluted them upon the platform with a wave of a deplorable felt hat, and went off up the town at a rolling walk, with the bottle swinging at his hip, and a fat rush-bag dangling over one shoulder. The plump lady gathered her brood, and waddled purposefully towards the lake-shore, on which the sloping sunlight lay greenly golden with the saturated life of leaves. And Garda drew the eye irresistibly northward into the mountains, to where its blue became merged in mist and distance and twilight, before the sun on the southern shores had even declined to roof-level.

They stood and gazed, by the barrier of stones which fringed the water, until Peter, pulled down to earth again by the drag of his rucksack upon a tired shoulder, shattered the stillness of their contemplation with a deliberate pebble of mutiny. Beauty on an empty stomach was too much for him.

'I'm hungry!' he said. 'Come on, let's go and eat.'

(3)

They bought some light beer and some rolls at a modest back-street bar, and some extra rolls and some peaches to eat in the bus, since according to Punch's time-table they had rather less than half an hour to spare, and he always liked to be at least ten minutes ahead of time. One bus would take them all the way up the lake to Riva, tucked among the mountains at its head, and a second would carry them on into the mountains, and drop them at Rocca della Sera at about half-past ten at night. At the Albergo Monte Gazza, they were assured, there would be a meal ready for them, in spite of the late hour. Meantime Peter, once installed in a rear corner of the bus, alternately munched salami rolls and dozed on

Punch's shoulder. Blessedly, there were seats this time, enough for all with a slight squeeze. They nursed their rucksacks, because the rack was already full of goods, but that was the only hardship.

They had not observed him among the people waiting, but suddenly there among the newcomers was the familiar stocky figure in the dilapidated hat, dangling the rush-bag and the Chianti bottle. He shuffled down the gangway and into the remaining corner of the back seat, beaming recognition at the full stretch of his gap-toothed smile. Once settled there comfortably with an elbow in Mab's rucksack, he fished out bread and cheese from the depths of the bag, and began to make a lengthy and leisurely meal. They all returned his smile readily, but the need for conversation was obviated by the talents of the bus, which proceeded with the maximum of noise, though with perfect efficiency. It was not one of the super-luxury coaches to be found on long-distance tourist services in Italy, but a veteran of the mountain roads, and had a brigand's manners as well as a brigand's hardiness.

After leaving Desenzano the road wound away from the lake, which was now beginning to fade a little from its improbable blueness to the rich but subdued purple of a good amethyst; but after a long detour it came back to a high shelf hanging above the western shore, and by a series of traverses to the shore itself, in a small seraphic bay of cypresses and white hotels. Who could want to talk, with such a spectacle passing outside the windows? They craned and gazed, first to the right, to marvel at the changing colours of the lake, of which the distant shore was now quite invisible in a shining haze, then to the left, at the glimmering convolutions of the shore, bright promenades, coloured cafés, gardens of marble and cypresses all strung along the edge of the water like a hem of pearls.

At first, and for almost an hour, it was simply one long, gracious town, with the wooded hills climbing steadily behind. Then the mountains drew in closely over the narrowing lake, and the distant shore rose out of the bright mist in blue planes of rock. Up the terraced slopes overhanging the road climbed lemon-gardens, tier upon tier, green waxen-leaved trees dark between the colonnades of white pillars which in winter would support a roof, but now reached stark fingers towards the sky, and held up nothing. Next, even these sharp slopes were left behind, and the road plunged into arched tunnels of rock, silent and softly-lit, into which the dove-grey evening light came glimmering through many pierced rock windows, trembling with the reflected motion of the water. In and out of the cliff the road threaded, glimpsing the first cluster of lights at the head of the lake, the tiny constellation of Riva; until the narrowing water rounded in a small sickle of shore, and the town sat about it gazing southward down the silver surface of Garda, as over an enchanted sea.

Inland of the little square, lined with cafe tables, the bus stopped to discharge its load. There would be, said Punch, about ten minutes to wait; in fact they waited twenty, but in a new and fascinating place that was no hardship. Half asleep, they hoisted their rucksacks out to the pavement, and stretched and breathed deeply again in the fresh and cooling air of the evening. Their neighbour with the earrings made a great gallantry of lifting Mab's rucksack out for her, and tried to take Phyllida's in addition, but she only looked over her shoulder at him, and laughed, and shook her head.

Under the pearly sky he gave them his broad, confident salute for the second time, and again wished them: '*A rivederci!*' Then he made for the nearest cafe, and in a few minutes they saw him ensconced under the coloured awning, now mysteriously fading into the single dove's-breast grey of the evening, the rush-bag in between his feet and a glass of wine in front of him. He was still there when they climbed into their bus for Mazzolo, and drew out of the square in a cloud of blue smoke; he already looked permanent, as if he had grown there, and would certainly be there until he shrivelled from sheer old age, centuries hence, and left a distant generation the job of grubbing up his formidable roots.

The bus climbed, crossed and recrossed the River Sarca in the dusk as it flowed southward to pour its waters into the lake; and then, coming face to face with the impossible sheer rock gates of its gorge, soaring two hundred metres into mid-air, the road began to double upon itself sharply as a hairpin, time after time until they lost all sense of direction; and after the fourth right-about turn, straightened itself out north-eastward along a high shelf above the deep scar of the gorge, in the distant hollow of which the river ran dark, silent and invisible. Sometimes the rock arched clean over them, just failing to make contact on the outward side; and after every such eclipse the light seemed to have dimmed perceptibly, until by the time they reached the comparative open of the high plateau it was already half dark. They strained their eyes to identify unidentifiable villages, but at long last knew their own by the soft oval glimmer which was the lake, lambent in its hollowed palm of rock and sand. Climbing up a zigzag path above it went a small, irregular pattern of lights, and a great, furry, blue-black darkness framing them, the lustrous live darkness of the forests.

'This is it!' said Punch, reaching for his rucksack, and

gently rocking Peter's head upon his shoulder, where it hung heavily asleep. 'Come on, liven up! We've arrived!'

Peter awakened to the promise of food and a bed, and clambered drowsily out of the bus on Phyllida's heels, to blink at the rising length of a narrow, convoluted street, faintly lambent with its own whiteness and the reflected light from the little lake. Shallow roofs, almost flat, made sharp incisions in a sky full of milky stars; all the creamy walls leaned backward a little from the upright, in a distinct batter, like the walls of fortresses in Arabia, and fingers of light played through the bars of their green shutters as in the strings of a mandoline. Green letters slipping askew upon the white end of a house spelled dimly: 'Albergo Monte Gazza'. Someone was singing, high and hard in the head, a woman singing on the radio; and the door was open, spilling light across the narrow paving and the channelled street. The only thing which seemed to have no right there was the large, low blue car just drawing in to the doorway as they crossed the threshold and entered the tiny hall.

(4)

Punch had no sooner stripped back the covering flap of his rucksack, and plunged his hand in for towel and soap, than he became suddenly still, all but the fingers of the questing hand, which halted, touched, wondered, and moved experimentally among the neat complexities of his packing. A most peculiar look came into his face, the wary, receptive look of somebody listening very intently, or trying very hard to remember. He said, in a tone which matched the look: 'That's funny!'

Phyllida and Mab were in the doorway, just making

55

for their own room, which was next to this one and its twin, even to the exact position of the two white-covered beds and the pattern of the net which curtained the windows. Peter was already splashing in the basin in the corner. All three turned at the tone of Punch's voice, and looked at him curiously.

'What's funny?' asked Peter, dripping water from his forelock.

Punch said in a low voice: 'Come in, and close the door.' And when it was done: 'Somebody's been in my rucksack! Better have a look at yours, too.'

There was a moment of thoughtful, but on the whole incredulous, silence. Then Phyllida said bluntly: 'You're imagining things. Why should anyone want to monkey with your things? And even if they did want to, how could they? The rucksacks have never been out of our sight since we packed them this morning in Turin.'

Punch spread back the flap and loosened the confining cord to its widest. 'Look! Do I, or don't I, know exactly where to put my hand on a thing, once I've packed it?'

'Oh, usually you do, sure enough, but good lord, even you can't be infallible every time.'

'Do you think I can't tell when things have been moved around in here? Look, I put my soap-case just here, tucked into the right side at the top, and tight into place, with the towel rolled just underneath it. You can see for yourself where it is now, over on the other side. Look!' He waved them indignantly close to the small table, in the centre of which the rucksack sat upright to be examined. The position of the green plastic case was certainly clear to be seen, but they were not convinced.

'After all,' said Peter reasonably, 'the ruckers have been heaved through windows, pushed around, sat on, kicked, used as cushions, heaven knows what, since we started out this morning. I wouldn't like to guarantee the position of anything in *mine*, after all it's been through.'

'You'd be wise, at that!' said Punch. 'But the way you shovel things in, nobody'd know the difference if a couple of ferrets had been fighting their way through it. But I do know where I put things, today or any other day. And that's where I didn't put it, and where it couldn't have slipped to, not after any amount of rough handling. It isn't only that, either. I could tell, as soon as I put my hand in. It isn't just that they've been shaken up more than usual – if that was all, everything would be more untidy and mixed up than it is. Look for yourself! The edges of things are turned up, just as if somebody's been feeling down in between.'

'Punch, dear!' said Phyllida, with offensive patience, 'You've had a long, hard day, and if you ask me, your nerves are just beginning to feel the strain after that other business. Look, we don't carry jewellery. We don't travel first-class. We haven't got a thing on us worth stealing, and what's more, we don't even look as if we have. Nobody'd take the trouble even to feel in our pockets, we'd be written off on sight. And in any case, just because of one bad experience, you can't go round assuming that the Italian railways are swarming with thieves. It isn't fair!'

'I'm not assuming anything. I'm just telling you, whether you like it or not, whether you care to believe it or not, that somebody's been feeling around in my rucksack. I'm just as much surprised as you are, I don't see any sense in it, I wasn't expecting it, and I can't guess why anyone should bother. I'm just telling you what I *know*. Somebody's had his hands in there since I packed it.'

'But it's crazy!' said Peter, unmoved by this display of certainty. 'It couldn't be done. We've had the things right under our noses the whole time. Even if there was any sense in anyone *wanting* to search them – and there isn't.'

'All right, you know it all, as usual! But that doesn't alter a thing. You look at your own things, before you get too cocky.'

Mab was already doing precisely that, crouching on the rug with her rucksack open before her, and carefully lifting out the upper layers of her small luggage. Her intense frown of concentration took no account of the heated but quiet wrangle proceeding round the table; but she effectively silenced it when she sat back on her heels and said, in her small voice: 'You know – somebody's been in mine, too.'

They all stared at her, instantly more respectful, since two people of independent mind are not likely to have the same delusion at the same moment. She pushed back the blonde feathers of hair from her forehead, and said anxiously: 'Really, you know! It isn't only a feeling. Look! My scarf was rolled round my mending things, right in the middle. Somebody's scratched his hand on the scissors, because, look, there's a smear of blood on the case, and even a drop on the scarf. Look, right inside the folds!' She spread out the light folds of silk, and uncovered a small, brownish blot on the diminutive compendium in which she carried all her sewing materials. 'He must have had his fingers right down into the middle of everything – but you see, he couldn't have been looking at what he was doing, or he wouldn't have run on to the scissors. He must have been doing it by touch.'

They looked at one another mutely for a minute, and then turned every one to his own rucksack in a fever of discovery, until the table and the floor were littered with small heaps of their belongings. No one bothered to argue the impossibility of the thing any longer, for there was the absolute evidence. They plunged instead, with unusual unanimity, to draw what conclusions they could as to the reason for the outrage. And presently Phyllida scooped up the nearest of her accumulations with a resolute hand, and dumped them back into her pack.

'Count me out! I'd be prepared to swear nobody's touched mine. Not because it's tidy – I'd think someone had been at it if it were. But I know my own touch, and it hasn't been disturbed. How about you, Peter?'

Peter looked dubious. 'I can't be sure. The more I look at it, the more I think it *has* been monkeyed about with. But maybe I'm just hypnotising myself, because you people have started this infection. I'm not evidence either way. I just don't know.'

'But has anyone actually had anything taken?' asked Punch.

No one had. Phyllida sighed: 'Just what I told you. They despised us, once they had a look.'

'But they didn't have a look! Didn't you hear what Mab said? Whoever it was, he felt his way round the packs by touch. Maybe he never even unfastened more than one strap, just enough to get a hand inside.'

The fog of bewilderment in which they blundered was clearing slowly, though it left them breathing a strange and unaccustomed air.

'But why?' said Mab, almost soundlessly. 'And when could it have happened? We had our hands on them practically all the time. And why leave out Phyllida?'

'Maybe Phyl's just couldn't be got at. *Was* there any time when somebody could have got hold of all the rest, but not of yours, Phyl?' But he remembered on the

59

instant, without waiting for any prompting from her. 'Good lord, yes!' said Punch, open-mouthed. 'The train at Milan! Like a dope, you kept it on. I remember heaving you up, and the thing was still on your shoulder.'

'Are you telling me?' said Phyllida. 'Once inside, I hadn't even got room to slide out of the strap and get rid of it, I was wedged so tight. All I could do was hitch the weight up on the window-ledge, and I had it sticking into my side all the way to Desenzano. Do you really mean to say—?'

'When else could it have been? They were all on the rack until Milan, and I don't think anyone could have tampered with them then, the train wasn't crowded enough. But when you're almost swamped under cases and bags, it might not be so very hard to slip your hands into one or two of them. If you're good at that sort of thing. That chap with the wine, for instance, who was being so darned amusing! Half the time you couldn't see his hands at all.'

'You know,' said Peter suddenly, 'I had a funny feeling I've seen that man before, somewhere. I know you often get that feeling without any reason, but anyhow, I *did* get it. Only I'm no nearer knowing where. I can't even see quite how it's possible, but still there's something about him awfully familiar.'

'We'd easily know him again, anyhow,' said Mab, 'what with his teeth, and his ear-rings, and his little-finger ring. Did you notice it? A thick, rough silver one, made like a thong and buckle.' She added with mild practicality: 'He followed us as far as Riva, you know. Even after he'd looked through most of our things. Because I can't think of anyone else who even had the opportunity, can you?'

No one could. In the bus they had held the rucksacks on their knees because the racks were full. And now that they remembered it, hadn't the friendly and helpful man lifted Mab's rucksack out for her at Riva? And hadn't he wanted to take Phyllida's, too, but for her invincible independence?

'Then he's still after us!' said Phyllida in blank astonishment.

'After your rucksack, by the look of it. But he did stay behind at Riva.'

'He saw which bus we took,' said Punch. 'Not that he'd know from that exactly where we were going to get off, but—Oh, no, damn it, we're imagining things now. He was just sitting among the luggage and taking advantage of his opportunities, that's all. Just a commonplace pickpocket. There can't be anything mysterious going on! Why should there? We're not mysterious. Nothing's been taken, because he didn't find anything worth taking.'

But no one was satisfied. No one said so; it didn't need saying; but the silence while they thought it out was pregnant with doubts. They were not in the habit of imagining themselves the characters in a melodrama, but the disturbing fact remained that they had recently been involved in one curious and violent incident, and could the more easily believe in a second. Peter was speaking for them all, however hesitantly they might acquiesce in his train of thought, when he said very flatly: 'Could he have been looking for something definite, do you suppose? Something we're supposed to have, even if we haven't really got it? Could it have anything to do with the business at Turin? Because nobody thought us worth following around until then, for all *I* ever noticed. And this comes awfully pat on the top of it.'

They had been so near to thinking the same things that Phyllida and Punch made great haste to argue in the opposite direction. But Mab sat on the rug in the middle of her scattered possessions, and frowned at the stained scarf in her lap, and without paying any attention to them, slowly and deliberately produced another rabbit from the hat.

'Another funny thing happened,' said Mab, 'in the train. When we climbed through the window at Milan, I was pushed right up to the forward end of the coach, and I went through to see if there was more room next door; but it was another first-class, and the door in between was locked. Only it had a glass panel in it, and in the corridor I saw a big man in a grey suit, and I thought – just like you with the other one, Peter – I thought I'd seen him somewhere before. He stood there for a minute, and then he went into a carriage and settled down. Well, I've only just remembered where I saw him the first time, and it's a very queer thing. You know when we were rushing to get out of the train at Milan, and I got tangled up with a man who was getting out of the next carriage? Well, this was the same man.' She looked at them simply, as if she had explained everything.

'What's so queer about that?' asked Punch.

'Well, only that he should get out of a second-class and into a first. We made a mistake about the coaches, but an Italian wouldn't have made the same mistake. So why choose to go part of the way in the second-class, and then change? Evidently he had a first-class ticket, so why not get in a first-class coach at Turin, in the first place? And he looked every inch first-class, too – well, I mean in the railway sense.'

'Well?' said Punch impatiently, as she paused again. 'Why do *you* think he changed?'

'I only wondered if he wasn't keeping an eye on us,' said Mab, almost apologetically. 'I can't think of any

other way to account for it. He was in the next carriage
from Turin to Milan, and in the next coach from Milan
onward. You see, he'd have to watch us, because he
wouldn't *know* how far we were going.'

'And did he get out at Desenzano?'

'I don't know. I hadn't remembered anything queer
about him then, so I didn't think to notice. But the other
man did. Supposing they belong together, then they had
us under observation between them as far as Riva, and
they know we took the road to Mazzolo. I don't think
it would be so very hard to find out the rest, do you?'

'My God!' moaned Punch. 'This is getting fantastic!
Now you're turning the whole sordid ordinary little
business into a grand conspiracy. Did they *look* as if
they belonged together? I ask you!'

'But of course, the trick would be not to look like it,
wouldn't it?' said Mab reasonably.

'I think,' said Punch, suddenly pushing his rucksack
away from him, 'the whole thing's poppycock. Somebody – maybe it *was* the bloke with the wine, he looked
as if he could do with a hand-out – somebody saw a
chance of lifting any bits we might have that would pay
for the trouble, found out there wasn't a thing worth
picking up, and threw us back. That's all about it, you
may bet your last fiver. The fellow came on to Riva
simply because it was to Riva he was coming, that's
all. And as for your first-class passenger, he jumped
into the second-class coach at Turin because he was
late, and the train was due out, and now he's gone
on to Verona, or Venice, or wherever he was going,
and I bet you what you like we shan't see him again.
Oh, let's forget it, and go and eat. We can't in decency
keep them waiting any longer, when they've been good
enough to lay on a meal for us at this hour.'

They remembered that they were hungry, and they

went, though in a silence not altogether of belief. They would have liked to be convinced, but Punch would have stood a better chance if he had really believed his own story. If, for instance, the big man had jumped in a moving train at the last minute, why hadn't he jumped out again and into his proper compartment at the first stop, instead of waiting for Milan? They all knew it wouldn't hold water. There could be an explanation, no doubt, but that wasn't it.

Their very late dinner, however, was waiting, and it was drawing near to eleven o'clock. So down they went by the twisted staircase which was so treacherously dark at the turn, and across the little hall, past the desk and the keyboard and the telephone box, and so through an unexpectedly modern glass door into the dining-room. The loose ends of all their problems trailed disconcertingly to trip them, but for the moment, at any rate, it was better to pretend that they noticed nothing, since every new idea produced new complications. After a night's sleep probably everything would look simpler.

Mab was the first to enter the dining-room, and the light within was so dim that she stood for a moment with her hand upon the handle of the door, looking round to discover at which table they were expected.

The room was quite small, but of an elongated L shape which withdrew one corner completely from sight. There were three tables in the longer shaft of the L, one squarely in the corner, and one, apparently, out of sight round the bend. That was all; and since all the light was concentrated in the short leg of the room she walked forward to the corner, and looked beyond. Peter was at her elbow, and he felt her check, and knew it was more than a mere hesitation over where to sit. He shut his hand gently over her wrist, and drew her to the table in the corner, where a very young girl in a black dress had just hurried to switch on a lamp for them. Mab obeyed his touch composedly, and when they were all seated, withdrew herself behind the heavy shade of the lamp to say, just above a whisper: 'Lucky for you nobody took that bet, Punch!'

Peter had already looked in the direction her eyes indicated, and Peter was the only one who could share her recognition. At the last table, out of sight of the door, sat a large, smooth man of unidentifiable age, beautifully tailored in light grey. He had arrived, she judged, about one minute later than their bus, in the long blue car. He was just finishing his dinner, and he looked across at them with only the gentlest and most remote of interest, his long, melancholy face serene, the fine, large hands which selected and lit his cigarette economical in movement and complete in repose. In the dingy little dining-room of the Albergo Monte Gazza, a mountain inn miles from anywhere, situation arduous for walkers and pointless for cars, tariff humanely adjusted to the purses of the penniless, his poise and finish made him a grotesque. He would have been about as inconspicuous dancing a fandango.

'That,' breathed Mab, without benefit of grammar, 'is him!'

Covertly behind the twilight of the lamp-shade they waited their opportunity to examine him more closely The longer they looked, the more clear did it become that this exceedingly square peg had not fallen into its present round hole by accident. He was, every inch of him, as Mab had said, a first-class person. If only in the railway sense of the word!

CHAPTER THREE

THE ASCENT OF
MONTE GAZZA

(1)

THEY went to earth in the girls' bedroom, and talked it over very seriously. Fantastic coincidences can occur, but no one supposed that this was coincidence.

'That settles it!' said Punch. 'He's here because we're here. People don't recur like this, in places where they don't fit at all, without a reason, and it looks as if we're the reason. To save my life I couldn't guess why or how, but we are. Whether the other fellow's anything to do with it or not, whether he's working for this one or whether he just took a chance on his own in the train, at any rate *this* one's after us. So now our problem seems to be this: What are we supposed to have that he wants? Any ideas!'

'Just that they seem to be on as bad a wicket as we are,' said Peter, chewing his knuckles. 'If they think we've got anything of value to them, they're barking up the wrong tree. What have we got to worry about? The moves are up to them, and they're wasting their time.'

Punch jutted his chin until it borrowed some of the character of his formidable nose, and said strenuously: 'I can't stand mysteries. I want to *know*. And besides, you said yourself, it all begins very suspiciously soon after that business at Turin. If it's got anything to do with that, I want more than ever to know.'

'Oh, yes,' agreed Peter, 'of course we want to find out anything we can that will help to corner the devil who knocked out the old man. But I don't see quite how we can set about it, until somebody else makes a move.'

'If we're supposed to be carrying something on us,' said Phyllida, after long and arduous thought, 'something we don't know about, then it seems to me the first thing is to find out if we've really got it. I don't see how it's been managed, if we have, but at any rate let's consider it as possible. Well, this fellow who knows what he's after, and knows how to look for it, has been through two of the rucksacks, at least, and didn't find it, because he's still after it. That's the theory, isn't it? So there remains my rucksack, and possibly Peter's. Well, all right, let's start by making sure that there *isn't* anything in them that we don't know about.'

It seemed to them all a foregone conclusion but they went through both packs with religious care, feeling along the seams, tipping out the last debris of paper-clips, safety-pins and string from the map pockets. Nothing new, nothing strange. Phyllida sat on the floor among the wreckage with a burning light in her eyes, and said:

'Well, then, so far, so good! The next thing is to find out if we're thinking along the right lines. Let's go out tomorrow, if it's fine. Let's go out all day, and leave all our things in our rooms, and give who-ever it is plenty of time to have a good old search. Doors duly locked, of course, or they'd smell a rat. Everything locked that has a lock on it. If we're on the right lines, they won't miss an opportunity like that. Your things may be let alone, mine will certainly be combed over pretty closely. And as we're on the lookout for traces, we ought to be able to spot the alien hand by now. Then at least we'd know we're not imagining things. We might even get an idea what it is they're after.'

'And suppose it *is* here?' said Mab. 'And suppose they find it?'

'It can't be here. Whatever it is, we should surely have noticed if we'd picked up something that didn't belong to us. And we've just looked, and there's nothing here but what should be here. No, they won't find it. Punch, where do you suggest we go? We may as well have a good day out while they enjoy themselves.'

Punch pondered, and suggested: 'We could go up Monte Gazza. If it's fine there's the most marvellous view up there, over half the Trentino. I'll get up early, and ask for packed lunches, and we'll take the smallest rucksack – yours, Phyl, I think – and take turns with it.' He reached his hand for it, and Phyllida, who had been negligently scooping tangled socks and underwear back into its main pocket, obligingly emptied everything out again upon the rug, and handed it up to him. Tightly but untidily rolled inside the two small cape-straps, her fawn raincoat arched across the flap. 'You don't want this, do you?' asked Punch, his fingers at the straps.

'Oh, I don't know, leave it on. My wind-jacket's very thin if it should be cooler in the evening, and anyhow, the thing's no great carriage. It doesn't get in the way at all, you can perfectly well leave it there. And here's my water-bottle, in case we need one. It holds more than yours. And now get out of it,' she said cheerfully, having arranged everything as she wanted it, 'and let us get to bed. The real show starts tomorrow.'

As if it was all just a game, thought Punch, as he closed the door of the girls' room very gently behind him, and followed Peter to his bed. But it was a queer kind of game which had brought Signor Galassi by way of an ambulance to his silent, screened room in the hospital at Turin. Maybe Phyllida, in the flush of excitement, could forget that part of it for a little while, but Punch couldn't. Not even for a moment.

He lay for a time listening to Peter's deep, even breaths, and watching the shining gauze sky outside the window, heavy with stars. Maybe they were on the wrong tack, after all. Maybe they'd put together a lot of disconnected incidents and a few flights of imagination, and made them into something which didn't really exist. Maybe they would come down from Monte Gazza the next evening, and find all Phyllida's belongings exactly as she had left them, untouched, untidied, and never a trace of the man in grey, or his car, or his supposed lieutenant. Punch had hypnotised himself into thinking so with entire success by the time he fell asleep.

(2)

The dawn appearance of Rocca della Sera, limpid and green and golden in the flooding sunlight of a perfect day, put every suggestion of the sinister out of their heads. Punch had not exaggerated. Below the hotel, in the oval bowl of the rocky valley, the little lake lay complacently asleep in the sun, aquamarine in the shadows, sapphire at the heart. Its near shore was of sand pale as ivory, and all the rest of forest, shading from the fresh, sunlit green of nut trees near the water, to the blue-black sheen of pine and fir higher up the slopes. Everywhere the soil, once broken, was ready to foam into narrow rivers of stones down every cranny of every valley, and high among the trees the weathered faces of rock began, lavish in amber and hyacinth and rose. And above these was the sky, carrying all these colours encrusted on its deep, immaculate blue, and turning the painted crests of the mountains into coruscations of antique jewellery.

The village climbed breathlessly up-hill from the eastern end of the lake, for two hundred yards along the Mazzolo road, and then gave up the struggle, and curled up in the shade of a high outcrop of rock beside the way. This cliff leaned backward a little from the road-side, looking due west, and by drawing to itself the last of the sunset light it had given the village a name, Evening Rock. Two improbable birch trees grew out of its crest, from crannies which looked too narrow to contain root or soil. Beyond it the road climbed more steeply, until it staggered over the pass towards Mazzolo, and coasted downhill again among the woods by a long and roundabout descent.

They followed this climbing way to a point just beyond the rock, and then turned aside by a path which more closely resembled a dried watercourse; and after the light which had awakened them early in their small white rooms, the warm green gloom of the woods took them. For a quarter of an hour they scrambled among boulders, and then the path smoothed itself, and narrowed to a ledge of leaf-mould, zigzagging methodically up the hunched shoulder of the mountain.

Twice they emerged upon tiny balconies of meadow, fine as lawns, looking over the steadily receding blue dewdrop of the lake. Once they walked for a time through spaces cleared of timber, where the bushes had grown high in the sun, and acres of wild raspberry canes were dripping with ripe fruit; and here, since they had no one to please but themselves, they stopped to pick and eat berries until they were surfeited. The sun climbed as they ate, and the raspberry canes steamed into the air with a rich spicy sweetness. They covered their heads from the direct rays, and climbed on.

It was nearly noon when they emerged on the rim of the high plateau of Monte Gazza, and the dwindling trees fell back into scrub, into heather, and finally left them standing in bare rolling uplands of springy turf, high in air and quivering with the impact of the sun. Looking back, they seemed to be walking on a level with the distant summits of the Brenta Alps, rosy and isolated and melodramatic as a mirage, far beyond the invisible valley.

In the shallow bowls of smooth grass two men and three women were working, scything between the frequent treacherous stones with beautiful close strokes, which left everywhere behind them a pattern of scallops, dappling the stubble with ripples like a painted sea. Two boys, barefoot and wiry and olive-brown, raked after them with wide wooden rakes, and their little stack, fenced with leaning poles against a wind which at present was non-existent, scented the air with a warmth of hay and clover and sorrel. They cried greetings across the plateau as the four wanderers passed, and Phyllida, ready to attempt any language on such a morning, shouted back unabashed: '*Buon' giorno, signori!*' The boys were delighted with her, and leaned on their rakes to gaze, watching her brightly and darkly all the way up the long, shallow bowl of grass. Past the stack, past the three ramshackle little brush huts where this haymaking party passed the summer nights, past the dull grass and twig fire bricked round to hold a cooking-pot, up towards the high rim of sky and outcrop rock, beyond which was the sheer drop into the next valley. They could feel it pulling at them already, the outward, downward surge of the golden air, plunging from the crest.

Suddenly a silver-green, creamy froth of edelweiss broke out in the turf all about their feet, and they were standing on the grassy shoulder of Monte Gazza.

'That's it!' said Punch complacently, as if he felt personally responsible for the prodigy before them. 'Well, did I tell you any lies?'

In front of their feet the ground fell away sheer to the floor of the valley, in less than two miles descending some four thousand feet. Fields, villages, roads were spilled there, far below, like the filigree detail of an aerial photograph, and a shallow little kidney-shaped lake with a hamlet tucked into its hollow side. Beyond these, another ridge of hills arose, high enough and sudden enough though it never reached the level where they stood; and beyond this was another deep folded valley, half invisible, but showing here and there between the crests of the intervening hills a silver glint of river which they knew must be the Adige, and in the lowest decline a slight haze of smoke and a pattern of streets, radiating like the spines of a cactus flower just growing out of its encasing leaf.

'Trento!' said Punch, triumphantly pointing, as if he had himself ordained it so. But on the shoulder of Monte Gazza he could be forgiven for feeling a little like a god, the flowering world which delighted him was so remote and small in its beauty.

They looked to the left, and saw the valleys narrowing, all the spines of mountain drawing together into one massive crest running northward away from them. They looked to the right, and the valley widened and widened, cupping two lakes linked together, and beyond these, great silver coils of the River Sarca like a shining ribbon on the green floor, another lake, very far off, and still beyond, what seemed first haze, and then sky, and then sea, withdrawing itself glossily from recognition into the silvery blueness and faint haze above.

'San Massenza,' intoned Punch, naming the lakes as they receded, in an intoxication of recollection, 'Toblino, Cavedino – Garda!' he shouted, reaching the mysterious presence on the remote skyline. 'Did you recognise it again? Well, isn't it wonderful? Did you ever see country look exactly like a map before?'

'You make it sound exactly like a map, too,' said Peter almost crossly, for he strongly objected to being bludgeoned into admiration, and suffered – or his friends did – from an absolute inability to exclaim. A pronounced judgment of splendour he might make after long and critical contemplation, but he would not be over-balanced into enthusiasms. However, he sat down like the rest of them among the sage-green velvet stars of the edelweiss, and nursed his chin, and stared contentedly; until he began to suspect that even the glittering landscape itself was a little too sure of its ability to impress, and recoiled, as usual, into his own unabashed physical nature, and announced that he was hungry.

'You must be related to the woman who got to the top of Snowdon, and said what a fine drying-ground it would make,' said Punch disgustedly; but he handed over Phyllida's rucksack resignedly, and was not five minutes behind Peter in unrolling the oiled paper from his omelette.

They ate everything they had brought with them, and then draped handkerchiefs over their heads, and fell asleep in the high heat of the afternoon. Only in the sudden stillness of the evening did they begin the return journey to Rocca della Sera.

Something had happened to the hot perfection of the day, something gradual and ominous. Heavy clouds had moved up over the western sky, apparently without wind to bring them, and a coppery glint had stolen over the sunlight. Then a cooler breath stirred out of the valley as they dropped down the first slope of meadow.

'Going to be a storm,' said Mab, looking up anxiously at a sky still half blue and serene.

'Won't break yet, I think,' said Punch, regretfully turning his back upon the prospect of half the Trentino. 'We'll make it back to the village in maybe two hours, and even before that we'll be within reach of some sort of shelter. But I think with luck we shall get home before it comes. Better step out, though.' He set the pace himself, one which Mab could just keep by breaking into a trot occasionally.

They had reached the patch of raspberry canes when the first drops of rain came, heavy and slow out of a suddenly still air; and though the shower passed quickly, only spattering them as it flew by, they all reached for their wind-jackets, and Phyllida crowed with glee over her forethought in bringing the old raincoat. Punch clawed it impatiently out of the straps for her, and shook out its crumpled folds with a frowning face. Peter often wondered how they were going to arrange things after they were married, with Punch wanting everything in the house neatly in its place, and Phyllida dropping things haphazardly wherever she ceased to want them for the moment, in the serene expectation of finding them where she had left them when next they were needed. But it would certainly be an interesting spectacle for the onlookers, and since Phyllida was so sublimely sure of herself as to be impervious to rebuke, the probability was that even the principals would live through it.

'You look like a tramp,' said Punch, when she had buttoned the dilapidated object round her shoulders.

'I am a tramp,' said Phyllida buoyantly, and smiled at him without rancour, and plunged on.

A moment later she stopped in her tracks, so suddenly that he cannoned into her. Her instinct when putting on a coat was to thrust her hands immediately and deeply into the pockets, for when she hadn't worn the thing for some time, who knew what treasures might be lying there forgotten? She'd found many a sweet that way. But this wasn't a sweet. It was something hard and heavy which hung solidly against her thigh, dragging at the skirts of the coat as she ran. Her face went quite blank with the effort to identify it. To Punch's irritated query she made no answer, but drew out and regarded with stupefaction the contents of her pocket.

A large electric torch, of a perfectly plain, sensible pattern, and a man's white handkerchief, never yet shaken out from its long laundry folds, but crumpled together over them into a loose ball. Phyllida had some large handkerchiefs, but none so generous as this; and besides, it had initials embroidered in one corner, A.G. She stared, and Punch, halted at her shoulder under the arching of the trees, craned curiously to see what had taken her attention.

'Good lord!' said Phyllida, 'have I been carrying that round on my rucksack? No wonder the thing felt a ton weight. Didn't you notice it when you shook the coat out?'

'Well, of course I did,' said Punch, 'only I'm never surprised at the things you lug round in your pockets. But what on earth did you bring along a thing like that for? Anybody'd think we were going pot-holing, or something drastic, instead of just walking.'

'Idiot, I didn't bring it. It isn't mine at all. I don't know where it's come from, or how I got it, but I

76

certainly didn't bring it with me. And why the handkerchief? Look, are those *my* initials?'

Punch said with a sudden gasp: 'My God, they're *his!*'
And as she stared rather irately at him for his obscurity,
he elaborated with less than his usual patience: '*His!*
Surely you haven't forgotten about him already? The
old man in the train – *our* old man. Arturo Galassi!
Isn't it plain enough?'

They stared at each other incredulously under the
green boughs, through which a few heavy drops still
slipped dully. Peter and Mab came back to the curve of
the path to find out what was delaying them, and seeing
them thus inexplicably intent upon two very prosaic
objects clutched in Phyllida's hand, padded curiously
up to be in the secret.

'What have you got there?' demanded Peter, all
eyes.

She held them out to him on her spread palms,
helplessly. 'Look! *His* initials! Punch just spotted it.
They were in the pocket of my coat. I didn't know,
I'd no idea, until I just stuck my hand in, and found
them. But they must have been there ever since it
happened.'

'But how could they get into your pocket, anyhow?'
asked Peter, gaping. 'You had the raincoat stuck in the
straps of your rucksack the whole time.'

'No, I didn't. Don't you remember, when we had to
run for the Customs at Modane – oh, but of course you
don't, you weren't with us then. It started to slip out
of the straps, because I'd displaced it when I shoved
my wind-jacket under, and I grabbed it out in a hurry,
and carried it over my shoulder. And when we got in
with you and Mr Galassi I stuck it in the rack beside
my rucksack—'

'And forgot it, and left it behind when we had to

77

move,' said Punch. 'It was just beside his cases, and, as usual, you'd only thrown it just on to the rack at all, and the skirts were dangling a foot overboard.'

'Yes, I know – that's why I had to go back at Turin. And when I got into the carriage I thought at first he was still asleep, and I grabbed the coat and stuck it back into the straps of my rucksack. I spoke to him, but he didn't hear, and it was only after that that I touched him, and – and found out—And afterwards, when we were answering all the questions, I never thought that my coat could have anything to do with it. Well, how could I possibly guess that an old coat mattered? But it must have been then that these were put into the pocket.'

'But didn't you notice that you'd collected some extra weight?' asked Peter.

'No, but you see, I just pulled the thing off the rack and rolled it up tight, all in one movement, crumpled it up anyhow and stuck it in.' She looked down at the skirts of the coat, which advertised the accuracy of her recollection by scores of creases. 'I didn't have time to realise there was anything different about it. And though it's big enough, it isn't so massive as all that. Anyhow, it wasn't there before. And you see for yourselves, the initials identify the handkerchief.'

'Then who,' asked Punch, for them all, 'put them there? Not Signor Galassi himself! Why should he?'

'No,' said Phyllida, thinking back very carefully. 'No. Somebody who thought it was *his* coat! Why shouldn't they? It was dangling from the rack just beside his cases, and it's quite masculine-looking. It wasn't as crumpled as this, then, and with only a foot or so of it showing, it would look fairly respectable. Especially to somebody in a hurry. Besides, there was no one else in the carriage – why shouldn't they take it for granted it was his?'

78

They looked at one another with intent, expectant eyes, remembering only one person who must have been in a great hurry on that occasion. Then Punch suddenly reached out and took the handkerchief from Phyllida's hand and, carefully probing its creases, and opening it into the long scarf it made in its original closely pressed folds, looked it over inch by inch. He collected from it two short, bright grey hairs.

'*His?*' said Phyllida in a whisper.

'Well, I can't be sure of that, but I think so. Don't you?'

'Then this,' she said in the same awed tone, and holding up the torch as if it might bite her, 'this is the weapon that hit him? Wrapped up in the handkerchief? Then it wouldn't break the scalp quite so easily, would it? At least, that's what I've read somewhere.'

'There's another reason, too,' said Punch grimly. 'That way, there wouldn't be any finger-prints. Even a man in a hurry might remember that – especially if he was used to that sort of job.'

They were all talking at once, quite suddenly, their imaginations turned loose upon this new evidence. It rained on them desultorily through the trees, and they did not even notice it.

'But why shove these things into my coat pocket?'

'Idiot, he thought it was the old man's coat.'

'Dolt, I know he did! But still, why choose to shove them in there? He could have chucked them out of the window, and made sure.'

'That wouldn't have been making sure. In a case like that I bet they'd comb the railway line from Modane to Turin – but a man's torch and handkerchief in his own coat-pocket – well, where have they got a better right to be?'

'Then why,' said Mab, in her small, clear, puzzled

voice, 'if it was so clever to ditch the evidence then, are they trying heavens hard to get it back now?'

This was a new thought, and they turned their doubtful, discovering stares on her, and found her frowning like a puppy anxious to do the right thing, but unsure of what is required. She always came in from a different angle from the rest of them, saw a different facet of the same event, and was apologetic about her left-handedness, and for ever hoping against hope to find herself, next time, among the orthodox. She said deprecatingly: 'There isn't anything else. It *must* be these they're after, don't you think so? They've turned down everything of our own, and yet they're still looking, and still following us. At least, it looks as if they are. And you see, by sheer luck they've missed the rucksack they really needed.'

'That's it!' said Phyllida, her eyes glowing with excitement. 'You've put your finger on it, Mab. This is the treasure they're hunting, I bet my last lira it is. And I had it tucked under my arm all the time our chum with the earrings was feeling his way through the other rucksacks. And I didn't even know I had it!'

'But why,' said Mab, apologetically persisting, like a discouraged but dogged child, 'why did they make such haste to get rid of the evidence then, and the next day follow us all across Italy to get it back?'

'Oh, I don't know. Leave that to the police. Maybe they found out it was the wrong coat. Maybe he reported back to the boss, and the boss said he was crazy, and told him to get it back at once. Maybe they want to dispose of it more safely.'

'There are dozens more questions, besides,' said Punch feverishly, fishing in Phyllida's rucksack for an empty bag from lunch, into which he carefully folded away the handkerchief with its two bright grey hairs.

'Did they know we had these, or were they just checking up on everyone who was around? And if they knew the coat had turned out to be yours, Phyl, and knew these things were in it, were they just hoping to recover 'em without our ever knowing anything about it, or did they think we'd already found 'em?' He rummaged for another sheet of soft paper which had wrapped peaches, and rolled the torch into it with great care. 'We'll have left some of our prints on it, but that can't be helped. Come on, let's get down to the village. We've got to get these to the police as fast as we can.'

He buckled the treasure away into Phyllida's ruck-sack, and set off downhill at his longest stride. Punch made up his mind slowly to the possibility of melo-drama, but he was convinced at last; and now, thought Phyllida, skipping delightedly after him with a pleased eye trained on his fiercely jutting chin, there would be no holding him. She looked forward to action, and plenty of it. It seemed a pity that the police had to be in it at all.

(3)

The real rain came just as they were scrambling down the stony watercourse above the road, plunging down the steepest places in showers of stones, and fending themselves off from trees and boulders. The coppery sky above the bowl of the lake opened in a flash of rose-coloured lightning, and a sudden steel downpour seethed across the water and slashed into the trees. Within a matter of seconds the leaves sagged under the weight, and water streamed through in cold, continuous streams, drenching them as they ran, pouring down their necks to the waist, squelching in their boots. Before they reached the road the watercourse was a watercourse again, and a swirling stream bore leaves and twigs stickily downhill about their ankles.

They splashed out on to the glazed surface of the road, and ran head-down for the village, stopping for nothing until they dived, gasping, into the dim little entrance hall of the Albergo Monte Gazza.

They shook out their waterproofs, none of which had continued proof against so much water in one go, and squeezed out puddles of rain from their hair upon the doorstep, and retreated wetly upstairs to strip, and towel themselves back into warmth, and wring out socks and shirts and drenched underclothing in their wash-basins. The rain continued to stream down the windows unabated. Punch padded across to peer out over the lake in search of a break in the clouds, but the sky hung dropsically purple, without a gleam of clean light, and the wind drew whip-lashes of spume across the muddied surface of the lake. He fretted, half into his dry flannels, scowling at the weather which had got in his way so obtusely. He said: 'Well, rain or no rain, I've got to go. This is urgent.'

'Half an hour won't make any difference,' said Peter.

'Not to the weather, by the look of it,' agreed Punch glumly. 'I don't know why I'm bothering to change – looks as if I'll be in the same state again as just now.'

'Oh, don't be an ass, you can't go out in this! You've got no more trousers to change into, if you do. And anyhow, you don't even know where you're going yet. Why go out and slosh about in the rain looking for the place, when you could just ask the girl in the bar, and have it all planned before you go out of the door?'

'What, with a phrase-book, on a job like this? I bet she doesn't speak English.'

'She does, a bit. Enough,' said Peter simply, 'for our purposes.' He smoothed his ruffled fair hair, just erecting itself fluffily after its wetting, and met Punch's eye brazenly in the mirror. 'Her name's Liana. She's sixteen. I was talking to her this morning, while you were in the kitchen getting the lunches out of the cook.'

'I see you were! But we don't want to make even your girl-friends too curious about this business. Don't forget that fellow's here, on our trail already. We're taking no chances.'

'That's all right,' said Peter serenely. 'She's on the dumb side, as a matter of fact. I can get what I want out of her, and she won't so much as know what I was driving at. As for curiosity, I don't believe she's got any. I'll go and do some prospecting. You wait here.' And he flashed away to the stairs, pleased with the job he had appropriated to himself. Punch let him go without encouragement, but he needed none.

Phyllida drummed with her finger-tips at the door a moment later, and came in without waiting for permission. She was in a state of high and pleasurable excitement, with a roused colour in her cheeks, and her eyes deeply lustrous. A pleased, even a complacent look illuminated her most irresponsible moments. She advanced upon him in a swirl of printed cotton skirts, announcing loudly and with great satisfaction: 'Well, it happened!' And when he stared at her for a moment without comprehension, she added: 'So you've forgotten, too! I suggested it myself, and we all went out all day to give the man a chance, and then we're all so preoccupied with this new evidence that we forget all about it. But he's been! Among my things, I mean. I left them so he couldn't miss leaving some traces. I left my powderbox with the powder tipped up to one side, so that if he moved it he couldn't avoid shaking a

83

few grains overboard. You know what a rim it leaves. If you wipe it off, unless you're very thorough, there's a sort of bluish matt smudge where the grains ran. And even if you're clever enough to blow it off, you're liable to let a little of it settle again in a wider circle. Enough, if you know what to look for. And I do. So we weren't on the wrong track, and we are being hunted for some precious thing we've got.'

'We know now what it is,' said Punch.

'You're not even surprised,' said Phyllida, put out by the grim placidity with which he went on drying his hair.

'I'd have been a lot more surprised if he *hadn't* had a try. Seems to me he wants these things pretty badly. I tell you what, Phyl, I shall be a lot happier when we've handed them over to the police.'

Phyllida opened her eyes wide in astonishment. 'Oh, but why? *I* was wishing we didn't have to do anything so ordinary. Oh, I know, I know! Citizens' responsibilities, and all that – and of course I know we must give them up. But I wish we could go on finding out the whole truth ourselves. And surely, the evidence couldn't be safer. There are four of us.'

'Well, there are at least two of them, and we don't know yet how many more there may be. But it isn't that I feel uneasy about us, and our safety. I'm thinking of putting the evidence where it can do most good. What matters is making good use of it.'

'Couldn't *we* make good use of it?' asked Phyllida gaily.

'Maybe. There's nothing to stop us trying – *after* we hand over to the police. But I'm not playing around with something that might make all the difference to catching the chap who hit the old man.' He set his square jaw firmly, and his eyes, dwelling on her almost aggressively, said further: 'Not even to please you!'

You never could tell with Phyllida. She might easily have tossed her head airily at him, said: 'Nobody's asking you to!' and sailed out of the room. Instead, she suddenly laughed, quite gently, and threw her arms round his shoulders and hugged him. 'Good old Punch! You never take your eye off the ball, do you? Yes, you're right, we've got to play it the safe way. It isn't just our game, and we've got no right to take any risks with it. OK, so we take the things to the police, and tell them everything we know, and everything we think we know. But there isn't a thing we can do until it stops raining, or at least eases up a little. So stop worrying about it for one hour, and come down to dinner.'

'It isn't quite time yet, anyhow. If the police-station is somewhere near, I'd rather get it over and done with. Then,' he said, with a sudden gleam in his eye, 'we can consider what *we* do next.'

Peter and Mab came in together from the landing, closing the door behind them with unwonted care. In a gingham frock, kept fresh by severely accurate folding through all the vicissitudes of the journey, Mab looked about fourteen. She looked round the room with a solemn, even a faintly reproachful eye, and immediately picked up Peter's socks from where he had dropped them on the floor, and draped them carefully on the towel-rail to dry. His plaid shirt she added to an array of wet clothing already arranged over her arm, collected Punch's also, and walked out with them without a word.

'It's all right,' explained Peter cheerfully. 'She's got an arrangement with Liana to get the cook to dry everything for us. Our shoes won't be so good tomorrow, but maybe it'll be fine and let us wear sandals. I told you that girl knew enough English to be useful. But it's no go about your trip, old boy, not tonight. You can forget

85

it until tomorrow morning. Sorry, but there it is! They haven't got any police-station here. Not even one little village constable!'

This was something for which Punch had not bargained. 'Then where do we have to go?' he demanded blankly. 'There must be a place somewhere within reasonable reach, surely.'

'Well, it depends what you call reasonable reach. The nearest station is at Sopramazzolo, so Liana says, and that's on the pass on the old road to Mazzolo, the one the modern road dodges by going umpteen miles round. She says it's a good hour on foot, and *not* for strangers in the dark, because though the path's safe as houses by daylight, there are some nasty drops in places alongside it. She's from up there herself, so I don't think she'd exaggerate the dangers – more likely to forget the worst, I should say. But there it is! It's either there, or right into Mazzolo, and that means tomorrow's bus, because you won't want to walk it.'

Punch, frustrated, considered the chances with indignation, and objected to being put off his course. 'Well, surely if one took it carefully – and we've got a torch.'

'We've also got more sense than to think we know better than the natives,' said Phyllida sharply, 'and we are not going playing the fool on a stormy night across precipices about which we've already been warned. So forget it!'

'We're not all going, anyhow,' said Punch, nettled. 'That would be advertising that we're up to something. You three are going to stay here and cover up for me, and keep an eye on *him*. But I don't see why I shouldn't get on well enough, with reasonable care. Anyhow, I could try it.'

'You won't,' said Phyllida firmly, 'if I have to knock you out with a Chianti bottle and tie you to the bed.

What sort of help do you think you're going to be, to the police or anyone else, if you go and get yourself lost or damaged in the mountains? No, we'll take every conceivable care of the evidence, and that doesn't mean dropping it over cliffs at midnight, it means keeping it safe and close here in our hands until we can safely get it to the police. Safely, my lamb, is the operative word. You said we take no chances. Right, we're taking none. You can stay here willingly or unwillingly until daylight, but believe me, here you'll stay.'

Rain slashing at the window, which was already only a slightly paler oblong in a gathering dusk of night and storm, argued more strongly than Phyllida's solicitude in favour of staying willingly. It would certainly be a dirty night on the pass; and after all, what good would it do anyone if he got into difficulties up there with the evidence in his pocket? There was no bus to Mazzolo until early afternoon, but if he set off immediately after an early breakfast he could be in Sopramazzolo by ten o'clock easily, and back by lunch, and if the others did their part, appearing and disappearing within the enemy's sight at discreet intervals, they could very well look like four instead of three, and he need never be missed.

'Well, I suppose one night won't make so much difference as all that,' he said grudgingly. 'All right, then, in the morning.'

'Now you do show glimmerings of sense. And I can quite see that a mass exit in that direction might be a mistake, and that somebody ought to stay here and keep an eye on the grey man. But surely two and two would be reasonable, wouldn't it?' She meant, of course, that she was coming with him, he could see it in her eye; and though there was no denying that he would have liked to have her company on the jaunt, he felt strongly that this was an errand better done alone, and that three on the lake beach, advertising half-nakedly in the sun that this was a rest day between mountain rambles, would be of more service than anywhere else. An innocent appearance was going to be of more value than the strength of numbers, he judged, in this contest.

'No, really, I'd rather go alone. There are good reasons. We've got to keep him happy about us, and don't forget, he's tried your luggage now for what he wants, and the field's narrowing. No, you've got to hover just in his sight all morning, while I slip over the pass. You've got to come and go as if you were — as if we all were having a lazy day, going no further than up the village to the film place, or for ice-cream, or into the bar for a drink. Try and look as if the fourth is always only just gone for a postcard and a stamp. You know how I mean.'

'I know,' said Phyllida, with ominous quietness, 'but I disagree. The one who goes from here with the valuables in his pocket is the one who goes into danger, if there is any danger.'

'But not if no one knows he's gone. I can be back before lunch, we can all four appear together at table, just as if I *had* only been up the village for stamps. You can do more to protect me by staying here than by coming with me.'

'Ridiculous!' said Phyllida.

'Ridiculous or not, that's what you'll do—'

'When you two have finished biting each other,' said Peter patiently, 'I'll deliver the rest of my recce report. I've been doing a little digging about our well-dressed chum in grey as well as about the location of the police stations around here.'

They gave him their attention immediately, not abandoning their fight, but only postponing it. 'From Liana? You didn't give anything away, did you?'

'What do you take me for? I got his name from the letter in his pigeon-hole in the key-board, there's a late afternoon delivery, and he hadn't collected. Nobody else was around at all. I spotted his room number last night, when he took his key. Name's Teodoro Monfalcone. So then I did a little pumping with Liana and the porter, to find out who he is. It seems he's never been here before, or anything like that, so they don't know him personally, but his firm has a name people have at least heard of. He's in some export-import business in Rome, dealing mainly in things like glass and bijouterie, especially between Italy and France. According to reputation he ought to be pretty rich. I don't want to discourage you, Punch, my lad, but you're going to have an up-hill job getting the police to believe a man like that had anything to do with a train robbery with violence.' He drew in a thoughtful sigh. 'Does that alter your ideas about him?'

Punch stared back at him heavily, thought for a long minute, and said flatly: 'No!'

'Good! It didn't mine, either. I can only think of one reason for a man like that being in a place like this, and it's a shady reason. If he wanted to stay in the mountains, he'd be in some big hotel in Bolzano, or up on Lake Como, or somewhere like that, not here in Rocca della Sera. But you're going to see the eyebrows rise when you suggest him as a suspect.'

'I shan't exactly do that. I shall tell them the facts we've noticed about him, that's all. They can believe it or not, I can't be responsible for their reactions.'

'It's time we went down,' said Phyllida, 'because we don't want to look too much like a conspiracy.

Since we've got to carry the goods on us, where do you suppose would be the safest place? Your pocket, Punch? Or my shoulder bag?' They tried both, and the sag of the torch's weight decided the issue. 'No,' said Phyllida, firmly retrieving the treasure, 'he'd spot it right across the room.' She shut it into her small leather shoulder bag, already well-filled with oddments, but kept in better order than the rest of her possessions. 'There, I won't take my hand off it, except to eat. Come on, we'll tell Mab all the arrangements after dinner.'

They met her on the stairs, just coming back from her errand, as demurely and seriously as if she knew nothing of secret conferences or crimes of violence. She made no protest about being the only one not in the know, but very practically turned about and led the way to the dining-room, for, like Peter in moments of stress, she was hungry.

They were the last comers, it seemed, for all the tables except their own were occupied. There was a nondescript individual sitting alone, who looked like some Italian version of a middle-aged and rather seedy commercial traveller. There were a fat married couple and their two small children; and beyond them, a young pair who, if married at all, were only recently married, for they appeared to be quite drunkenly in love. And round the corner in his secluded place, as Mab deliberately took her seat facing his way, the tall man in grey looked up from his dinner, and gave her the full calm glance of his gently melancholy eyes, and suddenly smiled and inclined his head across the lifted wine-glass in his hand. They saw it, they all appropriated it to themselves as a party, a little gesture of impudent amusement, patting them on the head, dismissing them as entertaining but unimportant children, whose interventions in his affairs could be indulged like mild sweets, without any ill-effects. They all accepted the supposed challenge, looking very erect and adult, bowing to him with the faintest and gravest of smiles in return. So he was inviting them to play, was he! He would see how quickly they would pick up the rules of the game.

But Mab sat there looking at him, being looked at by him, without a smile. Mab knew better. Maybe he had casually stretched out his large, easy, playful hand and stroked up their fur the wrong way, just for the fun of seeing them bridle and fuss and lick it back again; but the fingers of his glance had taken the opportunity of resting on her with quite a different implication, and their caress had been light, undisturbed, yet respectful. Her fur wasn't ruffled; he hadn't meant it to be.

She ate her dinner very silently. Something was going on which she did not understand. She had been too early and too long among the books, perhaps, and was coming rather late out of the bud. Being admired across a room, on terms of perfect assurance and equality, was something which had never happened to her before.

CHAPTER FOUR

ECCENTRICITIES OF THE LIGHTING SYSTEM
AT THE ALBERGO MONTE GAZZA

(1)

IN this high bowl of the mountains, even on fine days of summer, the night came rather early, and by eight o'clock in the evening artificial lighting was needed. Rocca della Sera was rather proud of the fact that all its lighting was electric, but kept a discreet silence upon its quality and reliability; for the plain fact was that the supply was woefully inadequate, and even when working, provided only a romantic twilight in which it was practically impossible to write, read or sew. The guests at the Albergo Monte Gazza peered at one another over dinner through a gradually deepening gloom, enlivened by occasional lurches towards complete darkness.

Liana, helping out with the serving of the dinner, said apologetically that across there in the mountains men were cutting a tunnel through the rock, to bring down water from the other side of the range and make more power, and when that was completed everything would be all right. In the meantime, her young dark eyes were screwing themselves into a perpetual frown, and from long groping in this half-light she misjudged distances sometimes in a way which made Peter, who was perhaps paying more attention to her than the others, furrow his own brow in indignant sympathy. She was sixteen, she said. She had been working in the bar, scrubbing and polishing, when he came down to breakfast that morning at half-past six; she had certainly been serving drinks the previous night after half-past eleven, when he had gone up to bed; and he rather suspected that she would still be hard at it tonight at the same time. The sun had been shining day after day for several months, hotly and lavishly, upon the Brenta Alps, and the visitors were all a rich golden brown; but Liana's round, good-natured face was as pale as cream, because she almost never went out. And she didn't seem to see anything wrong with it! Or at least, it didn't seem to have occurred to her that anything could ever be done about it.

Peter supposed that with something between two and three million unemployed in the country one hung on to any job, tooth and nail, right up to the edge of blindness. What a country! What a system, rather, to endure in such a heavenly country!

And yet there were things about it which restored the balance suddenly in the oddest ways, like the way the cook and the porter came into the bar among the guests at night, in the short interludes in their apparently endless duties, and put on the radio and danced to its music, everybody's fellow-guests and everybody's equals. Not that that would buy any bread, of course, but it was something very unlikely to happen in the same way in an English hotel.

The lamp on the table glowed, suddenly encouraged, and then lurched back into despair. In the bar, where people normally spent their evenings, it was usually rather brighter, and as soon as they had dined they began to move off in that direction. The glass-panelled door had just swung back from Punch's hand, and they were crossing the small hallway, when the lights suddenly went out altogether, leaving them in absolute darkness.

Instinctively they halted, feeling out for one another. Somewhere in the hall one of the children crashed into something – it sounded like a chair slurring along the floor at the blow – and burst into howls of fright, and the mother, groping towards the sound with excitable noises of comfort, evidently grasped someone who was not her distressed offspring, for a double stream of apology and embarrassment broke out together. Everybody was talking and exclaiming at once, and the darkness seemed to be heaving with people. Punch took his hand from Phyllida's arm to fend off a heavy body which blundered into him and almost knocked him off-balance. A stream of wasted words and a gust of garlic assailed him, and reach where he would, he couldn't find Phyllida again. It was altogether too opportune. A cool draught blew round his ankles, as from an opened door. A high-pitched voice appealed volubly for a moment's patience, a moment only, and the lights would come on again. And then, suddenly, incredibly, Phyllida gave tongue out of the darkness a yard or two from him, in loud indignant English:

'*My bag!* Punch, where are you? Someone snatched my bag! Right off my shoulder! Honestly, I felt it go. All my money's in it—'

A pained gasp from somewhere near to her was all too patently Peter despairing of her. But he recovered himself quickly, and said equally loudly, and with every impression of cheerful scorn:

'Oh, rot, you've just dropped it. Stand still a minute, and don't make such a fuss. The lights will be on again any minute now.'

Privately he groped for her, and gave her a vicious dig in the ribs for her stupidity; and with the greatest aplomb she lifted her foot and stamped hard upon his sandalled toes, and unfeelingly covered his smothered gasp of pain with a fresh outcry.

'What do you mean, fuss! Wouldn't you make a fuss if every penny you had went west? My *purse* is in it, I tell you, *and* my ticket home, and everything—'

'Oh, you've only let it slip off your shoulder,' said Punch, trying not to feel as alarmed and bewildered as he felt. If this disaster had really befallen her, why in the world was she going out of her way to advertise the urgency of her loss? But all he could do was to treat her lamentations in an offhand manner, and hope that he sounded convincing. 'It'll be somewhere round your feet, on the floor, if you'll only shut up and wait a minute, instead of flapping like a wet hen.'

'It isn't!' she shrilled indignantly. 'I've been feeling round for it, and I can't find it. I tell you, it was pulled off my shoulder, I *didn't* drop it. Punch, what am I going to *do* without any money?' But she grew quieter, as if his scornful optimism had not been without effect. Peter she had quite effectively silenced; she could feel him standing on one foot close beside her and tenderly nursing the injured toes of the other one. Serve him right for being so sure everyone else was a fool! She hoped he would be standing on both feet when the lights went up, and wanted to giggle at the idea of a stork-like Peter caught cuddling his wounds in mid-air.

The howling child had found its mother, and was subsiding in hiccoughing sobs. The manager was still making soothing noises and promising light; and suddenly the feeble bulbs lit up again, and cast a sick, pale glow over the scene of confusion, and instantly everyone became quite silent for a moment. And there was Punch with a strained and wary expression, gazing full at Phyllida and trying to judge from the look of her what had really happened there in the dark; and Peter, sulkily scrubbing his hurt toes up and down the calf of his other leg, and trying not to betray his intention of scragging Phyllida as soon as he could get her alone; and Mab standing quite quietly, exactly where the darkness had fallen upon her, and waiting to weigh and understand; and the authoress of all the commotion, looking ruffled and put out, and on the point of announcing her losses all over again. And there, alone relaxed and reposeful, was Teodoro Monfalcone in the open doorway of the dining-room, just retrieving Phyllida's shoulder bag from the floor, where it lay on its side, with the long strap dangling round the handle of the door.

'There you are!' said Punch bitterly. 'I knew it wouldn't be far away. You hooked it up in the handle. Snatched, my foot!'

'Oh, thank goodness!' sighed Phyllida, looking faintly ashamed of her agitation, and even contriving, heaven knew how, to flush prettily as Monfalcone bent his elegant shoulders before her and proffered the errant bag. His smile was friendly, if a little remote and vague, and the small gay gleam in his eyes was only gently satirical. He said in easy and assured English: 'I'm very glad it was not as bad as you feared, after all.'

Phyllida clutched her treasure firmly in both hands, and said radiantly: 'Oh, so am I! You know, it wouldn't be much of a joke, trying to get home without any money. Thank you, so much! I say, I do feel a fool, making such a scene!'

'Not at all! In a foreign country it is not funny to lose one's papers, even for only a few minutes.' His voice was soft, level and cool, like his glance, even distantly melancholy like it. 'The light here is certainly very trying – even when it works. You must come again in a year or two, when the new scheme is in operation, then it will

97

not play you such tricks.' He smiled, and nodded, and walked away towards the bar, into which the mother was just leading her recovered child by the hand. The radio was starting up within, and all the evening noises were smoothing themselves out into loud normality. The door closed between.

Phyllida made for the key-board. They couldn't talk here in the hall, or in the bar, or anywhere where they might be overheard. Punch had her by the wrist already, and was urging her towards the stairs. Up they went into the boys' room, which was the more remote of the two, and offered the better chance of hearing any approaching foot before its owner came into earshot of the conversation within the room. They didn't dare to speak, except for artificial enquiries whether no one wanted a drink, and loud wonderings whether their boots would be dry by morning, until they were inside with the door fast closed behind them. Then Punch demanded in low but heated tones:

'Now then, what in the name of fortune was the idea of going off at half-cock like that? You might as well have used a megaphone! Quick, open the confounded bag, and let's know the worst.'

Phyllida obediently opened it, and tipped out the fine confused contents upon the bed, where they all leaned over them, digging like terriers among the details of a complicated life.

'Here's the paper bag with the handkerchief,' whispered Mab, pouncing. '*That's* all right! But – I can't see—'

Neither could the others see it. Punch swept his hand through the litter, spreading it abroad with a low groan, but it was no use, the thing would have been too large to hide among such small fry as lipstick, compact and wallet.

'He got it!' he breathed miserably. 'Oh, *Phyl!* He's got the torch!'

(2)

Phyllida said never a word, but only sat there on the bed with her hands clasped in her lap, looking at her friends with a quite unreadable expression and, worst of all, without, as far as they could see, a trace of shame, or even of the belligerent self-justification which sometimes films over shame. Punch heroically shut his teeth on reproaches, and tried to say something which would make her feel better, though she did not look to him as if she were taking it very seriously to heart.

'Oh, well!' he said. 'We were taken by surprise. It could have happened to anybody.'

But the words stuck in his throat; and there was no reason in the world that he could see why Phyllida should begin to smile, affectionately, mockingly, sweetly, her eyes glimmering upon him in placid defiance of Peter's bitter whispered scolding.

'Could have happened to anybody, my foot! She *asked* for it, yelling around in the dark like any halfwit, and not even holding on to the thing tightly. We ought to have known better than to trust her with it, I suppose. But at least you might realise what you've done, and not just sit there grinning like a Cheshire cat, you – you dead loss!'

Phyllida looked at him with a remote sisterly look, as if she could have enjoyed slapping him, but had more important things to think about. 'I'm glad,' she remarked thoughtfully, 'that I trod on your toes, you nasty little boy. I hope they hurt. A fine, trusting lot of friends I turned out to have! Still, I dare say I'd have been just as stupid about it in your place. Look, then, and stop grizzling!' She reached a hand suddenly down the neck of her frock, and drew out from under her left arm, and flourished before their eyes, the identical torch for which they were mourning. 'And let me tell you, I was on pins the whole time that the silly thing would slip from under my arm, or show through my frock, or something. But if you didn't see it, the odds are he didn't, either. There was nothing else to do with it. I haven't the figure to stow it in front.' She stood the torch on its end upon her knee, and smiled at their relief and discomfiture and astonishment.

'I eat my words,' said Peter handsomely. 'Step on the other foot!' And he stuck out his impudent bare toes in front of her; but she was looking over his shoulder at Punch, with a teasing, delighted smile, pleased to see him flush as painfully as if he had reviled her like an angry bargee.

'Oh, Phyl!' he said, and was stuck for adequate words of apology. 'Oh, lord, I ought to have known you couldn't – you, of all people! But how could we guess? And you didn't say anything to give us a lead.'

'Listen to him! A fat lot of chance I had to give you any hints, with Monfalcone a yard away from me in the dark, and this idiot here groaning aloud in my ear and digging me in the ribs.' But she couldn't be angry with Punch, who had so nobly swallowed his chagrin and produced so thumping a lie in reassurance; and for his sake she could forgive even Peter. 'You might have had a bit more confidence in me,' she said warmly. 'Would I be likely to go up in smoke like that without a sane reason?'

'Well, but it sounded as if you'd really been taken by surprise, and just yelled without thinking. I'm prostrate in apology,' said Peter generously, 'but honestly that's how it did sound. And in the dark every squeak is so significant – if you know what I mean. Besides, how on earth could you know what was going to happen? I mean, how come the torch wasn't in your bag when he grabbed it? I suppose there's no doubt he did grab it?'

'No doubt in the world,' said Phyllida firmly. 'And I'll tell you something else, there's no doubt the lights went out because he wanted them out at that exact moment. I don't know how, I don't know who worked it for him, because it's pretty evident he didn't do it himself. But he called the tune, all right. The rest of the lights in the village didn't fail. Did you know that? From where I was standing I could see clean across the street by the little high window, and there was a naked bulb lit up there in the house opposite.'

'I didn't see it. But the whole thing was too pat to be any accident. Exactly what did happen with the bag and the torch?' asked Punch.

'Well, actually I didn't think very fast, and it could have been a bad show,' owned Phyllida, slightly frowning over this concession to Peter's distrust. 'You see, he was still sitting at his table when we moved off, and he didn't look in any hurry, so I'd no idea he'd followed us so closely, so when the lights went out, I—Well, it's a torch, isn't it? It just came natural to reach inside the bag for it and pull it out of the paper, and jolly well make use of it. So I did. Well, I didn't know he was on my heels, did I? And by sheer luck I always zip the bag up again, because it's a very deep opening, and when it's full I lose things if I walk round with it open. It's about the only tidy habit I've got, and I only got that one after I shed my whole powder compact once. Thank goodness it runs very quietly, and the kid was howling, and the manager was yodelling, and altogether I don't think the enemy could have heard it. So there was I with the torch in my hand, and suddenly the strap of the bag was flicked clean off my shoulder and down my arm. And I had to yell then or never, because honest people *don't* stand like mutes when their bags are snatched. You only keep quiet on occasions like that if you've got something to hide, and I wanted him to think we *hadn't*, and by sheer luck the bag wouldn't tell him a thing to contradict it, because the torch was in my hand, and I didn't think the bag with the handkerchief in would be identifiable by touch in the dark. And you see, I was right, because he didn't take it. So it added up to the desirability of yelling, pronto, if not sooner, and I yelled. Did I do right?'

'You did absolutely right,' said Punch heartily. 'And we nearly wrecked it, thinking you were going to give the show away! But good lord, how could we pick up all the threads at that speed? It's lucky you thought as fast as you did.'

'I didn't *think*, so much,' said Phyllida honestly, 'as act on instinct. I just let fly as I would if we'd known nothing about any torch – only perhaps rather more so – I hope it wasn't overdone,' she said with some anxiety, 'because I'm dead certain that's one man with an ear for false quantities.'

'Sounded all right to me. *Just* like a frantic tourist losing her money and passport in a foreign hotel.'

'Yes, maybe, but—Oh, well, hope for the best! Anyhow, he got the bag, and he made his search quite thoroughly and with plenty of time for it, and the thing he wanted wasn't there. In theory, she said gravely, 'he should now conclude that he's been barking up the wrong tree all the time, and we're as innocent as babes. I'm only afraid he already knows quite certainly that we're nothing of the kind.'

It seemed that the female half of the party had conceived a curious respect for the acumen of Signor Monfalcone. Mab looked at Phyllida, and wondered perceptively if that long glance across the room, that night, had seemed to her as personal as it had to Mab herself. Phyllida would have felt its effect less, because Phyllida was quite irrevocably, happily and suitably Punch's girl, but that didn't render her impervious. Women, however sensible, usually notice the men who notice them, and admiration is a point of intelligence when directed to oneself. But this illuminating and rather humiliating thought flashed through her mind and was gone so quickly that she had no time to examine it closely, and the exigencies of the moment closed over it instantly, and shut it from her memory. Only a faint uneasiness remained behind, the more disquieting because it seemed to be without a source, and she could not for the life of her remember afterwards when or how it had first assailed her.

'Well, anyhow,' said Punch firmly, 'he hasn't gained anything, and with luck, even if he did feel convinced before, he may be doubting his conviction now. It looks as if we won out on this round. But look, we're sticking to this evidence closer than a brother for the rest of this evening, all four of us. We *know* we've got something important now, or he wouldn't be so keen to get hold of it. And the plan for tomorrow holds. The only difference is, it's more urgent than ever. I'm setting off for Sopramazzolo as soon as it's light.'

'You must have some breakfast,' objected Phyllida, but without any very great conviction, for in the end he would certainly do as he thought fit.

'Oh, I can eat afterwards, that's not important. But the sooner I get to the police, the better for all of us. I shall go alone, and you'll cover up for me here, and keep Monfalcone happy. After all, if you watch him carefully, he can't do me any harm, can he?'

'What if he does leave Rocca della Sera?' asked Peter. 'Do we go after him?'

'If possible you can, but in any case try to find out where he's going. After all, if he takes the bus back to Trento, or something harmless like that, you won't need to follow him. Use your judgment! You'll see if he's only going down to bathe, or if he makes a trip into the mountains, or if he's only going up the village for a drink. If you think he's on my trail, keep on his.'

'But if he takes out that hired car of his,' pointed out Peter sensibly, 'we've had it.'

'If he goes out in that, it won't be by the way I'll be going, from all accounts! Anyhow, whatever plans we make, you'll still have to do the best you can in the circumstances, so it's no use trying to think of everything in advance.'

'At the police-station,' said Phyllida, 'perhaps you'll get news of Signor Galassi.' And after the little spurt of hope in her voice, her eyes suddenly avoided his, flinching from too intimate a recognition of her own reflected fears. The name always brought them back to silence, back to the reality of these matters, to violence, and greed, and the inversion of human and material values. It made Phyllida afraid for Punch, and she wanted to argue again, with more gravity, the desirability of moving two and two; but she had not yet succeeded in integrating the two worlds in which her mind now moved, and could not find the right key in which to pitch her appeal. Before she could find her way among so many complexities, Mab suddenly did her trick.

All this time she had sat there on the end of Peter's bed, looking from face to face, saying not a word.

Now with her usual look of blundering puzzlement and puppyish obstinacy she put her finger upon the unnoticed detail.

'The torch didn't come on,' she said.

'No,' said Phyllida, startled. 'I suppose I never pressed the button down fully, because it was then he snatched the bag, and after that, of course, I was jolly glad it hadn't flashed, because it would have given the whole show away. I just stuffed it down my neck, quickly, and hugged it tight under my arm, ready for when the lights should come on again. It was pure luck, really, that I never had time to switch it on.'

'I'm not sure,' said Mab, scrubbing her small nose upward with a thoughtful forefinger in an odd intensity of concentration, 'but I don't think it would have mattered. I think if it had shone, he wouldn't have been interested. I think he was looking for one that *wouldn't* shine. Because when you come to think of it, this is an awful lot of trouble to go to, just to recover a piece of pretty dubious evidence. No prints, you see, because it was wrapped up. And no *proof* how it got into your pocket in the first place. It could be anybody's. And even if it was shown to be the old man's property, that doesn't connect it up with anyone else. I wouldn't follow you across Italy for it,' said Mab weightily, 'even if I had hit someone with it. I'd just stay well away from it, and lie low. And so would he, if that was all. Isn't it funny,' she said, shaken, 'when you think we've had it nearly four hours, and haven't even thought to look inside it?'

Phyllida sat staring at her for a long moment without moving. So did they all, and then as unanimously turned their gaze slowly upon the torch. Phyllida snapped the button down fully, but no gleam responded. She said faintly: 'Isn't it crazy? I'm *scared* to open it now!' But she unscrewed the end of it with fingers trembling slightly in excitement, and tipped out into her lap, not a battery, but a roll of soft green felt, which fitted so closely into the case that she had to help it out with her nails. It was tied with a thin white cord round the middle and both ends, and when she had unwound these it uncoiled itself into a felt bag, with a small hard roll of something pushed firmly down into its base.

They were all holding their breath now, the four intent heads bent over her shaking fingers. She was too slow for Peter. He reached forward suddenly, and tipped the bag up into her palm by its bottom corners, and the hard roll in the base disintegrated into several small fragments, and tumbled out upon her startled hand a flood of blue and white fire, flashing from the facets of twelve cut stones, each as large as the nail of her finger. They counted them, and were speechless and dazed; counted them again, stared at them still, and still could not believe it.

There was no more mystery about the pursuit of a simple torch across the whole of north Italy. It was not only the blunt instrument, it seemed, but the motive as well. The incompetent agent on the train had searched everywhere but in the right place, and in panic at his victim's awakening had used the torch as a weapon for murder, and thrust it back into the old man's pocket; and his employer, on receiving the report of failure, had grasped the significance which he had missed, and set out to recapture the prize which had slipped through his fingers once by so narrow a chance.

Even on that first occasion it had escaped only by reason of that momentary panic. Perhaps the old man had made some sound which might have been heard, perhaps someone had been coming along the corridor. In such circumstances you don't stay to look in the last few possible corners for what you want, you run for your life to the nearest place of patent innocence, if not beyond. But to the other man, perhaps, the man who paid you to get something which he knew would be there for the taking, to him your life is still not the most important thing in the world. Not so important, say, as twelve matched diamonds of probably fabulous value, on their way from Paris to Turin in the keeping of an old and trusted man. So you are sent back on to the job, to Desenzano, to Rocca della Sera, to the ends of the country if need be. Why not? One of these little bits of ice and flame would pay the expenses bill with plenty in hand for the organiser. And if it would pay one man, it would pay others, as well, as many as were needed to make a success of the venture. There was no knowing, now, how many people were loose on the job.

Punch touched the small, dazzling things, and felt his finger-tips burn with their perilousness. Ought they to change their plans? Couldn't the things be put in some safe in the hotel until the police came? Couldn't he get rid of the responsibility tonight, instead of waiting for the morning? But someone had been in Monfalcone's confidence here, at least to the extent of removing a fuse to his orders; and how could one guess who it was, or feel safe with anyone in the house until that question was answered? Except, perhaps, Liana, who was almost certainly sweet and honest all through, but who was quite certainly too simple to be let into any important secrets.

No, far better to rely on an early departure and the vigilance of three resourceful friends here. There was an added reason now for haste, for urgency. They had all sensed it, he could see it in their eyes. It wasn't only heaven knows how many millions of lire they stared at in Phyllida's palm, it was Signor Galassi's honour.

Where he had pledged himself to carry those stones, those stones must surely go, and they four, whether they liked it or not, were the agents of their delivery. Nothing less would do.

'Put them away,' said Mab, quite softly. 'Roll them up again just as they were, and put them away. Now we know, at any rate!'

It was astonishing how little they had to say. No one admired the things, though in their spiky way they were beautiful. No one exclaimed, or got excited, or wandered off into questions and explanations. The time for volubility was over, and very certainly the affair had ceased to be a game. Until now there had been nothing they could do for Signor Galassi. Now they had taken over his trust, and it lay as heavily on their spirits as the storm clouds over the lake.

CHAPTER FIVE

AN ABRUPT EXIT IN
DUBIOUS COMPANY

(1)

PUNCH took every possible precaution. He slept with
the torch and its precious contents hugged against his
side in the bed, with a chair-back under the handle of
the door, in case the lock could be forced silently, and a
thin string stretched from the catch of the window to his
wrist, so that any effort to get in by that way should jerk
him awake in a moment. In spite of which complicated
and difficult set-up, he slept very well, and awoke only
when he had felt the uneasiness of the dawn reminding
him through a tangled dream of his good resolutions.
Then he got up at once, and dressed quietly; and when
he was ready, all but his boots which squeaked on
polished tiles, and must therefore be carried on the
first stage of their journey, he woke Peter, who opened
dazed blue eyes at him, and came to the surface with
dizzy suddenness from what seemed to be an infinite
way down.

'Is it time?' he asked, rising on one elbow. 'Do you
want me to do anything?'

'Nothing except to lie low until a reasonable hour for
breakfast, and then take care of the other job for me.
And look after the girls.' Punch had streaks of these
quaint outdated ideas in his make-up, they gave him in
Phyllida's eyes a sort of period charm.

'We'll be all right,' said Peter, scrubbing at his eyes to erase the sleep. 'It's you that's looking for trouble. Do you think the door's even been opened yet? It's only just daylight.'

'Doesn't matter, I'm not going that way. If I go through the window and along this balcony where they hang the washing, there's an iron staircase at the end, and only one window in between, and that isn't his. And the end of the house is dead blind, not a window in it. In two minutes I'll be in the trees.'

'You may need the maps,' said Peter, his mind clearing.

'I've got them. I've left you the district one, and taken the detailed ones. Now I'm going. If you *could* manage to miss Monfalcone at breakfast, so he won't know there were only three of us, so much the better. But with luck it won't matter, because I'll be almost in Sopramazzolo by that time.' He eased his string from the catch of the window, and coaxed it wide open with a finger under the latch, because it was stiff, and given to noisy movement when persuaded. The heavy growth of creeper along the slender iron railings of the balcony dangled its heart-shaped leaves against the pure primrose yellow of the sky before the sunrise. It was going to be a lovely, molten day. Yesterday's rain had all vanished as if by magic, the baked earth taking it thirstily deep during the night hours, after the fall had ceased. 'See you at lunch, with any luck,' said Punch, 'but if I'm not back, don't panic. We'll probably still be looking for an interpreter.'

Peter padded across to the window after him, and watched him climb through and slip along the tiled balcony with his boots dangling by their laces from his hand. At the foot of the stairs he must have sat down for a moment to put them on, for there was a full minute or more during which Peter could not see him moving through the patterned railings; then his head appeared again for a moment, his hand waved, and he was lost round the corner of the house. The morning remained absolutely still and silent. It had begun well; he was away, and not another soul stirring.

Peter crawled back into bed, but he did not sleep again. He had his own particular sense of responsibility, too, even if it was not over-developed like Punch's. He lay awake until the reasonable hour of a quarter to seven, and then went to call the girls, so that they could breakfast soon after seven, and with luck be out of the dining-room before Monfalcone came down. Of his habits they had no knowledge, having started their expedition of the previous day ahead of the normal hour for breakfast, and made a sufficient show of their intention to be out all day. But this, too, went according to plan. They drank their coffee and ate their rolls, and were out sunning themselves on the bench outside the door by the time he came down. Two of them ostentatiously in sight upon the bench, the third across the street angling for snaps of the women, who were already beginning their washing. They gathered with their bundles at the stone tank which lay back from the main street under a beech tree, close beside the tiny square where presently the fruit stalls and the linens and the fine expensive woollens would appear, in flower-beds of colour against the white walls. There were very few shops in Rocca della Sera, but there were always market stalls. Weekdays and Sundays alike, they flowered in the square, coloured awnings and paradisal fruit and iris-coloured shade.

Mab strolled with the camera, and from behind her sun-glasses kept an eye on the open door of the Albergo Monte Gazza, and the staircase within the

111

hall. Dim though it was inside, she could not mistake Monfalcone's shape when he came, his elastic run, like an unhurried but lighthearted cat, his easy movements and immaculate clothes. He was a resplendent sight this morning, in pale grey flannels and an ivory silk shirt, with a white sweater linked round his neck by the sleeves. He strolled into the dining-room, swinging massive white-rimmed sun-glasses in one hand; and round to the little terrace under the dining-room windows moved Phyllida, complete with book, to curl up in a canvas chair.

Peter spent the morning as a sort of liaison officer, making sorties up the village upon perfectly honest errands, leaving his three completed films at the shop for processing, bringing back bouquets of enormous ice-cream cornets for the girls, posting cards, buying stamps, trying to look like two boys instead of one in his frequent appearances and disappearances. Sometimes he was with Mab in the street, examining the beautiful sweaters and dresses of jersey on the woollens stall, and as astonished as she to find the equivalent of fifty and sixty-pound models being sold here from market booths. Sometimes he was foot-loose for a while, for the sake of conviction, far up the steep cobbled street taking pictures of the sunlit pattern of the village, green corrugations of shutters, white backward-leaning walls, shallow beautiful roofs with the perpendicular slopes of trees hung like improbable backcloths behind them; or down at the small square of the church, with its separate clock-tower, and the bright umbrellas of its neighbour cafe just opening brilliantly across the way. Sometimes he reported back to Phyllida, curled catlike and watchful in the sun under the hotel windows.

Monfalcone sat long over his coffee, and, even after it, went at first no further than the hard court behind the inn, where he displayed his exquisite clothes and quite impressive form in several rather tame sets against the male half of the young lovers. The boy was no match for him, and Phyllida felt that he might have dropped a game or two into his hands, if only to please the girl, who could hardly be enjoying watching the most wonderful man in the world soundly beaten in front of her eyes. But Monfalcone dropped games to no one if he could help it, and grew tired of trouncing the boy only when the sun climbed too high for comfort. Then he abandoned tennis, and vanished upstairs again, to reappear with a large towel draped over one arm.

'Do you suppose,' wondered Phyllida, watching him head downhill for the lake, and hanging back to give him a good start, 'that we could safely go and swim, too? I'd give anything to get into the water right now. But supposing he nips out again quickly, and gets away?'

'Doesn't seem to be trying, to me,' owned Peter. 'I never saw anybody look more like an innocent holiday-maker. Keep him in sight, and I'll dash up for the costumes. I don't see why we shouldn't enjoy ourselves, too.'

They followed the broad, immaculate back downhill among the casual strollers of the street, keeping well back out of his sight if he should turn; and when they came to the borders of the open beach, dazzling in the hot sun, Mab found herself a place in the grass under the rim of the trees, and lay down there to watch from cover, in case the quarry should indeed attempt a quick escape while the other two were in the water.

'You go ahead, honestly I don't mind. Better not all three appear, or he's more likely to wonder about the fourth. Though of course,' she added happily, 'Punch must have been there long ago, and there isn't much he can do about it now. Still, we don't want him alarmed, do we?' After she had said it, it seemed a singularly silly thing to say. Never in her life had she seen anyone look less capable of being alarmed than did Monfalcone, casually kicking off his flannels into the sand, and walking magnificently into the blue, clear water, in dark maroon trunks. Still, she knew what she meant, and it held good, even if she had not expressed it well. So she lay in hiding, while Peter and Phyllida splashed gaily into the shallows, and struck out into the delicious coolness.

But as this morning in Arcadia passed, and the sun climbed to its zenith, and the quarry lay in the sand baking his already golden torso after his swim, Mab felt uneasiness creaking like rheumatism through all the joints of her mind. It was past eleven o'clock, nearing twelve, and there was no sign of Punch returning. True, he had said they were not to worry if he remained absent rather longer than they had expected; but lunch was at half-past twelve, and by some curious consent they had all counted on having him back by then. It is never any use telling people not to worry, for worry they will, even on a sunlit beach among drowsy sun-bathers and playing children, by a pool in paradise.

They went in to lunch, after waiting ten extra minutes in case Punch should appear. They felt extraordinarily naked when they sat down only three in number at the corner table, within Monfalcone's interested vision. They felt his eyes, their large detachment, their deliberate and unmoved assessment of three very small, three quite pleasant but trivial people. They felt as if somehow, by being only three, they were letting Punch down.

'I don't like this,' said Phyllida softly, to the rim of her wine-glass. 'I don't care what he said, he ought to have been here by now. What's more, he expected to be.'

'Oh, there can't be anything wrong,' said Peter in the same suppressed tones, and with more confidence than he felt. 'I expect they've just taken longer over all the talk than he thought. Maybe there was no one who spoke English, just like he said, and they've had to wait for an interpreter. I bet you everything's OK.'

Phyllida had set her limit of quiet waiting, and it was already past. 'I don't believe it,' she said. 'There's something queer going on. If he isn't here by the time lunch is over, I'm going after him.'

'Give him until two o'clock. He *said* not to panic.'

'I'm not panicking. But I'm not taking risks with Punch. If anything has happened to him, we've got to raise an alarm by daylight, while there's time to find him. We can't give anything away now, it's all over for good or bad by this time. Come with me, Peter!' she said, on an almost inaudible breath, and with desperate gravity.

'Well, of course!' said Peter, studying the grapes he was just swirling round in their bowl of water. 'What do you think I'm going to do? But somebody has to stay here and keep an eye on *him*. He could still make lots of trouble. And if – well, if anything *has* happened – but it hasn't, it can't have, we haven't taken our eyes off him – but we've got to keep him still under observation, in case—' He let his minor whisper peter out altogether there, because the further implications were too obviously something with which Phyllida was already engrossed.

'I'll stay,' said Mab at once. After all, it was quite clear that she must. No one could expect Phyllida to sit back and wait while her friend and her brother hunted for Punch, and it was best that Peter should go with her, as the only other man available, in case there had been an accident, in case two people and a certain amount of physical strength were needed. 'I'll take care of him,' she said firmly. 'You're right, we can't let go of him now. You go, and leave him to me.'

'Mind you,' said Peter, pocketing a peach for future use, 'I'm betting you we're fussing over nothing, but it can't do any harm now. And even if he comes back by the other road, or something, and we miss him, Mab will be here to let him know, and in the end we'll have to come back, so they'll have nothing to do but wait for us. So if you're set on it, come on, we'll move off when you like.' And as they moved away from the table, passing behind Mab's chair, he stooped to whisper in her ear, with a sudden strenuous conviction that indeed something queer was going on: 'Stick to him like a leech, old girl. I've got a feeling in my bones something's due to happen.'

'I'll see to it,' said Mab mildly and clearly, as if she were reassuring him that she would collect his prints, or lay in some cigarettes for him, or something equally prosaic. And she looked up after his going, and met Teodoro Monfalcone's levelled grey eyes without a shadow in her own, without evasion and without any but the most placid of interest, as if she found him agreeable to look at but altogether irrelevant.

(2)

After Peter and Phyllida were gone, it became very quiet in and about the Albergo Monte Gazza. The sun was at its highest, the street empty and blanched to a dazzling whiteness, the pale walls of the houses quivering with heat. The women were all gone from the water tank, and there were no buyers at the linen and fruit stalls, only their sleepy proprietors nodding on canvas chairs under the bright orange awnings. Monfalcone went no further afield than the corner of shrubbery behind the house, where he lay in a deck-chair and drowsed with a handkerchief over his eyes. Watching him became so painfully easy that it set free too much of Mab's mind for thought, to follow the two sweating searchers up the mountain road she had never seen, and imagine them making all kinds of unnerving discoveries. She saw sheer drops, and Punch disabled at the bottom of them. Or, almost worse, an empty, silent, sun-drowned pathway, doubling among the rocks and trees and crumbling slides of scree, and nowhere any sign that Punch had passed that way. She hoped they would not be away too long, because it was obvious that after all nothing was going to happen here. But she had guaranteed to watch him, to stick to him like a leech; so she watched, until her eyes dazzled with watching.

She could afford to stare, because she had retired to the iron balcony above, and sat deep in the shade of the large-leaved creeper, well-hidden even if the enemy should look up. She rather hoped that he believed her to be gone after the others on some harmless expedition, for it was quite clear, of course, that all four of them were crazy enough to walk even in the middle of the day. At least, so far as he was concerned, she was absent. And if he should decide to move, she had the choice of two ways out of the house, and on to his trail.

Someone came out of the house, almost directly under her, and stood for a moment to look round. Mab did not lean out to see, but she thought it was a girl's step; and in a moment came Liana's high young voice, calling towards the trees: '*Signor Monfalcone! Prego, signore, il telefono!*'

Well, one didn't have to understand much Italian to know what that meant. And by the prompt flash of the large hand to whip the handkerchief from Signor Monfalcone's eyes, and the way he swung his feet to the ground and loped into the house, he had been expecting the call. Mab didn't like this development very much. If you observe a meeting between two people you can learn a lot, but watching one end of a telephone conversation, without the possibility even of hearing a word, is a tantalising business. All sorts of vital things can be arranged, all sorts of plans made, in a few minutes, without trace or sign left for the painstaking amateur detective stretching her ears outside the call box. Still, Mab kicked off her shoes and trotted along the passage in her socks to hang over the banisters, flattened against the wall on the blind side, and with her nerves at stretch for the first sound of an approaching foot from any direction. A drowsy silence filled the hotel, and through it maddening single sounds arose to plague her, the clash of the door of the telephone booth as Monfalcone let it close behind him, the tiny distant chime of the bell. And then silence again, while he talked.

It seemed to her that the conversation went on for a long time, but she knew that that was because her strained senses were so ardently clenched upon its silent passage, and time had slipped out of focus. But he came out at last. The door creaked, and clashed back again, his long, leisurely steps crossed the hall. She heard him call the porter, who came promptly from the kitchen premises somewhere, and there was a flood of Italian conversation, complicated by an odd echo which the staircase had; but she settled upon at least one word which meant something to her, and that was enough. She had only that morning called for '*il conto*' herself in the cafe, and she was not likely to forget that it meant the bill.

Such a stupor of consternation possessed her that she failed for a moment to notice that the light, long, purposeful steps were advancing upon the staircase. He had asked that his bill should be made out. He was coming up to pack. She came to her senses just in time, dragged herself backward out of sight of the foot of the stairs, and ran slithering down the glossy tiled passage and into her own room. She hoped he did not hear the door close, for she held the latch in her fingers, and let it relax very softly into place; but if he was very quick to notice, he might have seen the handle slowly turning as he reached the top of the flight. Mab crouched on the floor, listening until his door closed in its turn. She thought she could even hear the noise his big suitcases made as he dragged them out and let the lid of the first one fall back against the bed. Yes, it was true, he was leaving. He'd had a message, and he was leaving, now, at once, as soon as he could be ready. And it was something to do with Punch and the diamonds, as surely as her name was Mab Isherwood. And if he got away now, and the thread was broken, how were they ever to prove anything, how to knot up the ends again?

She didn't at all realise what she was going to do, until she suddenly noticed, rather as if she were still watching a stranger, that she had her rucksack open on the bed, and was stowing her rolled pyjamas and washing gear into the main pocket. Then her mind cleared a little, catching up with her fingers. A note pinned under Phyllida's top sheet couldn't be missed. So little to tell them. No notion yet of where she was going, just: 'He got a phone call, and left. Trying to follow him. Details later.' Maybe it wouldn't be needed.

Maybe the others would come back before Monfalcone left. She hoped so, because she hated to think of going away without knowing that Punch was safe, but she had to be prepared. It was lucky that she hadn't unpacked properly; her shoes were soon stowed in their special pockets, her towel was rolled just under the top flap. That was everything. She ran Phyllida's comb through her hair, and used Phyllida's powder, because she had packed her own. Her bright red wind-jacket made a brave splash of colour over her arm, primly clutched to her side. She looked harmless enough, almost too much like an earnest school prefect, she thought, giving her appearance a last critical examination before she slipped out of the room and down the stairs.

Monfalcone was still in his room. She could hear him moving about there, briskly but not hurriedly, and to judge by the cheerful half-tone tenor singing which accompanied his preparations, he was in high spirits. Something was going well for him. But one thing she certainly knew, he had not yet got his hands on the diamonds. Did that mean he was off to some rendezvous, that at some place appointed in the course of that telephone conversation he expected to have the booty handed over to him? He was very pleased about something, and considering he had crossed Italy for this one purpose it was not unreasonable to suppose that his present elation stemmed from the same cause. All the more determinedly, all the more obstinately, she resolved that she would hang on his coat-tails until she pulled him to a standstill. Let him be as clever, as patient, as subtle as he would in removing himself miles from the present scene before he touched the diamonds, he should not get free of her, and he should not get away with Signor Galassi's trust.

There was no hurry now, since she was ahead of him;

but she went demurely down the stairs, and out on to the doorstep, in the fiery white sunlight. It was nearly a quarter to three. The bus from Mazzolo for Riva came through at a few minutes after three, and it made a reasonable tale, at least, that she should be waiting for it; but if he delayed after it had passed she would have to think of something else, and think quickly. She had no qualms now; she felt capable of all manner of inspired lies. The truth was that for the moment the whole affair had lifted itself just out of the bounds of reality, and she was absolved from normal fears and limitations, like the central figure of a dream. The only snag was the uneasy consciousness one has sometimes, even in dreams, that this absolution is too good to last.

Maybe he himself was taking the bus, she thought for one surprised moment, for there was no sign of the long blue car; but then it came creeping round the corner of the house, from the alley just up the street, and slid silently to a stop before the door, and a bored-looking driver in his shirt-sleeves sat back and lit a cigarette. Did he know where he was going, she wondered? If he did, then Monfalcone was heading back in the direction of Riva and Desenzano; not necessarily to either of these, since the driver was hired with the car and could take care of its return, but certainly somewhere south, and that probably meant back to the railway. And here came the porter with the two big suitcases, and that quick step after him on the stairs was Monfalcone himself, just crossing the hall, halting at the desk.

The manager was there to see him off. And he was in time, for there was as yet no sign of the bus. So she had a story ready, and a slip of paper and her pen in one pocket, and the key of her room in the other. She felt at the pear-shaped wooden anchor of the key through the thin cotton of her skirt, and moistened her suddenly dry lips, because it was now or never. He had paid his bill, he had done something handsome about the porter, who was voluble in appreciation, though still with that faint, malicious note of mockery which she had noticed in the patronised Italian servant, temporarily tolerant of the craziness of the world in which the better man so frequently moves underneath, appreciative of its subtle revenges. She was becoming sensitive to these undertones, suddenly much more so because she was alone.

He was coming. She felt his tall figure drawing close to her shoulder, a perceptible warmth from him before she turned her head and looked up. She had never noticed that before, but all her senses were erected now in a more than normal sensitivity, both physical and mental. It did not surprise her that he should be looking full at her, and she met his eyes with a wide glance which at least had every appearance of candour. She stood on one foot like a shy schoolgirl, and began in a very delicate, probing voice: 'Excuse me – could I – could I ask a great favour of you?'

He was not in such a hurry that he couldn't stop to enjoy her, and he took his time over replying, as much with his eyes as his voice: 'Please, of course! If there is anything I can do—'

'It's just that—Well, I noticed the car was here waiting for you, and I thought that perhaps, if you're going down to the station at Desenzano – I was going to pick up the bus, but if you have room, and if you wouldn't mind at all—' Her small voice rose coaxingly upon the suggestion, her eyes lingered hopefully upon his face. Ridiculously, it was at that moment that she first began to wonder how much money she had on her, and into what sort of mess she was going to land herself without it; but there was no time to care about that

122

now. 'Of course, if I should be any trouble to you—' she hinted pathetically.

He said instantly, with resolution, with deliberate pleasure: 'I cannot imagine how you could be anything but a delight to me. There need be no difficulty there. But it is not to Desenzano I am going, unfortunately. If you want only to reach the railway, I could take you to the station at Verona, on the other side of the lake.'

She thought fast and accurately, and assessed chances with a calm which astonished her as she stood back to observe it. He was moving east to Verona, and his car was hired, so it was long odds he was going on by train from there; for the original necessity of sticking close to four penniless people who had to use trains had deprived him of what was almost certainly his normal means of transport, his own car. Her mind roved frantically along the railway line from Verona eastward, wondering how far, how far? Vicenza? Padua? Or all the way to Venice? How far would a respected business man think it expedient to go from the scene of a crime, in order to receive the proceeds in absolute retirement and safety? And it might not even depend on that, he might actually be going somewhere east upon some other business, killing two birds with one stone. But she had to make her case quickly, and with conviction, so it could be only guesswork. Plumping for what she considered his least likely destination, and what would certainly be the most probable for four eager novices fresh from England, she said:

'Oh, yes, that would be fine, because I should get there even quicker from Verona. You see, I'm going on to Venice to find a good place for us all to stay for our last few days. The others will come on tomorrow, but we hadn't made any arrangements about rooms,

.and we don't know the town at all, and it does take rather a time in a fashionable place to find something we can afford. So I said I'd go ahead today, and see to everything before they come. If I could really come down to Verona with you, it would help me no end. Are you sure I shan't be any trouble to you?'

He did not seem to be repenting of his offer, and she could not guess from his face how near she had come to touching his own plans. He stood smiling at her ever so faintly and contentedly; with the same critical admiration which had rested on her once in the dining-room. 'You will be charming and quite undeserved company, and it seems a pity that you will also make the journey seem much shorter. Please! I hope we can make you comfortable. Let me take your rucksack.'

She permitted it complacently, chattering thanks, radiant with her initial success; and as he was stowing the rucksack into the boot with his own hands, and with respectful care which it seldom got from her, she suddenly felt at her pocket, and gasped, and hauled out the key.

'Oh, I say, how awful! I was running away with the room key. Excuse me just one moment, I must take it back.'

Once inside the doorway she ran, terrified that he would follow her, hoarding the sounds of the boot being leisurely rearranged and closed upon her small luggage. Into the bar she scurried, and flattened her slip of paper on the glass above the postcards, under Liana's astonished nose, and scribbled madly: 'Venice. If not there, wait for me.' If there had been time, even, she had no more to tell. One of Punch's list of modest pensions would have a room for them, but how could she tell which one? And even if Monfalcone left the train midway, and she perforce after him, it was best that the other three should set off in good faith for the town to which she had sworn they were all going. Then their exit, at any rate, would be convincing, and if they did not know where to find her, she would at least have some idea of where to find them.

She thrust the scrap into Liana's hand, and the key after it, and the wonderful, vague, pathetic eyes blinked at her with surprise, but without question. She said: 'Please give it to Peter! To the young, fair one! Will you?' Extraordinary cunnings were coming to life in her, that she should so certainly know how impossible it would be for Liana to forget a message to Peter, or fail to deliver it faithfully. She even knew his name, for a slow, beautiful smile and a flower-like flush replied.

'Yes,' said Liana. 'Yes, when he come, I give it.'

Mab pressed her hand quickly and warmly, and fled. In the doorway she became again grave and demure, for he was just striding to the steps to meet her. It was done, she could go. 'Oh, lord!' she thought, getting into the back of the car, 'let me have enough money for the fare!' And she thought of having to borrow from Monfalcone, and for the first time she wanted to laugh, with a half-hysterical gaiety. The cushions surged, and he was sitting beside her, and again she felt his slight, strong, animal warmth faintly touching her bare arm. The driver threw away his cigarette, turned once in his seat with leisurely and arrogant curiosity to sweep them both with one large interested glance, and then let in his clutch and sent the car slowly forward from the doorway along the road to Riva.

(3)

They drove back into Riva by the way which Mab knew already from the outward journey, and there turned off to the left without passing through the town, and circled to come down to the lakeside on the sickle-shaped front at Torbole. From then on it was all magic, a drowning blueness of water on the right hand, dappled with coloured boats close to the shore; and on the left, first the chill granite faces of mountain closing down low to the road, in slaty strata inclined at an angle of forty-five degrees, then the great soft hills relaxing into folds of cultivation, terraces of olives silvery-green within their low stone walls, occasional lemon gardens; and then the wide, open bowl of the southern waters of Garda, rich with marble, and cypresses, and flowers, lustrous black and white and blue and green, all quaking in the highest heat of the afternoon.

They made polite conversation inside the car, reaching upward to catch the wind of their own going, through the open roof. How did they like Italy? Were they staying long in Venice? Had they been in the country before? He asked her nothing which might not equally well have been asked by some casual benefactor picked up on the road. She felt a little at a loss, a little light-headed, because she ought to have had some sense of danger, at the very least of excitement, and she had none. It was all so matter-of-fact that she began to wonder, in the stupefaction of the heat, if they had dreamed half of it, and made up the other half, concocting absolutely of their own will that sinister figure which was supposed to be Signor Monfalcone. She began to disbelieve in him, because she had put herself deliberately into this close contact with him, and behold, he was not here at all – not as they had created

126

him. This man asked the same sort of questions as had
Signor Galassi himself, perhaps a little more distantly
and coolly, but with the unmistakable touch of the
same passing sympathy, gracious, self-sufficient, fleet-
ingly moved by her youth and warmth and enthusiasm.
She was not at all afraid of him, though her memory
reminded her of many reasons why she ought to have
been; but though she acknowledged all these when they
thrust themselves back into her mind, she could not feel
any force in them. The sun was too bright, the world too
gay, the drinkers under the café awnings too content;
she could not bring herself to force those two opposed
worlds into focus.

And then, when they were nearing the foot of Lake
Garda, and the lush white hotels and villas were flowering all round them like magnolias, an extraordinary
thing happened. For some miles the heat had lain
heavily upon her senses, and the whiteness of passing
walls dazed her eyes. She fell asleep, leaning back into
the cushions; but she awoke, with a sudden, reasonless,
exaggerated awakening, with her head comfortably pil-
lowed on his shoulder, and the crisp scent of the silk of
his shirt in her nostrils. His eyes were on her, watching her start back into consciousness, with a curious,
amused tenderness. She felt it stroking her cheek, the
look of his eyes; and she was aware that for some
reason, or more probably for no reason, or none which
either he or she would ever identify, he had deliberately leaned towards her, to make a firm, smooth
rest for her head at the right level, his arm braced
under the slight weight, his other hand, with a touch
as light as a stirring of the air, steadying her forehead when she nodded forward at the motion of the
car, for she could still feel the faint warmth of his
finger-tips upon her temples, and the shadow of his

127

hovering hand passed from her eyelids just before she opened them.

Nothing like that had ever happened to Mab before. She had dozed on Peter's shoulder, on the way out from Paris, and he had let her, but the incident bore very little relationship to this delicate attention. She did not want to move too suddenly, to seem too aware of him, though her senses had never quivered to immediate perceptions of texture and scent and light as they did at that moment. Very gently, very circumspectly she sat up, and smoothed her ruffled feathers of fair hair with a confused hand, like a disturbed bird settling; and when she looked up at him with that soft, dazed smile, the devil of it was that she herself didn't know how much of it was acting, and how much was real.

'I say, I'm awfully sorry!' she said, flushing faintly under his contemplative gaze. 'How rude of me! Why didn't you wake me up?'

'Oh, but why? You were tired out with the heat, it is bad to be energetic in the middle of the day. And the weight was nothing. It is a mark of confidence, isn't it, to sleep in a person's care?' The mellifluous gentleness of his voice, in which she had formerly imagined she could detect a note of satire, now seemed to her no more than a curious natural charm of his, for his eyes were quite frank and serious in their regard.

'I suppose it must be,' she said, smiling, as she felt, rather stupidly; and she turned her head to look out at the landscape, so much simpler and safer matter for consideration. They had left the lake, and were travelling along a fine motor road, through wide meadows soon interrupted by eruptions of white buildings. Top-heavy hoardings, thickly spattered with leggy female posters in the American manner, offended her surprised eyes, and the traffic was becoming fast and continuous in both directions. They passed many fruit-stalls set up beside the road, laden with peaches as big as English turnips, and of an improbable golden colour.

'How long have I been asleep?' she asked, and suddenly she felt her first impulse of fear, an absurd one. How did she know whether he was taking her to Verona or somewhere quite different? She didn't even know what the road looked like, she wouldn't even be able to recognise the town when she got there. And it wasn't possible, after all that had happened, that he had accepted this jaunt on its face value, and actually believed in her innocent errand to beat up cheap lodgings for the party in Venice. He must know that she was there to keep an eye on him. Then how if he had accepted her in the spirit of simple gratitude for tactics which saved him so much trouble, and was disposing of her in the best way for his own purpose?

But the sun was too bright, the road too populous, the world too beautiful, and she simply could not believe in danger and violence for longer than a minute. She laughed as suddenly as she had trembled; she had not been made, after all, in a scale and kind suitable to anything but modest, unenterprising normality. Now, if it had been Phyllida, for whom incidents were almost all crises, and contretemps grew to the dimensions of adventures—Ah, then she could have believed in it. But she was Mab, and they were almost certainly going to Verona.

'You slept for nearly half an hour,' said Monfalcone. 'Tell me why you laughed.'

'Oh, just to think that I'm here, that all this is real, and I'm in the middle of it. Usually my life's rather dull, this is a beautiful change.' And she laughed again, and knew she could do it to order, in exactly that key of soft, pleased excitement, not even overstrung, only candid in its delight, like a child's laughter. And then she wondered if that was precisely what he was wondering about, how much of her was genuine, how much ran a little deeper than the depth his penetrating eye had explored. In short, what was she up to? Was that why he had accepted her small, childlike challenge on the steps of the Albergo Monte Gazza? Because he was puzzled, and wanted to probe and understand? Or merely because he was tickled by her cheek, and knowing himself capable of dealing with a dozen intrepid little girls meddling in his affairs, saw fit to amuse himself by teasing her a little by the way?

She turned her head, still laughing, and flashed at him with quite uncharacteristic impudence her violet eyes and quaint, crooked mouth. 'Now here,' she said sweetly, 'nothing is ever commonplace. Round every corner there could be an adventure – in Italy. Couldn't there?'

'And on every doorstep,' he said gently, smiling back at her lopsided smile, 'at least a most charming encounter. Perhaps – an adventure, too?'

So neither of them was any the wiser. It could have been a mere exchange of rallying compliments, or it could have meant much more; but it had been words wasted, for all she had done was to shed one skin of the defences her mind possessed against him. She blushed suddenly, and in fact rather becomingly, though this was one thing she could not do to order. 'Oh – not for you, I'm afraid,' she said, biting her lip. 'But just to ride in a car in Italy is exciting for me. Everything's so new, and so lovely.'

'You liked Rocca della Sera?' he asked, watching the road ahead.

'Oh, yes! I wish we had more time – and more money. I should have liked to stay there longer, but we did want to see Venice, too. Is it really as wonderful as people say? It doesn't seem possible.'

'More wonderful! Whatever they may have said, you will not be disappointed, I promise you. Look, we are getting near to Verona. In five minutes or so we shall reach the station, it is on this side of the town.'

The highroad, indeed, had almost become a street already, lined with shops and houses, and laced with copious traffic.

'Will you tell me your name?' asked Monfalcone suddenly.

'Of course! But it's not very nice,' she said sadly. 'It's Mabel Isherwood, but I'm usually called Mab.'

He gave her a sidelong, considering look, and said: 'It will do. Was she not a queen of fairies?'

It seemed to her, suddenly, that something had happened to him, as well as to her, in her sleep. To be sure, the conversation had not changed its character very much, but there were disquieting hints of intimacy sounding through it now and then, all the more disquieting because they were perfectly courteous, and even, in their remote way, perfectly direct. After all, you cannot slumber on somebody's shoulder, and then sit up and regard him as a perfect stranger. But she didn't like it; it confused her too much. She was glad when the car swept in to the right, round the vast open space before the new station at Verona, and pulled up by Cavour's statue. Now she was free, she thought, heaving a great sigh of relief. She must watch him still, but virtually she would be rid of him, and he of her, and she could go and sit in the corner of some second-class carriage to smooth the ruffled plumage of her mind, while he, no doubt, settled into an expensive reservation.

She had her thanks all ready as he helped her out. All she wanted now was for him to give her her rucksack, and let her run away into the crowds. But he was in no hurry about it. He climbed out, stretched his long legs after the cramp of the journey, and proceeded to pay the driver. Overpay him, rather, she thought disapprovingly, seeing the imposing riffle of notes which passed, and their effect upon the man at the wheel. He was so pleased with his customer that he followed them out of the car, all teeth and shining eyes and exclamations, and firmly put aside Monfalcone from so much as touching the luggage. With such a patron, probably the small exertion necessary to porter the cases to the right platform would be worth another tip. And it was, he slipped another note carelessly out of his wallet, laughing, giving the necessary instructions over his shoulder in rapid, liquid Italian which left Mab clutching at words and capturing none.

Had he mentioned Venezia? She couldn't be sure. Or the number of a platform? She tried to recollect, but everything had slithered out of her ears as swiftly as it slithered in. She had never yet so angrily regretted her failure to learn this beautiful, elusive language. She hadn't even taken Latin at school, to help her now with the inevitable echoes.

'Come along!' said Monfalcone serenely, picking up her rucksack by the shoulder straps before she could lift it herself. 'There's a train for Venice due out in about a quarter of an hour. You have a ticket already?'

'No, I have to book. Please, I've been enough trouble to you already, do let me take that. Don't worry about me, I shall find my train quite well, really.'

But he took her lightly by the arm, and marched her away from the formidable train indicator, through which she was just anxiously trying to find her way. 'Do not trouble about that, I know this station well, I can take you directly to the platform, and I think the train will be

132

in. Come, we must get your ticket.' But when they stood at the window, and she was just struggling to assemble the right words in which to insist on doing her own booking, he smiled down suddenly and brightly on her face of severity and distress, and forestalled her almost tenderly: 'You will let me do the asking for you? In a language one does not know, this is one of the hardest things to do gracefully.'

He asked for the ticket, and reported faithfully its price, and let her lay out the money herself so that she might be sure he had not tricked her into accepting even one lira from him.

That was the strangest, the most illuminating, the most crippling chivalry of all. She need ask herself no more questions now about how much he knew and how much he did not know of her motives. Their relationship was suddenly quite clear. If she had been to him nothing more significant than a casually pleasing young girl to whom he had given a lift, he would have paid for her ticket, quite gracefully, quite firmly, without regard to her protests. He was that kind of man. If she had been merely an agent of the enemy, a known spy in his camp, he would probably have done the same, as a means of drawing a red herring across her path, and causing a distracting wound in her conscience in all future campaigns of their not very evenly matched warfare. But he perceived her as something much more complicated and complicating than either. She was an enemy, yes, he knew it, and accepted it, but she was an enemy he liked and respected, in his amused way, too much to foul.

'Don't worry!' said his eyes, smiling at her out of the long, melancholy face. 'We'll fight on fair terms. You need owe me nothing. Look, your hands are not tied at all!'

It was then, of course, that she began to be aware that in fact they were tied very firmly, with a cord of whose existence he naturally would not know. For how can you take any delight in fighting a man who enters the contest with such a magniloquent gesture?

(4)

He led her straight to one of the eastward bays of the station, and put her into an almost empty compartment in a train labelled with reassuring clarity: 'Venezia'. She had not expected him to get in with her, but it was with a queer sensation of dizziness that she heard him saying, as he looked up at her from the platform: 'Excuse me if I leave you now. I am very sorry our ways have to part so soon, but I must look for my own train. I am going south from here, to Modena.' And without apparent eyes for her momentary start of horror, he continued gently: 'I hope you will find everything you wish for in Venice, and have a beautiful holiday there.'

She heard herself saying: 'Thank you, I'm sure we shall. I'm sure it will be even better than we expected. Thank you so much for everything!' She gave him her hand through the window, because she felt that he expected it, and instead of holding it for the formal moment, he bent his head and kissed her fingers. In a state of frenzy within, but demure as ever without, she watched him turn from her and move away lightly down the long platform, striding in and out of the groups of travellers, swerving round the refreshment wagons with their cellophane packages of grapes and peaches, and their gaudily coloured lemonades and inevitable and banal Coca-Colas.

Why had she let his selection of Verona persuade her

that he must be moving on eastward? Why hadn't she thought of this? South, to Modena! How should she ever find him there, or ever in time, if she lost him now? She couldn't afford to lose him, it was practically high treason if she let herself be paralysed by a chivalrous gesture and a sudden parry on its heels, like this. She must go after him.

She tore herself out of her stupor, and stood up to haul her rucksack out of the rack, bodily into her arms, startling the quiet old man beside her right out of the columns of his hitherto absorbing newspaper. She thrust fiercely along the already populous corridor, and jumped out into the dazzling early evening sunlight on the platform. Monfalcone was no longer in sight, and it was clear from the emptiness of the platform beyond the tunnel of the subway that he must have gone below. In the concrete corridors of the subway she might find him again; if not, she must look for the train to Modena, and trust to pick up his trail again on arrival. True, her ticket was to Venice, but in desperate situations such considerations go by the board. Let that problem be met when it arose, and not before.

She ran, and Mab, when she chose, could run with quite remarkable speed. She ran all the faster because, if Monfalcone emerged from some cavern on another platform in time to see her still haring down this one, she would have given away the whole game. She had to reach shelter before he came back into view; and then, since she could not rely on keeping him in sight below ground, she had to lie in wait and try to watch two ways at once, until the already familiar tall figure issued from one of the subways. Then she would dart down, and run him to earth in the correct train, and board it after him. But the smallness of her chance of catching sight of him among so many people terrified her, and not without reason, for she waited five minutes, six minutes, turning her head passionately this way and that, trying to watch every subway at once, and still he had not reappeared. He could not be in the concrete corridors still; she must have missed him.

Down she went, into the subway which crossed the entire station, sending up numbered stairways like feelers to the various platforms, each with its obliging label. A fine system, she thought approvingly, hurrying along past the names of half the cities of the north: Milano, Torino, Piacenza – Modena! She dashed up the stairs in a sudden panic lest the train should have left, and emerged, with rather belated caution hugging the side of the stairway, upon another wide platform, with a train drawn up on either side, and both steaming suggestively. And suddenly she couldn't remember, she couldn't remember which of these two ought to be the Modena train! Why hadn't she spared the extra second to make sure of the number, instead of leaping upstairs like a crazy puppy at the first triumphant sight of the name?

There were still a number of people moving about the platform, but there was not adequate cover for her to advance. She stood shrinking into the subway until a porter came along with a trolley of luggage, and slammed it down in front of the open van on one side; then she stepped forward to accost him with her single-word query, but it became unnecessary on the instant. She halted, staring at the case he was just lifting into the train.

Nothing is really coincidence, of course, everything has a cause. The case was large, expensive, of hide, but not unique; she would have passed it by and thought no more of it, but for the garish label in one corner, so new, so gummy, the child's picture of a little lake, and a little white village zigzagging up-hill from its shore, under a cliff of limestone decorated ostentatiously with two birch trees. 'Albergo Monte Gazza, Rocca della Sera', said the bright yellow lettering unnecessarily; and even in this oppressed moment she thought sympathetically how much those labels must have cost the proprietor, with all that printing, and so many lavish colours.

Well, if he had not been flattered and encouraged by the coming of so distinguished a guest as Signor Monfalcone, he would not have sought to use him as an advertisement; and if the porter had not been amply tipped, perhaps he would not so assiduously have stowed the luggage for his patron, and if the driver of the hired car had not been equally gratified, *he* might have been content to lift out the cases and drive away, leaving Monfalcone to find a porter on his own account – in either of which cases that gentleman of impeccable taste would certainly not have allowed this rather dreadful label to remain on his possessions for ten seconds after his eye first lit on it. But he hadn't yet seen it; and here it went, receding gaily into the luggage van of this particular train, and winking at her violently with its obstreperous greens and blues as it vanished, as if anxious that she should observe and understand.

She looked no further. To hunt for the man himself was perhaps to lose the only advantage she had. Let him go on congratulating himself on stowing her safely away to Venice, all she had to do was to stay within sight of this case, and follow it wherever it went, and it would bring her back to him in the end. She got into the nearest coach, and found a place in a corridor only gently filled, where at every stop she could lean out from the open window and watch what came out of the luggage van. Then she was satisfied.

And just in time, too, for in a few minutes the train

137

began to move; and pat upon its going the door at the end of the coach, that familiar door, opened, and through it came a very short, broad, black-avised guard, demanding tickets. Somehow she hadn't expected it so soon, and she was terrified because they were only just gathering way, terrified that he would take too much compassion upon a lost English girl, and stop the train, and put her kindly but firmly into the train in which, according to her ticket, she ought to be travelling. Besides, she wasn't English for nothing, she shrank from the scene, however friendly might be the spirit in which it would be conducted; she wanted to be mistress of the situation, taken for granted, an experienced traveller. Who doesn't, at eighteen years of age?

But there was no help for it. She fished out her ticket, and offered it self-consciously, getting ready to look imbecile even if he spoke English, getting ready to argue that he was mistaken, and not she, if extremes of lunacy should be necessary to lengthen out the error past mending. Then she would have to dodge him for the rest of the journey. Into the lavatory at the sound of his stentorian shout of '*Biglietti!*' after this, she thought – but even that's no sure refuge here, they knock on the door and ask you to pass your ticket out, I've seen them do it—!

Something incredible was happening! He had looked at the ticket, snipped a piece out of it, and handed it back to her without a word, and was moving on arduously into the next carriage, leaving her gaping at the slip of pasteboard as if it had suddenly answered back. Hadn't he seen? She was morally sure that he had, but she couldn't resist reconsidering the possibility that he had not. Then what was wrong with one or the other of them? She had followed Monfalcone's unmistakable luggage into this train, and he had told her he was going to Modena. He had told her—

She spent a long minute assembling a few probably incorrect but she hoped recognisable words. Trains were one subject on which the phrase-books were loquacious, and she had studied them conscientiously. There was no haste, for wherever she was going, she was going with her quarry still in sight; but she had to know. When she was reasonably certain she could string together something resembling the question she wanted to put, she turned to her neighbour, a round, merry man who leaned upon the window-rail by her elbow and hummed grand opera in an inappropriate light tenor.

'Prego, signore, dove arrivera finalmente questo treno?' she asked laboriously, hoping it would not sound as if she had any doubts of its successfully reaching her destination, but rather as if she had been stricken with a sudden natural curiosity to find out what happened to it afterwards.

The merry man answered cheerfully and promptly: *'A Venezia!'* and went on to enlarge and embroider, but she had heard all she could translate at that speed, and all she needed to know. Haltingly she produced her most expert sentence, lest he should waste his eloquence unaware: *'Non so parlare Italiano, signore – sono inglese!'* And promptly contradicted herself by attempting what she had already regretfully admitted she could not do: *'Credevo – che va uno altero treno a Venezia – piattaforma—'* Should it be *'baia'*? But never mind, so long as he understood. *'Piattaforma terza!'* She pointed back resentfully in the general direction of the bay where she had left it.

The merry man made a disrespectful face in token of what he thought of the other train to Venice. *'E lento – lento, quello!'* With short, broad hands he demonstrated

139

along the window-rail the extreme, the unreasonable slowness of that train. '*Ma questo – ah – è rapido!*' And his eloquent hand flashed along the rail with a realistic express noise, and arrived with a triumphant explosion of steam under her startled nose, which represented Venice.

'*Intendo!*' said Mab. 'I understand!' And so she did, much more than these brilliantly illustrated sentences. She understood that but for the business instincts of the proprietor of the Albergo Monte Gazza she would have been neatly side-tracked from the trail of Monfalcone, either to Venice by a train arriving hours later than his – wherever he intended to arrive on that interesting route – and misled into believing that he had gone to Modena; or, allowing for considerable enterprise on her part, to Modena, on a complete wild-goose chase, and with a ticket which would take a lot of explaining. And by sheer luck, without deserving it in the least, she had been led back to the right trail, and was here within twenty feet of her quarry's luggage, on the same train with him. And he didn't know it, that was the best of it. He didn't know it! It was he who had been thrown off-guard by his own tactics.

She stood leaning on her folded arms against the rail, and laughed aloud, a gay, high peal worthy of Phyllida herself. And the merry man laughed to see her laugh, for in his philosophy laughter was a fundamental good which demanded no reason for being.

CHAPTER SIX

A HUT ON THE
PASSO SAN ROCCO

(1)

THE rock path over the old pass to Sopramazzolo from Rocca della Sera made its first ascent from the road at an approximate angle of fifty degrees, up a gully of scree between old fir trees; and Phyllida took it at a pace which no experienced mountaineer would have approved, or expected her to keep up for long. Peter bore with her for a while, but when she began to pump badly, and still refused to slacken speed, he took her firmly by the back of her skirt, as she scrambled ahead of him, and hauled her to a standstill. She turned to say in a series of breathless gasps: 'Oh, don't fool about! This is serious!'

'I know it is,' said Peter equably, 'but if you think you're going to last long at that pressure, you've got another think coming. Show a bit of sense! You know perfectly well that going slower means getting there quicker in the end. Besides, we're supposed to be keeping our eyes open for traces on the way, or what's the good of our being here at all? All you've seen yet is the ground between your feet.'

'Well, we're hardly off the road yet. Nothing would happen here. I wasn't worrying about traces yet.'

But she knew that Peter was right, and sensibly settled back into her normal climbing stride, longish, steady, apparently slow, but it covered the ground at a surprising rate.

The path wound round into a shelf above a stony valley, narrow and poised high, so that slips of stones here and there had almost levelled it with the mountain-side. Liana had told no more than the truth when she had said that it was not for strangers in the dark. Only a trickle of water muttered querulously among the torrent of boulders below them; the valley was open to view, all its base a wilderness of whitish-grey against which the smallest splash of bright colour would have caught the eye like a banner. And after a while the path turned off and began to crawl up a rocky cleft to the right, where trees clung grimly in the inadequate hollows of soil, fed by the wind among sheer faces of rock.

The level of the path became crazy and blind here by reason of the difficulties of this broken country, climbing to fall again, falling to climb, here and there fenced in with wire ropes or wooden railings, some of which were already sagging into the void. Trickles of water made unexpected music down the cliffs, and a grottoed coolness breathed into the quaking afternoon air from crannies of vivid grass and fern. Then there was a sudden meadow, beautiful, smooth as a lawn, ringed round with the velvety, spiced silence of fir trees. There was no outlook, before them or behind; each section of the way existed by itself. Before they had covered half the distance to the crest of the pass, they had no sense of direction left.

But there was no sign of Punch, or for the matter of that, of any other human creature. Peter watched Phyllida's darting, uneasy glance, and said nothing, having nothing particularly comfortable to say. He didn't really believe that anything bad had happened to Punch, and yet he had certainly expected to meet him before now. Maybe he had gone back to Rocca della Sera at leisure by some easier way, and was already at the inn, and demanding explanations from Mab for their absence. Maybe! But Peter no longer felt quite so convinced that all was well.

In the middle of the meadow Phyllida suddenly stopped dead, and appealed passionately: 'We can't have missed him, can we? He couldn't have been lying hurt anywhere along this route, could he, without our seeing him?'

'Don't be silly!' said Peter, but without the usual intonation. 'I'm sure he couldn't. We're sure to find him if he's here at all. But you know, I still think it's more likely he's either being held up with official business, or else he's gone back another way, and is home by now.'

'Yes,' she agreed strenuously, 'I'll bet that's it. We're probably making all kinds of fools of ourselves, really. He'll be mad as hell when he gets back, and finds we've gone off at half-cock, like this.' A determined but rather dreary laugh saluted the thought. 'But some of those drops—' she said, and stopped, biting her lip.

'I know, they're hair-raising, but what does that matter when you've seen for yourself there's no body at the foot of 'em? Come on, fathead, let's get on a bit further. Anyhow, there's nowhere to fall down in this bit.'

Beyond the ring of resin-scented pines, warm as the wind from a herb fire, there was another crazy bend in the path, and another watercourse, a river of white stones with a concrete wall at its outer end to check flood waters in the spring. Not even a trickle threaded the desert of boulders here; only a shrunken puddle of water, baked at the edges into bricks of clay, lingered here and there in a hollow place. A raised causeway marched alongside for the length of what might, at some periods of the year, be a real little lake, but was now only an imaginary one, then climbed again and dwindled into a stony path, with the brave splashes of the Passo San Rocco route, blue and yellow, freshly painted on the bole of the first big tree beside it.

Soon they were scrambling again, this time up hard slopes under the trees, glazed an inch deep with needles. There was a final zigzagging climb among thick trees and bushes, the path making long blind traverses to get toehold in the slope, and then they blundered suddenly out into sunlight on a small, stony bowl ringed round with crumbling faces of dolomitic rock, rose-red in the heat of the afternoon; and in the middle of this bowl, set aside from the path, was a high square building of stone, set with two small, high windows, and pierced with a doorway like a tunnel, so thick were its walls.

'Hullo, what's this?' wondered Phyllida. 'Another little *rifugio?* Coca-Cola bar? Or what?'

'The *Baîto* something or other. Liana said there was one up here on the top of the pass, so it looks as if we're at the top now.' The path wound away past the hut and into the standing rocks, and there vanished in the complexities of the cliff wall, but its level at vanishing point certainly appeared to be descending.

'Would there be anyone here? If so, they might have seen him go by.' And Phyllida set off briskly for the deeply sunken door, across the floor of the stone amphitheatre.

'There won't be anybody,' said Peter, clattering resignedly behind her. 'Nobody lives at these places, they're only here in case anyone needs shelter, some odd time.' But he went close, and stared up with her at the low stone relief over the door, a pleasant but worn little Virgin and Child, after the long years of their weathering practically noseless. A glass jar stood on the ground by the slab of stone at the doorway, with a handful of withered wild flowers in it. 'Nothing here for us,' said Peter disinterestedly. 'Let's get on.'

Phyllida put her hands to the big iron latch, and lifted it with a great creaking clang, and pushed and pulled, but without result. 'Locked!' she said, and listened to the silence and turned away.

Peter was already round the corner of the *baîto,* and back on the path. Phyllida was in the act of following him, treading gingerly among the loose stones, for she had turned her ankle once on the way up, though without damage, when suddenly there was a splintering crash above her head, and a shower of slivers of glass scintillated down the wall just a yard in front of her and tinkled among the stones, and a large object hurtled past her to fall in the thin grass beyond the path, with a hollow thump and a dull echo. She had ducked her head into her arms instinctively at the crash, flattening herself against the wall, but came out of hiding as soon as the falling glass had settled, and looked up to examine a gaping hole in the high window. Peter had turned back with a startled shout and was running towards the dark object in the grass, and in a moment he picked it up with a whoop of delight, and waved it at her in the full transfiguring sunlight, and she recognised Punch's boot.

They scrambled for the door, protesting senselessly, in relief and laughter, that he'd let them stand outside the door and never said a word. They heaved at the latch, and pushed and pulled, and the door never stirred. Then suddenly Peter gave a yell of triumph, and reached up over the door, to a nail, encrusted with rust, which pierced the wall beneath the little stone Virgin. 'Look, the key! Of course it would have to be somewhere where people could get it at once, or what's the good of the place? Wonder why they left it for us, though?'

'Oh, thank goodness!' cried Phyllida in a vast sigh of satisfaction. 'Oh, Peter, why doesn't he make any sound even now? I can't hear a thing, can you? Do you suppose he's all right?'

'He can still heave a boot, anyhow. Look out, give me room. The thing's as rusty as the devil.' He got both hands to it, and it gave protestingly, and the door swung slowly and heavily inward, to release Punch's hoarse but reassuringly loud voice:

'My God, are you people stone deaf, or what? I've been howling my head off in here. I thought you'd gone.'

He came blundering through the doorway into the light, and stood shaking his head between his hands and grimacing. He was a little lame with only one boot, and Phyllida, half-laughing and half-crying, took him by the shoulders and steered him by the smoothest way to a rock on which he could sit. Peter, aware of the desirability of being somewhere else for a moment, and possessed also of an insatiable curiosity, stooped his head carefully under the massive lintel to have a look at Punch's prison. The thickness of the door, its solidity in the deep frame, awed him no less than the fortress-like walls. No wonder sound had no chance to convey itself past that barrier! Even the windows were up in the rafters, well above the level of the tallest head, and the walls smooth, and nothing at all within on which a man could climb, nothing on the wooden floor but a litter of dust and cobwebs and twigs. It appeared to him that a grown man, even if he could pull himself up to the windows, wouldn't be able to cram himself through them. And to find oneself locked in here, and see the latch move, and to shout, and shout, and get no reply at all—! Sound plays devilish tricks, but this one certainly couldn't have been intended when the place was built as a shelter in time of storm. What if Phyllida hadn't heaved at the latch? The one sound and movement which could communicate through this silent belt of massive wood and stone, and she found it by sheer blessed luck!

Peter's scalp prickled. He ducked his head and scuttled out of the stony chill of the *baîto,* just as Phyllida flew at him in a whirl of light-hearted reproaches. It had not been so helpful of him, after all, to wander off with Punch's boot still in his hand. He surrendered it docilely, trotting back on her heels to where the unlucky ambassador sat hugging his head.

Punch wouldn't look at them. He groped his foot into his boot, and dragged slowly at the laces, and occasionally gave his head a wincing, uneasy shake, staring all the time at the stony ground between his heels, with the hangdog look of a cornered criminal; and in a morose voice not at all unsuitable to the portrait he said hollowly: 'They got the diamonds.'

'My God!' said Phyllida, flopping down on the stones to tie up his boot for him, as if he had been her over-serious child, 'is that all? What do you expect us to do, beat you? Oh, Punch, my sweet idiot, if you only knew how crazy with worry I've been! And you can talk about diamonds! Poppet, I couldn't care less about the diamonds. Damn the diamonds, if you're all right! And what's more, old man Galassi would say so, too.'

But Punch couldn't. He cared passionately and wretchedly, from his heart outward, and he couldn't think of anyone else. He turned his face away from her, and said bitterly: 'I thought I was doing the best thing! And now we've lost all the ground we'd gained, and we can't prove a thing – not even that we're telling the truth.'

'Yes, we can,' soothed Phyllida reproachfully. 'We've got the handkerchief – haven't we? Punch, nobody's taken the handkerchief, have they?'

'I don't know,' admitted Punch dazedly, feeling dubiously in all his pockets. 'Honestly, I don't know quite what I am doing. I—' A small sigh of relief, but still a depressed sigh, greeted at least one good discovery. 'No, it's here.' He fished the crumpled paper bag out of the pocket of his shorts, and looked at it without any great favour. 'Well, that's something, I suppose. But the old man's stones are gone. I'd have given anything,' he said miserably, 'to hand them over safely – just to satisfy him. Even if he couldn't know it.'

'Well,' said Peter, reasonably but most unwisely, 'if only you'd listened—'

Phyllida turned on him a face of such ferocity that he left his 'I told you so!' uncompleted. After all, when people were like this about each other there was no knowing what they wouldn't do when roused. 'Say it,' said Phyllida through her teeth, almost silently but very clearly, 'and I'll slaughter you.' And having satisfied herself in one piercing glance of the temporary paralysis through shock of Peter's genius for indiscretions, she turned back to her problem child with quite another face, and gently felt where he was feeling, behind and above his right ear. 'What happened? We watched Monfalcone like hawks, every minute of the morning, and he hasn't been a step further than the beach, and nobody's been near him except just the hotel people, either. He couldn't have had anything to do with this. Oh, Punch, you've got the most colossal bump here! Did somebody *hit* you?'

'Of course somebody hit me,' growled the ungrateful

148

sufferer, wincing. 'Look out, it hurts like hell! What do you think I did, back into a tree? And then you idiots come and rattle the latch and walk away, as if you were stone deaf, and me bellowing inside like a sick bullock! I've been trying to get out of there for hours. We've got to go on to the police, it's more urgent than ever now.'

'Yes, of course! Yes, as soon as you feel better. But you must rest a few minutes, first. Anyhow, you're safe!' said Phyllida fervently. 'That's the great thing. How did it happen?'

Punch let her part the thick short hair from his wound, and examine with small explosive noises of indignation and sympathy the broken bruise which was oozing a few drops of sticky blood. He didn't really want to growl at her, it was only because his ill-temper eased a little his sick rage with himself, and that dark self-chastising grief and shame which she could never have felt on her own account, but by some gentle dispensation had no difficulty in comprehending when it assailed him. She, who had never been ashamed of anything in her life, or lost any sleep over irretraceable steps, no matter how misdirected, perfectly understood this other kind of conscience, because it was his.

'I got on all right,' said Punch gruffly, 'until I was coming up through a pretty steep slope of woodland somewhere here – I don't know how far he lugged me to the hut, so I don't even know where the thing happened, but the path was doing some sharp bends, and the undergrowth was pretty well closing it here and there, so I could never see far ahead or behind—'

'I know,' said Phyllida, 'we came up it, it's only just below those trees there. Hold on a minute, there's a trickle of water in the rocks back there, I'll wet my handkerchief.' She came back with it dripping, squeezed out the surplus, and folded it cool and smooth against the dull, hot pain at the back of his head. 'How does it feel?'

'Good! You know, it isn't anything, really, only it's given me the hell of a headache. I'll be all right now there's some air. Well, so I was coming up this bit at quite a lick, when on one of the turns towards the top – I could see the open sky through the bushes ahead – something comes crashing out of the undergrowth right into my back, and flattens me. I never heard a thing until he got me round the neck, and clamped his great ham of a hand over my mouth. I tried to hack back at his shins, but there wasn't hold enough on the slope, I only did for myself, and went clean off my feet, with him on top. It wasn't even much of a struggle. He gave me this on the back of the head, and I didn't need any more. And I came round on that filthy floor in the hut there, feeling like hell, and without the torch. That's all I know about it. I was out about three quarters of an hour, according to my watch – that didn't come to any harm, it's still going. Not like me!' he said bitterly. 'A fat lot of use I turned out to be at this sort of thing!'

'Don't be stupid!' said Phyllida, her voice much kinder than her words. 'It could have happened like that to anybody, however careful or however clever they happened to be. After all, we'd *taken* care of what we thought was the source of danger – there were three of us watching him. How could we guess there'd be other people already on your trail? Nobody can think of everything, or prepare for everything – not over a course like this. Besides, how could anyone know where to pick you up? We covered up all the traces as well as we could. No one but us *could* have known you intended coming this way at that hour.

150

And you made such a good get-away from the hotel, too. You didn't see any sign of anyone following you, did you?'

'No. But he must have been,' owned Punch dejectedly. 'I suppose if you know the country well enough you can take a few risks with short cuts, even on this sort of going, to cut a fellow off at the best spot for the job. Anyhow, he pulled it off. And they've got the diamonds!'

'You didn't get a look at him at all?' asked Peter.

'The first I knew of him was "crash", and he hit me in the back, and slapped his left hand clean over my mouth. Nearly pulled my jaw through to the back of my neck. No, I never *saw* a thing, except a close-up of the ground after he dropped on me—'

'But surely you got *some* sort of impression? I mean, you might know roughly how tall he was, you can tell if a bloke's reaching *up* at you or not. And you can tell if it's the weight of a big fellow, or not so big, that hits you.' Peter was rational, but his unwitting air of having been frequently attacked from behind, so often indeed that he knew the art of eyeless recognition backwards, had a certain lack of tact.

'I can do better than that,' said Punch; 'if you'll shut up a minute I was going to tell you. This bloke clutched me from behind, and I was just opening my mouth to shout, which I suppose was what he expected, and there were his fingers trying to pull my front teeth down my throat. So I bit them. Damn nearly broke my teeth, he had a great thick ring on the little one—' Their twin gasps of enlightenment were music to his ears. 'Yes, it was him,' he said, with sour disregard of all the grammar he had ever learned. 'Old Sparafucile's turned up again.'

Peter, sidetracked even in the middle of his gasp of

recognition, asked densely: 'Old who? Is that his name? How did you find out?'

'No, of course it isn't his name, idiot! But I had to call him something. You can't go on for ever giving a description of him to show who you mean. And if he isn't a hired assassin,' said Punch feelingly, 'he's the next thing to it.'

'Oh, the bloke in *Rigoletto*,' sighed Peter in comprehension. 'Well, OK, it's as good a name as any. But are you sure about him? There could be other men running round with rings on their little fingers.'

'There could, but they wouldn't all be following us. He was, and *this* fellow was. Besides, he was the right sort of heft and height, only a lot stronger than I'd expected. It was like being collared by a bear. And anyhow,' he said, with the first warmth of sheer satisfaction creeping grimly into his voice, 'if we can get our hands on him we can soon find out for certain, because this bloke's got my marks on him. Maybe the ring has, too, if the silver's soft enough – but we were struggling, and my teeth slid off the ring, and I got two of his fingers. Hell of a way to fight,' he said disgustedly, 'but what else could I do? And he wasn't too particular, anyhow, leaping out on me from behind, like that.'

'Darling,' said Phyllida, getting back into her old form, 'I'm sure even the Marquess of Queensberry would absolve you. Maybe I ought to care about the diamonds, but I can't. I'm too relieved to find *you* safely. You don't know what awful things we've been imagining.'

'You don't know what awful things I've been imagining myself,' admitted Punch, looking over his shoulder at the square grey shape of the *baîto*. 'I tried climbing to the window, but there's nothing to get hold of. I tried to find a nail or a bit of metal in the muck on the floor that would do to pick the lock, but nothing doing there, either. But now I see how near the path we are, I'm pretty sure he meant me to be found easily enough – after he'd had time to get clean away. He left the key in position, and after all, if you'd gone the length of going to the police this is one of the first places they'd have looked, being about the only building on the route. Maybe he had strict orders to be pretty careful – after the other one.'

'The path isn't used much,' said Phyllida doubtfully. 'We never saw a soul all the way.'

'No, maybe not, but you wouldn't see many on the main street in Rocca della Sera at this hour. Nobody moves about in the middle of the day. I did meet a few people this morning. I'm sure it's used a fair amount. No, honestly, old girl, I don't think he really wanted to do for me. Only it didn't feel so certain when I was inside. Thanks for pulling me out, incidentally,' he said gruffly, 'I never heard you at all until you heaved up the latch, and then by the time I got to the door you were going away again. It's practically a sound-proof box.' He sat up and gave his head an experimental shake, disarranging Phyllida's cold compress. 'I'm all right now, I can make it. We'd better push on.'

'If you feel up to it.' She turned his face to the light with a disrespectful hand under his chin, and sponged at his mouth. 'He marked you, too. The ring's cut your lips – quite a gash here on the bottom one. I suppose you were too busy even to feel that.'

'Has it? I didn't know. I had a mouthful of blood, but I thought it was his – I'm sure most of it was.' He scrubbed uneasily at his mouth with the back of his hand, and said: 'My God, I must be filth to the eyebrows, after lying about on the floor in there. Am I fit to show up in the village?'

She wiped his face for him with her wet handkerchief, turning him to her convenience by his short and curly forelock. 'You're grubby, but you'll do for the police. Do you really feel fit to go on? Say what you like, you weren't feeling so hot, my boy, when you came out of gaol.'

'Yes, I'm all right. What's a headache, anyway? I can walk.' He was off already down the path, heading across the bowl of rock towards Sopramazzolo. His legs still felt uncertain under him, if he would have admitted it, but he had got his wits back into working order, and that was all that was required to drive him, and his friends too. He couldn't wait to get to the police with the tragedy of the diamonds. He couldn't forgive himself for all the wasted minutes he'd already spent sitting stupidly among the stones, free but not yet reintegrated. The hired assassin had gained a start of nearly eight hours, but still there was no sense in sitting in despair while the eight became nine. Punch blundered downhill on his shaky legs, nose-forward after his revenge, mad to reclaim his reputation; and Phyllida, who had abandoned all her feelings of responsibility for Signor Galassi's honour at the first breath of a nearer anxiety, skipped uncomplainingly at his shoulder, ready to retrieve him if he foundered, loyally involved through his conscience if no longer through her own. It came to the same thing in the end.

(2)

There were two police officers in Sopramazzolo, and neither of them spoke English. The senior was a grey, wide, lethargic man of about fifty, whom everything excited, in a pleasingly serene way, but nothing could surprise. The junior was a thin youth with much more to say for himself, and a nervously active manner, but though he got off the mark much faster with every question and every move, he never arrived any earlier at either answer or action. They were both big, in the mountain fashion. Punch reflected again how misleading is the conception of all Italians as little men, and how many he had already seen who topped six feet, sometimes by several inches.

The older man wasted no time in calling in his son, aged perhaps somewhere in the late twenties, who spoke perfectly good English, and would have liked to launch into a description of his experiences as a student in England if his father had not held him good-naturedly to the point. So there were no difficulties, after all, in the telling of their story. The other two left it to Punch, because he was so obviously keyed up to make a brief, accurate and clear job of it, and if it helped him to forget that his head was opening and shutting, they were content that he should have that relief. He did well, and he wasted no time over it, and all they had to do was offer confirmation or an additional detail here and there, to fill out the picture.

It was nice talking to a man who couldn't be surprised. The young one wrote copiously, and interrupted frequently. The old one listened, nodded, made an occasional brief note, heard everything to the end, and then – and Phyllida loved him for it, though he was probably only having a look for himself, to see that they were telling the truth – came over and turned Punch round with his back to the window, and fingered the still oozing bruise. He gave a soft, rich, sympathetic little chuckle, patted him on the shoulder, and said: '*Si, poveretto!*' And to his son he added a rapid flood of instruction which despatched him from the room, to return presently with a glass of cognac, which Punch obediently swallowed.

The younger officer was already on the telephone, making one torrential call after another, with his voluminous notes in hand; and surely half the Trentino would presently be out after a short, square dark man with bad teeth, with a scratched silver ring buckled round the bitten little finger of his left hand. At least their whole story had been believed; and it seemed that the grey-haired man, even if he functioned only in a small village in the mountains, was perfectly conversant with the problems of the rest of the country's police force, for he patted Punch again in a commending way as the brandy vanished, and sat back, and told them, in Italian which his son quickly turned into English:

'Signor Galassi has already spoken of these diamonds, they are being sought everywhere. If you did not deliver them safely, at least you bring the first news of them. Until now we have had no lead at all.'

'He's spoken?' cried Punch, sitting up straight in his surprise and eagerness. 'You mean he's better?' He had been afraid to ask until then. And he reached out, quite without knowing he did it, and clutched Phyllida's hand, and pressed it delightedly.

'Yes, he's better. Yesterday he was conscious for the first time. His first thought was of these stones he was carrying for his firm. He should have delivered them in Turin. It is very much on his mind that he failed to do so. But he is better, and he will live.'

The relief was so great and instant that only then did they realise how heavy and dark the shadow had been. Even the diamonds, even Punch's abject defeat, though he could not quite be rid of it, at once seemed to matter less. Much Signora Galassi would care, or

Antonia, or Francesca, or the young boy who was still at school, about twelve shiny stones, when their invalid had opened his eyes again and called them by their names. Phyllida hugged Punch's hand, and gleamed with joy. Peter's incandescent smile widened and widened until it spanned his whole face. And yet, thought Punch fondly, how fine it would have been to remind the old man of his friends in the train by suddenly restoring his lost trust, and making him free of every charge on him. And all through his, Punch's, inadequacy, the chance was lost. No grand gesture for them. And besides, he had this personal account to settle now, and it would nag him until he discharged it, yes, even in good moments like this one.

His head was a little better, and his mind clearing accordingly; and he recovered the courage and self-confidence to remind the policeman that they had found certain reasons to view one other gentleman with suspicion. What about Monfalcone?

Well, what about him? The policeman sat serenely in his chair, and smiled sceptically but kindly upon his inexperienced assistants. He caught the eye of his junior across their heads, and the two exchanged twin looks of indulgence and disbelief. A wealthy merchant in bijouterie and glass does not ordinarily meddle with violent robbery in trains, nor drive up into the mountains to compromise himself by being seen with wanted characters near the scene of fresh crimes. He comes, he comes, certainly. Garda sees him by the thousand, he colonises the lakeside hotels of every mountain town, making a second strange world there, as alien as the moon from the hard-working poor who inhabit the low dark tenements a hundred yards higher up the village. But he does little more energetic or ingenious than play an occasional game of tennis, or take a daily swim, between sessions of sunbathing and lengthy, many-coursed meals. The policeman knew the type well, for he was a mountain man; and perhaps of the two methods of robbery, direct and legal, he had more respect for the former; but he did not make the mistake of confusing them, or supposing that they often habited together.

'Into his movements, too, we shall look. But you say yourself that he cannot answer for today. I think that in him you have no more than a little string of coincidences. But possibilities must be examined.'

But they could hear the scepticism in his voice, and knew that this, at least, was not considered very much of a possibility. Still, they could do no more, they had told everything they had seen or heard or even thought in the matter, and now it was up to the police. There was a certain feeling of deliverance and peace at the moment, though later probably they would begin to want action again, and to calculate the chances of picking up the trail of Sparafucile for themselves.

'I suppose Signor Galassi couldn't tell anything about the man who hit him?' asked Punch, not very hopefully.

'No, nothing. What could we hope for? The instant he opened his eyes he would be struck down. He knows nothing but his own anxiety, that he was in charge of the diamonds, and was robbed of them. Besides, he is not yet in condition to be questioned too closely. Later he may remember more – but I doubt if he will ever tell us much.'

Somebody hammered on the shutters outside the window, which looked out on a narrow little courtyard behind the house; and the interpreter, with a flashing smile at his father, slipped out of the room, to return with a grey little elderly man in his shirt-sleeves. He looked out from under a fall of grizzled hair, with deep-set grey eyes in a wrinkled and weathered face, another mountain man, leisurely and adroit and silent of movement, for all he looked old and infirm. He greeted the police officer with the very few and offhand words which pass only between old friends, and asked something which evidently referred to the three young English people, for he turned his deep, bright eyes upon them all in turn, and switching suddenly into English on his own account, repeated the question in their direction:

'Well, which one is it needs me?'

They were a little startled, because he did not look like a doctor, but the policeman turned him placidly towards his patient. The old man tilted Punch's head to the light, and went to work on him with assured and unsurprised hands, saying nothing; but his silence was neither morose nor professional, merely the companionable silence of one who normally speaks little. The policeman talked, looking up at them occasionally across his table, between fits of writing, and sudden exchanges with his junior, who was still wrangling with the telephone.

'Doctor Rossi learned his English,' explained the interpreter proudly, 'from prisoners of war, when he led them across the mountains. Two years of the war he did this work, secretly at night, and in the day he was our doctor here. Many Englishmen he took north, to their next guide. Also Italians and others who had to leave the country, while the Germans were here. That was a busy life for an old man.'

Phyllida and Peter stared at the doctor, upon this recommendation, with round eyes of respect and excitement. Punch turned his head furtively to catch a glimpse of the untypical hero out of the corner of his eye, but all he could see, before the large, lean hands turned

159

him firmly back again, was still a shabby old man in his shirt-sleeves.

'Keep still!' said the doctor. 'I am going to cut your hair. Great luck for you, young man, that you have so thick a thatch, or you would not now be in such good health. Don't be afraid, your curls will grow again quickly enough. And don't pay too much attention to Tommaso. I was four years in England before the war, and my English was as you hear it before I came back to these mountains. From your soldiers I learned to enlarge it with many untechnical words one does not hear in hospitals, that is all. Still, now!' And Punch was still, feeling the small scissors working steadily round his wound, and seeing, by Phyllida's looks of silent regret, how the short strands of hair fell. He was growing sleepy now from the cognac, but the twinges of soreness from his broken crown kept him from nodding.

'But I say, did you really lead escaping prisoners through the mountains?' asked Peter eagerly.

'Here in these villages you will have harder work finding someone who did not,' said the doctor, and satisfied him no further.

'But in the last months,' supplemented Tommaso, 'the doctor took to the hills for all the time, because the Gestapo came looking for him—'

'Hush!' said the doctor, 'I have delicate work, and my hand will shake if I must be eaten in this way with great eyes. Enough, I am a wonderful person! Now be still!' And everyone obeyed him, though it could not be said that they stared less ardently than before as he gently completed the dressing of Punch's head. 'There, go home and go early to bed tonight. If you must sleep on your belly to have comfort, do it, but sleep. I shall give you something to help you. After a long night you will be all right. Perhaps a little headache if you tire yourself too much tomorrow, and for a few days still this sore head. But you have a fine thick skull, and a bullock's constitution, you have no great damage from your adventures. How far must you go to reach your supper?'

'To Rocca della Sera,' said Punch meekly.

'Better you should not walk so far. You have already enough.' And indeed Punch, in relaxing, had also wilted a little, and looked ready for his bed even at six o'clock in the evening. The doctor went into consultation with the policeman, and presently Tommaso translated their decision:

'I shall drive you on in the doctor's car to Mazzolo, and put you safely into the evening bus back to your village. This evening it will not be filled, and you will travel in comfort.'

This last rather obscure remark they understood better when they had seen the doctor's car, which was ancient and battered beyond belief. However, it was still competent to deal with the mountain roads. They packed their invalid into it, made their farewells all round, and were driven away at a rattling rate towards Mazzolo.

(3)

'Weren't they *nice?*' said Phyllida, as they walked up from the square towards the Albergo Monte Gazza. 'Don't you feel happier now, Punch? They did seem to know what they were doing, and they listened to us, and I'm sure they're on the job already. You'll see, old Sparafucile will be arrested before he ever gets out of the district.' She had been chattering cheerfully all the way from Mazzolo, but Punch had grown steadily more and more silent and glum beside her, and she was afraid that he had sunk into a new passion of self-reproach now that the reaction had set in. She linked her arm into his, looking at him furtively along her shoulder. 'Don't feel bad about it,' she said. 'Nobody blames you about the silly diamonds, and anyhow, we've done everything we can, now, so don't go on fretting.'

'I'm not fretting,' said Punch crossly, 'I'm not even feeling bad about that, particularly. I just feel bad, period. But it's all right, really. All I need is a long night in bed, and a rest day tomorrow.' He gave her a tired, apologetic smile. 'Been a long day!'

'It has for you,' she said, hugging his arm. 'Poor old Punch! Dinner and bed, and that's all for you tonight. Except that Mab will be waiting on the doorstep with her tongue hanging out. But we'll do all the talking, and you can go to bed.'

But Mab was not waiting on the doorstep. Peter was already ahead by a dozen yards, looking for her, and the open doorway of the inn was a dark and empty oblong before his eyes. He skipped up the steps, and looked round in the hall, and there was no one to be seen but the cook, just scurrying back into her kitchen after coming up for air. Peter halted in the empty room, gave a soft whistle which she would recognise for his, cocked his head on one side and waited in vain for a reply. He turned to meet Phyllida and Punch in the doorway.

'She isn't around. Do you suppose he led her off on a line somewhere? It's bang on dinner-time, I hope she isn't far. I'm hungry. I was ready to bet anything that everybody'd be home and eating at this hour.'

'Maybe she's already in the dining-room,' said Phyllida. 'Anyhow, she'll come. We'll go and clean up a bit, and then we'll look for her. Anyhow, Punch will have to go straight in and eat, because he must be famished.'

She started up the stairs, still holding Punch by the arm. Peter was about to follow, when the door of the bar opened, and Liana put her head out, anxiously, and somehow with the subtle suggestion that she had been doing the same thing at every opportunity for the last hour. She saw him, and the rich, rosy colour flooded her innocent and plaintive face, and the beautiful hesitant smile came slowly to her lips.

Peter said: 'Hullo!' and smiled back at her, though rather distractedly. 'You haven't seen Mab, have you? Our little blonde girl?' He was so used to using his hands to eke out his words that by this time he did it naturally, sketching the miniature outlines of Mab upon the air between them with rapid flourishes.

'Yes, I see her.' Liana fished inside the neck of her blouse, under the printed cotton overall she wore, and brought out carefully a very small and closely folded scrap of paper. 'Please, I have here – for you.' She met his eyes with her wide, blurred gaze as their fingers touched, and the delicate colour mantled on her soft cheek-bones, and burned there. 'She say, give it to Peter. I wait a long time.'

'Yes, we have been a long time. I'm sorry, Liana, you've been anxious about it. Thank you!' He opened it, a little clumsily because something about Liana's half-blind look always upset him, and especially at such close quarters. 'You don't know where she is now?'

'I think she is gone,' said Liana, and trembled at the startled upward jerk of his head. 'A long time ago, maybe three o'clock, she is gone.'

'Gone?' said Peter blankly, and stared sharply back

to the paper in his hand. It took a lot of believing, but it made its point in the end.

'Venice. If not there, wait for me.'

He read and re-read it, and it didn't seem to tell him much. He would have thought she could have been more explicit than that, and at least said what had happened to send her off across the country alone. For he supposed that was what it meant? Venice. Even of her destination, it seemed, she was in some doubt herself. He must show this to the others, quickly, and see if they could make any more of it.

'It is – not all well?' asked Liana anxiously.

He looked up, and shook the frown of desperate concentration from his forehead in order to please her. Apart from the necessity to keep this closed within their own small circle, one could not involve Liana, of all people.

'Oh, yes, everything's fine. Just a change of plans, that's all. There's nothing wrong.'

'You will go also?' said Liana with a discouraged sigh.

'We must, very soon. Perhaps tomorrow. I don't know yet. I must talk to the others about it. When we are rich,' said Peter, smiling at her, 'we'll come here again, and stay a long time.' He gave her hand a quick, light touch, and turned towards the stairs. 'Thanks awfully for taking care of the message for me.'

He ran upstairs two at a time, leaving her looking over her shoulder after him rather sadly as she went back to the bar.

Phyllida and Punch were washing, and making a fairly sketchy business of it; and no doubt they were still expecting to see Mab already at table when they went down to the dining-room, and had therefore made no great search for any other sign of her. Peter broke in upon Punch's hasty splashings with the note outspread in his hand.

'Look! She left it with Liana for us. "Venice. If not there, wait for me." She's gone – Liana says about three o'clock this afternoon – gone to Venice at a moment's notice, by the look of it. Here, see for yourself.' He thrust it into Punch's still wet fingers, and ran to call Phyllida from her solitary preparations next door. 'Phyl, come in here, quick. There's a note from Mab. She's gone!'

Phyllida's voice from within the half-open door said: 'I know! That makes two notes, I just found mine. Trouble is it doesn't say *where* she's gone.' She sounded perplexed, and put out, and the next minute appeared in the doorway looking no less so, and sucking her finger. 'We had a landlady in one of our digs who used to read all the notes we left for each other, and so we started pinning them under the bedclothes to diddle her. I just remembered. Scratched my finger on the pin. But now we're not a lot wiser.'

'Well, don't stand there shouting about it on the landing,' hissed Peter. 'Come on in, and keep your voice down.' And he drew her into the other room, and shut the door.

'Doesn't matter now,' said Phyllida simply. '*He's* gone, too.'

'Who? Monfalcone?'

'Who else? Look!' She proffered the message Mab had left in the bed, and they put their heads together over it, and read: '"He got a phone call and left. Trying to follow him. Details later."' And then, a characteristically punctilious afterthought: '"Please pay my shot. Will settle later."' They looked up over the scrap of paper with eyes kindling into speculation and excitement once again, for the decision to go on interfering had evidently been taken for them in their absence, and again they had an honest stake in the business, something they couldn't abandon, something they couldn't leave to others, no, not even the police. 'Well, I'm the details later,' triumphed Peter. 'Look, she found out where he was going – or at least she believed she'd found out. "Venice. If not there, wait for me." And she left this for Liana to deliver because she hadn't time to dash up here again. That's it! He was going, and she didn't dare take her eyes off him. But she'd have to risk losing him somewhere on the way, wouldn't she? Unless he took the bus. Do you suppose he would? Didn't seem his line of travel. There's a colossal gulf fixed between his kind and the good old hoi-polloi, I fancy.'

'If Liana knows what time she went,' said Punch, 'maybe she saw the exit. Could you do a bit of pumping, without giving too much away?'

'I'll try. But she'd know Mab was going, anyhow, if she flew into the bar to leave a note for us. She may not have seen a thing beyond that, you know the poor kid lives in the bar day and night, practically. But I'll try.'

'We'll have to go after her, of course,' said Punch, mustering his battered wits to attempt command of this changed situation, and feeling them dazzle and ache in protest at the effort. 'But we can't go tonight. We couldn't get down in time for a train.'

'We can't go tonight,' said Phyllida sternly, 'if there were fifty trains. You've got your orders for tonight. But we can go in the morning, and we shall be in Venice by early afternoon, at the latest. How are we going to find her, even if she is there?'

'She'll go to one of the places we listed up as possibles, surely. She knows a good many of the names and addresses, after all the talking we did about it before we came away. And she's got to stay somewhere. We can split up and try them all until we do find her.'

'If a phone call sent him off at five minutes notice, like that,' said Peter, 'it looks as if it was news of the things he was after. I reckon Sparafucile rang up to tell him the diamonds were in the bag and make a date to meet him with them somewhere. And what's more, it looks as if Mab thought so, too. Anyhow, she didn't intend losing him. Punch, old lad, with a lot of luck and some fast movement you may get your revenge for today, after all.'

'But why go so far?' wondered Punch feverishly.

'Well, why not, for thousands, maybe millions, of lire? Isn't it worth it? Well away from the scene of either crime, and maybe well away from any business places where he might be known. A man like Monfalcone can't just make an appointment with a hired thug – one who *looks* like a hired thug, too! – in a hotel where he's been staying, or meet him in a wine-shop, or anything like that, now, can he? He daren't risk being seen with him. And after all, if you've already got certain information the diamonds are yours, and you can trust your man, why spoil the ship for a ha'porth of tar? *I'd* be super-cautious, too, in his place.'

'Besides,' pointed out Phyllida, 'she wasn't sure about Venice, she only thought that was where she had to go. Well, all we can do is go after her, first thing in the morning, and when we've actually found her maybe we shall know what to do next.'

So they went down to dinner, for they were very hungry; but after all, Punch lasted no longer than the end of the risotto, and then his weariness and the doctor's sedative overcame his hunger, and he drooped away to his bed, and after a few painful but increasingly sleepy experiments with the position of his head upon the pillow, drifted away into deep sleep.

Peter waited until Phyllida had followed Punch up the stairs before he made his approach to Liana. His instinct in these matters was sound, quite apart from the fact that he didn't want any sisters cramping his style. But within five minutes he was tapping softly at Phyllida's door, and imploring her in an agitated whisper:

'Phyl, can I come in?'

She opened to him, already in her pyjamas, and closed the door behind him lest their voices should penetrate Punch's exhausted but uneasy slumber. She had put out the light, and a milk-white glimmer of moonlight lit his face for her, and made it a mask of comical consternation. 'Whatever's the matter?' asked Phyllida, laughing at him a little, because nothing could possibly have happened in five minutes to alter things very much.

'About Mab,' said Peter directly. 'I've been talking to Liana.'

'Well, what's wrong? You look as if the poor girl had given you a shock. I don't see—'

'Well, I don't quite know if it's bad or good, I don't know what to make of it. Only I can't help being worried about her, a bit, because what can she *do?* I mean, all by herself, against a man like that—'

'Oh, Mab knows what she's about, all right,' said Phyllida comfortably, 'even if she does look about as competent as a primrose. She knows what risks to take and what to let alone, she won't get into any trouble.'

'Well, that's what I thought, too. But now I'm not so sure. Because Liana was rather surprised when Mab gave her the note all at once, like that, and she went out into the hall to see what was happening, and she saw them go—'

'Them?'

'Them!' said Peter very firmly. 'Just like that! Liana says, Monfalcone was just helping Mab into that big car that brought him here, and she was smiling, and talking to him, and then he got in beside her, and they drove away towards Riva. Yes,' said Peter, 'that's why I'm wondering if she really does know where to draw the line. She didn't just go *after* him: she went *with* him!'

CHAPTER SEVEN

BENVENUTO,
AN ANACHRONISM

(1)

THE train stopped only twice before arriving at Venice, and at neither stop did the hide suitcase emerge from the luggage van. At Vicenza Mab watched from behind her window, keeping carefully within the corridor, so that she might not be seen by her enemy, if he should be leaning out in search of evening papers, or fruit, or wine; but the activity at the van was desultory, and she never had to wonder if she had missed the important item. So far, so good.

Between Vicenza and Padua her mind began to work with more precision, and she laid out her armaments coolly, as if she had been doing this kind of thing all her life. Her wind-jacket was cherry-red, and even when rolled inside the straps of her rucksack could be distinguished at a hundred yards; he could hardly have stowed it into the car at Rocca della Sera without noticing it. That must be hidden. Her frock was a printed seersucker in two blues and a grey on a white ground, not particularly distinctive, she thought it would pass unremarked with a little help. There was a thin blue cardigan inside her pack, one she had not worn at all in the mountains. She fished it out, and put it on, stowing her wind-jacket inside in its place. Her hair also would be easily recognisable, once she ceased to be totally surrounded by people taller than herself – it was her usual state, but could not be relied upon for ever. She pulled out her favourite white scarf, printed with quite beautiful and economical sketches of convolvulus in heliotrope and green and black, and tied it over her head, hiding her fairness. She had been in Italy long enough by this time to realise that its excellence of design, which would have made it stand out in England, fitted it suavely into the pattern here, where dress prints were almost all works of art, and the occasional ugly commonplace drew the eye as at home the occasional grace.

In this disguise, she thought, and as one in any case not expected to be on this train, she should escape notice. Especially if her friend the merry man, whose action vocabulary was by no means exhausted yet, should happen to be going all the way to Venice, and could be induced to carry her rucksack off the station for her. To which end, not without shame, but not without pleasure, either, for she liked him, she made herself very charming to her neighbour for the rest of the journey. They played a game which needed only very few words, and those the ones she knew best in his language. He sang her bits of opera, Verdi, Rossini, Donizetti, Bellini – and as soon as she recognised the air she joined in. Occasionally he defeated her, but every success of hers delighted him so much that he helped her out with the few failures, and between them the time passed very pleasantly. And he did not get out at Padua, and neither did the hide case. After all, her guess had been inconveniently accurate when she had meant it to go reassuringly astray. It was for Venice the enemy was bound.

The earth grew dull and flat, and brought them slowly through a flat, brownish town, and a queer sudden growth of oil storage tanks; and this, according to the name-board on the platform, was Mestre. Before she had done wondering at it, it slithered inconspicuously away, and the long, serpentine, dust-coloured line of land ran out into the long, soft, iridescent, glimmering line of water.

They were in the lagoon, they swam on its bright, surface, so low to the waves that she expected to hear the slur and wash of their progress feathering away on either side, but the water remained limpid and still, shimmering with reflected blue and pearl and iris from the sky. Across this placid mirror, close under the lee of the train, a slim grey causeway of road ran with them, cars scudding along it towards an opening water-lily which spread its leaves afloat upon the silvery distances. Low and elusive and faint and soft along the ghost of the sea, the ghost of a city slowly took shape; and that was Venice. Coloured like the sea, or like the sky, or like a delicate smoke or a dancing heat-vapour drifting between the two, it glimmered and dissolved before Mab's enchanted eyes, and she did not believe, at this first vision of it, that it could ever be reached.

It was a wonderful feeling, to be in an amphibious train, there was no awareness at all of any railway line running under them. But the mirage of a city, the cloud and dew city, grew nearer, and resolved itself into real buildings, of solid materials which could no doubt be touched, like any others. And for fully five minutes Mab suffered the only misgivings of disappointment which Venice ever caused her, and dreaded that she should never again find it as ravishing as at first sight, when it was inaccessible as Atlantis.

The carriage road swerved to the right, and left them, heading for the Piazzale Roma, the lost cars' home of a town with no use for wheeled traffic; and the train, suddenly surrounded by walls and sidings and platforms and people, just like anywhere else, ran on into a perfectly ordinary station. She could hardly guess as yet that this would be practically the last ordinary thing of any kind which she would see for several days; and if she had realised it, it would at once have become extraordinary.

Now at the last moment she did not know how to proceed, and it seemed to her that in the very moment of success she ran the greatest risk of losing her quarry. If Monfalcone collected his cases himself, it was long odds he would hire a gondola to convey him and them to whatever hotel he proposed to honour. And there were various difficulties in the way of following him by the same method. For one thing, gondolas cost money, and she had no idea of how much money she was going to need before this expedition was over. For another, even if she had been rolling in lire, she had not the very faintest idea how to say 'Follow that gondola!', she had not a dictionary; her phrase-book was dumb on such abstruse subjects, and, above all, she was not sure that she had the requisite nerve. She could do all kinds of crazy things herself, but she curled up at the idea of displaying them before others. Life just isn't like that. So on the whole it was just as well that she didn't know the words. But it meant that she had to think of something else, quickly.

If the porters from the hotel collected the cases, the position would be much the same, for they would sail off from the landing-stage in the hotel boat, and she would be left with no means of following. If you use the water-buses, the little nonchalant *vaporetti* which scuttle across and across the Grand Canal, tacking like water-spiders, you can hardly expect to keep your eye on one particular gondola for long, even if it is moving in the same general direction. But if Monfalcone's luggage was carried off in this way, then she might, with luck, see the name of his hotel somewhere on the caps of the porters.

Alternatively, since he would then have no luggage on his hands, Monfalcone himself might not be particularly anxious to go straight to his hotel. It was just a chance. The evening, tenderly coloured and soft as pearl, was just folding down like cool gauze after the heat of the day, and he was newly come into the town, and bored from the train, and maybe he would want to stretch his legs, and sit over the Grand Canal somewhere in the open, and have a drink, before he went home to dinner. In which case, whether he walked or took the *vaporetto*, she could keep an eye on him. But there were too many ifs for her liking.

However, she edged along the corridor very slowly, waiting to see the gaudy label among the cases now being hauled out from the van, and fiddling with the straps of her rucksack to account for her slowness. And when she reached the doorway, there by the luggage van in full view was Monfalcone himself, and a young man in a casual sort of half-uniform at his elbow, just picking out the cases he indicated. She avoided being pushed out of the corridor by hooking the frame of her rucksack into an open doorway, and succeeded beyond her hopes because an extremely fat lady was just trying to get through the doorway, and provided a jam which took some three minutes to disentangle. By the time she finally detached herself, with profuse apologies, Monfalcone was striding away towards the exit, his light grey felt just visible above the heads of the crowding passengers, and the young porter was collecting the luggage of another guest to add to the cases he had already set on one side. There was no name on him anywhere that Mab could see. All the more reason for keeping that elusive grey hat in sight, she thought, and began to hurry.

The merry man took the rucksack from her very firmly, and slung it upon his left shoulder. She was obviously not to be trusted with such awkward things. He asked her, as she skipped alongside him, if she was boarding the *vaporetto,* and with her eyes on the grey hat she calculated the chances rapidly, and said that she was. Monfalcone appeared to have no qualms at all about her, was not looking round to make sure he had got rid of her, but taking it for granted. She did not think she need even have bothered to change her colour scheme, but it was as well to be on the safe side.

They came out from the station, which was dark, and blinked in a renewed light brighter than they had remembered it. And before she had any time to prepare herself for it, there they stood on the embankment, with the Grand Canal opening resplendently before them in gleaming amorphous blues and greens and olives and silvers, and the tottering palace fronts of marble and inlay leaning over to look at their faces in it, and the mooring poles, top-heavy, striped, lantern-headed, bristling outside the doorways in the cobalt-shadowed water, and the sudden bunches of piles propped together like drunks holding one another up outside an English pub after closing time.

And the gondolas, the veritable long, graceful, silent shapes she knew already from pictures, there in their dozens; but all shabbier than she had imagined them, and all dingily black, like light insouciant hearses. The edges of their seats were worn and scratched, their cushions leaked at the seams, their gondoliers were middle-aged men with teak faces, in a rig reminiscent of *H.M.S. Pinafore*, instead of slender, dark-eyed youths in white shirts and knee-breeches, with coloured scarves round their heads. But the odd thing was that the magic was intact in spite of all these puncturing facts which ought to have shattered it. They moved graciously along the water, the long oar creaking softly in its slanted rowlock, the boatman leaning forward on it lazily with his bared brown forearms, and his weight swaying from foot to foot in a rhythm which seemed much slower than the motion through the water. Elegant, aloof and self-sufficient even in their shabbiness, they cut the air with their sharp comb prows, and the water with their narrow hulls, and remained wonderful.

The merry man heard her laughing in incredulous delight, saw her clasping her hands to assure herself by touch that she was indeed here, alive and awake; and he was as gratified as if he had arranged the whole show for her himself. He launched into a panegyric of which she understood not one word, though she felt its theme and tenor without benefit of language; and by the time she had recovered her wits and looked round for the grey felt hat which she was supposed to be following, she knew she had let the thread slip out of her hand. Monfalcone was nowhere to be seen. It was terrible! Here was her friend asking her where she wanted to go, and the *vaporetto* just sidling towards the landing-stage, and she had lost her quarry in the crowds, and dodge and dive and turn as she would, she could not find him again.

She had a bad moment of panic and chagrin, and actually only boarded the boat because she could not think fast enough of a way to get out of it reasonably. The merry man had her rucksack on his shoulder, and was waiting to buy her a ticket at the window, and it was one of those awful moments when the whole attention of the world seemed to be centred upon her, and unable to move on until she spoke and acted. It takes a lot of courage then to stick fast upon your own preoccupations, and let events continue petrified.

She said weakly: 'Lido, please!' on a cowardly compromise between despair – because to leave here now without finding him again was to admit defeat – and obstinate optimism – because it was the most distant stop, and therefore if he should be on board, or if she should see him on the embankment, she would at least be equipped to follow him as far as she could possibly go. And when she had trotted down the short, echoing wooden stage after her friend, almost the first person she saw ahead of her, just rising from a corner of the bench and folding his paper away under his arm, was Monfalcone.

He must have booked his ticket, gone straight down to the stage, and sat down to read, just as the first vision of the Grand Canal had driven him from her mind. Behind a newspaper every man is anonymous. Mab hung back until he had stepped aboard the boat, and following cautiously, watched him make for the outer rail, and lean upon his hands there to stare across at the Corinthian front of the Church of San Simeone Piccolo opposite. She felt calmed, now, and capable. That first slip should be the last.

The merry man had hoisted her rucksack on to one of the luggage racks built into the superstructure of the boat, and luckily felt compelled to stay near enough to guard it, or he would certainly have wanted to show her every building on either bank of the Grand Canal. She stood close beside him, using him as a shield between herself and the enemy; and when he left her, with many farewells, at the Rialto, she was ungratefully glad, because at once she felt free of every necessity for normal speech or behaviour, free to give her whole mind to the campaign she had in hand. From now on it was between the two of them, Monfalcone and Mab Isherwood.

(2)

On that first trip Mab scarcely saw the Grand Canal, she was so intent upon Monfalcone's elegant back. She had a confused impression of endless riches of soft pastel colours, palace after palace in tints of rose and amber and pearl dyeing the waters of the canal, and dappling the shadows with broken images of their ogival window-frames and fretted loggias. She saw in the drowned shade of the little waterways, narrow between high palace walls, the occasional green of trees looking out from secret gardens, in a city where all the rest of the spectrum was spilt recklessly, but green was jealously hoarded. All down the reversed S of the Grand Canal, from the single steep span of the Rialto Bridge, with its double row of shops, to the Academy, from the Academy to the Church of Santa Maria della Salute, with its dome wreathed in excited whorls of stone, and the little squat Abbey of San Gregorio tucked under its flaunting shade, she ached to use her senses, and could not spare them for Venice.

She could not even gaze as she would have liked when the canal opened out beyond the Salute into the great shining floor of the Basin of San Marco, and beyond the cool stone outlines of the island of San Giorgio Maggiore the soft, glimmering water stretched away into melting distances where sky and islands and lagoon all dissolved in one vaporous trembling of lavender and iris light. For suddenly her quarry was moving regretfully away from the rail with his chin on his shoulder, and his eyes on that seductive vanishing point where water and air become one element. The *vaporetto* was drawing in to a stop on the left, and Monfalcone was preparing to go ashore.

So were a considerable number of other people, luckily. Mab craned between their heads, and caught her first glimpse of the Ducal Palace and the Piazzetta, with its two white columns rearing into the evening light above long, long ranks of gondolas, and the beautiful, rosy palace-front stretching away beyond, looking over the wide silver bowl of the lagoon towards the Adriatic. A crazy building, with its heaviest storey at the top and its lightest at the bottom, just to show that in Venice there were no rules which could not be broken; its vast pale forehead freckled pink and white, its open arcades below tapering away into the ground in columns without bases, as the mooring poles tapered away into the water. And as he stepped ashore at the landing-stage – which he did in the manner of true-born Venetians, stepping off with apparent carelessness into the blue while the boat was a yard and a half from the stage, and arriving neatly on the edge with its inward swing – Teodoro Monfalcone suddenly looked up at San Teodoro on the top of his pale granite column, and smiled, and raised his hat in salute. Mab liked him all over again for that. That was the hell of him, that he was always doing things which made her want to like him, in a situation in which her feelings ought to be irrelevant.

She hoisted her rucksack, and followed him along the hollow-ringing stage, and on to the Mole, hanging well back among the crowd, and just keeping him in sight. Now that he was on dry land she felt happier, for she had the whole of the Piazzetta in which to manoeuvre, thronged with strollers in the cool of the evening, quivering with pigeons, surrounded by shadows – cover enough for a regiment. With her eyes fixed firmly on the striding figure ahead, she padded along in the lee of the library, passed the Sansovino *loggetta* without a glance, which she knew to be more or less blasphemy, and turned into the vast irregular quadrilateral of the Piazza of San Marco.

A band was just assembling itself with soft experimental breath somewhere in the middle, but the middle was so far away that the musicians were only audible, not visible. In between strolled the evening thousands, and the hundreds of café tables, spread out with mathematical precision upon the enormous paved floor, were just beginning to be populous. At one of them Monfalcone sat down, stretched his long legs with every appearance of pleasure, and smiled happily upon the scene, and drank, without haste, two delicately coloured concoctions unidentifiable within Mab's experience. He looked as if he might stay for a long time; but let him be as long as he would, she would still be there.

She lingered under the arcades, looking into the fabulous shop-windows at laces and linens and glass and mosaics which she would never be able to afford, and remembering the instructions of her elder brother: 'Don't shop round San Marco, you'll pay through the nose if you do. Go to the shops in the back-streets round San Zaccaria, or near the Rialto.' Unnecessary advice, for if the others didn't find her in a day or so she wouldn't even be able to pay her hotel bill – when she had a hotel, of course! But the things in the shops were glorious, only expensive in proportion to the amount of money she possessed, not to their own beauty. Come to think of it, that was probably the trouble for about ninety per cent of the Italian people, too. The shops were still open, and it looked as if they intended to be open all night. If she lingered too long at one window, even here, someone would come out and smile at her beguilingly, and enter into pleasant but purposeful conversation about the goods in the shop. So she kept on the move, avoiding the most brightly lit windows, and waiting for Monfalcone to finish his drink and feel hungry. She was growing tired, she would be glad to find a bed for herself, and a dinner, too.

He paid at last, and left his chair, and walked away out of the Piazza by the narrow brilliant streets of shops at the corner of the Basilica. Here was an unrelenting glitter of glass and jewellery sharp as thorns and vociferous as an annual fair. She had studied the map pretty thoroughly, and was a little surprised to see him heading into the modest quarter of San Zaccaria, but he turned off from the shopping streets at only a short distance from San Marco, and brought her into a small, quiet and rather beautiful square, with a stone wellhead and a sudden grateful plane tree; and there was a high garden wall of dark-red brick, with more green heads nodding over it, and a discreetly lit house-front with the sign over the door: 'Hotel Truffaldino'.

She hesitated to enter the square until he entered the open doorway, so she lingered just within the mouth of the *calle*, where the lights of the shops dwindled into the small receding frontage of a modest café and bar, with two tiny trees in pots in front of its door, and a few little tables ringed round with a thin chain in the angle of its neighbour wall. From there she could see the doorway of the hotel without actually being in the square at all, and in front of a café you can sit for hours on comparatively little money without being conspicuous. She made an approving note of the place, liked its raucousness and its gaiety, which filled the evening air with laughter and a rather loud but very good-humoured babble of voices. But she would just like to reassure herself, before she ventured to leave him even for a short interval, that Monfalcone was really going to settle down and spend an hour or so over his dinner, so that she would know where to find him again.

She walked round the edges of the square, and past the hotel doorway. The clerk at the reception desk was just confiding the guest to a porter, she saw the key change hands. Lucky that the hall was so small, and the doorway so wide. Now surely, surely she could make a dash for her own dinner.

She halted in the dark mouth of the next *calle*, to consider where she was. This way ought, if she had not lost her sense of direction, to bring her back on to the embankment of the Grand Canal; and somewhere there, clinging to the Riva degli Schiavoni by one precarious corner, was a dingy but reputedly comfortable little pension which figured towards the top of Punch's list. Good because it was not very far away, better because it was at any rate one of the first places at which her friends would enquire for her, best of all because they spoke English there. Her rather tired spirits rose at the thought, and she began to hurry.

With a landmark like the Grand Canal and the Basin of San Marco, you could not get lost. She saw the great, soft, violet sky lightening before her at the end of the dark *calle*, and emerged gladly into the promenading crowds on the Riva. After that it was easy enough to find the Pensione Loredano, merely a matter of walking along the Riva and examining every dark lane which led inland from it, until she found the name. A very old house, leaning on one side like a crooked, brown

183

old woman, with some improbable acute angles in its make-up, and the stucco on all its walls except the facade peeling away from the brick in patches. Its lit windows looked comfortably bright, and the girl who sat at the little desk, placidly reading a book, had a pleasant face and an unprofessional manner. Her English was perhaps a little tricky, but it worked if one listened carefully; and there were two double rooms free, and though it was rather late, there could be dinner into the bargain.

Mab felt better. She washed, in real hot water, in a little bedroom which looked out over the narrow, dark *calle*, and then went down to eat a quick but hearty meal in a dining-room which was simply the front half of the hall and lounge curtained off, with only a gauze veil across the wide window, between her and the glimmering evening on the lagoon.

As soon as she had eaten, she went back to the little *campo*, and sat down at one of the outdoor tables of the corner bar, where she could watch the door of the Hotel Truffaldino without herself being seen. She ordered a *cappuccino*, trying out one of Signor Galassi's tips. 'If you ask for your coffee in this way,' he had said, 'they will think you are Italian.' She knew they wouldn't, but she was feeling good, and wanted to make a flourish of her knowledge, to show that she knew just the modest amount of milk which would produce the true *cappuccino* brown. And the waiter bowed, and smiled, and didn't spoil it. The coffee came, and was strong and good. She sat over it for a long time, steadily watching the hotel. One or two people passed in and out, but none of them was Monfalcone; she knew his outlines too well now to make any mistake.

The little café seemed to be a haunt of boatmen. At least a dozen gondoliers were drinking and laughing and arguing inside, with a great deal of cheerful noise, spreading their elbows across the small tables. Most of them were quite elderly, grey-haired, with deeply lined and weather-beaten faces. They looked, apart from their singular uniform of white drill sailor blouses and wide-brimmed straw sailor hats with trailing red and yellow ribbons, exactly like the old men who sit on upturned boats in the sun along any small harbour-wall or stony beach in the English west country; and they looked as if they knew all the same stories known to those old men of the sea, even if they told them in louder voices and with more gestures. She could not help diverting part of her attention to these near neighbours of hers, when nothing happened across the *campo* for such a long time. And then she noticed – who would not? – the one who was different.

He was young, perhaps in his early twenties, perhaps younger still, and exceedingly good-looking; beautiful, in fact, was the just word for him. He wasn't drunk, but he had, she judged, been doing rather more than his share of the drinking, though it had only raised a becoming dark flush of colour under his fine cheek-bones, and given his large and lustrous black eyes an additional spark of which they had no real need, being sufficiently brilliant for all respectable purposes already, and fringed with long, curling black lashes in the grand manner. His hair was black, and curly, and rather disordered after a lot of horse-play in which he was curiously both the leader and the butt. She couldn't quite make out what was going on, but it seemed to her that his friends were pulling his leg rather boisterously, and he was divided between sulky resentment of their pleasantries and vicious delight in some entertainment which he was putting on for their benefit at someone else's expense. He was making more than half the noise himself, and seemed to be exulting in it until someone prodded him a bit too close; and even then he laughed, only rather angrily, like a child who has started a stone rolling downhill, and now can't stop it, and is still more than half-tempted to give it another gleeful shove even when he catches up with it for a moment.

Besides what nature had done for him, he was very fine in his dress, too. His white blouse was really white, and fairly new, and the broad-brimmed hat which dangled behind his shoulders had bright new yellow ribbons. Of these things also he seemed disposed to make fun. As for the older men, they were teasing him without malice, as they might have done a hot-tempered small boy, to make him display his tantrums, and his mettle, and his wit, all at once.

He was the first gondolier Mab had seen who fitted into the imaginary picture of Venice. He might dress like the others, he might have a certain amount of cynicism and a confident swagger, but for all that, he wouldn't have been out of place among the ruffles and fan-tailed coats and tricornes of Goldoni. Straight from the eighteenth century! He was the hole in the cloak of reality, keeping the illusion not only alive, but visible. In Venice there is always one somewhere within view.

She was aware that she was being studied, too. English girls must be fairly usual, even in this quite untouristic spot, at least since the ones with no money began to come, the ones who walk, and use the *vaporetti*, because they can't afford to go from church to church and gallery to gallery by gondola. But perhaps they were not quite so usual alone. Or perhaps it was just her miniature size and primrose pallor which made her conspicuous. At any rate, in their perfectly gracious and uninhibited way the patrons of the café were filling their eyes with her, in the intervals of teasing their mascot; and the boy himself, though full of his own concerns and spites, had not failed to notice her. His dark eyes strayed in her direction with increasing frequency and mounting curiosity. She felt that some of the conversation was beginning to circle round her, too; and though she would have liked to talk to the boatmen in other circumstances, she did not want them to call too much attention to her now.

She almost wished that Monfalcone would come out and lead her away into the city, but he did not appear. And the fine young man with the yellow ribbons was just strolling into the doorway, between the two little trees, to get a breath of air and a closer look at her. She felt his eyes, curious, appreciative and assured, studying her gravely; and clearly she felt the small, quick flame of his interest burn up and burn steady.

He had a long, soft stride which brought him to her table without any sound. She looked up at him rather helplessly, annoyed with him for distracting her attention and making her conspicuous when she had so much need of concentration. Her wood-violet eyes looked half-defensive and half-defiant, trying to frown him away, anxious at least not to encourage him; but for all that, he was encouraged. She set her small, lopsided mouth severely, and prepared her one Italian sentence, in the hope that it would finish him; but he took the wind out of her sails by saying in English, in the frankest and warmest of voices:

'The signorina is staying long in Venice? Excuse, I have seen that the signorina is English.'

'Yes, I'm English,' admitted Mab, rather weakly.

'You are staying perhaps a week here? You will need a good gondolier. I am a good gondolier,' he said with superb simplicity. 'Hire me!'

She kept her eyes fixed on the shaded orange light

187

of the Hotel Truffaldino, and said politely: 'Thank you, but really I don't want to hire anyone. I shall only be here a few days.' But even to her own ears her voice sounded daunted. If only people would sometimes conform to one's ideas of them, things would be so much easier; but they kick over the traces in every direction, and even when they say approximately what one might have expected, say it in such an unexpected way that the right answer sounds hopelessly wrong.

'All the more you will need me,' said the beautiful young man cheerfully. 'To see everything in a few days you must have an expert guide. I know Venice like my own hand, every *calle* I know, every *campo*, every *rio*. I am a good gondolier, I speak good English, I devote to you the whole day while you stay here.'

She could not help laughing, though she shook her fair head until the gleaming pale gold fronds of hair danced at her temples. 'Really, I can't hire you even if I wanted to. And besides, I'm sure you must have other much more profitable customers who'd be quite willing to hire you.'

He threw them over his shoulder with a disdainful flick of long olive fingers. 'You say the word, I leave them flat. I am the boatman for you.' And with a sudden flashing of strong white teeth he drew up a second chair from the next table, and sat down opposite her. 'Look, I tell you! I have an American who wish to paint me – so, as you see me! Today it is begun. Very easy work, very much money, perhaps for three, four days more, only to stand in my boat under the Ponte dei Sospiri and take his money. You say the word, tomorrow I do not go. You say the word, I go no more.'

She was shocked, and looked at him squarely with her big, honest, reproachful English eyes, and he was not abashed at all, he only delighted in her as in something even daintier and stranger than he had foreseen.

'You can't possibly let him down,' she said severely, 'if you've made a bargain with him. Of *course* you must go! How could you think of spoiling his picture, when he depends on you?'

He made a wickedly derisive face. 'I spoil nothing. He cannot paint, he wastes time and money. What picture will it be, from such a man who takes me – me, only because I have this pretty face! – Oh, long time I live with this face, I know it is pretty! – and makes me to stand in my boat under the Ponte dei Sospiri? Is that an artist, do you think?'

She saw his point, and had to bite her lips in order to refrain from laughter outright. 'All the same,' she said obstinately, 'he *might* be good.'

'I have been painted,' said the young man serenely, 'by some who know well their trade, and I have learned what is an artist. He is not.'

'Still,' said Mab, looking over his shoulder at the hotel doorway, 'if you promised him, you must go. And in any case, I'm no use to you. I don't want a gondolier, really. I'm sorry, I'd like to be able to afford one, but I can't. You'd much better stick to your bargain.'

He leaned his chin in his hands, and studied her face all over with a close, serious, gratified attention, quite without insolence, though at such close quarters it was rather embarrassing. 'Because I have this face,' he said reasonably, 'I am not therefore to be a doll for all the maudlin old men who like to play with me. Paint!' he said with indescribable scorn. 'I take his money, because it is good, and I must live, and my mother, and my two sisters, and my old grandfather also must live. But I am not a doll. I am a gondolier. I do not like this way of living.' And he looked at her with so

189

much indignation that she felt personally responsible for his predicament, and oddly ashamed that she could not rescue him from it. And her big purple eyes dilated and darkened with sympathy, and the corners of her crooked mouth drew downward in extreme gravity, and he was enchanted.

'I shouldn't like it, either,' she agreed honestly, not pretending to misunderstand him, though she retained a strong impression that this young man could more than hold his own with any middle-aged patron, of however unwelcome tendencies. Still, even putting the job at its best, she could understand how he chafed at having to stand still and be made into a monkey for the sake of some amateur's vanity. 'But really, I'm no use to you,' she said seriously. 'You'd much better look for—'

She stopped, her eyes fixed in an intent stare over his shoulder. Monfalcone had appeared in the doorway of the Hotel Truffaldino, and was leisurely descending the three steps to the level of the *campo*. The light silhouetted his tall figure clearly for a moment, as he stood considering which way to go, so lightly and casually that it seemed he had nothing in mind but an evening's stroll in the town; but for all that, she must follow him. She stood up, and turned her head quickly to look for the waiter. When she remembered her companion and looked at him again, he, too, was on his feet, and his quick eyes were looking where she had looked. 'I'm sorry,' she said, 'I have to go.'

'He expects you?' said the young man, displeased but dignified in his chagrin.

'*No!*' said Mab, horrified, and met his eyes with a desperate solemnity. 'You don't understand at all. He doesn't know I'm here, and he mustn't see me.

He mustn't! It's awfully important. You wouldn't do anything against me, would you?'

'*For* you,' said he, with a sudden relenting smile, and a downward sweep of his long lashes, 'I will do anything. He comes this way. Go into the *calle* opposite, where it is dark. It is blind, he will not go that way. Go! I will pay what you owe.'

She whispered: 'Oh, thank you!' and pressed a fifty-lire note into his hand, and ran across into the deep shadows, before Monfalcone had passed by the stone wellhead and drawn near to the lights of the bar. The young man watched him stroll by into the warm night, watched Mab slip out of her dark doorway and steal after him along the shadowy edge of the *calle*. When they were gone, he looked down at the note in his hand, and frowned angrily:

'Now why,' he said to himself softly, 'should a girl like that have so much interest even to hide from such a man? And why does she follow him? He is not even young.' But he paid for her *cappuccino*; for, after all, she had trusted him. 'Still,' he said resentfully to his own mind, '*I* am *much* nicer.'

(3)

By the time Mab saw Monfalcone back into his hotel at something after midnight, and crept home to her own little room in the Pensione Loredano, it seemed to her that she had walked through the whole of Venice. She almost hated Monfalcone for the first time, because she had walked and walked and walked after him, without even being able to enjoy the delectable scenes through which he led her, and tired herself almost into falling asleep on her feet, and all for nothing. He hadn't even spoken to anyone, except a waiter on the *riva* near the Rialto. He'd simply come out to enjoy Venice by night, and probably he had succeeded in his object, but by the time she had kicked off her sandals all sensations of pleasure had faded from Mab's mind.

However, she lay on her bed at last, drowsing in the rich hot night, and recovered her contentment for very pleasure in being at rest, even though the inexhaustible human noise which echoed upward shatteringly from under her window kept her awake for more than an hour after she had lain down. Before she had left England she had collected two opinions on Venice which had proved to be equally false, even in her first evening. A critic had told her that Venice stank, but she had found already that even the smallest and most stagnant *rii* had generally only the rank, watery smell of any small English harbour, without even the accompanying fish-market smell which so often dominated her memories of these.

Now she learned that the silence of Venice is equally a misrepresentation, based apparently merely on its lack of wheeled traffic. The people were anything but silent, had not even a silent period during the night as far as she could hear. They made up for the lack of cars without much trouble, and the tiny streets, maybe four feet wide between buildings five and six storeys high, made tremendous rising echoes, doubling and redoubling voices not notably subdued even without their amplification.

It seemed to Mab, before she finally sank into a deep sleep, that most of the business of Venice, its love-making, its quarrelling, its social life, was conducted in the *calle* under her window. But once she fell asleep no pandemonium could awaken her again until the light found its way in and lay brightly on her face at about half-past six in the morning. She awoke refreshed, as if she had slept for a much longer time, and rose at once with full remembrance of the task to which she must return.

She breakfasted soon after seven, and then set off through a gold and silver morning, back to her little café on the *campo*. The sun was already hot on the Riva, and the air over the lagoon was a glittering mist, radiantly ascending, leaving the surface of the water clear. Mab's single-track mind was so intent upon Monfalcone that she did not remember her friends until she was half-way along the *calle*, in the deep dawn shadows; and then she thought how she had left them no word, and how they might arrive before noon, while she might be heaven knew where about the city, and in need of them.

She scuttled back to the pension, and wrote a bald little note, addressed it to Phyllida, and left it with the nice girl at the desk. When they read it, they would be as wise as she was; wiser perhaps, since they knew already the half of the story which she had left behind, and at which she could only guess. She didn't let her thoughts linger upon Punch, because speculation was useless in that direction, and unnecessary fears even more so. She had a job to do, and could be most useful by seeing that it was done properly.

Then she ran all along the *calle* until it widened into the first tiny square, and there were people there, and already a stall of silk scarves shimmering with bright colours. It was still quite early, she did not think Monfalcone would have breakfasted yet. She took the most retired table outside the café, sheltered by the angle of the house and the tired little tree in its wooden tub, and draped her scarf over her hair to be less noticeable. Since leaving him the previous night she had not thought much about the young gondolier, but now she did wonder anxiously if she had given him enough money for the coffee. She hoped he wasn't annoyed with her for taking him at his word and pushing the note into his hand, and running away like that. But all the same, she rather hoped she wouldn't see him again. He was nice, but he was a complication. She looked round furtively to see who was inside the café, but there were only a few of the older men drifting in and out as yet. She ordered a *cassata*, which perhaps was rather extravagant and not very suitable for so early an hour, but it was large, and she could make it last a long time if necessary.

She had no more than reached the first layer of fruit inside the ice-cream, when a shadow fell over the table, and a remembered voice – it could almost be called a familiar voice already – greeted her with: *'Buon' giorno, signorina!'* and an olive hand laid upon the table before her, with deliberate gravity, a five-lire note and a two-lire piece. She looked up, with a curious mixture of pleasure and reluctance, into the face which its owner had scornfully admitted to be pretty. It looked, if anything, more sulky and hard-done-to than ever, but it smiled at her, so she was evidently not the cause of the general gloom. 'It is yours,' he said, 'from the money you gave me.'

Mab remembered the old grandfather and the mother and the two sisters who must live, and understood that this ought to have been a case for acknowledging a small service in a practical way; but she understood even more strongly that even if it ought to have been, it was not. An unpractical way, perhaps, but not a practical one. So she took the money, flushing a little, and smiled back at him, and said: 'Thank you very much for helping me last night!'

'It was all right?' he asked, warming. He needed very little encouragement.

'Yes, thank you!' she said, sounding a shade doubtful about it.

'And this morning you have not changed your mind?' He reached for the back of another chair, and turned it towards her table. 'The signorina permits? It will be of use. At such a lady seated here alone he might look carefully, but with a companion – no, he will not look.' He sat down, and folded his arms along the table, and regarded her squarely, and a spark of pleasure lit in the depths of his discontented eyes. He was as fine as on the previous evening, with his yellow ribbons trailing low from the hat slung on one shoulder.

'You are going to model for your painter?' asked Mab, with careful and respectful gravity.

'If you will not hire me, what can I do? It is money, it is work. But if you will hire me, then he can go—' He forbore from giving the painter's destination, but she could guess at it.

'I should be glad to have a gondolier,' said Mab patiently, 'and I should be very glad to hire *you*, if it was at all possible, but I assure you it isn't. I'm not here for sightseeing, exactly. And even if I were, it would have to be on foot. I'm just no use to you, you'd much better look for someone else. I just haven't any money.'

'Money!' said the young man with princely scorn, forgetting his old grandfather, and his mother, and his two sisters, as if they had never existed. 'Money I get as my duty, yes, the last lira, from these people who have too much of it, these people who think everything can be bought. But between two people who have a respect to each other—' He snapped his thin dark fingers disdainfully, ' – what is money?'

'But you must earn money,' said Mab, bewildered, and in spite of herself flattered, too.

'I must earn enough to live. But also I can stop when I have enough. Look, when you need me, when you want to go in my boat, only go to the Mole, and ask there for Benvenuto. What you wish to see, I will show you. You understand, there is not between us any question of money. If I am not there, someone will come to tell me. Everyone there knows Benvenuto.'

She could believe it. What she did wonder was how he lived at all, if he often took such an arrogant fancy to a prospective customer. 'You're very kind,' she said, meeting his black eyes with her serious iris gaze. 'But you see, there's something I have to do here, I can't go to look at the town yet.'

'I understand,' said Benvenuto, glancing briefly over his shoulder to where her eyes were always returning, even while she talked with him. 'And is there then nothing a friend can do to help you also with this thing?'

'Thank you very much, but I don't think there is. I can't explain, it's very difficult. But if I could think of anything to ask of you, I would ask it.' She flushed under his kindling eyes, but wouldn't look away. She smiled; it was all a little ridiculous, but he had meant what he said, and she had accepted it.

'And if you need my help, you will ask for me? You will remember my name? Benvenuto?'

'I'll remember,' promised Mab.

'And you will send for me?'

'Yes, I will.'

He smiled brilliantly. 'If you call to me, be sure I shall

come.' And he seemed to be aware, she thought, trying not to study him too obviously, that on this disinterested gesture he should rise and leave her; but he did not want to do it. A warm human curiosity was burning up in him, and at the first wind of encouragement reared as high as his lips, and even if it spoiled his flourish he could not resist indulging it. 'What is he to you, this man?' he asked jealously. 'He is not even young like you, he is nothing, he has only money. You should not look at him.'

'I don't look at him because I like him,' said Mab, intent upon the doorway of the Hotel Truffaldino, where someone was just emerging into the sunlight on the steps; but it was not Monfalcone. Not yet!

'Why, then? Is it better to look at what you hate?' asked Benvenuto reasonably.

'You mustn't ask me about him. I can't tell you anything.' She looked round for the waiter, and summoned him with her eye, for someone else was just following the first man into the light, over there across the *campo*. Monfalcone came into sight, and halted to light a cigarette and feel the first sun upon his face. That was good, it gave the waiter time to reach her table and accept the note she proffered, even to fish for change, which he did with strategic slowness. She waved it back into his pocket with a small motion of her hand, not because she believed in big tips, but because it was considerably more important now that she should get out of sight quickly, and she couldn't wait for a mere twenty lire. But it was a tactical error, for it kept him by her side bowing her away from the table with copious but still slightly ironical thanks, when she would have been glad if he had gone back into the café and left her to fade away inconspicuously.

This time she did not look at Benvenuto at all, but

slipped straight past him and across to the shade of the awning which covered the shop doorway opposite. Under pretence of looking at the wine-bottles and cheeses and meats in the window, she looked into the *campo* and saw Monfalcone descend the three steps, pause to inspect the lines of the wellhead, and then turn and saunter towards her. He was coming this way again, probably into San Marco for his morning stroll and a drink, and a look at the promenaders. He didn't intend to take a boat, or he would have gone by the other *calle* straight to the Riva degli Schiavoni. That was good; drinking or shopping or walking, round San Marco she could easily keep him in sight.

She turned back quickly, and walked a little way down the dark alley which ended in water, and there stood in a deep doorway, with the pungent watery green smell of the dirty little *rio* in her nostrils, and high above her head the narrow blue sky festooned with washing; and blessedly no one appeared to inform her kindly that she could not get out by that way. She saw Monfalcone go by, crisply and jauntily, very large and very immaculate in a suit of fawn-coloured linen which it should be very difficult to lose sight of, even in a crowd. Altogether, things were going quite well. She walked sedately out of her refuge, and set off after him.

(4)

Under the Bridge of Sighs, against the prison wall, where the morning sun reached gloriously, Benvenuto stood leaning lightly upon the oar of his boat, making believe to be going somewhere at a rapt, romantic rate, though in fact all he did was ride a yard forward and back with his weight on the oar, to amuse himself and annoy his patron a little. The painter sat in a small barge, just clear of the shadow cast by the Ponte della Paglia, and over the parapet of this little bridge hung a ridiculous arc of staring faces, since almost everyone crossing from the Riva to the Mole stopped to watch for a few minutes. They had all of them seen painters at work before, if they had been more than a day in Venice, but they stopped just the same; and Benvenuto considered it a pity that they could not be found something better to do with their time.

He had nothing to look at but this array of idiot faces, and the tantalising glimpse of the lagoon and San Giorgio Maggiore through the arch of the bridge; the squat prison wall with its grim little grilled windows on his left hand, and the lower reaches of the Ducal Palace, the Renaissance side, on his right, with two doors open immediately upon the water, and all the stones of the wall carved out into heavy bosses, streaking the reflection in the green mirror with shadow and light. High over his head the closed stone corridor of the Bridge of Sighs arched shallowly between palace and prison, a little like the face of an owl stuck there between the buildings, with two staring square window-grilles for eyes, and a shell-like ornament of stone for a beak, and stone volutes for ruffled feathers on its crest. Benvenuto thought nothing of it, but was glad that its height above him caused his patron to paint from the body of a low boat at a reasonable distance. Even if he had to raise his voice to make himself heard across the water, it made no difference, for his voice had no lower tones in any case, as his mind was without sensitivities.

He was not as senile as Benvenuto's description had led Mab to believe, this old man who thought he could paint. He was maybe nearing fifty, but certainly not beyond it, and a big, lumpy fellow, but running to seed unnecessarily early. His complexion and his saggy eyes looked as if he had drunk just too much for just too long to be able to hide the effects ever again, even if he stopped the habit at once. His waistline looked as if he had fed lavishly but not necessarily well all his life, and all the lines of his face and body were just getting filmed over and thickened and muddied with flesh, so that even his big undershut jaw looked more like elephantiasis than determination. Though he had a lot of money, he liked to dress Bohemian, but after years of practice he still looked as if he had put on his corduroys and sandals for a fancy-dress party rather than for work. He had never found anything or anybody yet without a price in dollars clearly marked on him somewhere, and because he was not short of dollars he had always got whatever he wanted; but the difficulty was always to continue to want, or even to recognise as something he had once wanted, the thing he had thus acquired. So he was as far as ever from being contented, though it was always someone else's fault.

He had a way of calling: 'Hey, Benvenuto!' with the transatlantic lilt on the third syllable, like someone playing Cellini's patron in a Cecil de Mille film, which made the owner of the name wish, secretly and fondly, to submerge him in the dirty water of the *rio* before he could finish the word. Some day he thought he would; not necessarily today, because he was thinking of something else, and did not want to disturb himself from it too drastically. He was thinking how the little girl like a tiny pale-gold hill-crocus would say 'Benvenuto', for she had not said it at all yet, and his imagination was free. Her voice was as quaint and grave and small and clear as her person, as delicately shaped and as definite,

and came with honest roundness from the very front
of her personality. Such a voice would be charming in
Italian, firmly and earnestly tripping over the double
consonants, with the solemnity of a small child playing a
grown-up game, in which every rite must be performed
exactly or a spell would be broken.

'Hey, keep still, can't you? What's eating you this
morning? And keep your head up! Do you think I'm
paying you to look at your face in the water, Nar-
cissus?'

'*Si, signore!*' said Benvenuto with sublime indiffer-
ence, and lifted his disdainful dark face and smiled bale-
fully upon his patron. 'At what then should I look?'

'Look where you're supposed to be rowing. Or if you
must have a focus to keep your chin off your chest, look
at me.'

'The pay,' said Benvenuto in Italian, with a glittering
smile, 'is not enough for such unpleasant work. I will
look in the water which stinks only a little, and has not
so dirty a colour.' But he had obligations to himself,
and he said it only for his own pleasure, in a voice too
low to carry to the gallery on the bridge. One cannot
take advantage of a man who claims to know Italian,
and therefore cannot demand translations, by exposing
him to laughter without any remedy. Between these two
everything was fair, but to invite others in as an audience
was something Benvenuto could not do, because it was
beneath his own dignity.

'Close your beautiful mouth, Benny boy,' said the
gentle artist, 'and keep it closed if it kills you. I don't
need any sound effects from you. Your face is your
fortune, and that's what I'm paying you for.'

Benvenuto looked down his straight nose with a
glittering eye of disdain, and went calmly back into
his own thoughts. Where was the little creamy-gold

crocus of a girl now, how far away from him on the heels of her tall acquaintance, whom she followed not because she liked him? And why, then, did she follow him? And to what curious difficulties would it bring her, where perhaps there would be no Benvenuto to help her? She had promised to come to him for help if she needed him, but he might be a long way from her when at last she called to him. 'Benvenuto!' in her little, clear, honest voice would be delightful, would be enough.

'What's the big joke?' asked his patron suspiciously, observing the dreamy smile of pleasure which he had not requested nor paid for. 'Tell it out loud, and let's all share it.'

Benvenuto unlocked his lips merely to say: 'I am told to close my mouth. You wish already that I should open it again?'

The gallery on the bridge appeared to him, all at once, to be composed entirely of Americans on their way to the Ducal Palace, all with unending leisure to stare at him without even paying, all rather like this man in the quality of their voices and the opaqueness of their eyes, always looking at him from the outside, as at a specimen under glass, and of course marked with a price if ever they should wish to acquire him. He fixed his eyes upon the bright glistening water of the Basin of San Marco, seen under the bridge on which they stood, and even there a clean, smart efficient Coca-Cola barge went suddenly, smugly by, manned by two young men in a sort of semi-military uniform, with the inane red and white advertising strip on their caps.

His patron was saying: 'I don't need any bright conversation, but I don't like that grin. If you've got anything on your mind we ought to know about, give! Don't keep it to yourself, let's all have the benefit.'

'*Si, signore!*' said Benvenuto with mellifluous sweetness. He shifted a little on his perch, turned his remarkably handsome head to follow the stern of the barge out of sight, and with considered grace spat eloquently into the Rio di Palazzo.

CHAPTER EIGHT

DEPARTURE
AND ARRIVAL

(1)

PHYLLIDA had roused the boys in good time for breakfast, asked for their bill in advance, made sure of the time when the train left from Verona, and doubly sure that the bus from Riva would catch it, and done everything which remained to be done so that they could leave immediately after breakfast; and then at the very last moment, when they were assembled expectantly in the square among a dozen or more other prospective passengers, and the bus from Mazzolo was due in precisely three minutes, Peter had to do his trick.

His mouth fell open with consternation, he clapped a hand to his forehead, and gasped: 'Oh, *lord!* My films!'

Phyllida, recognising the symptoms at once, took firm hold of the nearest strap of his rucksack, to make sure he should not get away. 'Too late!' she said. 'You've had it!'

'What films?' asked Punch, coming out from under a cloud of headache which was still, but dully, cutting him off from the world.

'I left them at the shop yesterday morning for developing and printing. They'll be ready this morning. I've *got* to go and get them,' he said in dismay, and when Phyllida tightened her grip he slid his arm out of the strap, and let his rucksack drop to the dusty ground, with Phyllida still foolishly clinging to it.

'Sorry, old girl!' he gasped back over his shoulder, already running. 'Won't be two ticks – *Must* get them!'

'There isn't time!' shrieked Phyllida, starting one despairing step after him, at which he only ran the faster. 'You'll miss the bus,' she cried after him, less warning than threatening.

'I shan't!' came drifting back defiantly on the breeze, and Peter tore up the curving street of Rocca della Sera in the direction of the photographer's shop, and rounded the corner by the washing tank, and disappeared.

'Silly idiot!' said Phyllida raging. 'All for a few wretched snaps which probably won't come out, anyhow, not worth bothering about. Oh, isn't it typical of our Peter!'

She would not, perhaps, have made so much fuss about vagaries which she usually accepted as normal in her brother, if she had not been feeling very much the temporary head of the expedition, and more responsible than usual. Punch was recovering, but Punch was in no case to lift the whole load today, everything must be kept off his shoulders. It was she who must worry about getting them all safely to Venice, and finding Mab again; though it was true that she had assumed the responsibility entirely for herself, without consulting Punch in the matter, and it was possible that he, on the other hand, considered himself to be still in control.

'Oh, he always falls on his feet,' said Punch, reminding her of what she herself had once said. 'If he keeps up that pace there and back he'll be here before the bus.'

'If he isn't,' said Phyllida, 'he'll have to follow by himself, the best way he can. We're not waiting for him. As if a few photographs mattered as much as all that!'

'Oh, well,' said Punch mildly, 'nobody wants to leave
'em behind if there *is* time to collect. I'd hate to be done
out of a film myself, after all the trouble of taking them,
and looking forward to seeing the results, and all that.
He'll make it, all right.'

'He'd better!' she said darkly.

More and more people came bustling along to the
square, where every morning the bus loaded until its
springs – such as they were – creaked and sagged under
the weight. Anxious eyes trained on the bend of the
cobbled street saw no sign of Peter returning, and far
up the Mazzolo road a fierce low roar was announcing
the approach of the bus.

At the crest of the street the low roar was augmented
by a high rattle, like a local dance-band hotting up.
Still no Peter, but a dozen other late-comers took
the warning, and came scurrying out of alleys and
doorways, as the bus surged round the bend and pulled
up in a cloud of dust by the shoe-stall. And instantly,
for two people who got out, two dozen lunged forward
to get in. Punch hoisted his own rucksack and Peter's,
craning to see above the mêlée to the corner by the
barber's shop, where the street climbed out of sight.

'What can we do?' cried Phyllida, at the last moment
torn between two anxieties where she had acknowledged only one. 'Can we ask him to wait? Oh, Punch, I
don't know the words, do you? But we *can't* wait for the
next bus,' she agonised. 'There's Mab to think about.
She may be getting into all kinds of difficulties. Oh, why
doesn't he come?'

'Get in!' said Punch briefly, hoisting her towards the
heaving tail of the procession, which was shortening by
jerks like the tail of a very fat worm hauling himself
into his hole. The bus bulged, but continued to swallow
gamely as the last solid matron planted her foot upon

the bottom step. Phyllida looked towards the driver, looked again desperately up the street, and hesitated between her two preoccupations, unable to make up her mind to go or stay.

'Get in!' repeated Punch, almost lifting her aboard, and leaping back from her elbow to gesticulate at the driver, and yell frantically across the roused roaring of the engine: '*Uno momento! Prego* – wait a minute! There's one more! *Ancora uno! Uno altro viaggiatore!* Understand? One – more—'

The engine snorted and lurched. The driver leaned out to wave both hands and shout back, in what appeared to be a high fury, but was probably only a slight expression of regret that he could not comply. The sheer impetus and weight of high-speed Italian almost swept Punch from the step, as the water coming down at Lodore might brush a leaf from its path; but he hung on grimly, bellowing appeals against the tide, waving back madly up the street to indicate that the missing traveller would appear magically from that direction. The driver shouted still louder, the passengers began to join in, the bus began inexorably to move.

Punch put one foot on the step and went with it, but hanging back with all his weight and all his voice, in a passion of suggestion, as if he hoped the bus might be susceptible to sympathetic magic. And suddenly Phyllida shrieked that Peter was coming, that he was here, that it was all right. Two dangerously optimistic statements, for he was still a hundred yards away, running like a marble down a mountain, and the bus had got its neck well into the collar, and was gathering way.

Phyllida, who had just sufficient standing room to get both feet on the top step, leaned over and poured agitated entreaties into the driver's ear, imploring him not to leave Peter behind for the sake of a mere twenty seconds – no, not even twenty, only ten. He didn't understand a word, but it distracted his attention, and between yelling back at Punch and arguing over his shoulder with her, he forgot to drive. Peter came alongside just as he recovered his concentration and the bus sprang forward; and Punch got the truant by the arm and the slack of his shirt, and dragged him aboard, and fell down on the steps with him in a tangle of bodies and rucksacks, with Phyllida clutching at them both to prevent them from falling out again as the bus swept round the bend. By the time they had sorted themselves out they were roaring along at full speed, the little lake a glimmering eye of blue winking at them from the starboard beam; and the hubbub within was settling down into a steady loud babel of voices, only a little ruffled with the wind of past excitement.

Peter was too blown to speak for the first few minutes, but when he had tucked his shirt tidily into his shorts again, and found the least cramped attitude on the steps, and got the door shut, he drew breath deeply, and gasped with odious cheerfulness: 'Lord, that was a near thing! I say, thanks awfully for keeping him, I wouldn't have made it but for you.'

'If it had been left to you,' said Phyllida, shouting above the steady din, 'we'd none of us have made it. And the next time you do a thing like that, you've had it. We shan't lift a finger, you can jolly well make your own way on.'

'Well, what did you expect me to do?' demanded Peter, injured. 'Go off and leave the films here? I wasn't going to give up all that work for nothing, why should I?'

'You should have thought of them earlier. You knew how important it was that we should get off at once, you *knew* Mab might be needing us. And all you care about is your piffling films, to hell with everything else! Much you care what kind of a mess Mab may be in at this very moment!'

'I *do* care!' yelled back Peter angrily, all his pleasure and triumph evaporating with sickening suddenness. He was ready to be conciliatory, but she wouldn't have it like that, so he could be nasty, too. 'Only I know Mab's got plenty of sense, and doesn't panic every time something gets sticky, like you. Anyhow, I caught the wretched bus, didn't I? And I never asked you to hold it for me. You could have shed the beastly rucksack and left me behind, if that's how you feel. I can get to Venice without you to hold my hand.'

'Without any money, either?' asked Phyllida un-kindly.

'Without any of *yours*, anyhow. I can hitch-hike, and be there as soon as you. This is the last time I come away with *you*,' he said bitterly, making the largest gesture of rejection he could think of at the moment.

'It may be the last time you get the chance,' said Phyllida just as tartly.

Punch held his head, which had suffered from the shouting match and was now rattling like dice to the motion of the fierce old bus. 'Shut *up!*' he said, 'the pair of you! What's the use of fighting about it now?'

Phyllida deflected her attention, but not her anger, indeed she found new fuel for it in Punch's tight-drawn brows and heavy eyes. 'Your head's aching again! Oh, Punch!'

'It's nothing much,' he said forbiddingly. 'It'll go off presently. Let me alone!'

'If you hadn't had to hang out and scream at the driver to save *his* beastly neck,' said Phyllida roundly, 'we could have got a seat, at least it would have been better than being shaken about on the step, like this.

But of course he thinks of nothing but his old films – and they're never even any good!' she added unworthily.

'Of course, everything's my fault,' said Peter, pale with sulky rage, 'even his headache now!'

'Well, isn't it? He could have been sitting down, at any rate, if you'd shown any thought.'

'Shut *up*!' snarled Punch, holding his head together between exasperated hands. 'Isn't there enough bloody din without you two snapping the whole time, as well?' And in a moment he said more resignedly: 'Sorry, Phyl, I didn't mean that, but I just can't stand any more screeching. Do be quiet and forget it.'

'Sorry, too!' said Phyllida, and was quiet, but she did not forget it. She gave Peter a look which was as eloquent as all her words, and much more effective. He wriggled round to get out of range, but however he turned, someone's elbow or knee stuck in him, and that made him aware how bad this sort of travelling must be for Punch in his present state. He felt guilty, and rather wretched, and all his pleasure in collecting the snapshots had oozed away, so that he didn't even wrestle his hand round to the back pocket of his shorts to fish them out and look at the results. In the shop he had stopped for nothing but to pay, and to thrust the little blue packet unopened into his pocket and run for his life. But he had meant to take them out once they were all safely in the bus, and examine them, and show them to the others, and get a small but perfect pleasure out of them as he always did. And now it was all spoiled. Phyl wouldn't look at the things, and Punch didn't want to be bothered, and wouldn't get any fun out of them; and so dismally did this alter things for Peter that he himself didn't care much for them any more, didn't even feel any curiosity. He clung to the best handhold he could find, and looked miserably at the incredible road of rock and gorge and river flashing by. Maybe later, in the train, they'd all relax and come round, and the atmosphere would ease again.

Still, it couldn't be called an auspicious beginning to the journey to Venice. He almost wished he'd done as he was told, and abandoned the wretched films; they weren't worth all this unpleasantness.

(2)

At Riva they had about a quarter of an hour to wait, but they were still hardly on civilised speaking terms, and besides, they had to be on the alert for the coming of the next bus because a lot of people were waiting for it. And then Phyllida grew crosser than ever, because she fought for a seat for Punch, and pushed him firmly into it, and within five minutes his nice nature had got the better of him, and he had given it to a young woman with a baby in her arms. To tell the truth, Phyllida would have been astonished if she had succeeded in keeping him seated much longer than that, in a crowded bus, but she was in a mood to be angry with him even for being the person she expected him to be, and with equal perversity took out her annoyance, not upon him, but upon Peter. So the atmosphere remained still, with the uneasy stillness of stormy weather, and Peter remained in disgrace.

At Verona they had to hurry for the train, but when they found their platform they were lucky enough to get seats, and had reasonable space all the way to Venice, so the gloom lightened a little. Punch dozed most of the way to Padua, and awoke there to say that he felt better; and Peter judged the time ripe for a gesture, and hung out of the window to buy fruit and drinks for them all. Phyllida accepted a peach, and sailed out of her displeasure with disconcerting suddenness, as if she had forgotten all about it; as, practically speaking, she had.

'Where do you think Mab's most likely to go for a room?' she asked. 'And what do you make of her going off with him? Do you think it was just a way of following him close, or what?'

Punch shook his head, refusing to guess. 'Better find her first, and let her tell us about that.'

'You don't think,' said Phyllida slowly, 'that she could possibly still be with him? I mean, it sounds crazy, but so it did when Peter came in and said she'd gone off in the car with him. And after all, he has to be reckoned with, too. Suppose he smelled a rat? Then she's put herself right in his hands.'

'I don't know,' said Punch. 'All we can do is to find her, and that's quite enough to start with. I'm not even going to try and work it out, not until we can talk to her again. Every time I start putting the bits together, they fall some way that makes no sense, so what's the good? She went, and she seems to have known pretty well what she was about. And she left us word to follow her to Venice, and here we are doing it. That's all I know. But the sooner we get hold of Mab again, the happier I'll be.'

'How do we set about it?' asked Peter, coming into the discussion rather cautiously, rather circumspectly, to avoid reminding anyone of his late banishment.

'Let's have a look at the map.' Punch unfolded it upon his knee, the plan of the city afloat in its lagoon like a heart-shaped leaf on a long stem, with the reversed S-bend of the Grand Canal threading it from north-west to south-east. 'When we get there, we'll go all together to the Rialto, by the boat, because it's a place you can find blindfold from either end once you've been there.

Then we'll split up, and go three ways to tackle all these addresses I collected, because there are eight – no, nine – of them, so we might lose a lot of time if we all stuck together. Whoever strikes oil, books for us at the same place, if she hasn't done it already. Then we'll all meet at the Rialto bridge again – somewhere definite, say at the foot of the steps on the east end of it – and if we haven't found her by then we shall have to consider the next move. But I hope she'll be at one of these places. If you find her, bring her back with you if possible, and if not, bring the news at any rate. OK?'

They agreed, and between them chopped up the list of hotels and pensions into three reasonable districts. Phyllida took the three addresses which lay near the Rialto and San Stae, Peter two on the Riva degli Schiavoni and Ca' di Dio, and one in San Zaccaria, and Punch three scattered in the south, between the Zattere and the Academy, because that was the most complex of the three districts, and he knew it a little already. They passed the map round, and memorised their routes as well as they could, finally bestowing the map itself upon Phyllida, because Peter had not even to go out of sight of the Grand Canal, that infallible landmark.

'What time do we get into Venice?' asked Peter.

'Round about half-past twelve, I think.'

'Do you think we could have lunch quickly some-where, before we separate?' asked Peter wistfully. Breakfast had been very early, and he was not finding grapes very filling. He regretted now refusing Liana's offer to get something from the cook for him for the journey, but it might have been a little awkward explaining it, and he was not particularly anxious to have anyone notice, just yet, that his favourite cycling club badge was missing from its place on the flap of his rucksack. What business was it of theirs, anyhow, where he left his badges, or who wore them afterwards?

'Yes, we'd better. There's a reasonable little restaurant I know near the Rialto. We'll eat immediately we get there, and then push off to find Mab.'

To this programme they adhered, as soon as the train steamed into that unexpectedly banal railway station, and the exit led them immediately afterwards to the rim of the Grand Canal. Punch was recovering his elasticity by that time, and would have liked, in other circumstances, to act as guide to this delectable city; but now his heart was not in it, because of Mab. Their job was to find her, not to look at churches or admire gondolas. The sun shone radiantly upon Venice, the soft, luminous air shimmered above and the olive-green, cobalt and russet water trembled beneath, and the enamelled palaces quivered with their own fantastic colours and the mirrored light from under their feet; and every tack of the *vaporetto*, every turn of the Grand Canal, every brief glimpse into the little *rii* which fringed it, took the breath away with flashes of wonder and delight. But there was no time to stand and stare. Later, perhaps, but not yet.

They had lunch at Punch's tiny restaurant off the Rialto, and then separated on the steps of the bridge, agreeing to meet there at two o'clock, or as soon afterwards as they could manage it. Those whose field of operations was easy and near would not be long in exhausting their three addresses, and Punch would rush back to join them as soon as possible after the hour, even if he could not be on time.

Peter went back to the landing-stage, and bought himself a ticket for the Arsenal, as the most convenient starting point for his search; which was the chief reason for his finding Mab's trail only at his third port of call.

Working back towards San Marco, he threaded a way through the café tables and souvenir stalls of the Ca' di Dio, with the Basin of San Marco outspread on his left hand like a shining sea, two naval vessels anchored well out beyond the Customs House, and the island of San Giorgio Maggiore rooted upright and fortress-like and aloof in the shallows off the tip of the Giudecca.

The waters of Venice were no more real and ordinary than the land, for through all those miles and miles of rippling silver the earth showed faintly, rosily still, and even the glitter of light over the lagoon was here and there rather a glitter of wet sand than of trembling water; and not content with being the illusion of two elements, it must complicate these with the shadow of a third, for the shallows, like mirrors, held moving, sailing clouds in a quiet limpid blueness of air. Shoal and cloud and wave melted together, shifting, embracing, vanishing, reappearing, until the light was liquid and the water was level light. And on this insubstantial but miraculously permanent foundation Venice floated, all its walls alive with the mobility of water.

Peter roamed along the embankment, looking at the gay stalls of glass ash-trays, and little chromium gondola paperweights, and plastic cigarette-cases; and at the flat brown house-fronts, with shallow graceful roofs and arched Gothic windows. He found the first pension and asked for Mab, without result; found the second, and was held up for a little while because the man behind the desk spoke no English. But she wasn't there, either, and no one had heard of her. He went on, and over the bridge to the Riva degli Schiavoni, looking for the third house.

The Pensione Loredano, said the small canopy over the dining-room window of the dark, golden-buff house on the corner of the fourth *calle*. The door was round

216

the corner, in the crooked long front which folded back at an acute angle into the tiniest of *campielli*, only just big enough to hold a wellhead and a narrow way round it on either side. It looked an encouragingly modest sort of place, without any flourishes. Peter went in, and asked the girl at the desk if Miss Isherwood was staying there. Even before she smiled promptly and said yes, he had a feeling that he had arrived.

'Without doubt you are Mr. Hazlitt or Mr. Thorne!' said the young woman. 'Miss Isherwood takes also for you a room. And there is a letter.' She presented it, and there was Mab's own unmistakable handwriting, as round and definite and normal as the noonday sun. He clutched it eagerly, and began to thumb it open.

'She isn't here now?'

'The signorina went out quite early, and has not been back yet.'

'You don't know where she went?'

'I am sorry, no. Perhaps her letter will tell it.'

Peter read it through.

'Dear Phyl—' He hadn't noticed until then that it had been addressed to Phyllida, but it didn't matter. 'Dear Phyl, I've taken two double rooms for us here. *He's* staying at the Hotel Truffaldino, Campiello Grigio, just inland from here. I shall pick him up when he leaves there this morning, please keep an eye on his hotel in case I lose him. No one made contact with him yet, as far as I know. When he walked out I felt sure he'd had word about you know what, and was going off to get them, so I asked him for a lift to the station. He knew there was more behind it, and tried to sidetrack me to Modena, and it's only by luck he didn't manage it, so now I'm all right unless he actually sees me, because he doesn't know I'm here in Venice. Don't worry about me. Even if I don't get anything for all my trouble, I'll be in tonight, and tell you all about it. Hope Punch is all right. Mab.'

Well, that was perfectly satisfactory. She was all right, she had the quarry in sight, and all they had to do now was to keep constant watch on both the Pensione Loredano and the Hotel Truffaldino, and make sure of contacting Mab as soon as she returned, and picking up the trail of Monfalcone if he came back without her. Peter's spirits bounded high. He took his key, and quickly dumped his rucksack, for why carry that a step further than he need? Then he made haste out to the *vaporetto* with Mab's note, to reach the rendezvous at the Rialto on time.

There was no hurry, however, for it was only a quarter to two, and he doubted if either of the others would be ready ahead of the hour. So instead of going back to the stage at which he had landed, he walked on towards the fascinating rosy frontage of the Ducal Palace, and the lofty red-brick tower of the Campanile, with its white arcades and pointed crest jutting high above the roofs from the still invisible square beyond. In any case, no boat was coming just yet, so he might as well see all he could.

The Riva was very wide here, and richly sown with café tables and coloured umbrellas, and little wooden stalls selling sweetmeats and souvenirs and silks, postcards and plaster galleys and snowing globes, peaches and green figs, and vermilion-middled melons like green bowls of blood. Along the edge of the glittering noon water boatmen ranged and wrangled, about all manner of little wooden stages; and if half the Venetians themselves had wisely moved into the shade for a sleep, yet the *riva* had life enough, visitors both Italian and foreign, who strolled, and embarked, and shopped, and drank, the length of its brilliant whiteness. Periodically they had to draw inward to cross the intersecting *rii*, by the white stone bridges which clung close to the buildings. Peter climbed the broad steps of the third of these, gazing up at the dappled rosy face of the palace beyond, and found himself standing within twenty yards of the famous outline of the Bridge of Sighs, there in the half-shadow and half-light of the *rio*, poised between the palace and the prison.

Here all good tourists stop to stare. Peter was a good tourist; he spread his elbows along the parapet, and stared dutifully, and was not disappointed. The *rio* receded into most sombre and suggestive shade between the two high enclosing walls, and even the water had a grim, evocative sound, lapping softly against the steps of the doorways down there.

Something was floating on the green surface close against the palace wall, and knocking gently against the stones. It had, as far as Peter could see, no possible business there; it was a canvas perhaps rather more than a foot long, and a little narrower, floating face-upward in a corner where the wakes of passing boats had washed it, and going gently round and round. It was half covered with paint. Peter almost dangled over the parapet by his toes to see what was on it, but it kept shifting, and all he could make out was the shape of the Bridge of Sighs, all very pat and conventionally unconventional, and a lot of daubed colour which left a faint iridescence on the water as it washed over it.

He'd seen a good many things floating on the *rii* of Venice already, even in one trip along the Grand Canal and this short walk, wicker bottle-cases, fruit husks, discarded flowers, wood shavings, cabbage leaves, a dilapidated straw hat; but this was the oddest thing of all. People so seldom have sound instincts about their own attempted works of art. Peter thought he would have liked to see the superman who summed up his own muse so accurately, and slung it overboard. But he had no time to range any further into the unknown hero's motives, for the *vaporetto* was just nosing up the *riva*, and he had to run down the steps on to the Mole, and race for the landing-stage.

CHAPTER NINE

EDUCATIONAL TOUR
OF THE DUCAL PALACE

(1)

MONFALCONE appeared to be going somewhere definite this time, even if he was going by a rather roundabout way. There was something about the back view of him, a spring in his step, a gaiety in the swing of his broad shoulders, which filled Mab with a vague, uneasy excitement. Even if he stopped to handle silks in a shop doorway, or to drink a glass of beer at a back-street bar claiming to serve Italian Pilsener – whatever international curiosity that might be! – or to savour for a moment the heavy, drunken smell of all the raw-flesh melons on the fruit stalls, still his figure, even when halted, seemed to keep a strung tension and an onward impetus, as if his mind did not halt. He had been looking sleepy and suave, like a panther relaxed in the sun, ever since they left the *vaporetto* at San Marco the previous evening; but now he had got up and stretched, and was beginning to pad away somewhere, silently, silkily, after prey. And if he had time to kill, and went slowly, with many little excursions by the way, yet he knew where he was going.

When he got to the Square of the Lions, by the corner of San Marco, he stopped to look at his watch, and apparently decided that he was still too early for something, for he went to a table out on the patterned centre of the Piazza, and spent twenty minutes over another drink. He looked at the enormous and rather obtrusive Campanile, and seemed to ponder going up it, but decided against. She saw, from under a shop awning and the veiling folds of her convolvulus scarf, the little shrug of his shoulder.

Now he was looking at his watch again, and deciding, though still without haste, that he might as well go. He paid his bill, producing in the waiter the usual symptoms of slightly ironical gratitude, and then walked leisurely across towards the corner where the Basilica attached itself to the Ducal Palace. Through the elaborate stone gateway, in company with a steady stream of morning sightseers, Monfalcone passed, and into the courtyard of the palace itself. The back view of him even began to look like a tourist, the right enquiring cock of his shoulders and head, the lifted chin, the earnest appearance of the back of the neck, intent on culture at all costs. He was enjoying putting on the perfect act, because he loved his own infallible effectiveness as an artist does his art.

So, at least, thought Mab, as she stepped through into the coolness of the cloister after him. At the moment she looked like a certain kind of very young and earnest tourist herself, one who has a fixed objective in view, and means ploughing through the guide-book until it is located, and then making a bee-line for it, regardless of anything in between.

It was quite a good place for following someone, oneself unseen. So many people were moving about in the great stone courtyard, in and out of the arcades from brilliant sun to brittle shadow, rubber-necking up at the long Renaissance façade of the eastward side, or the Baroque clock-tower under which she had entered, or climbing about the two enormous wellheads to find good places for taking photographs. A lot of English people among them, and even more Americans; different as chalk from cheese, the voices, the clothes, the attitudes.

Monfalcone moved across in the stream of new-comers towards the vast staircase which climbed to the loggia on the eastern side of the court; and Mab followed at a discreet distance, small and insignificant behind a party of five Americans, who provided a fine tall screen for her if he should turn to look back.

In the centre was a middle-aged man in a white silk shirt and an expensive summer suiting, with camera and field-glasses dangling from his neck, and a pair of gold-rimmed spectacles half-way down his nose; on his left a thin, stringy woman who ought not to have put on a very Italian sun-dress in a beautiful but bizarre print, but unfortunately had; and next to her a brash young man with buck teeth, who was not impressed. He had a guide-book under his arm, but didn't consult it, because he knew all about Sansovino, and Rizzo, and the Giants' Staircase already, and if the rest of the family didn't, he was quite willing to enlighten them. On the middle-aged man's right walked a rather bony but very graceful girl with brass hair and sun-glasses, who also wore a sun-dress, but with even less bodice than her mother's had, and not very much more shoulder to put inside it. However, at least she looked as if there might still be sap inside the willowy limbs. And the fifth member of the party, but perhaps not of the family, was an adoring young man whose round shoulders and stoop were probably due to his desire to be near the girl, since he would have been more than a head taller if he had stood upright. Mab judged that he had been walking constantly at the sharp right elbow for a long time now, and it had gradually got him like this; it was

223

noticeable that even his stoop had a cant to the left. The girl had a guide-book, too, and was reading aloud from it, and everyone was listening religiously, except the sceptic on the extreme left, who interrupted only when he was in a position to put the guide-book right.

At the top of the staircase they crossed the loggia, and came to a pay-box and a turnstile. Monfalcone had paid already, and was crossing the dark entrance hall inside, and passing out of sight through a door on the right. Mab thought optimistically, as she put down a hundred-lire note: 'Oh, well, the others will be here today, they'll at least give me a chance to go and change my last travellers' cheque.' She resisted a temptation to squeeze past the Americans and hurry into the next room, to make sure that Monfalcone was still within sight; and it was fortunate she did, for the first few rooms proved to be empty except for paintings on the walls, and so small that it was well to keep one doorway in between herself and her quarry.

The impressions she retained of the Ducal Palace afterwards were very strange ones indeed, composed of a long list of names of rooms and names of painters, together with a catalogue of the Doges as voluminous as the skirts of their painted robes; in which abstruse subjects she was instructed throughout by the girl with the guide-book. Visually it was a procession of rich and sombre colours, gilded ceilings, pneumatic cherubs, cobalt seas, scarlet gowns, and in the greatest room of all a great restful darkness of grandiloquent green, like a forest night, in which the lighter colours swam diminutive as stars. Perhaps if she had looked closely at the walls themselves, instead of at Monfalcone within the frame they made, she would have found that the dark prevailing colour was not even green at all; but the memory of it was green, and cool, and soothing, after so much gilding and plaster.

The constant procession of sightseers kept, by and large, much the same even pace throughout, and was steered along in the same general direction, though the profusion of doors made it possible to linger, and skip rooms, and still catch up again if you had lost time. So for most of the way the American family remained between Monfalcone and Mab, even though many others flowed about them from room to room. There was a sprinkling of young, penniless English students, in shorts and bush blouses and thin wool sweaters, and girls in short skirts and stout shoes and cotton shirts, all of whom looked as if they had walked here, or hitch-hiked, or perhaps cycled most of the way. Mab wondered absurdly if there was a cycle shed in the Piazzale Roma, as well as the garage. Some of these young people were inelegant in an innocent and accidental way, as if they had been caught gardening and had no time to change, and were rather anxious, in these sumptuous surroundings, to hide their bare knees behind some graciously full Italian skirt. Some of them clashed about the glazed floors defiantly, glorying in their informality, and superbly sure that their entry rendered the fashionable unfashionable, here as everywhere. And some were all warm, wide, intelligent eyes and open, eager senses, and had no idea or concern what they were wearing, so long as it covered them tidily.

There were great numbers of Italians, too, for even Italians go sightseeing. Representatives of both Italian worlds were there, and when they were put in one room together it became even clearer than usual that they had nothing whatever to do with each other. It seemed an ethnographical curiosity that they should speak the same language; that was something which investigators should take up as matter for urgent research. In front of the vast, overwhelming, deep-sea-green and rich gold Paradiso of Tintoretto, Monfalcone stood almost side by side with a short, square, bull-necked, leather-skinned workman, and the poles could not have been farther apart than were these two men.

So Mab was thinking, as she hovered well back from them, with a moving mass of people about her, and the American family arrayed five in line just in front of her, with guide-book spread; and the uncomfortable effort to reconcile the two worlds made her concentrate rather more than she might otherwise have done upon the back view of the short, square man. And then her heart gave a distinct leap into her throat, because she was almost sure she knew him. When he walked she would be quite sure. Even if he had put on a comparatively respectable dark jacket, and washed his neck and hands, and left the deplorable hat at home, she would be quite sure. Short, dark, square-set men of Italian features no longer looked all alike to her; this one looked only like himself, the powerful, jaunty back view she had watched receding up the street at Desenzano, the air of rooted permanence she had observed in him by a café table at Riva, these were his own, and no one else's.

She moved a little to the left, to see him in profile. The American girl was just reading out decisively from her book: '—a bold composition, full of force and warmth, the largest oil-painting in the world.' On this last statement her voice achieved a note of outrage, almost of disbelief, at finding the largest of anything strayed unaccountably into the wrong hemisphere. 'Imagine that!' she said.

'But it gives no dimensions,' commented her brother, with a sceptical smile.

The workman turned a little, looked Monfalcone up and down with a bright, undaunted eye, and showed her the unmistakable brigand's moustache, the thin gold wires in the ears, the weathered olive face and marred teeth, of their acquaintance of the train. So now she knew who had telephoned, she knew whom Monfalcone had come to Venice to meet. In one of those shapeless pockets reposed Signor Galassi's twelve diamonds, the price of his kind, frank, civilised life. And she had just one job to do in the world, and that was somehow, anyhow, to interpose in the moment when they were to be transferred to the well-fitting pockets of Monfalcone. She knew now what she had to do; it only remained to do it.

(2)

So now there were three people treading surreptitiously on one another's heels all round the Ducal Palace; not hurrying, not paying any attention to one another, but all through the gilded, painted rooms, with their dizzy procession of Tintorettos and Tiepolos and Veroneses, keeping the same stealthy distance between them. Once or twice Mab lost the Americans for a few minutes, but they always turned up again when the great rooms narrowed into corridors, and drew the vagrant streams of humanity together trimly for the next stage of the journey. So Mab's education continued to proceed by leaps and bounds. She had never in her life acquired so much concentrated information in so short a time. And the girl's large, good-natured, humourless voice was useful, for it helped to cover and obscure the movements of lesser people within her orbit.

The square back view of the man with the rings

in his ears proceeded solidly out of the Sala dello Scrutinio, and back towards the Golden Staircase. The high white arch, encrusted with plaster and gilt, spread its grotesque splendours above him as he went down the steps; still slowly, still looking about him, like all the others who moved like a receding stream in the same direction. After him drifted other sightseers, and among them Monfalcone, who had turned his back upon the last of the Doges at the precise moment when his creature went out of the room, exactly as if he had eyes at the back of his head. And small and insignificant behind the five Americans, elbowed by a comfortable Italian couple and their bored little boy, Mab followed.

The little boy was being querulous, and no wonder, after the miles he had tramped unentertained over the shining floors. His whining, and his mother's gentle, vociferous coaxing, made a pleasant European counter-measure to the American voices, which by this time were affecting Mab much as the Coca-Cola barge had affected Benvenuto. She felt ashamed of her own nervous irritation with perfectly inoffensive individuals, but the truth was, she supposed, that she was strung up for the coming crisis, and must quiver with hypersensitive revulsions from the mere knife-edge of sunlight and shadow on the terrace, if nothing more definite offered.

Queerest reaction of all was her distinct thrill of sheer touristic anticipation at sight of the pointing notice: '*Alla prigione*'. She thought, as all the uninitiated think, that she was about to cross the Bridge of Sighs, and like all the uninitiated, she was taken in, for suddenly the company ahead dived into a narrow corridor in the wall, and descended into a fold of stone, and behold, they were going down to the nasty little Istrian stone cells under the sumptuous apartments of the palace itself.

The narrow steps, deeply hollowed, flared dimly out of a bare greyness, lit with artistic inadequacy, where the shadows of sightseers made giants and dwarfs on the walls, and complicated every movement with doubts as to where the edges of things really lay. The American girl gave a little gasp of: 'Oh, John!' and clutched at her admirer's elbow because the steps kept changing their shape with the slipping down of shadow on shadow. And suddenly Mab's spine prickled coldly, and she was sure that this was where it would happen, whatever it was that was going to happen. She was so sure of it that she pressed forward in a panic that she might miss it, and slipping past the American father on the stairs, mingled with his straggling family.

They fumbled in the tricky light along a narrow rock corridor, and on either side there opened in the rock slits of doorways, into which everyone must step over a high coaming, and beneath which every head must bow very low, unless it happened to belong to a person as diminutive as Mab. Glancing through the first doorway, she saw a cell cut out in the stone, hardly bigger than a box, hideous and quite bare except for a small stone slab. A niche high in the wall held a dim light. Mab liked the Serenissima even less than she had thought, she decided at sight of that period interior.

Monfalcone – thank God he was so tall and she so small! – was still in her sight, and closer now, and up to this moment he had not slackened nor turned aside. She kept her eyes on him, saw him glance in at this doorway and that, as some of those shuffling along ahead of him stepped in over the stone coamings to gape at the poor relics of names and miseries scratched in the walls. Now there was only one person between Monfalcone and the man with the rings in his ears, and only John and the girl, closely linked together in the narrow space, between Monfalcone and Mab. And over all of them the dim dazzle of shadows flickering and changing, dazing her, terrifying her that she was going to miss the key moment.

But she did not miss it. She saw the man with the rings in his ears turn into a cell on the left, and peering under John's arm, like a desperate gnome, she saw him sit down on the slab just to the right of the doorway. She had only a six-inch slit of the interior within her vision, his bent left knee, the skirt of his coat, his arm to the elbow, and the end of the stone slab, but on these the light within the cell shone clearly. He had taken something from his pocket and stood it up on end beside him, where a hand reaching in could abstract it easily; as a certain hand surely meant to do, just as soon as the fat matron in between had rolled by on her swollen ankles. Blessedly, she was slow enough to give Mab a clear glimpse of the thing just before Monfalcone could reach the doorway, just before he could stoop his handsome head and gaze idly into the cell without entering it, as everyone else was doing by this time, for they were all alike – stoop his head inside and block the doorway for only one second, and scoop up the prize without anyone being any the wiser, and without exchanging one word with an improbable-looking acquaintance resembling a hired brigand.

The object standing on end beside the brigand's left hip was a large electric torch, and one which Mab had seen before. And there was no earthly reason why it should be there, unless it had twelve diamonds still within it.

It could not be said that Mab thought at all. She registered a sudden brilliant impression of what was happening, like a flashlight photograph: the fat matron just wavering out of range, Monfalcone just doing a

230

neat left incline and bending his head beneath the stone lintel. She never had time to think. She simply launched herself forward with all her weight into the middle of John's back, reached a hand to involve the girl also, shrieked faintly: '*Scusi, signore!*' and sent the pair of them and herself reeling heavily into Monfalcone.

John gasped: 'Oh, pardon me, sirr!' and engulfed him in a wildly flailing arm. The girl echoed Mab's shriek half an octave higher, and fended herself off from the wall, thrown back helplessly against two heaving shoulders, at which she clutched indiscriminately. They staggered together a yard and more past the gleam of light in the doorway, fantastically lit and hidden again. Behind them Mab made a confused babbling without words, except a stream of '*Scusis*', and went on making it longer than in fact she need have done, and to the point of imbecility, for with the first shriek and lunge she had dived over John's hip into the cell, and snatched away the torch like a gold pear from a Grimm pear tree, and was now burrowing like a frantic mole between John and the wall, to get past the spilt trio before they recovered their balance. The dark man's hand, clutching after the flown treasure, actually pulled at a fold of her skirt, but the thin cotton slid out of his fingers, and by the time he had scrambled from the cell John was sprawling between them. They were making rather a lot of polite, apologetic but breathless noise, and that helped her. She even had for a moment a delicious sensation of triumph as she heard Monfalcone grunt when John's gawky elbow took him in the wind. It was the first time he had ever been off-balance, in any sense, in her presence, and she was sorry she could not stop to enjoy it. Sobbing with excitement, she wrenched herself through the little heaving space left for her, grazing her arm along the wall, slithered round the fat matron, and hopped with impatience behind the father, mother, and querulous little boy, who were all moving in one solid mass, and with maddening slowness.

Everyone had looked round at the uproar, but it was not unheard-of that some clumsy person should fall over his own feet in a dark passage, and they were all moving on again placidly, disbelieving in sensations. Only a few odd, distorted echoes still made the air uneasy, flying over Mab's head. She hugged the torch under her breast, and sidled round the family, almost overturning the disgruntled little boy, to whom she apologised crazily in English, with a brief, mad smile. Under a raised arm she ducked, and round a loitering student with his head thrust into a stone doorway. She had noticed clearly only one thing. To go back and climb the stairs against the tide would have been impossible, but there must be another way out, because the procession of visitors nowhere seemed to turn on its tracks. Therefore she had only to cut through it upon the same path as fast as she could, and she was out of the cells and out of the wood.

A few yards can seem ten miles. She came to where the stone corridor ended in another stone corridor cut at right angles. She paused only a fraction of a second, to decide that the tide was moving to the right, and making only idle investigations to the left; but as she turned to the right she could not resist looking back, to see how much start she had. And that was her great mistake.

He was there not three yards behind her, coming purposefully and silently after; but until that moment he had not known on whose trail his vengeful nose was laid. She saw it clearly now by the flame which lit in his face, as she looked straight into his eyes across the oblivious shoulders of strangers. He knew her. It had needed only one look at her, any time this last twenty hours, and he would have known her; but this was beyond recognition, a steady electric stare at close range for a fraction of a second only, but she would never forget it. That long, melancholy face of his was as gaunt and hard as a lantern, and his mournful eyes lighting violently at sight of her were the flame in it, and it was a flame which would burn. And his mouth, that faint, satiric-romantic mouth of his with its delicately arranged flowers of speech, was like a thin steel trap shut coldly on something alive. It was like looking at a different man, and yet something about him felt just the same to her; it was only that she had not looked closely enough before.

She tore her fascinated gaze away from him, and put her head down, and began to run madly to the right, along the half-lit corridor of stone, diving between people who walked too slowly, ducking under arms, squeezing round the fat, swerving round the thin, in and out like the proverbial dog at the fair. She wondered numbly why he did not raise an alarm, shout to the people in front to stop her, but realised in the same breath that thieves do not cry 'Stop thief!' in public places, for fear of too many questions arising, especially when the stolen property will take as much explaining as do twelve fine diamonds. No, it was still between her and him, and if she could get to the police ahead of him she could at least ensure that the prize should be held pending enquiries into her story, and probably scare him off altogether. There was a charge of attempted murder he wouldn't want to meet, there was his own valuable respectability he wouldn't want to jettison if he could find a way of retaining it. No, he wouldn't try to bluff the police into taking part in the game on his side. It was between Mab Isherwood and Teodoro

Monfalcone to the finish; the fight was still on, and still private.

Ahead, on the left, there was daylight flooding in. She plunged towards it joyfully, and emerged abruptly from the stone corridor and the artificial light into a broad landing, with a flight of stairs running upward on her right hand, back into the body of the palace, and on her left a wide-open door, through which she almost darted in sheer relief before she noticed that it gave upon water. She pulled herself back with a starting heart, and turned to run up the stairs.

Three stairs from the top, a long way above her and taking his time, the man with the rings in his ears was coming down; crook-armed, like a sailor or a wicket-keeper, rolling purposefully from step to step, and grinning at her merrily with the full tale of his piebald teeth, down he came to meet her. He must have doubled back against the tide to the terrace, and rushed along here to cut her off, while Monfalcone followed to drive her into the net. And now there was nowhere to go, nowhere at all that wasn't covered only too well, except the doorway on the *rio*, where the green water quaked right to the lip of the step.

People past whom she had elbowed like a rude child in the dark were now emerging and staring at her, and she saw Monfalcone's face again for a moment over their curious heads. He was smiling, creamy-smooth and plaintive and civilised, like a well-bred cat. He was deliberately tantalising her, approaching at leisure because the road was closed and there was no haste, letting her wonder, and hope, and run about looking for a way out.

Mab ran to the doorway, and looked out, and there was the reflection of the Bridge of Sighs arching across the *rio*, close beside her feet. And there, against the squat prison wall opposite, a solitary gondola rocked gently, as the gondolier leaned idly on his oar, a resplendent gondolier, a sulky gondolier, who scowled down into the water, and made absent patterns in it to amuse himself, and yawned hugely just as her eyes fell on him.

She remembered, she knew him, and her heart gave a great bound of joyous laughter.

'Benvenuto!' she shrieked across the Rio di Palazzo. 'Quick, Benvenuto, help me!'

CHAPTER TEN

FLIGHT
BY WATER

(1)

WITH Benvenuto thought was often unnecessary, his instincts and senses worked so beautifully by touch. He heard his name called, and by the voice of which he had been idly dreaming, but not as he had imagined it, gently and demurely. Not at all! It was a healthy, wild, urgent young scream, shrill with desperation. And all it did was shake his reactions off the mark more rapidly and smoothly, without any reasoning or any questions. Such a lot of time is wasted in asking and answering questions, even privately within the mind.

Everything happened at once. He looked up at the shout, and saw her, and shouted back in a great wave of enthusiasm: '*Si, signorina!*' And his weight was on the oar, and the prow of the gondola swinging over to cross, with a silent green wave lifting sidelong from its passage, before the echoes of his name had slid out of his ears. The girl was standing on the extreme edge of the step, groping out towards him with one agitated hand, and looking over her shoulder, and making little frantic jumps as if she would leap into the water. She was very frightened, and yet she was laughing, too.

The gondola came about in a beautiful wide arc, and swept to her side, and sent a heavy, oily lip of green washing over the rim of the step and up to her toes. Benvenuto leaned, and his long left arm took her cleanly round the waist, and snatched her aboard just as hands were reaching for her, and voices, many voices, were shouting. It was all confused but pleasing to him. It was better than anything he had dreamed. Her arm was on his shoulder as he swung her into the boat, and her warm, soft breath was on his cheek, sobbing and laughing: 'Oh, Benvenuto!' as the gondola slid snake-like along the doorway and left the pursuers clutching at air. One was the tall man she had been following, and his hands had missed her only by inches. The other was no one Benvenuto had seen before, and of no account. Neither of them, in fact, was of any account. He steadied the boat a moment to lift her down into the cushions, and her arm slid down his with excited confidence, and her hand parted from his wrist with wild gentleness. Benvenuto wished to sing.

During these ten or twelve highly satisfying seconds he had completely forgotten his patron. But now he was aware of a high, enraged bellowing behind him, which had already penetrated the girl's confused senses, and was causing her to sit up in the cushions and look back in anxiety to see what new reinforcements were coming to harass her. Benvenuto looked back, between the slowly sliding walls of palace and prison, and there was the painter standing up in his moored barge, dancing up and down with rage, shaking fist and brush after them, and roaring: 'Hey, you, Benvenuto! Come back here! You cheating little yellow swab, you! Come back, or I'll sue you! You heard me, come on back!'

Benvenuto waved his hand, leaning back graceful and delighted from the stern of his gondola. '*Addio, signore!* The picture I shall see at the Biennale!'

'Come back!' howled the artist, tugging at the moorings of his barge, and rocking it with his rage until the water slapped heavily at its green old sides. 'You won't get a cent out of me, do you hear? Not a cent, unless you come back here this minute!' The knot defeated him, he pulled and savaged and stamped, and water washed aboard among his upset colours and brushes.

'I am a patron of the arts,' shouted Benvenuto. 'I give you what you owe me. When you live on your art, you will need it!'

The answer was a wave of half-inarticulate invective, on which Benvenuto turned his back squarely, and leaned forward on his oar with taut forearms and smiling face, looking down at Mab, where she knelt among the dingy black cushions, staring back past his legs, over the pointed stern of the boat, to the receding chaos they had left behind. Not yet very far behind! Not yet far enough! 'Oh, ought we really to leave him?' she wondered guiltily. 'He'll tip the boat over. I don't think he's safe.'

'He has thousands of dollars,' said Benvenuto, rowing strongly away from the scene of his apotheosis. 'Therefore even if he falls into the *rio* he is in no danger – unless perhaps he will be torn apart by the gondoliers fighting to rescue him. Do not think of him. What happens with those other people?'

They had not moved from the step of the palace doorway, nor raised any such rumpus, once she was gone, as the deprived genius was raising over the loss of his model. Monfalcone stood at the edge of the water, looking steadily and fixedly after her in her flight, and now she was too far away to see the expression on his face, but his stillness and quietness were not reassuring. And the other man had been shouting up towards the Ponte della Paglia and the Mole, and to some purpose, for already another boat was nosing its way in under the bridge.

'A gondola is coming for them,' she said, crouching among the cushions as if still trying to hide herself. 'It has two gondoliers rowing it.'

'No doubt there was no motor-boat at hand,' said Benvenuto, leaning into his oar with more energy still. 'Even so we shall have need of haste. He means to have you, this man.'

The arriving boat might have picked up its passengers and the trail together with more speed if it had not been for the baulked artist, who had been wrestling with his moorings with more fury than science all this time. It was no longer worth his while to pursue Benvenuto, but he could not endure to be thwarted, even by a rope. He had paid for the barge, and it ought to obey him. The knot gave, and slipped treacherously into the water just as the double-oared gondola was drawing in past him to the step. He wrenched hard on the oars, and the barge came round and fouled the gondola, and rocked in a torrent of Italian invective and oily green canal water. The low easel bowed, and went over the side, the canvas lit with a flat, derisive plop, and went swirling round and round towards the wall in the eddies from the oars. The artist uttered one wild scream, and leaned to snatch at it, but it was out of his reach, and he was left cursing it, and Benvenuto, and Venice, and Italy, and all places and people that were not U.S.A., as the two gondoliers drew their craft clear and steadied it at the palace doorway.

'They're aboard now,' said Mab, between laughing and crying. 'Oh, Benvenuto, I've ruined you! He's lost his picture, it fell in the water. He'll never forgive you. And I can't even pay you for all you're losing with him, not until my friends come—'

'Now I am rowing for pleasure,' said Benvenuto magnificently. 'Think no more of him, that is nothing.

But watch those others who follow us. They are already away?'

'Yes, they're coming after us. With two,' she said, looking up at him anxiously, 'will they go faster? Surely they will?'

'Yes, but there are many ways, and we may have luck among the traffic. It is a pity,' he said, with some anxiety himself, 'that this *rio* is straight for such a long way. But when we can turn aside we shall lose them.'

She hoped so, but it seemed to her that the boat behind was gaining on them already. How could one man out-row two? She turned in the cushions to look ahead, between the high enclosing walls, with stucco peeling from them here and there now in sad, bald patches, and troops of tiny children playing on the unguarded steps of blocks of dark tenement houses. Not far from the palace to the slums! Washing drooped across the sky from window to window, wads of cloth or sheets of cardboard were stuffed into the frequent broken panes of the lower windows. Old boats, some half waterlogged, lay in under the scrofulous walls, barges rocked softly under open warehouse doors, loading and unloading, with a mess of straw and packing round them in the water. They overtook one gondola, then another, were overtaken themselves by a wicked little motorboat, snobbishly tilted of nose and brazen of finish, which lifted them out of its way on a diagonal bounding wave, and disappeared under the bridge ahead in an arrow of spume. Now they met a few gondolas, and one or two barges carrying mounds of greenish-yellow melons, and Mab hoped that they could be lost among this to-and-fro and in-and-out of traffic; but whenever she looked back the other boat was still heaving steadily along after them, with such a fixed intent that she felt sure every man aboard it had them clearly in his eye.

They slid under yet another bridge, and the *rio* bore to the left gradually, without branching, and very shortly after emptied itself into another and slightly wider waterway crossing it at an irregular angle. Here there were more boats, and with a quick double-turn, more hope of eluding pursuit. Benvenuto put on speed, sending them in and out of the shifting barges and gondolas as fast as he dared, taking some long chances by the way, and getting some rude remarks hurled after him in consequence; but to these he merely replied as briskly, in Italian which it was just as well Mab could not understand, and wove his way onward without once diverting his eyes from the path they were singling out ahead.

'Are they in sight?' he asked, as they shot out into the wider *rio* and took the right-hand way, almost turning back at an acute angle upon their own course.

'No, they're not round the curve yet.'

'Good!' said Benvenuto. 'Here we must make speed to shake them off. At least they will not see which way we go.' And he continued to swing the oar at the longest and fastest stroke he could make. It looked easy, but she saw that at this pressure it was not. Sweat began to gather on his beautiful forehead, and his damp black curls shook down over his temples heavily with every stroke. She looked up into his face with a little anxious frown, and said: 'Couldn't you rest a little now?'

He looked down at her briefly, and smiled, but even the smile was shaken a little out of line by the rhythm of his movements and the haste of his breathing. 'Later!' he said, panting. 'We are still within sight from the turn.'

'You're very good to me,' she said suddenly, her large eyes steady and wide upon his face.

His smile deepened and warmed richly, but all he said was: 'Are they at the turn yet?'

They were; she saw the long body of the boat turn into the curving *rio*, and knew it by the two gondoliers. When she raised herself among the cushions to look more intently, she could distinguish the figure of Monfalcone amidships. And just as she found him, his boat, which had hesitated which way to turn, set its nose firmly to the right, and swung into speed again.

'They've seen us,' she said, slipping low down in the boat and pulling the scarf back over her pale hair. 'He's got field-glasses, I saw him using them.'

'Then keep out of sight, and when we have again turned I shall change myself a little. Have they gained on us?'

'No, lost a little, I think, because they lost way at the turn through looking for us. But they're coming ahead now.'

She looked ahead, and the next leftward bend of the *rio*, with a very narrow stream joining on the right, seemed reassuringly near. Also there was an agreeable amount of water traffic here, which hampered the bigger boat, on the whole, more than it troubled Benvenuto; so they lost no more of their lead before they swept round the bend and out of sight of their pursuers for the second time. Then Benvenuto suddenly stripped off his blouse, and dropped it into the well beside her, on top of his beautiful hat, and bent to the oar again in only a thin white singlet, already wet through with sweat, for it was nearly one o'clock, and the hottest hour of a hot day.

'So, that is better!' he said, smiling at Mab.

'But you're very tired,' she said doubtfully. 'Couldn't you put me ashore somewhere, and let me fend for myself? It would be better for you.'

'And worse for you, I think. They are too near. And you do not know the city. You would not have a chance.'

She thought so, too, to be truthful, but she did not wish to make shameless use of him just because he was crazily chivalrous. She hesitated, looking up at him with furrowed brows and hesitant lips; and as she felt her way through all the things she was not sure she wanted to say, Monfalcone's boat sheered suddenly round the bend. Crouched low, she said: 'They're nearer, they're coming!' There were not even many boats in between, and the light over them was brighter, because they were passing through an open area. A large square, with a church and a campanile, spaces of trees, and an embankment which ran alongside them for a while. No narrow, twisting *calle* down which she could dive and be lost, even if she could get ashore unobserved. 'I'm sorry!' she said. 'I seem to be on your hands for good.'

'I find it good!' said Benvenuto in his princely way. 'You have not told me, yet, where you wish to go, when we are rid of these men.'

'Anywhere, it doesn't matter. I only want to get away from him. Then I can go to the police, anywhere, I don't care where, they'll have to listen.'

'To the police?' he said, opening his fine eyes very wide, for they had never been great friends of his.

'Yes, but, you see, he is somebody, and speaks their language, and I am nobody, and don't. I *must* get in my story first. He's so clever – if we started even, he could lie so wonderfully that they'd believe him. But if I could have time to explain properly they'll *have* to investigate, because it's too serious to fool about with.' She watched the pursuing boat, and was not sure if they were already identified, but she feared they were. Benvenuto's slender figure was in its way as unmistakable as her own blonde head.

'They are nearer?' he asked.

'No – at least, only a little. Why do you do so much for me?' she asked in her turn, quite simply. 'You don't know anything about me.'

'Tell me,' said Benvenuto, 'what I need to know to help you. Don't tell me any more. I know already, very well, what kind of person you are.'

(2)

They threaded the multifarious traffic of a busy corner, passed on to swing into a narrower and quieter *rio*, which smelled rank and green, and looked almost still. Few boats here, and their passage had left a clean swathe in the middle of the water, while all manner of small rubbish and a faint oily scum lay against both walls. Small children squatted in dark doorways, staring at them with great eyes all the time they were passing, without excitement and without wonder. Between the close dark walls the sky was so far away that it hardly seemed to belong to the great luminous day they had left behind them.

'Why does he want you?' asked Benvenuto.

'He doesn't want me, really. He only wants this.' She showed the torch, which all this time she had hugged to her. 'He'd be glad not to be bothered with me, if he could get hold of this.'

'But what is there in a torch, that he should want it?' he asked curiously, his eyes leaving the dinted case to rest with confidence upon her face.

'You won't believe me,' said Mab helplessly.

'I shall believe whatever you tell me.'

'There are some diamonds in it. It's an awfully long story. They were stolen on a train, and we got into the case quite by accident. An old man was nearly killed. Now I've just stolen them back again. All he wants is to get them back. And all I want,' she said, 'is to get them safely to the police.'

'Are they in sight?'

'No—Yes! They've just turned in after us. Can we get out of this *rio* soon?'

'In a moment.' And they came out of the brick and stucco tunnel into daylight again, and swerved to the left, and were again among gondolas, and barges, and a motor-boat or two. A little *campo*, with stalls of fruit, melons cut open, blood-red in the green husk, scarlet and gold peaches; a small stone wellhead under trees, and a glimpse of a café full of gondoliers resting from the noonday.

'Then if you had not that torch,' said Benvenuto, thoughtfully, 'he would no longer follow you. You would be safe.'

'Oh, no, he isn't interested in me, I'd be safe enough once I parted with this.'

'They are gaining on us, are they not?'

'They're just coming round the bend. They have gained a bit.'

'Listen to me! I cannot keep up this speed. We must try some other way. If we separate, you and I, and this man believes that I have what he wants, then they will follow me?'

'Yes, I suppose they would. But then *you'd* be in danger.'

'Then let us make him believe it. It need not be true. You with the diamonds can be slipped ashore and go quietly to complete this business, with no one to follow and trouble you. And I with the torch will lead them away from you.'

'Don't be silly!' said Mab. 'They wouldn't care what they did to you if they thought you'd got the stones. And if we can't get clean away from them now, you couldn't get away without me, either. You'd get hurt.'

'I could keep clear of them long enough for you to get away. I could lead them a long way from you, while you go to the police. Afterwards, why should I run any risk? If they become too troublesome, I could give up the torch.'

'Yes,' she admitted, her eyes lighting. 'Yes, you could do that.'

'I do not like to leave you, even in this way, but I think for you it will be safer. I am growing tired.'

'I know! Oh, Benvenuto, what should I have done without you!'

'Listen, then! We are getting near the Fondamenta Nuove – I shall let them gain on us slowly, so that when we come to the landing stage they shall be close behind us. You must slip out what is in the torch, and hide it secretly, and then, when I shall tell you, give to me the torch. They must see you give it, but it must seem that you do not wish them to see. Then I shall quickly put you ashore. It is best it should be there, because from there I can turn back by the next *rio*, very close, and lead them back towards San Marco, right away from you. They can be busy in the south, while you speak with the police in the north. It will do?'

'It will do perfectly. Only I don't want you to get hurt.'

'I shall not get hurt.'

'And I must see you again. I must tell you everything. When you have shaken them off, will you go to the place where I'm staying? The Pensione Loredano, on the Riva degli Schiavoni. Do you know it?'

'I know it.'

'Some friends of mine will come today, two boys and a girl. You will easily find them, three English students. Tell them what's happened, please, if you get there before I do. Say you come from Mab.'

He had slackened his exhausting speed a little, and already had let the pursuing boat creep nearer, not only to give the appearance of flagging strength, but also to hoard his energy for a convincing dash away from the landing-stage when he had landed her, so that her enemies might be reassured that in hunting him they were after the right quarry. So he had leisure to look at her, and enjoy the unquestioning candour with which she gazed back at him, and the earnest concern of her eyes as she gave him his instructions. 'Mab,' he repeated dreamily. 'It is your name – Mab?'

'Yes – well, a shortening of my name. Will you go to the Pensione Loredano, please? I should like the others to know you, too. And I must see you again. I must know that you're all right.'

'I will go, and I will tell them. How near are our enemies? Can they yet see us, and what we do?'

'Getting near. About thirty yards behind—' She crouched low, and unscrewed the end of the torch, and drew out the little roll of felt cloth, still tied with its three tapes. She felt the stones through the bag, and was sure they were as Punch had left them. 'I wish I could show you! It was so wonderful, the way you never turned a hair when I said diamonds.'

She thrust the little roll into the breast of her dress, and pinned her brooch carefully through a fold of it to make sure that it stayed in place. It was not bulky if she kept it there firmly between her breasts; nor conspicuous, if only she could keep her hands from it. The best way was to keep them in her pockets. She screwed back the cap of the torch, and raised herself again from the well of the boat, where she had crouched for cover, to look back and count the yards which now separated her from her enemies.

'You are ready?' said Benvenuto, rapid and low.

'Yes.' She looked over her shoulder, and saw the great pale shallows of the lagoon opening out beyond the end of the *rio*, bluish white and without an outward rim, sea into sky. The *rio* itself widened suddenly, so that the sky's shining pallor filled its waters with reflected light, between the trembling prismatic colours of mosaic and marble, and the cool sudden green of occasional trees. A bridge, with the characteristic crescent arch of Venice, spanned the end of the waterway like a white drawn bow aiming an invisible arrow at the sky. Beyond it the colours of water and air met without any variation.

A flight of steps came down to the waterside from the end of the bridge. 'There?' asked Mab, bracing herself.

'Yes, there!'

She raised herself in readiness, her heart suddenly beating very high into her throat.

'Now give it to me!' whispered Benvenuto, and leaned down to her, his slender shoulders arched over her as if to hide her from the following eyes. He could hear the soft rhythmic splash of the oars very close behind, and leaping up to a faster stroke now in the expectation of a capture. They slid to the foot of the steps, slowing, trembling, touching. She put her hand up, as if only to steady herself by his arm, and laid the torch in his palm almost too smoothly, for she was suddenly terrified of being obvious. Her fingers touched his for a moment with a warm, hard pressure, she lifted herself over the side by his hand, set foot gingerly on the slippery damp stone at the bottom of the steps, and ran quickly upward towards the embankment.

No one cried out in the boat which was thrusting so eagerly up astern of them; but just for a second she had seen Monfalcone's face very clearly, not fifteen yards from her, and leaned forward towards her to diminish the distance by force of will. His eyes fixed, but quite cool, without any little flames in them; his face relaxed and perfectly calm, not drawn taut like an overstrung instrument. He was sitting easily, the discarded glasses already cased at his side; she saw them as she stepped on to the stone. At that distance he could not miss the implications of her sleight of hand. She only hoped he would believe them. He would see only a brief glint of the chromium case as Benvenuto slid it feverishly into his pocket, freeing his hand again for the oar. And then a new flight. And she did not matter, she was only something which had got in his way – not even worth kicking, if she could be once again removed from his way without so much exertion.

But she did not stop to look back until she had reached the white, wide, sun-bathed stretches of the Fondamenta Nuove, and crossed the width of the bridge over the *rio*. She stood for an instant on the edge of the stone embankment, just as Benvenuto's gondola flashed from under the bridge, and bore away to the right at its best speed, bound for the mouth of some neighbour *rio* which would carry him back into the complicated waterways of the city. She ought not to have stayed even to make sure of this, and he gave her a momentary frown for it as he shot by, but the last she saw of him was a brief flashing smile of great confidence and reassurance, and then the graceful lunging shoulders and pliant back receding rapidly. All in two seconds, for she had no more to spare. She heard following oars, heard a voice from under the bridge; and she ran back from the edge, and across the pavement into the shelter of the house-fronts, and shops and booths and people, into the beautiful, glittering Venetian normality which she had lost since morning. And even then she went on running for a few minutes, by fits and starts like a capricious bird, until she felt that she had dissolved herself into the hot, half-peopled afternoon, and was invisible among the souvenirs, and the fruit-husks, and the happy, languid women by Venice's northern sea.

(3)

She was astonished to find that her knees felt wobbly under her now that the strain was temporarily over. It is, perhaps, the best time to let them wobble, but the sensation was none the less disconcerting to Mab. She had been very frightened for the past half-hour, but too busy to realise it, and it was humiliating to discover it now. She told herself that she was merely hungry, for by rights she should have been thinking of lunch before this; but she knew the real cause of the tremors very well. Under the awning of a stall which glittered with little glass figures, and mosaic boxes, brooches and shell gondolas, and transparent plastic cigarette boxes in the shape of grand pianos, she paused to recover her breath and her composure, and to get her bearings in a part of the city which was entirely strange to her.

It was easy to lose her mind's anxieties for a few minutes, like a wave broken up among variegated pebbles, in the shoals of these minute jewelled toys. The grand pianos actually played a tune, a tiny tinkling eighteenth-century tune. And it was nice to be ravished with triviality after a whole day of preoccupation with things too big for her. Or it would have been nice, if she had not still been anxious about Benvenuto.

Since every way was a new way here, she thought it best to go on along the *fondamenta*, to be sure of putting a longer rather than shorter distance between herself and Monfalcone, in case some accident should turn him back on his tracks. She walked demurely, thinking hard behind the immaculate serenity of her little, irregular, delicately-coloured face. Her scarf had slipped back on her shoulders, and her ruffled feathers of hair curved softly against her cheeks, as pale as primroses. She was wondering, deep within her blonde nordic isolation, wherein she was about as inconspicuous as an icicle in Africa, what was the Italian for police-station, and if she would be safe in making some Italian-sounding word from the English, as in this obliging language so often proved to be the case. It was a good principle, it worked nine times out of ten, but the tenth time could be a bad let-down. Mab touched her brooch, to see if it was secure, and fingered the small, hard roll of treasure between her little breasts, while her knees grew steady under her, and she drew breath more easily, beginning to feel safe.

This was the Fondamenta Nuove, then, another great promenade strung along the lagoon on the northern side of the city, not as wide or as fashionable as the Riva degli Schiavoni, but still a populous place. The lagoon stretched away from it north-eastward, whitely blue, with a curious walled island rising out of its pale levels at some distance from the shore, all red brick and white crests, its long, low, flat lines echoing the long, low flatness of the sea. Until you have seen the

Venetian lagoon, thought Mab, you have no idea how
very flat water can be – like a field pond produced to
infinity, only without the shadows and reflections which
give a pond greenness and deceptive depth. And yet
so fluid, even without movement, so variable without
apparent variation, that one need never grow weary
of watching it. It unrolls itself stilly to the sun, and
dissolves its distant rim in air to make all one, and
yet with subtle gradations of colour makes clear where
every shallow lies, where every channel runs like a
river, where every cloud passes. A silvery, sleeping
chameleon, an optical illusion. The island seems as
often as not to be Laputa, anchored in mid-air, rather
than San Michele, the cemetery of Venice. And there
are always other islands in sight, far away where the
elements lose their distinctness, where air is below,
and water above, and the occasional glimmering flats
of earth can disguise themselves as either. And even
then you are never sure whether these are veritable
islands just breaking – no, no more than touching –
the surface, or whether they are only shallows where
the sands show through.

Boatmen along the *fondamenta* offered to take Mab
out to look more closely. Large motor-boats rocked
alongside wooden stages, for the regular services to
these northern islands start from here. The first, according to the notice on the stage, ran to Campalto, the
next said: 'Cimitero – Murano'. And besides the service boats, there were others running round tours for
the benefit of visitors, as presumably they did all the
summer long.

Mab felt better. Everything here was so normal and so
bright, the sun in its zenith, the very stone of the houses
drowsy with warmth. She stopped beside another stall
of souvenirs, for the most feminine of reasons, because

253

several mirrors were hung outside its end wall, and she was recovering to the extent of feeling concerned about her slightly dishevelled appearance. Flat mirrors, rounded mirrors, mirrors framed in glass or in painted fishbone ornaments, showed her half a dozen copies of her exceedingly grave and fair little face, and her hair rubbed up into creamy feathers, like a half-fledged chick. She frowned at it, and fished out her comb from the pocket of her frock, and began to tidy herself.

A strand of her hair was over her eyes, and the comb poised in her parting, when her one uncovered eye perceived in the mirror before her a tall figure in fawn linen, which was bearing down upon her purposefully and silently in a diagonal line from the shelter of the shop awnings, across the embankment. Her mouth fell open in sheer horror. It wasn't possible! She had looked back several times, and seen no sign of pursuit, no familiar figure anywhere among the shop-gazers and strollers along the *fondamenta*. Yet half a dozen distorted images of Monfalcone came sidelong and serene out of the deployed mirrors, advancing upon her with a small and charming smile, and deadly intent eyes.

She swung round, and the images all fused into one frightening reality. In less than a minute he would have had his hand on her arm. She began to run, the comb still in her hand, but there was nowhere to run to. She couldn't get to any of the *calli* which offered shade and hiding there across the embankment; he was in between, gently driving her towards the water again. His advance had been planned awning by awning, doorway by doorway, to cut her off finally from that warren of back streets, and he had not moved out into the open until he could get between her and every way of escape. And you cannot even run madly along a promenade in the heat of the early afternoon, without becoming too conspicuous for comfort. An appearance of guilt might be fatal to her prospects of being believed, if it came to her story against his.

A boat's siren, an important little hectoring note, hooted at the end of the next landing-stage. A big motor-boat, already filled with people, was just casting off, but if another few hundred stray lire happened to be wandering by in somebody's pocket, so much the better, and it was worth a suggestive last peal on the siren, on the off-chance. In the middle of her momentary panic a beautiful instant placidity of reason dawned again. You can at least run madly for a boat which is just leaving, without being thought either crazy or a suspicious character.

She swerved along the bounding planks, and waved her hand. The boatman was just standing with the rope eased in his hands, one foot on the low gunwale, one still on the jetty. He reached a large hand to heft her aboard, and let the rope uncoil in the same instant; and there was a yard of water between the boat and the wooden piles by the time she had jumped down into the well.

There was just room to sit, and she sat, for her knees were trembling again, and not with running. Nor with the characteristic throbbing reverberations of small, well-loaded boats, either. She sat rather shakily between a thin dark Italian girl and an old woman in black, and felt reprieved. She thrust the comb hastily into her pocket, shook back her half-tidied hair, and felt uneasily in her bag for her purse. She had no idea where she was going, nor how she was to get back, nor whether she had enough money to pay the fare, but nothing seemed to matter, except that she was here, in this little moving island of disinterested, harmless, ordinary people, with a widening stretch of water between herself and Teodoro Monfalcone's long, gentle, assiduous hands and sad, predatory eyes.

She looked over the side, soothing her eyes with the beautiful lines of the deep furrow their passage cut into the water, and the long, straight feather of spray which hissed outward from the cleft, like the unexpectedly turbulent blood of the lagoon spouting from a wound. They lay low in the water, she could easily trail her hand; and the spray was warm as bath water. She looked back, following the widening wake to where it still lapped imperceptibly at the distant piles of the jetty.

A small motor-boat, one of the water-taxis which scud about at such insulting speeds among the dignified gondolas of the city *rii*, was just boring outward from the shore with its flat glossy nose on the same course. She could see the young boatman standing upright at the wheel, a boy in his shirt-sleeves, with streaming dark hair. The man who had hired him she could not see for a moment. Then he, too, stood up, to focus field-glasses forward and stare steadily through them, and not at any island upon the skyline, either.

After all, she had hardly needed to see him. She knew very well who he was. Now keep your hands away from your brooch, Mab, she thought, he can see every move you make through those glasses, and he already has far too good an idea of how your mind works, or he wouldn't be here at all, but heading south on Benvenuto's tail. She supposed he had sent his creature to take care of Benvenuto, but that must mean that he had reserved the most likely field of search for himself, here, hard on her heels. Yes, he knew too much about what goes on in the minds of people who are not quite fools, but not quite clever enough, either. The middle ways of the human mind, the ordinary, decent human mind in emergencies, held very few secrets and very few surprises for him. He was too damned clairvoyant by half.

The truth was that something odd was happening inside Mab's mind at this moment, something he didn't know about. She had been frightened, excited, even amused, in a queer oblique way; but now she was becoming annoyed, and that was quite a new reaction.

So it wasn't ended at all, but just about to begin all over again in some new island arena, dodging through a nerve-racking pursuit in which she was alone and without voice, and he had the language, and the lie of the land, and the plausibility of his own respectability all on his side. But she'd survive it and keep him from getting the diamonds, and get them safely back to the city, too, if she had to elude him through the whole archipelago.

With blunt brown fingers the second boatman thrust a paper ticket under her nose, his palm suggestively lifted. Her heart bumped, and the worst moment of all was when she opened her purse and began to count out the remaining notes, in horror that they would not reach the daunting amount printed on the ticket. Eight hundred lire, good lord! Not really so much as it sounded, of course, but heart's-blood to Mab just now. Some ridiculous imp inside her mind wanted to giggle, sitting back and beholding her in more terror of a slanging-match with the boatman, over fifty lire, than of a final fight to the death with Monfalcone over twelve diamonds and an obscure principle. But it didn't happen. Not quite! When she had paid, she had exactly twenty-three lire left in the world; but the sense of relief at being spared that awful, trivial humiliation was wonderful.

She stared at the ticket in her hand. So she was going on a round trip to Murano, Burano and Torcello, it seemed. She and Monfalcone.

She looked back, and he was lounging at ease in

his tiny boat, ambling along just on the port beam, where he could keep her under observation without even using his glasses. The boy was looking bored and sulky, because he could have passed the trippers' boat like a greyhound, and yet the signor did not wish it. He must be one of those queer people with oddities about speed, though he looked normal enough. Mab settled down to survive the long leisurely scrutiny, which was almost certainly meant to tease her into nervousness or doubt. He was smiling, genuinely smiling, she could just distinguish the curve and shadowing of his lips. Something came over her. She untied her scarf, and waved it at him deliberately, letting it trail in the air-stream of their passage in a long arc of heliotrope and iris and green, like a banner.

Signor Monfalcone was always punctilious. He raised his hat, and returned the grave inclination of her head. You could almost hear the bell ring for the beginning of the next round.

CHAPTER ELEVEN

ATAVISTIC BEHAVIOUR
OF BENVENUTO

(1)

BENVENUTO turned south by the Rio dei Mendicanti, and made his best speed down its busy bright length, without once looking back, after that first rapid glance behind at the turn, to make sure that the other boat was on his tail. He flashed among the leisurely gondolas bringing visitors to the Campo San Zanipolo, and crossed its wide, sunlit spaces, where a flight of white steps led upward from the water, and two parallel white lines inlaid into the pavement conducted the landing visitor obligingly straight into the doorway of the church of S. Giovanni e Paolo – the compound San Zanipolo for short. The great Gothic face of the church glowed in the sun, the façade of the hospital opposite arched its three semi-circular pediments, and its doorway, and the added arch above the doorway, and all its window-frames, in an extravagance of astonishment, Colleoni on his pillared pedestal gestured and scowled; and Benvenuto had passed and vanished in a moment. Buildings closed in snugly to the *rio*, square and embankment were left behind.

Concentrating on keeping his speed and managing his course, Benvenuto still did not look behind to find out how much start he had. If he had looked, he might have lost a few yards of it. No, his job was to lure them away from where the girl Mab was, as fast and as far as he could. Only when he began to leave the more frequented *rii* did he finally look back, to make sure that the pursuers were near enough to follow his manoeuvrings. And though he found the distance nicely adjusted to his purposes, and the two gondoliers still rowing sturdily and incuriously wherever they were bidden, stare as he would he could not find the tall man in the boat. There was the other, the square and dark one, the one of no account, leaning forward with his hands on his knees and his eyes fixed on his quarry; but the one who mattered, the big one, he was gone.

Benvenuto stopped wishing to sing. Where had it gone wrong? Why had not that man been convinced, and done as he was expected to do? And where else could he be now, but on the heels of the little fair girl, somewhere along the Fondamenta Nuove?

He rowed on, to keep clear of the enemy while at least he thought what to do. It had not been a complete failure, for if the tall man had not been altogether taken in, he had certainly been in doubt; doubt sufficiently strong for him to send his lieutenant after Benvenuto in the boat, while he himself jumped ashore after Mab. But the reservation of this assignation to himself was not reassuring. And now there was no further point in leading this fellow away from her. All that mattered was speed in either getting back to her himself, or getting other help for her. Yes, thought Benvenuto, flashing his bright young eyes over his shoulder at the squat figure in the other boat, it is time for you to make an exit.

He knew every *rio* in Venice, and knew where he could leave all normal traffic behind, and have elbow-room for less orthodox practices. He bent to the oar again, and made a couple of rapid turns from the frequented ways, losing the hired gondolas first, and then most of the barges and freight boats, until he was driving his boat silently and darkly along a narrow *rio* between high tenements, in a green gloom dripping with washing. The water was thick and almost stagnant, drifting with straw and rubbish, and smelling strongly; but here and there a narrow blind *calletto* came down and stopped in a flight of slimy stone steps slipping down into it. To one of these landing-places Benvenuto drew in, and tied up his boat.

The pursuers were not far behind, but he had time to make all fast before he jumped ashore and darted up the dim deserted alley, where windows at which no light ever entered stared into one another across a mere metre of twilit air, and every little twisted iron balcony upstairs had a line of laundry attached, because this minute drying-ground had to be multiplied as many times as possible in order to be adequate at all. The cobbles were hollowed deeply, for they had not been renewed in many centuries; but Benvenuto knew even the worn places in them, for he was very near to his own home.

He was half-way along the *calletto* when feet came pounding behind him, heavier feet than his, running in shorter strides, and rousing echoes which eddied upward and upward in broken time from wall to wall until they blundered out into the daylight, six storeys above. Only one man running. That was as he had calculated. Gondoliers need not question the instructions of those who hire them, but neither is it any part of their business to make themselves parties in their patrons' affairs once they are ashore. They are hired as boatmen, not mercenaries. These two had stayed in their boat. Maybe they had been trusting enough to wait the return of their passenger, but more probably the other one had already given them money, or they would not so placidly have let this one get away from them without paying. All was as Benvenuto preferred it; one man against one man, and on ground which he himself had chosen. He ran lightly, and fast, for he wanted to gain as many seconds as possible before he reached the corner.

The turning was invisible until it was reached, being no more than a tunnel in the wall, sliding away to the right at an obtuse angle, first bridged by the upper storeys of the houses, then open remotely to the sky. Benvenuto dived down it like a rabbit into its burrow. The passage was only a dozen or so metres long, and at the end it emptied itself into another *calletto* hardly wider or lighter than itself, running parallel to the one by which he had approached, and ending similarly in the water of the *rio*. A yard from the sharp corner at this second turn there was a deep doorway; two yards round it on the way back to the waterside there was another as deep. Their juxtaposition pleased Benvenuto's sense of fitness. A fugitive smoked out of one hole at close range does not immediately dive into the next, but tries to put distance between himself and his fear. It could not be apparent to the pursuer in this case that Benvenuto was not, strictly speaking, a fugitive.

In the snug and odorous darkness of the alley he flattened himself into the doorway, and waited, breathing long and gently after his exertions, and smiling to himself. In a moment the dark man crashed into the mouth of the tunnel, and paused there, casting a long hunchbacked shadow along the stones. He could move softly enough when he chose, he slipped a few yards nearer along the alley without a sound, more rapidly than Benvenuto altogether liked. Also he had something in his hand which made a faint metallic sound when it touched the iron grille of a blind window, as he felt his way along the wall. In his left hand, Benvenuto noted. That can be a little disconcerting to a right-handed man, it means he is either left-handed or ambidextrous. And Benvenuto had no knife. Well, he would have to do without one.

He let a movement show, merely as a stirring in the shadows, when the enemy was only a few yards into the alley; and as the ape-like shadow jerked forward along the stones in a lurching run, he leaped out of his doorway and round the corner, and went to earth in the near side of the second doorway, just in time. Frozen into absolute stillness, holding his breath, he waited with confidence his justification; and it was just as he had reasoned. Seeing the victim start out of shelter and dart round the corner at speed, the hunter at the same speed plunged after him round the corner and hotly on his supposed trail, not anticipating a stop as abrupt as the start had been. His weight carried him past the corner of the doorway before he even knew it was there, and Benvenuto lunged out of hiding and fell on him from behind with added weight which drove him forward from his balance. Benvenuto's left hand accurately found its hold on the other man's wrist, his right arm closed low round arm and body, and clenched there. Had he had a third hand, he might have bothered to use it to cover the grunting, swearing mouth, but most likely he would have found some more practical use for it. Thieves and the accomplices of thieves do not scream for help when attacked in the back streets of Venice or any other city. Not, at any rate, until they are afraid for their very lives, and therefore have no preferences in the matter of who saves them.

They fell together, and rolled along the cobbles, and Benvenuto wound his long legs round the other man's knees, and hung on like a monkey. His opponent was very strong, and had not been rowing at a pressure beyond normal for the better part of the last hour, as he had; and though he pulled back hard on the hand which held the knife, until he thought the starting muscles must surrender and release it, the hard brown fingers held on grimly. Their two locked arms flailed up and down, the blade made sparks along the cobbles, and once turned viciously and gashed Benvenuto in the thigh. The prisoned right arm, tethered at the elbow, heaved and strained and jerked, using its hard bone to press back into Benvenuto's side, and sometimes as suddenly prising forward to try and whip the knife from his other hand, when their convulsions brought it nearer. And all the time his mouth threshing against the stones pronounced unimaginably filthy things about Benvenuto's ancestry. He had more breath to spare than Benvenuto had.

They inched their way painfully along the alley, like a single hurt animal threshing about in distress. Benvenuto felt himself tiring, and was moderately sure that if he did not dispose of the knife in a few minutes more it would stand a good chance of disposing of him. He could not break the hold by sheer strength. Instead, he dragged hard backward upon the resisting arm once more, and suddenly, when its pull against him was at the most desperate, reversed his weight and smashed down hand and knife hard against the cobblestones. The impact of the blow fell on the edge of the knife, and sent a jarring shock up into the fingers which held it, and away went the knife, and clattered a yard out of reach of either of them.

The noise it made seemed great, because the struggle had proceeded in comparative silence. No one had stirred in the alley apart from themselves, no one had looked out from either door or window. Now a girl came out on a second-floor balcony, and looked down on them through her dark hair for one instant in silence, and then slipped quietly back and closed the window quietly and furtively behind her.

Benvenuto shifted his grip, and that was his mistake. If the fingers were nerveless for the moment, the arm was not, it whipped away from him, and the hard bunched body sprang and rolled from under him, and recoiled to grapple with him on different terms. Disorderly, and with more noise, they groped at each other's throats on the ground, and unexpectedly Benvenuto received a knee in his stomach, and curled over upon it, retching. He drove his head hard into the enemy's still vituperative face, and was pleased with the grunt which ended the flow. But he felt sick and winded, and could not keep his hold when his opponent thrust off hard from him, and prised himself to his feet. Benvenuto clawed after him upon the ground, and got a boot hard in the hollow of his shoulder, but he embraced it round the exploding pain, and heaved upward with all his strength, hoisting his enemy backwards to fall with a dazing crash against the cobbles. The crisp, neat, hollow crack his head made against their roundness was music in Benvenuto's ears. He went half-way to meet the recoiling spring, and it did not come. The man lay quietly blinking up at him with an idiotic blank smile, stunned, stirring his hands vaguely along the ground.

Benvenuto fell on his knees beside him, hauled him over on to his face, and dragged his wrists together behind him, quickly, before he could recover his senses. The stringy tie round the victim's own neck provided the nearest means of securing his hands, and when that was done. Benvenuto dragged the jacket back over his shoulders and knotted the sleeves round him for added insurance. The feet began to jerk feebly;

having no other means of hobbling them, he knotted the shoe-laces together and dragged the ends tightly round both ankles. Then, pleased with himself, he looked round for the knife.

He hadn't heard the little boy come out of the tenement doorway, but there he was, squatting on the step with the knife in his hand, and studying them over it with an observant but unexcited stare. About seven years old, dressed in next to nothing, with a black fringe of hair dangling into his grave and elderly eyes, a child not to be surprised by anything, but deeply involved in the manifold significances of everything. He looked back unwaveringly at Benvenuto, and surrendered the knife when a peremptory hand was held out for it. He did not say anything at all.

Benvenuto said: 'You want to earn some money?'

The child looked patient, sceptical, but willing to listen to reasonable offers. He said at length: 'How much money?'

Benvenuto felt in his prisoner's inside pocket, and extracted a well-filled wallet. He was careful not to let the child see how much was in it, but dangled a hundred-lire note in front of him, and suggested sweetly: 'For this you could find me some pieces of rope?'

The child considered silently, and then got up from his heels, and went back into the dark doorway. All was silent inside. In a few moments he came out again and proffered, without a word, a coil of dirty but adequate rope. When he had the note securely in his other hand he finally released his hold upon his merchandise, and sat down on his heels again to watch Benvenuto make an efficient job of tying up his captive. The victim was just coming round, and beginning to mutter confused curses in Benvenuto's direction, but he did not yet know what had happened to him, and before he could focus and use his voice more violently, Benvenuto had diverted an unclean handkerchief and the misused tie to another role, and reduced him to grunts again.

'You still want to earn more money?' suggested Benvenuto. The child waited, alert, impervious and practical.

Benvenuto dangled another hundred-lire note. There was no need to be mean, since the money did not come out of his pocket. He extracted also a thousand-lire note, and displayed it in his other hand.

'On the *rio* there—' he pointed: '—is a gondola with two gondoliers. This man owes them money. Take this and give it to them, and tell them they can go, he does not want them any more. Do you understand?' He watched the large eyes pass unchanging from one note to the other, and perfectly understood what went on behind the eyes. 'Give the money and the message, and you will have a hundred lire, and no trouble. But if you keep the money and do not deliver the message, you will have a thousand lire with trouble, and soon only trouble, and no lire.'

The child silently held out his hand for the thousand-lire note, and went off at a sudden and headlong but still silent run. He was on safe ground. Benvenuto was not likely to vanish, and leave a bound man, obviously of value to him, lying in the *calletto*, and he could hardly take him with him at any very startling speed. The boy was away several minutes, during which the bundle on the ground began to jerk helplessly. Benvenuto watched it, and felt satisfied with his work; and presently the child came back, and held out his hand for his pay.

'When the gondola passes there,' said Benvenuto,

nodding towards the blind end of the alley, 'you shall have it.'

The child, secure in his virtue, sat on his heels again in the doorway, without complaint, but kept his eyes upon the money; and in a minute or two the soft plash of oars rippled past, and they both saw the boatmen and their craft unconcernedly withdrawing. Benvenuto was glad he had not sent more. They must have been paid already, and handsomely, as he had thought, or they would not have gone away for a mere thousand lire, after all the work they had done for these unpredictable patrons.

He handed over the hundred-lire note, which vanished promptly to join the other one, inside the thin leather belt which held up the minute and tattered trousers. There were eight more thousand-lire notes in the wallet, and some small change. Benvenuto, after a moment's thought, rapidly transferred seven of the notes to his own pocket, leaving the last for the sake of appearances. It seemed a pity that all should be wasted.

He took his captive by the folds of his coat, and dragged him gradually along the alley to the waterside. Then he went back gaily through the dark, secret *callette* for his boat, and brought it alongside. From his place on the steps the child watched with remote and large-eyed interest as the inert body was stowed carefully aboard, and tucked out of sight under the seat, with Benvenuto's blouse wrapped round his head. Perhaps in the self-contained little mind which he kept somewhere behind his silence he was wondering to what destination the man under the seat was bound.

He would never have guessed it correctly, however, in a lifetime of wondering. Benvenuto was taking his prisoner to the police.

(2)

It was nearly half-past two when Benvenuto walked into the Pensione Loredano, and looked round him for someone of English appearance. It had occurred to him, in a rapid assessment of the priorities as he threaded his way south, that some confirmation of his story from an independent quarter might be not merely helpful, but necessary, and would save time in enlisting police help for Mab. Especially he did not wish to have the questioning turned too closely in his own direction, in view of the seven thousand lire reposing in his trousers pocket. So he was here looking for the three students. He had tidied himself a little, and put on his blouse again, at the risk of giving his captive a slightly increased chance of uttering some muffled sound; but with his bruised face and the slit in his thigh he remained a slightly bizarre figure, especially as his eyes were glowing with a light of wild contentment and wilder urgency, which did not belong properly to the twentieth century at all.

Phyllida, who was buying postcards from the girl at the desk, noticed him at once, and nudged Punch unobtrusively to call his attention to this very striking specimen. They had just come down from their rooms after a rather sketchy wash, and were waiting for Peter to come in from the *riva,* so that they could make their plans and disperse to their various duties – one to locate and watch the Hotel Truffaldino, one to stay here close within call, one to shake a loose leg through Venice with an eye open for Mab; when this quite unknown and improbably beautiful young man walked in, summed them up in one glittering glance, and said in serviceable English:

'You are the friends of Mab? I have come from her.'

With this for his only credential, he was on perfectly

safe ground. They leaped to meet him without hesitation, their eyes lighting ardently. Phyllida cried joyfully: 'You have? You know where she is?' Punch demanded: 'Is she all right?'

'I do not know where she is now,' said Benvenuto, 'I do not know any longer if she is all right. An hour ago I have left her on the Fondamenta Nuove. We have to find her again, and quickly. It may be there is trouble. We must go soon.'

'We'll go anywhere, now, this minute,' said Punch promptly. 'We've been looking for her. But what's happened? How did you meet her?'

'Has there been trouble already?' asked Phyllida, paling at the sight of the bruises and the unmistakable dark stain lengthening down Benvenuto's trouser leg. 'You're hurt! What's been happening? You must get that attended to, at once.'

'It is nothing,' said Benvenuto scornfully, 'only a scratch. We cannot spare time to notice that. We have to get to Mab, it is all that matters.'

'But that was done with a knife,' she said, unable to keep her eyes from the blood.

'Yes, but she was not then with me. With her I hope all is well. This was only a small fight, and the hurt is nothing. But there is another man following her. A big man, with good clothes and much money. You know him?'

They looked at each other, and both said: 'Yes!' Punch said quickly: 'Look here, sit down a minute in this corner, and I'll get Peter. We'd better all be in on it, and know what we're doing.' He dashed out impetuously to the *riva*, and left them to hide themselves behind the palms in the corner of the minute lounge; and in a few minutes he was back with Peter on his heels, sparkling with eagerness.

Benvenuto told his story. They heard him out without any interruptions, and he told it in remarkably few words.

'I have drawn off this one man, but she is left there in the north, and this more dangerous one follows her still, and already it is more than an hour she is left alone to deal with him. Now I think first I will go back there at once, then I think, no, with you I can go to the police, we shall have better protection for her, and a fast boat. It will take a little time to make them understand, but when they have understood it will be time saved. Alone,' he said with superb simplicity, 'I could not make a very good story for them. It is a little unusual, this affair as I know it. But you can tell what I do not know, and together it will make a case.'

'And you have the torch?' asked Punch, intent.

He drew it from his pocket and showed it. 'Better, I have also the man. He is in my boat. I have his knife. He attacked me, and for that they can take him, and once having him, they can examine well if there is more against him. And he may perhaps talk of that other one who pays him, because it is better at such a pass to look after oneself first.'

'This chap you've got,' said Peter, glowing with excitement ' – there's a good chance we may know him.' He caught Punch's vengeful eye, and said: 'Sparafucile, I bet you!'

'So much the better,' said Benvenuto, rising and hitching at his belt. 'Let us go, then, there is no time to waste.'

He led them out of the pension, and along the *calle,* and through the little *campo,* and round another unobtrusive corner, until he brought them to the dark little *rio* where his gondola rocked gently in the faint wash inland from the Grand Canal. 'Get into the boat! I can take you straight to the police by water, and it will be more private so.' With a gesture of one foot he indicated the bundle which lay uncomfortably in the well, almost out of sight under the seat. 'That is the man. Look at him! There is no one to watch, and if there were, now it does not matter. Do you know him?'

The body, hauled out and propped against the boat's side jerked and contracted viciously under their hands. Benvenuto's knots had held, even though the child's rope had proved to be mouldy and frayed here and there. Grotesquely wrapped up in his own coat, tied together like a fowl in the market, with his mouth lengthened into a wider grin than usual by his scrawny red and blue tie, which he had almost managed to chew through, Sparafucile glared back at them from under his shaggy black hair, and made awful inarticulate sounds, like a deaf and dumb man trying to speak. If looks could have killed, the boat would have been full of bodies.

'That's him!' said Punch positively. 'We all know this chap, all right! I can make a charge against him myself, he laid me out and took the diamonds, up in the mountains.' And yet, when he ought to have been hugging himself in spiteful glee, he found himself almost sorry for Sparafucile. It was right that he should be defeated, but it seemed unnecessary and in slightly bad taste that he should have to look quite so ridiculous. 'Not much point in the gag now, is there?' he suggested uncomfortably. 'Plenty of us here to take care of him. Couldn't we take it out?'

Benvenuto stepped aboard and thrust off with one hand from the wall. The oar creaked in its rowlock, and without more sound they were away. 'As you please!' said Benvenuto, shrugging an indifferent shoulder. 'At least you will not understand what he says. But if you give him teeth he will certainly bite you.'

'That would be only tit for tat,' said Peter light-heartedly. 'Punch bit him once.' He recollected that in fact it had happened only yesterday; it seemed more like a month ago. 'Let's see if you really did mark him,' he said, and plunged upon Sparafucile's pinioned hands, twisting them to bring into sight the third and fourth fingers of the left hand.

There was the silver buckle ring, with a shallow bright dint in it across the tongue of the buckle; and both fingers carried clearly enough the marks of Punch's teeth, on the third only a glancing scratch, but on the little finger two small distinct holes punctured and just healed over on the inner side, and on the outer side a whole semicircle of tooth-marks, broken again in the recent struggle, and oozing blood, where Punch had got a good hold and hung on grimly.

'That identifies him on at least one charge,' said Peter triumphantly. 'They can check with the police at Sopramazzolo about it, if they want to, and it'll all tie up. And we can tie in Monfalcone with him over this business of yours today, and that involves him as a receiver of stolen goods, at the very least.'

'Yes,' agreed Punch, more soberly, 'if only we had our hands on Monfalcone. But we haven't. And we haven't found Mab yet, either.'

He unknotted the tie from Sparafucile's mouth, and withdrew the unpleasing object, whereupon the hand-kerchief was immediately spat out over the side of the boat, and a stream of soft, imaginative and obscene adjectives after it. Peter let go of his hands, and let him hunch his shoulders flat against the boards once more, and there he sat darkly glaring, and indulging his embittered fancy in exploring, unknown to them, the remotest obscurities of their parentage.

Benvenuto said in Italian: 'You are a fool! If you tell

all you know, you will get off very easily. You are only small fry. Do you think he is going to take any trouble for you? Why, then, should you do more for him?'

'I tell you nothing,' said Sparafucile, 'and I tell them nothing. There is no charge you can make good against me, any of you. We have had a fight, you and I, but why, and who began it? Your word is no better than mine, and these frivolities, they have nothing to tell, they were not there. You will get nothing out of me.'

'There is another charge. This boy says you have also attacked him in the mountains, and robbed him. He has already told his story to the police there, and your hands are marked as he has said they would be. Is not that evidence?'

'Did he see me? Does he claim to have seen me? Can one not get such marks in Venice, too? And what is it, this charge? A common assault, and he is unhurt. Is that a hanging matter?'

'You think,' said Benvenuto smoothly, swinging gently on his oar, 'that it will be worth being in prison a little while, because he will pay you well and compensate you when you come out. But it is a mistake. How do you know he would not cheat you, even if you did save him? But in fact he will be in prison himself. You will get nothing out of him to make your future safe. So why not be reasonable, and look after yourself? Let that one take care of his own skin, you take first care of yours.'

'I know nothing of this one you speak of,' said Sparafucile scornfully.

'Don't be a fool! There will be no pickings for you out of the diamonds, they are going back where they belong.'

'You're raving! What diamonds?'

Benvenuto sighed and shrugged. After all, this could

wait; what mattered was to get to Mab, and in pursuit of that objective he was prepared to argue even with the police, if need be. There would be time afterwards to convince this fool where his best interests lay.

'We come into a busier part now,' he said, turning the boat in a soft arc of ripples round the corner of a red-brick garden wall. 'There will be boats. Sit close about him, and do not let him be too clearly seen.'

'What has he been saying?' asked Phyllida anxiously, as they threaded a way through the gliding gondolas of San Zaccaria.

'He says he will deny everything. He will have stories ready, perhaps, to prove he was somewhere a long way from all these happenings, except for this of today. He thinks that if that other one gets off, he will pay him handsomely for a prison sentence. If there were a worse charge – if he were afraid for his life, and not only for perhaps a few years in prison – he might tell a different tale.'

'There might,' said Phyllida, 'be a charge of attempted murder. Would that change his mind, do you think?'

'It is possible. Perhaps even his trust in this other man is not so great as he thinks now. If he cools his head a few days in a cell it may be different with him. But this of the murder I do not know. What is it?'

'It happened in a train, when the diamonds were stolen. But we haven't any evidence, we're only sure it must have been him. And the man didn't die. But the police needn't tell him that, need they?'

'But it will need something more than only being sure,' said Benvenuto regretfully.

'I know! We can't even prove that he was on the train, or even in that part of the country. And he didn't get the diamonds then, really, although I said that was when they were stolen. He made a mistake with them. It's a

complicated business, we shall have to tell you all about
it later.'

'So also said Mab,' he agreed, smiling rather ruefully.

'I wonder,' said Phyllida in a low voice, 'what's
happening to her?'

'I wonder, also.'

Another turn brought them into the *rio* where he
proposed to leave the boat. They untied Sparafucile,
leaving only a twist of rope tight round his wrists, to
make sure that he should not elude them at the very
door; and Peter and Punch between them got him out
of the boat and up the watery steps. It was quiet
there, a tail-end of street with a shop or two, and a
few passers-by with interested but undisturbed faces,
looking after them curiously as they came up into the
calle. Benvenuto tied up the boat, and leaped past them
up the steps.

'You'll have to do the talking,' said Punch, 'and
translate for us.'

'I will do the talking. Only bring him safely,' said
Benvenuto, and stalked ahead of them into the police
office.

(3)

So in the upshot here they all were, on board a large
police motor-boat, boring a way northward through the
water-traffic of the middle afternoon: Phyllida, Peter,
Punch, Benvenuto, and three police officers, besides
the one who was at the wheel. Mab's private army,
hurrying to the rescue.

This time they went north by the easiest and most
direct way, crossing again the sun-blanched space of
the Campo San Zanipolo. The great limpid flats of

the lagoon opened before them, and the level red and white walls of the island of San Michele, glowing in the radiant light, rose secretive and mysterious out of the shining water. It seemed queer to see an island with walls right round it coming sheer out of the sea; but even so, when they came to think of it, did Venice itself arise, created upward laboriously stone by stone in a diversity of buildings, with its foundations under the water. The most elaborate, the most permanent, the most justifiable and lovely artifice of the world.

Under the silver, quiet water the shallows showed faintly flushed with rose and gold. Benvenuto pointed ahead to the next bridge, as they nosed along the *fondamenta*. 'There I landed her. His boat followed me as we planned, but he had landed, and I did not know it.' He reported as much to the policemen once again.

'Good!' said the senior of them, briefly. 'Here we may find someone who will remember seeing her. Such a girl could well be noticed here. Come ashore with us – these your friends also. You will know best how to describe her.'

They drew in at the next landing-stage, and left only one man with the boat. They scattered among the cafés and booths which were open there all the day, and the boatmen along the little jetties, making everywhere the same anxious enquiry.

'Did you see a fair-haired girl in a blue and white checked frock come along here about two hours ago? *Very* fair, with short flaxen hair, and a pink and white skin?'

'She came up from the *rio* there, and began to walk along this way. She had a scarf with a pattern of convolvulus flowers round her shoulders. No stockings, and she wore sandals.'

And when they had gone into every detail without

eliciting any light of remembrance in the willing but puzzled eyes, Benvenuto would add: 'A very, very little girl – so—' His eloquent hands described delicately in mid-air the level and span of Mab's waist, the boyish suppleness of her figure, the height and poise of her blonde head. 'Like a pretty child – very serious—She looks straight before her, and her mouth is a little on one side, but grave. She is beautiful. If you had seen her, you would have remembered.'

They progressed slowly along the embankment with their questions, until at a wooden kiosk of glass and trinkets they struck a spark. The man behind the arrays of beads and ash-trays and figurines was middle-aged, but not yet too old to have an eye for a girl. He smiled fatly, and kissed his fingers.

'I saw her! She stood here by my stall, and combed her hair at my mirrors. A little piece of sweet candy! Too nice a mouthful for that one who was trotting on her heels.'

'You saw him, too?' asked Benvenuto, flaring into excitement. 'He was so close to her?'

'Is she your girl?' asked the stallholder curiously, looking him over with a bawdy eye. 'Well, she did not like that fellow much, either. She took one look at him, and ran. He should be looking worried, not you.'

'What was he like, this man?' asked Benvenuto, making sure.

'Oh, one from the south, perhaps. A fine, tall man in a light linen suit. A lot of money went to make him.'

'He was close on her heels here, it seems,' said Benvenuto rapidly in English to the others, whose eyes were all fixed on him trustingly, like three well-trained spaniels round their feed. And he went on urgently in Italian: 'Where did she go when she ran from him?'

The stallholder nodded placidly towards the edge of

the water. 'To the boat. Not the regular one, but it runs very often at that hour. I know it well. I saw her jump on board, just as it was casting off. It goes to Murano, to the glass furnaces, and then on to Burano and Torcello, a round trip for the afternoon. At about five o'clock they will come back,' he said, chuckling. 'It is not so long for you to wait.'

'And the man?' demanded Benvenuto, flashing with impatience. 'Did he also take the boat?'

'He had no time. I watched, because of the way she ran from him, so I saw all. No, he was too late to jump on board with her, but he took a little motor-boat, and went after her. He was not easily discouraged, that one!' he said, and laughed again slyly at Benvenuto, whose dignity and fire had become quite formidable under this treatment. But there was no time for argument.

He turned on them with a hasty translation, already hurrying them back towards the boat. 'She is gone to the islands with a party of sightseers. He has followed her in a small fast boat, he can join her at any point where they land, unless perhaps she can find there among them someone to help her.'

'Can we overtake them?' asked Punch, striding beside him.

'By this time,' said Benvenuto, rapidly calculating, 'they will be perhaps nearing Burano. They will make a stay there, long enough to visit the lace school, and the church. I think it will be best for us to go straight to Torcello. By the time we can reach it, they will be already there. But come, we shall tell the police this news.'

They conferred again excitedly, and Benvenuto made his point. 'I have done this trip sometimes, I know the times, they will be always ahead of us if we go to Murano at all, it is off the track. Better to go to Torcello at once, then we should arrive very soon after them, while they are still there in the Duomo.'

'Something may happen,' one of the policemen reminded him, 'before they reach Torcello.'

'I know it. But then in any case we cannot prevent it, we can only try to undo it. But if she can avoid him until Torcello, I say we can be there in time to prevent it.'

'Yes, it may be best. If we get no news of them there, it is not far to return to Burano.'

They were off again, heeling out across the limpid grey pearl waters, outward from the city into the infinite soft vaporous spaces which never knew whether to be sea or land or sky; a wonderful warm wind in their faces and their hair, a taut grey wave arching up the side of the boat within easy reach of their fingers, like the muscular warm heaving neck of a grey colt with a white mane. The policemen sat forward, or stood to stare ahead more intently, dreaming, no doubt, of diamonds and promotion. Phyllida sat on the side of the boat astern, drawing her hand along in the water for the love of feeling the strong, concentrated tugging of their counter-current; but she was thinking of Mab. They were all thinking of her, and they were all very silent. There was a certain amount of comfort and peace of mind to be got out of the presence of the police, and the turning over of their cause to its proper guardians; but the fact remained that they had started it, and now Mab was trying to end it alone. They had never meant that to happen.

'He wouldn't hurt her,' said Peter suddenly, staring ahead under corrugated brows of uncertainty. 'Why should he want to? It wouldn't do him any good to hurt her, and I don't think he's the sort to be uneconomical about things, do you? If the worst comes to the worst, he'll only get the diamonds, *she'll* be all right. He's not such a fool as to commit two crimes where one would do. Any more than he'd pay double for things.'

Phyllida said unexpectedly: 'He does pay double for things. Haven't you noticed? He pays double for services of any kind – he tips double. I expect he paid Sparafucile double. It's a kind of investment – establishing an aura round himself. He might think it an investment to be lavish with his little revenges, too. It isn't only to build up the idea other people ought to have of him, it's to build up the idea he ought to have of himself, too.'

'Oh, you're getting too subtle,' protested Peter. 'Besides, if he can get the diamonds, all he'll want then will be to get as far away as possible as soon as possible. He won't waste time being nasty, however much it boosts his idea of himself, when it puts his neck in danger. He'll just get out, the quickest way.'

'She won't give the diamonds up easily,' said Phyllida. 'That's what I'm afraid of. I know her! She looks so pliable, and she's as stubborn as a mule when she takes on something like this.'

'She'll be all right,' said Peter strenuously. 'Of course she'll be all right!'

But he did not look quite convinced himself, and Punch continued to say nothing at all. They looked steadily ahead, waiting already for the first glimpse of the distant islands, as the boat rounded the open gates of San Michele, and swung north-eastward across the lagoon.

CHAPTER TWELVE

MAB AT
MURANO

(1)

MAB examined carefully all her fellow-passengers in
the boat. None of them looked at all English, none
of them was speaking English; only an Italian chatter
surrounded her. 'I'm still on my own,' she thought.

They had left San Michele far behind, slipping down
lower and lower into the mother-of-pearl water; and now
the boat was speeding along a wide marked channel,
studded out with wooden piles, leaning together in
threes and bound with iron. Outside these boundaries
the vast fantastic shallows undulated, pallidly glistening
with the sand just below the surface, and the reflections of wispy clouds floating above. And here on
these bewitched banks, miles from anywhere, men
and women were wading about with nets, with trousers
rolled up and skirts kilted to the knee. After all,
thought Mab crazily, perhaps we could have walked
to Murano.

Although it seemed a beautiful, flat silver emptiness,
it was astonishing how populous the Venetian lagoon
really was. Though Monfalcone's boat dangled behind
them like a pendant on a chain, others of its kind
passed them from time to time at speed. Rowing-boats,
sometimes manned only by tiny boys who stood leaning
their breasts on the oars to move them, lay out softly

in the navigable shallows. Fishing boats rocked at rest, or stirred lazily along the open channels with slanting red-patched sails angling for the wisps of breeze, small dinghies nosing after them like calves after the cow. Copper-coloured fishermen naked to the waist looked up from their work for a moment as the motor-boat passed by, and tipped back their broad-brimmed straw hats to stare incuriously after it for a moment. They seemed to have all time and all space at their disposal.

Mab sat resting in this queerly peaceful interlude, watching the horizon which was Venice fade out behind them, until it was only an almost imperceptible line of blue dividing sea from sky, then not even a thread, only a memory, like the place where an outline in a sketch has been erased. Presently there would be another faint hair-line rising into view ahead of them, and they would draw in to another landing-stage, and get out of the boat, and she would be again as vulnerable as ever she had been; but now, while this respite lasted, Mab relaxed and enjoyed herself. She was surprised that she could do it, but there it was; there was nothing she could do in advance to defend herself, so why worry?

The old woman in black, who was plump and grey-haired and comfortable to look at, offered her a bag of green figs. Not, perhaps, the ideal substitute for a missed lunch, but Mab was grateful, and bit gladly into the soft, warm greenness and the gelid gold within. She said: '*Grazie molto!*' so nicely that the old lady was encouraged to pour out a flood of Italian upon her, but when she found that it was not understood she lost interest, and kept contact thereafter with only an occasional benevolent smile or nod. If only there had been one person who spoke English, thought Mab regretfully, even a very little English, I could have

attached myself to her firmly for the whole trip, and
that would have helped a lot. But no, they knew she
was English, of course – she was quite resigned by now
to the knowledge that it was perceptible at a quarter of
a mile – and if they could have spoken to her in her
own language, any of them, they would have done it
before this. They were well-disposed, they smiled at
her whenever she caught an eye directly; but she was
cut off from them by a barrier which precluded any
intricate confidences. And it was going to take more
than smiles to fence her off from Monfalcone, once
they landed at Murano.

How do you tell somebody who can't understand you
in words that you are being hunted across the lagoon by
a capable and ruthless man who will not hesitate to kill
– why was she suddenly so sure of that? – to get what
he wants?

After that one impudent and rather silly gesture of
hers, she took care to look at him only very rarely,
and with calculated restraint, only a glance at and
through him to the horizon, to observe what he was
up to without seeming to be disturbed about it. He
lounged in his boat very much at ease, watching her
with a cool, composed smile, willing to catch and hold
her eye if she would have let him. It amused him to
amble behind her skirts in this languid manner, waiting
to cut her out from the party at leisure. He had plenty
of patience, and until now it had probably always been
well rewarded.

A new dark line began to grow out of the pearly
distances ahead, first only an accentuation of the faint
blue colour of distance itself, then a flush, then a thin
dark redness, a wound in the soft watery colouring
of this amorphous world; then a positive red-brick
wall, less severely neat than at San Michele, a high,

factory-like wall, a working wall, with no glazed finish, no decorations. A wooden jetty stood out from an open doorway in it, set well above the level of the water. To this the motor-boat drew round with a flourishing curve, and a small middle-aged man jumped up in the bows, and began to deliver what sounded like a brief introductory lecture. As they all listened to him with respect, she concluded that he was something for which they had paid in the eight hundred lire. This, she thought, attending to him with even more devout concentration than that shown by the people who could understand him, is the man to stick to.

He led them, still talking, up the wooden steps, and across the stage to the doorway. Mab, trotting at his heels and paying abject attention to every wave of his hand, looked back only once, to see Monfalcone's boat just lying-to beyond theirs, since there was no room for it to come alongside the stage. The bored boatman steadied it with a hand, while his patron stepped lightly from one boat to the other, and so to the steps. She did not look again. Her business was to stay in the heart of the group, safely immured among innocent people. And her greatest anxiety just now was that they would keep going into places where there would be something more to pay. Twenty-three lire wasn't going to take her very far, and after that the party might stream through some alluring gateway, and leave her naked, so to speak, on the doorstep. And his hand would be smooth and prompt and solicitous at her elbow. She would, to put it plainly, be sunk.

But at this doorway no one asked for any money, to her relief. Through the red-brick wall they went, and along a resounding wooden platform past two open doorways on the right, through which there emerged from nondescript wooden buildings a blaze of colour and light which dazzled her eyes. Now she knew why they had come here. It wasn't the island of Murano they had come to see, but the glass-works and the showrooms of the industry. These last, however, were being saved up until last, fireworks for the finish. Everyone peered and blinked as they drew abreast of these glittering glimpses, but the guide, unshipping his large sun-glasses from his nose, marched straight ahead, past a wilderness of discarded scrap and a rubbish-heap of glass debris, into a rather dark and intensely hot cavern beyond.

There was a small furnace in the middle of the cave, and about it darted half a dozen men and a round dozen small boys of perhaps nine or ten years old, plunging long rods into the orange-hot glow, and withdrawing on them globes of molten glass. These they manipulated nonchalantly the width of the room, twirling the rods and evading one another's backs by casual inches, to roll them vigorously on tables, plunge them slithering into patterned moulds, and occasionally blow down the hollow rods into the mass.

An old man, the star of the show, sat with a pair of pliers in his right hand, drawing out a graceful handle of soft glass at the neck of a vase, and pressing it into the exact shape he wanted with one touch and twist of his tool. The economy of his movements was something of which he was perfectly aware, and he was used to making the most of it for an audience, too. He sat there methodical and leisurely and rather exhibitionist in the middle of a little teeming hell, in which the entering visitors wilted and gasped. The little boys, like the minor imps of this hell, padded about busily with their globes of fire, rolling and dipping and shrilling at one another; their elder devils stalked round them twisting out ropes of molten glass with revolving tongs, even as they manoeuvred their dangerous cargo across the room, the lengthening coils of gold swinging like skipping-ropes.

The cavern, besides its heat, was dingy and dirty, and altogether an unpleasant place; and what the nine-year-olds were doing there was more than Mab could understand. They could not be beyond school age; maybe they were children of some of the workmen, allowed to come in and pass their time here during the holidays; for certainly they did not seem to her to be suffering from any compulsion in the matter. They were working very hard, and their grubby singlets were soaked with sweat, but they were doing much as they liked, having a try at everything, and looking pleased and important about it. They rolled and twisted and plunged, and trotted back and forth to the furnace, with every appearance of enthusiasm, and had little interest in the visitors, who seemed to represent to them merely a fresh series of hazards between themselves and their objectives. A lump of molten glass on the end of a heavy rod, however, used as a lance by a determined child, clears the way with miraculous rapidity.

Nevertheless, something in Mab's mind, some lingering devotion to the conventional views of the English, asserted severely that at that age they ought not to be here, that this dingy oven, even if it baked prodigies of beauty and colour, was no place for children, and would take a good deal of the colour and beauty out of them if they spent their time in it. She looked at them with rather worried and doubtful sympathy, but all their response was to shrill at her importantly to get out of their way, as they pattered across to lower their Chinese lanterns of fire on to the benches, and roll them into long cooling shapes of vermilion and gold.

The guide talked, in a high, loud voice because the

babel of voices and bustle of movement gave him such formidable competition. Mab clung close to his elbow, listening faithfully to every word which fell from his lips, and looking grave and intent, as if she had never been so interested in her life. She didn't understand a word, and even her thoughts were on very different things, but no one would have guessed it from the devoted solemnity and singleness of her attention. This little greyish man was her ticket to safety, and she stuck to him devoutly, as to the very stuff of her life. Covertly from behind his shoulder she saw Monfalcone enter the cavern, and mingle casually with the fringes of the circle; and gently he moved between the darting children and the sweating men, watching everything with a detached and contemplative eye, and sighing at the heat. As he moved round in one direction, so unobtrusively did Mab move round in the other, keeping the mass of the party between them, but never going far from her mascot, the guide.

She couldn't quite make out what he was likely to do. He was in no hurry about it, he seemed to be content to keep her under close observation, without bothering yet to cut her out from the crowd. He was going about it in his own patient way, avoiding the possibility of scenes which might involve these other people. If it came to that, no doubt he would attempt it with grace and efficiency, but he wasn't courting it. And he knew, better than she, these places to which they were bound. She realised that already he knew also at what precise point he would separate her from the flock, and by what means. That was why he could afford to make bright, teasing eyes at her between the scorching globes of glass, and to stretch her nerves by deliberate tantalising advances and retreats. It wasn't to happen here; here he was only amusing himself a little, and continuing the process of wearing her down, nerve by nerve.

She watched, with a fixed and painful concentration, as the old artist in glass, surrounded now closely by the kind of gallery he loved, went rather condescendingly through a few of his tricks. He drew out a few fine strands of glass from a small globule on the end of a rod, bent them into vigorous curves with a negligent touch of his pliers to each, joined on another shred from a rod which an eager boy proffered, and stood up on the bench a small glass horse, three inches high, with arched neck and waving tail. All this she observed as if her life depended on it; but all the time she was thinking: 'This is probably the last place where I can rely on being safe. So if I'm going to make the diamonds safe, it's here I've got to do it. If it comes to one against one I shan't have a chance, so why not face it?'

No use wondering how Benvenuto had fared, though she hoped he was all right, and wished she had had time to thank him properly. No use wondering if he had found the others, and what they could any of them do about it even if he had. No, she had no time for any consideration outside this one problem.

'If he gets *me* into his hands, still he *shan't* get the diamonds. I've got to get rid of them somehow, quickly. I've got to get rid of them here. The next place may be too late.'

(2)

The old man heaved up his long pipe like a trumpet, and blew a little bubble of glass, blew it bigger and bigger until it was bigger than a football, and almost invisible but for a gleam of identifying light here and there. Then he put out his hand, and grasped it, and broke it into little pieces at the touch, so that scraps of it like curious bright cellophanous ash drifted among the spectators. Mab put out her hand with the rest, and caught a fragment of it, so light that it rose from the mere wind of her fingers stirring, so brittle that it shattered when she tried to hold it. Everyone exclaimed in wonder and interest, and the old man smiled and plumed himself like a dingy black bird, and began to make another figure. The little horse stood on the bench arching its beautiful, disdainful neck, a drop of pure water-white coolness in this furnace.

Mab thought: 'Could I post them somehow to Punch at the pension? But it would mean packing them, somehow, and even in the boat, where I might be able to do it without him seeing, I've got no way of packing them. Ashore he'll never let me out of his sight long enough. If I tried to get to a post-office I'd have to leave the party. He'd have hold of my arm inside two minutes.'

No, that was no good. And if she gave someone her last twenty-three lire to post them – even if she had the means to pack them – it would not even be enough. Quite apart from the possibility that she might choose her messenger badly, and lose the diamonds for good and all. She wouldn't have hesitated to entrust belongings of her own to the general good feeling of the Italian people, but picking on a chance ally and giving him this precious trust was quite another matter. It was the honour of all of them by this time, their self-respect, their faith in justice, too much to give away as lightly as a mere personal treasure. Besides, it could be dangerous to the messenger, it might only transfer her own troubles to a perfectly innocent person. It was, in fact, out of the question.

'No,' she thought. 'I might be able to post a card to

Punch, to say where I've put them – in case I don't get back quite according to plan. That's a better idea. I've got postcards in my bag, some I bought in Rocca della Sera, and one or two stamps left, too. I could write that in the boat, and post it or get someone else to post it on Burano. But I've got to ditch the diamonds here, if only I can find a good place to hide them. And I've got to put it over by myself.'

The guide flourished a hand towards the door by which they had entered, and made some further explanatory speech at which the old man gave him a gratified smile. The party began to make its way back to the showrooms, heaving great breaths of the fresher air in the doorway; and there, unostentatiously but suggestively displayed upon a bench close to the door, was a plain glass bowl to receive the practical earnests of their appreciation, which evidently they were expected to show in the usual manner.

It was astonishing, and even a little ridiculous, how guilty Mab felt at the idea of passing by that bowl without putting something in it. There was no compulsion at all, no one even watched to see who did and who didn't pay for his entertainment, but that made it even worse. She kept her twenty-lire note, and dropped in the three lire; but it was a mistake, because she looked up the next minute to see Monfalcone watching her across the bowl with a curious, scalding little smile. He hadn't missed, of course, the significance of her hesitation over the open purse. Very likely he knew exactly how much she had left in it; quite certainly he knew that it wasn't much. Probably he dropped a hundred-lire note over her miserable offering, but it was typical of him that he didn't do it until her back was turned.

She passed on after the others into the showrooms, very much aware of him there almost within touch of her, only perhaps two or three people in between. Now that she had resolved quite finally to separate the safety of her charge from her own safety, she was less afraid of him. Was it possible that what she really feared was defeat at his hands? Not because her own pride was liable to suffer for it, but because it would mean the overturning of her faith in justice, and in the decent ordering of things. And had she, perhaps, accepted some less comfortable but more adult view of the world and events, when she accepted her own responsibility for seeing that, in this one case which had fallen into her hands, things should indeed be ordered decently?

She passed through the open door on the left, into Aladdin's caves. Mere plain wooden sheds outside, inside the whole spectrum broken and sparkling and scintillating in a million points of light. Two large rooms, all their walls lined with shelves, and on the shelves bowls, vases, sets of glasses, great cups, dishes, trays, mirrors, bottles, glass figures, sometimes in whole intricate groups, sometimes singly. Chandeliers dripping with lustres lit the dazzling scene from the ceilings, elaborate candelabra from the walls. In the centre of the room on tables were laid out glass jewellery, ash-trays, more and more glasses and bowls. At first when she entered, Mab was not clearly aware of any of these details, but only of a dazzle and shimmer and blinding brilliance which dazed her eyes, a glitter in which facets were lost, and only the single brightness remained.

She took care to put the nearest table quickly between herself and the door, but Monfalcone maintained his cool distance, and made no attempt to come nearer to her. He watched as closely as ever, and here it was made easier for him by the plethora of mirrors; but she was becoming used to that by now, and her smallness helped her to evade too exact notice. She followed the guide, who knew where every museum-piece in this treasure-house was to be found, and could tell long incomprehensible stories about them all. To these she listened as devoutly as ever, because by that means she could always be snugly in the middle of the group which surrounded him, only her head and shoulders visible to her enemy. All she had to do was keep her eyes fervently fixed on the guide's face, and her expression under perfect control; and her hands, between the warm, plump Italian bodies which surrounded her, could be doing whatever they pleased, and he would be no wiser.

In a corner of the first room, admiring a set of resplendent gilt and blue glasses, she unfastened her brooch unobserved, and tipped the diamonds out into her palm from their bag; then the party disobligingly moved on into the other room to see some new prodigy, before she could tie up the bag again, and she had to trot along with them, clutching the little bundle tightly in her other hand, until the guide burst into song again over a massive cut-glass mirror which had some story attached to it. While he told it, she managed to get the bag tied up again in the same form as before; but she was so afraid of dropping the diamonds that she had to put them loose into her pocket while she pinned the roll back into the breast of her dress. The strain was considerable. She found her hand shaking, and let it lie in her pocket for a few minutes, guarding but not touching the stones, until it recovered its steadiness.

If only she had not had this on her mind, she could have spent the whole afternoon here with great delight. The colours were so delicate and glorious, rose and iris and flushed pinks and ambers and blues; and when they came into the second room a great

294

many of the shelves were full of elaborate figures, dancers and gondoliers, market women and gypsies, shepherds and shepherdesses, animals, trees, flowers, from the wild, stream-lined simplicity of the modern fashion to a brittle filigree delicacy as extreme as that of Dresden china.

Perhaps, after all, complex fancies like these would pall if you lived with them, thought Mab. Such formidable things, for example, as this glass market-girl, a foot high, with a basket of fruit on her hip, might be fascinating to look at here, in this setting, but not to possess, and certainly not to live with. She was one of the filigree ones, sparkling uncomfortably from head to foot, the fruits in her basket so cut and faceted that they flashed like jewellery. Mab liked better the little glass horse which had taken two minutes to make. And perhaps, on the whole, the effect of the whole display was a little too frothy, like endless sundaes instead of food. There was no modern heavy moulded glass, none of the vases thrusting upward in strong, leaf-like pressures, like the best Early English capitals, or curving spirally into an organic life of their own, like a rising wave, such as she had seen sometimes in glass from other countries. Here no one had paid enough attention to the other qualities of glass, its solidity and tensile strength, because they were all preoccupied with encouraging it to glitter. Which it did superlatively. But it can glow, too, if it is allowed, and it can soothe as well as excite.

The guide was still in full spate, but in the middle of his commentary he looked at his watch. Evidently he had one eye on the time-table for the trip, and evidently their time on Murano was almost up. Mab looked from her secure corner at Monfalcone. Yes, his eyes were on her, and at no great range; but he could not come nearer at the moment, even if he wished, because she was well hemmed in by seventeen or eighteen people, pressed closely against the shelf where the market-girl flaunted her dazzle of colours and offered her basket of fruit.

It was now or never. She felt deeply into her pockets, and collected together the little heap of diamonds into her hand. She let her eyes meet his directly, and stare back unsmilingly at his sweet but chilling smile, as she lifted the treasure out of her pocket.

(3)

When they trooped back to the boat the very landing-stage seemed to dance under Mab's feet. Perhaps it was partly hunger, but she felt curiously lighter and less stable; as if, she thought honestly, she had just been sick. A sense of ease, but a precarious one – half the indifferent ease of feeling: 'I don't care now!' And in her situation that was not at all a safe thing to feel.

One thing still held her by a thread of anxiety. Supposing he should suspect something, and fail to follow her away from Murano? She had some bad moments over this when he fell back rather far behind the party as they thudded along the wooden stage and down the steps into their boat; but it would be inviting the very thing she feared to seem concerned about it. All she could do was bet hard on herself, her luck and her acting, and sail away from Murano without a backward glance. And if that did not fetch him after, then in any case she just wasn't up to this kind of thing.

The worst moment was when the extremely bored young boatman in Monfalcone's boat, seeing the trippers already climbing down into theirs, looked up to the stage above them, and seeing no sign of his patron, resignedly cast off his own boat and stood away to permit the larger one to proceed. Then she really felt her heart sinking; but she was like a plunger at the bad moment of a race, who has laid his money, and must let the weight of his belief in himself thrust on his fancy more doggedly than ever when it looks hopeless, simply because in any case there's no going back and laying the money again. So she took her seat in the boat, and trailed her hand over the side, and kept her face resolutely and eagerly seaward until they were well away. Then, because it was either won or lost now, she suppressed the feeling of sickness inside her, and looked back.

The little boat was there, dangling like a pendant on a chain after them, and Monfalcone seated and smiling in it, watching her across the lace and foam of their wake.

Her heart rose like a bird, and a great sigh swelled into her throat. Now she could go on believing in herself. If it killed her! And be damned to him, now she was sure that he should never, never have the diamonds. He never could, short of a long and exhausting search, unless she told him where they were, and that was at any rate one thing which she alone could decide, no matter what he or any other creature might choose to do about it. Obstinacy, not in itself any real relation to courage, could be made to serve the same purpose on occasion.

And so for the next move, since the whole effort had not, after all, lost its point. She fished one of her Trentino postcards out of her bag, and wrote a very brief message for Punch, and addressed it to him at the Pensione Loredano. There were a few stamps left in her wallet, and though she wasn't sure of the inland postage, what was enough to take a card to England must surely be more than enough to see it safely delivered in Venice. She stamped it, and put it in her pocket, so that she could get rid of it quickly at need. If she did not manage to post it, or get someone to post it for her, before Monfalcone made his pounce, she must do something drastic – eat it, if necessary. It was now almost as valuable as the diamonds themselves, but at least easier of disposal.

The high red wall dwindled into the milky-grey water behind them. They headed north-east across the lagoon, between the wide-set piles which marked the channel. Intricate as a road map, the whole lagoon was laced with these deep waters – canals, she remembered, was the right word for them here – between which the pale banks rose glimmering, and lay just below the surface, and the fisherwomen waded about in the warm water with their big nets. In the deep marked roads island freight boats butted along stolidly, and the imperious water-taxis darted flourishing tails of spray.

Mab thought, as she slipped her postcard away: 'How unfair, that I should make this trip just when I can't appreciate any of it!' And she wondered if it would come back to her more plainly, like living it all over again with a quiet mind, when the stress was over.

Another island appeared like a mirage in the hazy air ahead, and grew steadily clearer and larger until they began to coast along another high wall, and Mab thought for a few minutes that they meant to land here. But no, it was only that the canal crept closely about its north-western shore to avoid shallows. This was not Burano, after all, but San Francesco del Deserto. Cypress trees looked darkly over the wall, the first strong green life she had seen, the first stubbornly upright growth in this waste of horizontals, except, perhaps for the masts of the little island ships, which kept so fine a tension against all the mild recumbent levels of quiet sea and floating land.

As soon as they had rounded San Francesco, they saw ahead of them, and at no great distance now, an archipelago of large water-lily leaves of land, no higher than the water, only of a different texture. Then two abrupt points, towers still tiny to the view but wonderfully significant. Drawing nearer to the outspread leaves, the boat began to run along a wide waterway between flat green meadows, and presently there were boats lying-to by the roadside, draped with their patched russet sails. Their naked masts looked unnaturally high. Now the land on the right rose a little, began to feel its solidity, and to bear buildings, tall along the waterside, staring out with rows of windows across a narrow embankment where children squatted playing. A round-headed water-tower looked over the shallow roofs. A narrow *rio*, with a paved *fondamento* along either side, turned in between the houses to bring them into the heart of the island.

A sense of desolation came suddenly upon the air as soon as the boat swung inward, a faint sinking of the heart, a less faint revulsion of the nostrils. Maybe Venice did not stink, but Burano did. The *rio* was dirty, weedy, and afloat with all kinds of rotting rubbish, and a strong and nauseating smell rose from it in the hot sun. The embankments presented a row of house doors, all open, all faded and dingy upon faded, dingy interiors; and the women who sat in them, the very children who played in front of them, looked dingy and faded, too, quite without the grace and insouciance with which the poorest in Venice presented their squalors to the world. This was a miserable and a neglected island, where poverty seemed to have gone beyond the edge of that country where gaiety can live.

The boat put them ashore at the embankment on the left, and they walked along it for perhaps fifty yards, and then a large paved square opened on their left, and on their right a bridge crossed the *rio*. Here were a few fruit-stalls set out under awnings, and a drifting wash of rinds and peelings and leaves and rotting fruit in the waters of the *rio*. Even the displays had a half-hearted and not very clean look about them, and even the cafés in front of the quite well-built shop-fronts did not seem to care whether their checked cloths hung straight on the tables, or whether their wooden chairs were clean. As far as hopes and illusions were concerned, thought Mab, clinging close to the guide's elbow as he turned left into the square, Burano appeared to have had it!

She was well aware that Monfalcone's small boat had brought him beyond the spot where they had landed, though she did not think that noisome *rio* would be much to his fastidious taste. She was not surprised when he stepped ashore near the bridge, at the precise moment when the party was passing, and joined himself unobtrusively to its fringes. She still kept her distance from him, though it was less urgent now. Was there, she wondered, anything he could do about it if he saw her post her card, and guessed that it had some bearing upon what he wanted? What would *she* do, in such a case? Go to the post-office, and say she had dropped something in by mistake, and could it please be recovered? In England that would be at any rate possible; here, and with Monfalcone's ready hand wellstocked with money, no doubt it would be child's play. No he had better not see it go. Either she slipped it in quite unobserved, or she must trust it to someone else; and this, too represented a risk. And yet, if she was not to get back to collect the diamonds herself, she must, for her pride's sake, for her soul's sake, make it possible for someone else to retrieve them.

In the meantime, she followed the guide, and kept her hand upon the card in her pocket. And the enemy, suavely patient, sauntered behind, waiting for his cue.

CHAPTER THIRTEEN

THE ANTIQUITIES
OF TORCELLO

(1)

BESIDES its air of general decay, and a species of fly which bred on the *rii* and could outbite a dozen mosquitoes, Burano possessed a church with a spire almost as far out of the true as the leaning tower of Pisa, and a school of lace-making. It was to the latter that the visitors were taken, presumably because it produced something which could be sold. But as far as Mab discovered on her way there, the island had no visible postbox.

Nor did the lace-school do anything to relieve the deep depression into which she was sinking. They trooped through an open doorway in a building almost opposite the church, and into a narrow white hall; up a flight of stairs, and into two plain, light, white rooms, where two or three black-gowned nuns rustled about softly, and perhaps fifty girls sat stitching lace. The place was cleaner than disinfectant, and yet had a curious, musty odour, perhaps of unnatural silence and submission. The children filled her with a kind of superstitious horror, as if by some aberration of science their childishness had been extracted, and only their physical and mechanical possibilities left. They did not chatter, they did not laugh, they did not even smile, but only looked up warily under their eyebrows, and stared faintly, and went on stitching. Even their gravity had no tension about it, as has the solemnity of children absorbed in what they are doing. They looked at her through a glass, and very darkly. She was no more real to them than they were to her. It was impossible to imagine them running, or dancing, or playing with skipping-ropes. It was impossible to imagine them ever raising their voices, or their eyes without reserve. Difficult, in fact, to imagine them doing anything except sitting here, efficiently and joylessly stitching infinitely fine flowers and leaves of lace into the corners of handkerchiefs. Everything else in them seemed suppressed.

A few older girls and women were among them, but most were about eleven or twelve years old, and the smallest dwindled down to seven or eight. There were several who looked no more than seven. As the visitors moved among them, stooping to look closely at the work they were doing, they raised it meekly, scarcely looking up, scarcely answering when they were addressed. Mab went close, too, her horrified curiosity aroused. She found that some of the smallest girls were merely making practice stitches in pieces of material, with larger needles and more substantial thread; but she also found children of about eight who were apparently fully fledged embroiderers. The intricate point lace they made was done entirely with the needle, and the single stitches they were putting in were almost invisible to her sight. She wondered what happened to the eyes of these infants, after a few years of this work. Even if they worked only a couple of hours a day the effects must be bad. She wondered, too, how soon they began to draw money for their work, since the handkerchiefs they made were on sale at the end of the room at very handsome prices. But these were questions she had no means of asking, and questions which might not be too well received even if she knew the words to express them. And what shocked her almost more than their probable exploitation was their obvious perversion into little automatons, without the natural devilment to whisper and giggle together in the back rows, without a smile among them, without a single bright critical look to spare for those who came in and stared at them.

She backed away from them, ashamed to make one of the starers. It could have been quite different if she had spoken their language, but just to stoop over the wretched children and peer at their handiwork was something she could not do. She backed almost into Monfalcone's arms, and turning her head at the last moment, moved aside half sick with shock towards the table of laces displayed for sale.

For a few minutes she had forgotten him, and there he was quite still and silent and at ease, standing at the top of the stairs, looking absently into the white, bare room. Her eyes as she trembled and turned had looked deeply into his, her skirt had almost brushed him. All her nerves started at the touch, and she knew she was afraid of him; not just excited or nervous, but deep-down afraid. She stood looking at the delicate buttonholes and flowers and motifs of lace on the table, and her knees were shaking under her.

A thin dark woman smiled encouragingly at her across the table, and pointed out the beauties of a spray of white roses, and when she did not look very responsive, offered a handkerchief of which almost one quarter was drawn and stitched into lace. It cost only nine hundred and fifty lire! Mab thought of her remaining twenty, and wanted to laugh, and the next moment felt tired and defeated, and wanted to cry. As if either would do any good! She avoided the bright predatory smile with a pale parrying shake of her head, and moved to another small table, where perhaps she might be left to recover herself in peace.

Outside the window the paved square, this corner of it almost deserted, stretched away to the drunken spire of the church, and beyond was the limpid water and watery light, the spread lily-leaves of meadow with their moist paths round, and even a little round straw-rick marooned among the seas.

Mab looked at this shining placidity, and wanted to get away out of this horrible room full of bewitched children, but her enemy stood at the head of the stairs, and she could not pass him. Maybe it made no difference, maybe she would be wise to forestall his moment, bluff past him and go and post her card as if he didn't exist. Maybe if she made the effort the spell would be broken, and there would be nothing he could do about it. Fears are often like that. But she was still afraid. She could feel the pricking of her flesh when she had brushed near to him. She knew that if she tried to pass by him and go down the stairs he would turn and go with her, and his hand would take her arm. It would not be the time and place he had chosen, but no doubt it would do. When she remembered her sleep on his arm as they drove down by Garda, she felt sick with incredulity. And when she thought of the three she had left behind in their innocence at Rocca della Sera, she felt a hundred years old, and a thousand miles away from them.

And there wasn't any way out, or any way back, except straight through this problem, and straight past this man. She felt that when she reached the others again, if she ever did, she would be so changed that they would not know her.

The party was tiring of the spectacle of maiden

306

industry, and beginning to move again towards the door. One or two of the women bought posies and handkerchiefs. They were delicate and finely made, some of them even beautiful, but Mab thought she could never get any pleasure out of the possession of such a frivolity, never look at it without seeing all those rows of blank, unchildish faces, and lowered eyes, and flying hands. She was glad when the guide collected his flock, and marched off down the stairs. She hoped Monfalcone would move away ahead of them, but he stood and waited for them all to pass, and she gave him the width of the stair, and no glance of her eyes at all. Down they all went, and out at the open door, and she thought flatly: 'That's that! It doesn't look as if I'm going to be able to send this card, after all.'

There was a café just at the corner, with little tables out on the pavement before it; and some of the party moved resolutely towards it, and sat down. Perhaps it was a regular break in the thirsty business of sightseeing, perhaps they were just a little thirstier or a little more determined than most parties. At least they meant to have their drink. And since they were already ordering beer, the rest of the party also drifted to the tables and sat down to wait in comfort, the guide among them. It was a certainty that someone would buy him a drink.

Mab hadn't enough money even for lemonade, probably not enough for soda water. All she could do was stroll unobtrusively through the tables to the shelter of the shop-fronts, and make believe to be interested in them. By which means she rounded the corner into the main part of the square of Burano some fifteen yards ahead of her unhurried pursuer, and ran her shoulder hard into a veritable letterbox on the wall. She stared at it for a second without comprehension, and then whipped her postcard out of her pocket and thrust it into the open mouth as if her life depended on it. It didn't matter who else observed her action and thought her mildly crazy; *he* was still ten yards away round the corner, and even he couldn't see through bricks and plaster. She moved on at the same speed, looking calm and rather tired, and not at all as if she had just delivered her soul. Herself she could hardly believe it, it was suddenly so peaceful. Unluckily she was already becoming used to the treacherous brevity of that peace. She walked across the square by the fruit stalls, and from there she turned to look back at her enemy. Her small face looked pale and drained, and a little astonished. She was smiling.

(2)

From Burano to Torcello is only about ten minutes by boat, and among the archipelago of islands and shoals all the way. This time everything was different. No built-up embankments of houses and shops and stores, no wall, but open green country lying flat to the water, yet bearing hedges and crops like any other meadow land; and vaguely seen to their right as they coasted along this Netherlandish shore, there was a square, high tower, just distant enough, just white enough, to seem to melt into the colouring of the sky.

Mab sat and looked at this tower throughout the crossing, watching it draw nearer and put on detail, because it was, she thought, the most beautiful thing of its kind she had ever seen. It was strong and plain, and almost certainly very old, without any of the graces and flourishes of newer campaniles; just the pleasing shadows and variations brought to life by its indented walls, and five cool dark eyelets of windows strung down the left side of each face, and at the top an open arcade deeply cut under the shallow square red roof. The shadowed eyelids, the slant of the roof, the string of dark loopholes, these came into sight first, then the slight shadows pouring down the fluted walls, which in spite of their elegance had the solidity of a fortress. Mab's eyes, when they had the whole outline clear, could find no fault in its proportions anywhere. It soared nobly, it ceased firmly, it tapered with restraint and boldness, and the eye was satisfied. Afterwards, when she read in Punch's guidebook that one third of its height was supposed to have come down in an earthquake to bring it to this state of perfection, she could well understand nature's gesture of exasperation.

She lost sight of it again for a time as they drew in to the land, and lay rocking gently by a stone landing-stage, at the mouth of a small green *rio*. Green for the right reasons this time, for it ran between a high tow-path on one side, and a green hedge on the other, and its banks were grass and meadow flowers, like any small English survival from the early canal days. Path and *rio* curved gently away inland together, and a few gondolas, manned by wrinkled old men, waited to ferry passengers from the landing-stage to the heart of Torcello.

This was the last stop, thought Mab, and from here they would go directly back to Venice. Here, therefore, whatever the conditions, it was not going to be so easy to evade Monfalcone, because here he did not intend to be evaded. Had he really wished it, he could have made the opportunity at Burano, in those last few minutes when she had crossed the square and cut herself off for a brief time from the party. But he had

309

not wished it. But now here was Torcello, and after that there was no other port of call, unless he meant to shepherd her back to Venice and be there to meet her when she disembarked on the Fondamenta Nuove. And something about the quiet, solitary tranquillity of Torcello certainly suggested to her that for discreet encounters, for little chats with unwilling people, this was much more the mark than Venice.

She no longer looked back very often, because she knew he was there, even knew by this time how he would look when she turned her head. Instead, she bent all her energies on staying in the centre of the party; and when they climbed out of the boat, and it seemed that the greater part of her companions intended to walk along the *rio*, her heart rose with relief, because the path was narrow, and she could still immure herself between pacing couples, where he could not come at her without making himself rather more conspicuous than she believed he would wish to be. But he did not try to reach her. He seemed to have forgotten that she was there. He simply dropped into one of the gondolas, and was rowed up the *rio*, in style under a striped and tattered awning.

If the older people had walked more quickly, she thought, walking would have been a speedier way of reaching the piazza; but since they dawdled, and her speed had to be theirs, the gondolas rippled by and kept a short but lengthening lead all the way. And now, provided they did not have to pay more than twenty lire to gain entry somewhere, she thought, she would stay in the very middle of this innocent group until they stepped aboard again.

The path had not led them very far when its slight curve brought the tower into sight again, nearer now, and with a long red roof close to its foot on their side, and other tiled roofs clustered about it. On the left of the path one or two houses stood, with fruit trees climbing their end walls, and outspread gardens flanking them. On the right, the edge of the path hung over the *rio*, and beyond a rising bank of grass and bushes the meadows stretched away gently. Once, half-way along towards the piazza, the *rio* was spanned by a fairy bridge, a large segment of a circle in stone, almost without parapet, a thin white rainbow. Then there were more houses alongside the path, and here and there women sitting before them with little tables spread with fruit and laces for sale, and lace pillows in their laps. They looked poor enough, the houses were dilapidated, the *rio* had its share of litter and needed cleaning out. But the air of abandonment to misery which had made Burano so distressing was not to be found here. People smiled, and sat placidly in the sun, and ate fruit. The children shouted and ran, and had lively eyes. Torcello might be indigent, but it was certainly not depressed.

The *rio* curved to the left, and another rainbow bridge flew across it to bring them into the little piazza, with fruit gardens on their right hand, and all the antiquities of Torcello spread out before them. Nearest to them, a curious Byzantine church, with an open octagonal cloister all round it, and above the shallow red-tiled roof of this projection, the roof of the church proper climbing by odd-shaped clerestories to the circular lantern, with its flattened conical hat of ridge-tiles. Beyond this, across the piazza, rose the great level roof and powerful, plain, barn-like body of the Duomo, and at the distant end of this, there was the tower itself, whitely immaculate, so near that the batter of its walls was exaggerated, and all but the edge of its red roof had vanished. There were trees, scattered richly among the buildings, and in the grass which covered the piazza there was a stone wellhead, and the broken shaft of a cross.

But no catalogue of its contents could explain the particular atmosphere of Torcello, nor suggest what the tower perfectly expressed, how its roots came up out of the remote and unpathetic past, pre-Venetian, still aware of the Serenissima as a conglomeration of mudbanks hardly higher than the surface of the lagoon. There was nothing sad about it, nothing decayed, hardly any nostalgia for the dead and gone days when the whole civilisation of the Adriatic had stemmed out of this place, and the stones of its threatened city had been carried away to build that other city. Torcello had survived splendour to achieve this serenity, and it did not seem to be aware of any great loss in the change. Some places cannot decline without a kind of death; but Torcello was alive, and vigorous, and still interested in living. Perhaps that was why it had remained so beautiful.

Monfalcone's gondola was just rowing gently back when they crossed the bridge, and the man himself was nowhere to be seen. What did that mean? Her palms pricked. She was sure he could not be far away; but evidently he was not expecting to be returning to his boat yet, or he would have asked the gondolier to wait, and made it well worth his while, too. She had felt his eyes on her for so long that she could feel them still; and if he thought that his apparent absence would lure her from the centre of her unwitting bodyguard, he was very much mistaken.

They crossed the green, and taking a narrow path between the two churches, Santa Fosca on their right, the Duomo on their left, turned in at the wide, dark doorway of the latter: and there was a little elderly custodian in his shirt-sleeves, sitting by a table with a roll of printed tickets. A vast breath of coolness came out from the stone interior, and a glimpse of unexpected Grecian columns, and black and gold mosaics with great, blank, tragic Byzantine eyes. Mab wondered anxiously how much money was required of her, and craned to look at the tickets. Fifteen lire! She could manage it. She was practically in sanctuary.

She was almost the last to take a ticket, only the old lady in black and a middle-aged couple remained behind her. Or so she thought until a long left hand closed gently on her wrist, and put back the twenty-lire note she was just in the act of offering, and the long right hand which was its fellow laid down with equal gentleness a fifty-lire note in its place.

'*E anche il campanile!*' said Teodoro Monfalcone in his soft, caressing voice. '*Due!*'

Her breath stopped for a moment at the touch. She turned her head, and looked blankly into his eyes, which were cool and limpid as his voice. His fingers circled to the under side of her wrist, his arm enclosed hers solicitously. She wondered why she didn't do something about it, now, before it was too late, now, while there were people all round them, and the little man was unconcernedly tearing off two different tickets for them. Twenty-five lire each – the two churches and the tower! Somehow she'd been so sure he would not approach her until no one else was within earshot; and all the time it was as simple as this! Why not? He was the only bilingual person present. He could say what he liked in English, and continue to look at her with that gallant, assiduous, escort's smile, and the only way she could shatter the illusion was by opening her mouth and screaming without restraint, until they sent for a doctor, or a psychiatrist, or an interpreter to find out what ailed her. And now that it came to the point, she couldn't do it. She opened her lips, and that was as far as she got. She couldn't do it!

She wanted to laugh, it was so ridiculous. My God, she thought, for all you know it's your life! Isn't it worth making a scene for? And it was, but the practical difficulties remained, and she couldn't get round them.

'Oh, come!' said Monfalcone, smiling at her. 'You can't really be surprised, after all that's happened.' He took up the two curling blue tickets, and slipped them into the pocket of his jacket, and left his hand there with them. 'I shouldn't cry out, my dear, or try to break away, or do anything spectacular, if I were you. I have a revolver in my pocket here, it is loaded, and if you make it necessary, I am prepared to use it. You might not be the only one to have reason to regret setting things in motion – you would certainly be the first. Do you understand?'

She said: 'Yes.' Her voice was small and numb with shock, and sounded a long way off. In her heart she didn't believe him. He wasn't so deeply tangled with trouble yet that he could afford to add murder, here in broad daylight with a dozen witnesses. Why should he take such a shattering risk? He was bluffing! And yet, she thought, deep within herself, these things happen, you read about them in the papers. Thwarted gangsters get their enemies at all costs, even the cost of their own lives. And for such petty treacheries, too! If it's the last thing I do! – that was the phrase. It would be the last thing Monfalcone would do, but for all that, maybe he meant to do it. And how can you be sure? How can you be sure if a man's bluffing? And unless you're sure, how can you stake your life on it?

No, she didn't believe him – or at most she only

314

half-believed. The terrible thing was that half was quite
enough to keep her silent. His hand was drawing her
away, back from the cool doorway of the Duomo, along
the path towards the cloister wall, and the door in it,
and the tower beyond; and she was going with him,
step by step, slowly but helplessly, like a sleepwalker.
She was letting herself be led away, without a word,
without a cry. And it wasn't even a sensible, sane
fear for her life that kept her quiet, not at bottom.
If she'd even known any of the right words, words
like 'murderer' and 'thief' and 'help', she might have
raised the courage to scream them aloud and risk his
gun and his determination, but all she knew, all she'd
asked for when she had the chance, was '*Prego!*', and
'*grazie molto*', and 'How much are the peaches?' and
'A cup of tea, please!' A cup of tea, my God!

So it was just a scream, or nothing. And twice
she'd opened her lips, and been unable to get out a
sound. It was too fantastic, too silly, too embarrassing
to contemplate. The sun was shining, the little man
was still handing out tickets, nice, dull, commonplace,
comfortable people were gaping at the Last Judgment
on the cathedral wall, everything was sleepy summer
normality. She would have liked to know that she had
the guts to behave like a lunatic when that was the sane
thing to do, but she hadn't – she hadn't! Every nerve in
her shrank from facing it, and her mouth dried up, and
she couldn't scream. Was it possible that people died
for their inhibitions? What an inglorious sacrifice!

'You're behaving very well,' said Monfalcone, sweetly
as to an indulged child. 'I'm glad to find you so sensible,
I should very much dislike having to spoil something
so charming. This way! It's quite near, you see. Just
a little private talk, and everything can be cleared up
very satisfactorily.'

They were through the door in the wall, the cloisters and Santa Fosca fallen behind, the voices receding. She managed to make her throat work. 'Someone else may want to climb the tower, too,' she said.

'My poor child, don't build on it. There is no lift here. One walks, by square ramps inside the walls. I think your companions are too hot to want so much exercise. And too fat.'

They had reached the base of the beautiful tower, and the door in it stood open upon a deep darkness, after the radiance of the sun. He thrust her through into the gloom, and entered after her, and the door closed heavily to behind them. He had her by the wrist still, and for a moment he kept her there in absolute stillness, and she guessed that he was listening for any sound of movement or voices above, to be sure that they had not shut themselves in with some energetic sightseer. The silence inside there was profound, it seemed to grow more intense as the darkness lifted a little from the eyes. The hand at Mab's wrist drew her back a little towards the door. She heard the key turned, a smooth but heavy sound.

While his fingers were relaxed a little, as if to transfer their strength to the right hand which was just forcing the key round in the lock, she tore her hand out of his hold, and sprang away from him towards the dark corner where the ramps began. There was nowhere else to run to, but the moment she was out of his clutch she knew it really made no difference.

She heard him laugh in the darkness beneath her, but useless as it was, she went on, stumbling up the occasional step at the corners, running up the gradual and easy slope of the ramps, wanting only to get away from him. Even five minutes out of his touch, a dozen clean breaths without sight or sound of him, would be worth the effort. She passed by loophole windows at almost every corner now, and their light threaded the wide interior of the tower, with its internal arches on her left hand pressing strongly upward, and their great shadows patterning the opposite walls with solemn and austere shapes. She could still see even things which had no bearing upon this desperate problem of her life and death, and she saw that in its gaunt dark nobility this tower was as beautiful within as without. While she lived, and if she lived, she would never forget it. And strangest of all, it was something which neither he, nor the fear of him, nor weariness, nor hunger, nor any other distress could spoil for her. She loved it as she ran. While there was time, she loved it.

(3)

Sound travelled inside the tower without exaggeration and without diminution. When she paused for a moment and held her breath, she could hear clearly but softly the light, unhurried sound of his feet upon the few steps at each turn, and then the even softer, the almost imperceptible few paces in between. He was coming up after her at a leisurely speed; and as he climbed, he talked to her with all the gentle coaxing of a mental nurse with an amenable patient. He was very sure of himself. Hadn't he every reason to be?

'Don't be foolish, Mab! The case is very simple. You have something I want. I mean to have it. Far better to be sensible, and hand over the diamonds to me without any fuss.'

She did not answer, but only went on climbing, more slowly now because she was a little out of breath, and also because with every step it was borne in upon her more clearly that there was no point in running away. Since every minute gained might, just wildly and laughably might, be useful, she would keep ahead of him as long as there was anywhere to go, but to lengthen her lead was only to waste breath and invite herself into panicky country. She became very quiet, and crept upward close under the wall, slipping quickly past each window, or creeping under it, to cast no shadow which might be seen from below. Occasionally she saw, deep in the well of the tower, a faint shifting of light and dark which marked where he came after her.

'Your manoeuvre with the torch was good,' said the gentle, disembodied voice beneath her feet, 'but not good enough. I know you kept the stones. You do not abandon a job half-done, I know so much about you. Don't think I'm trying to flatter you, my dear girl. It isn't a virtue, any more than a limpet's tenacity is a virtue, it is only a constitutional disability. But it has a certain unreasonably admirable quality about it. And it makes you calculable. I should be grateful for that, at any rate.'

She went on along the wall with shut lips. Her mind was beginning to work again, or at least to be in condition for work; the trouble was that there was nothing for it to do here. Nothing was left of any service except this very obstinacy on which he had just placed his accurate and hurtful finger. But that was still functioning. She hugged the wall, and stole steadily upward.

'If you had not looked like a baffled child,' complained the voice, with plaintive amusement, 'you would never have been allowed to stray so far into my affairs. But one cannot go on for ever making concessions. The time has come to put a stop to you, my dear little girl. We are no longer playing a chivalrous game. Give up the diamonds, and you will be none the worse. You shall even come out of it on the credit side. And after all, you need not be too hard on yourself for wishing to be sensible. Who can blame you? The door is locked, and we are alone here, we have plenty of time to talk things over between us in a reasonable way.'

He was silent for a few moments, so completely silent that she thought he had stopped to listen, but then she saw his vague shadow cross the opposite wall. She thought how easy it would be to stage an accident here, where no balustrade shielded the inner side of the ramps. True, they were wide enough to be very easy of passage everywhere, but two people abreast, and a stumble or a slip on one of the steps, and how easily one of the two might go over the edge into the dark. And what a safe threat to use as persuasion for an unwilling tongue! Except that then the tongue was never likely to tell anything of use again. That had always seemed to her the weakness of threatening people with valuable secrets too far. And in that, too, lay the strength of obstinacy. It looked as if it might be put to the test, with herself as the subject of the experiment. Her hand was further strengthened by another consideration. People who obligingly tell their secrets on the promise of immunity are, on the whole, more likely to go over the edge than those who keep them for further bargaining – for endless bargaining, that is, until they can get their own price.

In fact, so long as she held her tongue she might have some uncomfortable moments, but she was not really very likely to die. And tomorrow the postcard would be delivered at the Pensione Loredano, with the

Burano postmark on it, and other people would begin
to embark for the islands.

'You are not being very kind,' mourned the voice,
tenderly, 'to put yourself to so much needless incon-
venience, and me to so much pain. You are tired after
your long day, I know. Give me the diamonds, like a
sensible girl, and I will take you back to Venice, and
send you home safely to your friends.'

It sounded so true and so delightful that she was
desperately glad she had put it out of her power to
accept the offer. Now she was impervious even to the
temptation to sell out, since she had parted with the
merchandise. She could have laughed about it, if she
had not already regulated herself to silence and evasion.
Even a laugh would have given something away. Time,
time, time, she must lengthen out time – not because
it offered very much help, but because nothing else
offered any.

She had reached the last ramp. She came out upon
an empty floor beneath the roof, with light climbing
in dimly through all the deep, pillared loopholes on
all four sides of the tower. Touching the outer stones
with a white brilliance, it came dwindling inward the
thickness of the walls, and arrived within already grey
and subdued. Only on one side the rays of the sun came
in, narrowly between the thick columns and under the
deep stone brows, and made a pattern of long gold
bars diagonally across the floor. Outside the windows
the radiant air sang, swooping down from the level of
her eyes to the shining shallow waste of water, and the
floating leaves of land; to Burano, a serrated blue line
tapering away in two directions from its lurching spire;
and beyond, to a hairline of horizon wavering along the
shimmer of the sky. She retreated slowly and silently
into the brightest corner of the sunlight, nearest to

life and the warm touch of the day, and there set her
shoulders firmly back against the stone and waited for
him. There was nowhere else to go now, she had arrived
literally at the end of her tether.

Rising slowly out of the dark, his handsome, melancholy face turned in a slow arc until he found her,
standing there silently in the sun with her eyes fixed
on him. She wondered what quality in her look drew
out of him that slow, intimate and secret smile. Maybe
things had not really run down into such a drawn-out,
deliberate tempo as she believed, maybe it was only
some abnormality in her senses which caused her to
stretch her nerves against their imagined slowness. It
seemed to take him an age to mount the last step, and
cross the floor to where she stood.

Looking down at her with the delicate and ominous
smile still on his lips, he held out his open hand in
front of her.

'If you please, the diamonds!'

His voice was as sweet, as respectful, as punctilious
as ever. She looked at the large, shapely fingers which
had guarded her forehead so tenderly from the shaking
of the car by Garda, and shook her head very slightly, as
if it mattered that she should spend only the irreducible
minimum of energy in resistance.

'You make it very difficult for me,' he sighed, and
plucked the small bag from her hand. She watched him
go through its contents, with a blank, detached look,
as if it meant nothing to her; but it did not take him
long, not long enough. The tempo was speeding up
again, she could feel it pounding in her ears with an
ever-accelerating rhythm and a louder beat.

He shut the bag again, quite softly, and put it back
into her hand. She took it, and made no other move.
'How silent you can be,' he said, leaning over her,

'when you please. And why? Like a little animal which thinks it has only to be still and silent to be also invisible? Or perhaps to be taken for one already dead?' His hands explored the pockets of her dress, felt at the cuffs of her short sleeves, and the hems of her scarf, where a small package could be knotted under the folds without showing. She did not draw away, but her body shrank a little wherever he touched, fastidiously, without her knowledge. 'Why do you make a virtue of resisting what is inevitable?' he said with gentle reproach. 'You could have spared us both a distasteful memory, since it is all for nothing. Are you so afraid of me?'

After all, it was a relief to speak. She said: 'No!' in a small and equable voice. It was a lie, but astonishingly it did not sound like one.

'Sometimes, however, it is intelligent to be afraid.' His hand flattened itself, large and intent, against her breast. She felt the fingers start and close, and suddenly she put up her own hand, and tore out the roll of felt and her brooch, and a fragment of her dress all together, and threw them through the loophole at her shoulder. They vanished into sunlight and silence; and Monfalcone laughed.

'My dear child! My poor child! A bag containing twelve large diamonds would fall in a very different manner from this empty one. You should have replaced the weight with a few pebbles if you wanted to be convincing. Nor would you choose to throw it out from the side nearest to the water, if it had anything of value in it. If it had been enough for you only to spite me, you could have dropped them into the Rio di Palazzo and saved all this labour and distress. But that was only a part of what you wanted, wasn't it? Not even the greatest part.'

His hands completed the exploration of her little, thinly-clad body, perfectly detached, like an artist's hands, even touched with cold delicacy her hair, but it was too short and fine to make a hiding-place for anything so bulky. Her shoes were only fragile sandals, a few straps, and nothing more.

'Where are the diamonds?' he asked, taking her by the shoulders in his two large hands.

'I haven't got them,' she said simply. 'I left them behind a long time ago.' She drew her head back against the wall from his too near, too sombre eyes, and turned her face aside. Now there was really nowhere else to run, except back into her silence, which it had been pleasant to leave for a time. His face, inclining towards hers slowly, was slipping out of focus. His weight was on her breast like a cold, insistent caress. 'A long time ago,' she said in a declining sigh, and closed her eyes.

'Where are they?' he repeated, with no stronger emphasis underlining the softness of his voice. His right hand slid up from her shoulder and stroked its way deliberately into the hollow of her throat, and closed there slowly. His weight lay more heavily on her. Her ears with the pressure of his fingers began to fill with sound, a steady, distant roaring like the sea on a reef. His left arm closed hard round her shoulders, and the fingers gathered slowly the fine fall of her hair, and pulled her head back.

Pain began like a cloud, all round her head. She opened her lips, struggling for breath, and suddenly his lips were on them, closing down in a long, soft, calculating pressure. His fingers about her neck relaxed, only holding her with a strong, stroking motion, and in her hair she could feel his touch now hardly lighter than before, yet immeasurably changed. From a gesture of deliberate cruelty to a luxury of equally deliberate gentleness, as the eyes change in an unchanging face, and make everything new.

She felt weak with surprise, and with something else which was more than surprise; and to hold herself upright from the dizziness of astonishment she groped upward and clung to his coat. His voice with a note of chiding sweetness was whispering in her ear: 'Little fool! Little bird! Did you not sleep on my shoulder once, and feel safe? I have never killed. Do you think I should begin with you? A creature so dainty, so charming, so sweet! Did I not fight fair? And now at the end you are afraid of me!'

His lips were smoothing her cheek when she heard the first sound from below. The blood pounding in her ears did not shut it out any longer. Rapid feet on the stairs and the ramps, a long way down, a lot of feet running upward with a long way still to go. Then she understood. Everything! Even things which had been going on inside herself, and had made no sense until now.

Her hands relaxed from him, she didn't need support any more. She stood there in his arms listening to her army running up the stairs, and waiting for him to realise that in this crisis he was no longer effective. She was almost sorry for him, because it was going to come as a shock. She ought to have been so easy.

'As if I could hurt you!' he whispered against her cheek. 'Since I looked at you across the supper tables in that little inn, I have been more than half in love with you. Did you not know it then? And now you would believe that I could harm you for a few diamonds!'

Oh, yes, it might so easily have succeeded, all the more because in the heart of its monstrous perversion of truth there yet existed a truth to be perverted. His fine, treacherous hands stroked softly down the line of her cheek and chin, and drew ice after them where they had intended fire. But she knew still, in the touch of their bitter cold, how the fire would have melted her senses. She stood curled inwardly into her own humiliation and pain, too sick as yet to speak or move.

The quiet small sounds came furtively up the well of the tower, hurrying to her assistance. Who but the police could have extracted thus silently a second key for the locked door? Other visitors desiring to enter would have knocked and shouted. These had tried the door quietly, obtained entry quietly, quietly climbed the ramps, not to precipitate what they had come to prevent. With his hand at her throat, deafening her with her own blood, Monfalcone had heard and understood the first stealthy sound. And acted upon it! Give him his due, he had acted upon it without hesitation and with his usual bold efficiency. Only, as it happened, she had somehow developed the ability to connect pretty quickly herself.

She could translate him fluently now. 'I have never killed. Do you think I'm going to begin now, with nothing to gain but a little emotional satisfaction, and probably my life to lose? When I can turn your susceptible little heart round on to my side with a kiss, and a little soft talk? And find a dozen legal loopholes to slide through before I ever come to trial on the evidence they can put together without you! What an unpractical fool I should be to kill you instead of kissing you! It's cheap enough, because you're really not displeasing!'

There were no treasons too mean for him, not even that.

She stood patiently and weakly, drooping her hands and turning her face aside, waiting for him to take his arms away from her. She said in a dim, indifferent voice: 'You're wasting your time. I've heard them, too.'

He stood back from her then, and his hands quitted her slowly. They stood looking at each other for a minute, while the feet climbed nearer.

'Yes,' he said, with a dark smile, 'yes – I see you have. I should have known you better! Yes, the victory seems to be yours – if you can keep it – or if the law can keep it for you.' He put his hand suddenly into his pocket, and took out the revolver, and weighing it thoughtfully in his palm, selected the loophole which gave most nearly on the water, and hurled the gun out with the full swing of his body and arm behind it. 'Your word against mine,' he said smiling crookedly at her. 'It's hardly worth the argument, is it? And if I could not buy you, believe me, my dear little enemy, there are many people and many institutions which can be bought. Not in the currency I offered for you,' he admitted wryly, 'but in coin I can part with more easily.'

He came to her slowly across the sun-barred floor, and touched her forehead again, lightly, tenderly, with his finger-tips. 'I am glad,' he said, in a very low voice, 'that you were not for sale.'

She only looked at him mutely with her wide, exhausted violet eyes, and had nothing to say. The footsteps on the stairs were drawing near now, voices breathing indistinguishable English and Italian, in elusive whispers.

'They will be anxious for you,' said Monfalcone. 'Shall we go down and meet them, or wait for them here?'

She did not believe she could have walked across the floor yet, but it made no difference now, for they were very near, and she could hear Peter's voice in a breathless half-tone, and a few quiet words in authoritative Italian. She said, in a queer, clear, loud voice, towards the head of the ramps: 'It's all right! We're here, both of us. Everything's all right!'

All the voices sprang out of their dark abstinence together, Phyllida's high above all crying: 'Mab!' and again: 'Mab, are you OK?'

'Yes,' she said, suddenly thawing with the relief of it, and began to tremble uncontrollably. 'Yes, I'm fine!'

The whole sound of their advance, voices and steps and movements, surged over the level of the last ramp like a triumphant wave, and out they came gushing from the dark, Benvenuto, three policemen, Punch, Phyllida, Peter. She tore herself away from the wall, and took a step towards them, and light and shadow in a fierce, whirling pattern went round before her eyes, and the stones heaved, but she reached somebody's hard, indignant, unsubtle arms, and was held up bodily for a minute, until the strength came back into her legs. Phyllida was hugging and feeling at her, crying passionately: 'He hasn't hurt you, has he? You're really all right?' Peter was coaxing cheerfully and excitedly: 'It's all over now, old girl, you beat him hands down. He can't touch you now!' And there was Punch's gruff voice adjuring them not to hustle the poor girl, and Benvenuto's calling her by soft, cajoling Italian names, *mia diletta, mia piccola, bionda mia*.

Other voices, too, in rapid and satisfied Italian, and then the calm, familiar tones of Monfalcone's voice, not protesting, not complaining, but cool, civilised, amused, calculating already, she thought, by what modulations of bearing to disarm certainty, and create doubts in these first witnesses, with what subtleties of law to sidestep a conviction, or at the worst whittle down a sentence. And how to conserve untouched the profits up to date, for capital to be exploited afterwards. What circumstances could not be persuaded could be bought, and what could not be bought could be arranged. She did not doubt that he would come out of it almost without a scratch.

She opened her eyes, and lifted her face from the willing shelter of Benvenuto's shoulder, and looked at Monfalcone. Two of the policemen had a light but wary hold on his arms, but somehow he contrived to stand as easily between them as if he had hired them as a bodyguard. He was looking steadily at her, and his eyes were full and calm, and gently melancholy, as once when he had looked at her across the width of the dining-room at the Albergo Monte Gazza, and startled her out of the bud.

But was it fair, was it fair, that she should open her unpractised petals for the first time to such a bitter frost?

CHAPTER FOURTEEN

THE APPARATUS
CANNOT LIE

(1)

THEY led her solicitously down the ramps, up which she had scrambled without aid or comfort; and half-way down she was discovered to be shaking with sobs. The revelation dismayed everyone, and produced demonstrations of anxiety, indignation and affection which, to tell the truth, she would have been glad to do without. It was nice to be surrounded by friendly people again, after so long of being alone and on the run, but her equilibrium had been too severely upset for her to be able to respond in normal ways, especially as none of them could ever be expected to understand why she was crying. So they got no thanks for their well-meant efforts; and this was all the more disturbing because Mab had never been a temperamental little thing, but on the contrary exceedingly reasonable.

'But, darling, what's the matter?' pleaded Phyllida in dismay. 'He *didn't* hurt you, did he? And it's all over now, he didn't get the diamonds, thanks to you – he *didn't*, did he?' For of nothing as yet was there any certainty, no questions had been asked or answered. 'Mab, where *are* they?'

'No, of course he didn't get them,' sobbed Mab. 'I know where they are, we've only got to go and pick them up. I sent a p-postcard from Burano – to tell Punch, in case I didn't get back—'

'Oh, darling! But you are back, and it's all over now. So that's all right, isn't it? And Mr Galassi is better, and going to get well – they told us in Sopramazzolo. So there's nothing in the world left to cry about. You're safe, and we beat him – at least, *you* beat him. Goodness, you ought to be on top of the world!'

'I know!' said Mab. 'I'm all right, really. I wish you wouldn't fuss!'

'Well, but whatever is the matter then? We don't like to see you like this.'

'If you must know,' said Mab, goaded into making something the matter, something which could be understood on the old terms, 'I'm bloody hungry!' Because it was such unfamiliar language, she said it very loudly and fiercely, but surprisingly she herself got some comfort and stability out of it, because she was reminded how very true it was; and once remembered, in spite of emotional complications this healthy, earthy distress proved not unimportant. 'I haven't had anything to eat since breakfast,' she said plaintively, 'except a green fig. And I didn't even stop for much breakfast.'

They installed her in a small room in the museum below the Duomo, and gave her wine and cakes and fruit, and let her rest and recover herself; and presently she told the whole story of her small odyssey for Benvenuto to translate to the police. She did not have to see Monfalcone again, for more police had already been called to take him back to Venice; and the last memory she had of him was of that backward glance over his shoulder as he was led down from the tower, and of a hollow darkness of regret in his eyes. Which might or might not be as false as all the rest of his demonstrations of regard and liking for her, but which nevertheless existed in her memory with a power of its own.

'He had a gun,' she said. 'He threatened to kill me if I didn't go with him quietly, but when you were all coming up the tower he threw the gun out of the window, on the side nearest the water. But maybe they could still get it back. He said it was my word against his, and more or less suggested I should say nothing about it, because he could tell a better tale, and I shouldn't be believed against him.'

'This he will certainly try,' agreed Benvenuto, with a curl of his lip, 'and who can say he will not succeed?' But he translated faithfully. 'They ask, did he touch you? Did he try to hurt you?' And his voice and his eyes burned with a far from impersonal concern upon this point. A faint flush touched her cheeks, which had been pale with weariness until now.

She had made up her mind to tell the exact truth about everything which had happened, but when she reached the momentary darkness and the traitorous kiss it was quite impossible to keep to her resolve. She could not speak about that. What difference could it make? If they had a case against him, it would not be helped or hindered by leaving out this one crime, since it had been committed against no one but herself.

'He took my bag, and searched it, and then my pockets, and then he was feeling through my dress, and I snatched the roll of felt out, and threw it out of the window. I hoped he'd believe the diamonds were still in it, and run down to recover them, but he only laughed. He knew by the way it fell that they weren't there. And when he kept asking me, I told him I'd left them behind a long time ago, but I wouldn't tell him where.' She looked down into her cupped hands from the furious brightness of Benvenuto's eyes. 'And then he took hold of me by the throat, and by my hair, and – well, I don't know what he would have done – I suppose he meant to hurt me, enough to make me tell him, but then he heard you on the ramps. And he – he let go of me, and began to say that we'd have a hard job to make a case against him that he couldn't talk or buy his way out of. And then you came, and it was all over.'

Benvenuto called Monfalcone by the ugliest name he knew in English, which was quite ugly enough to make Mab blink and Phyllida suppress a chuckle. Then he translated what she had told him, but with his eyes still on the round dark bruises on her throat, and still inflammably angry. 'I am sorry,' he said on his own account, 'that it is with the other one I have to deal, and not with this man.'

'It doesn't matter now,' she said, 'it's all over.'

The policemen wrote busily, and asked more questions. 'They wish to know,' said Benvenuto, 'if you now feel strong enough to come back with them to Murano, and then you shall be taken home. But if you are not yet fit for this, you must rest a little longer here.'

'Oh, no, I'm quite all right!' She rose readily, even eagerly. 'We ought to go quickly, I'd hate it if someone else found them before we could get there, and I'd wasted all my trouble.'

Long since, Mab's tourist party had left Torcello, reassured that their missing member was accounted for and in good hands, and Monfalcone's young boatman, informed of his passenger's misfortunes, had shrugged an indifferent shoulder and gone off home with an equanimity which announced clearly that he had been paid in advance, and handsomely, for the time he had already spent in that gentleman's lavish services. This return trip on board the police boat was very different from the outward journey. Mab sat between Peter and Benvenuto, the centre of everyone's assiduous attention, even the policemen making her occasional compliments, for if all went well at Murano they would be fairly in line for promotion.

It was early evening, and the sunlight over the lagoon was turning to a deeper, richer, less dazzling gold, when they lay rocking alongside the jetty at Murano once again. Mab led the way up the steps, and along the wooden platform to the doors of the showrooms; and suddenly, hearing all those eager feet thudding along where she led, she was visited by the first astonished prick of pleasure in the situation. The centre of the scene, the heroine of the hour! Her smile had begun rather wryly, but it flowered into a real smile when she plunged into the corner where the glass market-girl stood on her shelf. After all, it was fun, in a way, to be made a fuss of like this, and fun to be the only one who knew where to find a fortune.

She herself had difficulty in seeing the diamonds, and suffered a momentary stab of horror at the thought that, after all, someone else had discovered and removed them. But her tentative fingers soon found the first, then the second, then the third, there among the glitter of glass fruit in the basket. She felt into every cranny, and counted them solemnly into her palm until they were all there: twelve pieces of strange, cold, glassy fruit, bluish white, a handful of greed and coldness of heart. The glitter of the market-girl's basket was hardly diminished at all by the loss of them.

She put them into the hand of the nearest policeman, and stood looking at them with a slight, worried frown. 'It was the best I could do. I had to get rid of them quickly, and I thought the best place to hide a small glitter was in the middle of a bigger one. And it's all right – they're all there!'

But it had already ceased to be fun to her. Somehow the sight of those fragments of precious ice turned everything to reality again. They were the symbol of her victory, perhaps; they represented Signor Galassi's peace of mind, his self-respect and theirs, and a minor triumph of human decency. Or perhaps only of human pigheadedness! How could she tell? She knew only that she had done the only thing she could do, and by luck and faith it had come off; and that nothing was as simple as it had seemed to be, not even right and wrong. In this fight as in every other, the ground had shifted imperceptibly during the battle, and brought her up in the moment of victory facing in a very different direction, seeing a very different landscape, from that which she had expected.

She was glad when the diamonds were carefully stowed away in a deep official pocket. She was glad that Signor Galassi should have them back, more than glad that he should be on the road to recovery; but without a scratch or a visible injury she had paid more for those pebbles than anyone else would ever realise, and more than she liked to remember. And she didn't want to see them any more.

'Could we go home now?' she asked, looking up at Benvenuto with a suddenly tremulous face. 'I'm awfully tired. Ask them if we can go home now.'

(2)

They had to spend half an hour more in the police office, clearing up a few last points, and confirming their statements through the offices of an interpreter somewhat more orthodox than Benvenuto had proved. Then they were dismissed with profuse compliments and thanks to their pension.

'All the same,' said Benvenuto regretfully, as they walked back slowly through the iris and gold evening to the Riva degli Schiavoni, 'it is as I have told you. That one with the knife, he will not say one word, he refuses to know anything. I have heard them talking about it. He says he was in Milan when your friend was hurt in the train, and he will bring people to prove it. They are sure he lies, and all these his witnesses will lie, but how to show it? And this Monfalcone is very well able to look after himself. If his man will not speak, they will have trouble ever to get that one into prison, I think.'

Mab thought so, too. He had as good as told her so. But in a way it had ceased to be as important to her as she had thought, because whether he won or lost on this throw, the fact remained that he had bid for something, and had not got it. Not only the diamonds. Oh, no, much more than that. He had staked on his ability to twist her round his finger, and lost on it; and though she was well aware that she had not mattered in the least to him at the beginning of the experiment, something told her that she had mattered very considerably from the moment it went wrong. Presently she might even be able to get some satisfaction out of that conviction, but just now there was no flavour about it that was not bitter.

She let them all talk, but she herself was very quiet. Benvenuto took her arm stealthily as they chattered, and she suddenly remembered how very little he had said, for such a volatile and voluble young man, about his own end of the adventure.

She looked up into his pleased dark face, and said, in a low voice: 'I've never thanked you properly for everything. I don't know what I'd have done without you. And after all, it was you who got hurt.' She looked down ruefully at the slit in his trouser leg, dark and stiff now with dried blood. 'I'm so sorry! Is it very painful? I do wish you'd stopped to have it dressed.'

'It is quite nothing,' said Benvenuto gaily. 'It is already closed, and I am very healthy, and it will heal quickly. Do not think of it.'

'And – and I'm afraid you've lost a lot by helping me, too. I'm awfully sorry!'

'Do not be sorry!' he said happily. 'I have been very joyful to help you, and I have not lost anything.' She would have been disposed to argue about this, remembering the overturned easel and the swearing painter, but there was something about Benvenuto's smooth, inward smile which warned her not to dig too deep behind it. He looked a little like a small boy who has been at the jam, but has washed his face in time. 'And now,' he said blithely, 'you will be able to come in my gondola, and I shall show you Venice. If you are not too tired, come tonight! For an hour only, before you sleep? You need not walk even the length of one *calle!* Tomorrow we shall go all together to look at the city, but tonight I wish to take you on the Grand Canal alone. You shall rest and be cool, and no one shall trouble you. Will you come?'

She thought willingly and warmly of all she owed him, but her senses were even more strongly aware of his voice lowered cajolingly to reach no ear but hers, and of a simple, sensuous flattery in every note of it which was something her outraged nerves wanted achingly, and would not let her refuse. 'Yes,' she said, 'I'll come. After dinner I'll come out on to the *riva* and look for you.'

'I shall be there waiting,' he said, and went off in high delight to his obscure and crowded little tenement home in the back streets inland of the Rialto, to make himself even more beautiful than usual.

So there they were once again, the four of them at table together, newly washed and brushed, and uncommonly hungry. It was too early yet for them to do their best and most voluble talking over the excitement of the past two days; that would come later, back in England, when they had got everything in focus, and inexhaustible relays of audiences to stimulate them to an imaginative presentation of events. For the moment they were content to have lived through it all, and to be able to relax after it, and to have Venice still before them.

Punch had changed for dinner, but Peter had been in too big a hurry to do more than tidy himself and brush his dusty shorts. Venice had virtually no dust, but the journey from Rocca della Sera had left him plenty. Even the brushing, however, had been done in a rather sketchy fashion, and never reached his hip pocket, or he might have recognised the flat paper rustle from within. As it was, his re-discovery of the films did not take place until almost the end of dinner, when he choked over his wine at some joke of Phyllida's, and failing to find a handkerchief in his side pocket, felt round to the back one in case he had at some time secreted one there. And there instead was the flat blue packet, now warmly curved to the outlines of his anatomy; he fished it out and stared at it blankly for a moment before he even recognised it.

'Good lord, I'd forgotten all about these! What with all this excitement, I've never even looked at them.'

'Which are they?' asked Mab, with warming interest.

'The last ones from Savoy, and some from the train, and then in Rocca della Sera. I collected them this morning, just before we came away. Only this morning! Fantastic! It feels at least a month ago.' He began to shuffle them out from the packet, and pass them

337

round the table. 'Here's a good one of you on the Grande Chible, Mab. But this one I took from the station when we left isn't so hot. All foreground and telegraph wires – I ought to have known! Pity, because the light just then was wonderful.' He passed it on, and bent a critical eye on the next. His eyes opened wide; the quick, incipient grin faded before an expression of white, wild astonishment. 'Good *lord!*' he breathed, and sat staring for a moment in absolute silence.

'What's the matter?' asked Punch.

'Nothing's the matter! Everything's marvellous! Everything's almost too good to be true!' He turned the snapshot about and dangled it before their eyes. 'Recognise a friend of yours, Phyl? And I've got another of him, too, I remember.' He relinquished the print which was causing him so much incoherent gratification, and scrabbled frantically among the rest until he found the second one. 'Not quite so good as that, but it's not bad, either. And anyhow, it's the other profile, so it'll be useful.' He presented it with a triumphant flourish. 'Well?'

No one would ever again be allowed to curse Peter for upsetting time-tables over photographs; never, at least, without being reminded of this affair, and put to helpless silence. The three attentive heads leaned closely together over two prints in slightly faulty focus, owing to the cramped quarters in which they had been made: Phyllida and the Customs man of the Turin train, leaning on the window-rail and studying passionately the Valle di Susa and the little town of Chiomonte. On the one they had been caught in right profile, he the nearer of the two, leaning assiduously at her shoulder; on the other, in left profile, and part of his face slightly obscured by her hair, but to make up for that there was a very clear close-up of his left hand and arm, spread solicitously round Phyllida with the fingers resting on the rail; and the most noticeable thing in the picture was the heavy silver ring on his third finger. It was made in the shape of a buckled thong, and there could not be very many exactly like it in Italy, unless the law of averages had gone a little mad.

'Sparafucile!' said Punch, gaping at the dark profile and the obtrusive ring. 'Good lord, and it *is!* When you come to look at this chap closely—'

The trouble was that they never had looked at him closely until now. Not even Phyllida could have told you more about him than that he was of medium height and very broad-built, dark, and decorated with a large moustache. With the longish dark hair combed into shagginess, the well-trained moustache frayed into a brigand's brush, the skin darkened, the pierced ears sporting rings, the beautifully white and even dentures removed, the well-kept nails massacred, and a liberal allowance of stain or dirt to treat his hands and arms – with these alterations, and the substitution of ancient and greasy working clothes for the smart uniform, there went Sparafucile as large as life.

All the apparatus he would need in addition would be very considerable acting ability, which evidently he had at command. And nothing can change a man so much as the assumption of the whole manner of a different kind of man.

'Well, here goes his alibi,' said Punch, 'proof positive he was on the train, and in that coach, too, just after the attack. There couldn't be a better way of boarding a train at Modane and travelling in to Turin than in Customs uniform. Why, he'd be virtually invisible all the way, except to the real Customs man. That's the only person aboard that he'd have to stay away from, and I dare say they'd studied out beforehand exactly where *he* was likely to be during the journey.'

'My God!' breathed Peter, remembering, 'he must have been half out of his mind when I slipped past them to take this first snap, and almost went into old Mr Galassi's carriage. What a half-hour we must have given him between us!'

'Nothing to the one he's got coming!' said Punch, sweeping up the photographs in a large hand. 'Come on, Peter, we're going back to the police station. If this doesn't make him open his mouth and blow every gaff there is to blow about Monfalcone, nothing will!'

But it did, before the evening was over. For after all, a master who has promised adequate compensation for a short retirement from the world can hardly expect the same loyalty when the period of retirement shows every sign of being lengthened by many years. In such circumstances it is every man's duty to consider his responsibility to himself, and make provision accordingly. Once things have reached this stage, it may even be as well to go the whole hog in involving your employer, because the longer he is under restraint, the longer will you be safe from any little counter-measures he may be contemplating.

Phyllida was sitting alone in the lounge, rather reluctantly mending socks, when Peter and Punch came back at last, fat and glossy with satisfaction, erupted round the obscuring palm-trees, and fell upon her in a rapture of news.

'It worked! He's still talking, and by this time Monfalcone hasn't got a shred of reputation left to his name. This wasn't the first robbery he's planned. Old Sparafucile's busy as the dickens now, pulling his own chestnuts out of the fire.'

'All those he can haul out without burning his fingers

too badly,' supplemented Punch, grinning. 'It seems he's been working for him for some years on this sort of job – no small fry, connoisseur stuff every time. They've found out his real name, but I can't remember it, and it seems he used to be an actor, in a small way—'

'And Monfalcone's got a most efficient information service working among the Italian firms with agencies in France. The police are having a marvellous time there now.'

'In fact,' said Punch, 'it looks as if we've got him, after all.'

'Yes, and, Phyl, they were on the line to Turin, and they let us speak to the hospital.' Peter's eyes were brilliant with excitement in a vividly flushed face. 'We talked to Francesca Galassi. She says he's going to be all right. She says he's better today, already, but you can't think, she says, what a difference this will make to him. They let her tell him about it, though he isn't fit to talk much yet. She said he remembers us, and he wanted to thank us, and she says if ever we come to Turin, please come to see him, he'd like us to. He told her to say: "*Mille grazie!*"' He laughed, and hugged Phyllida briefly and dangerously, escaping impalement on the darning needle by a narrow inch, and looked round with sudden bright realisation. 'Mab gone to bed?'

Phyllida readjusted Punch's sock on her fist, and smiled at it pensively. 'Well, not exactly! She's gone out.' She slanted a complacent glance up at their obtuse masculine astonishment, and laughed. 'Don't look so flabbergasted! Couldn't you see it coming? She's out somewhere with Benvenuto.'

Brought up short against the complexities of women, 'I thought she said she was tired!' said Peter blankly.

'So she was, what's that got to do with it? She'll come back pretty well asleep on her feet, but never mind,

341

he'll do her good,' said Phyllida, placidly clairvoyant. 'That boy is exactly what Mab needs tonight. Better-looking than Monfalcone, younger and more attractive than Monfalcone, at least as good at flattering a girl's ego, and as safe and sweet as the other one wasn't! What could be better?' said Phyllida blithely, tugging the needle through a congested spot of mending in the heel of Punch's sock.

They looked at her in awed silence; sensing which, she remembered rather late that she was thinking aloud upon a subject which might reasonably be expected to be beyond the scope of mere males, and from the bewilderments of which, perhaps, it was rather her part to shield them. 'Never mind!' she said kindly, as nurses say it to children beset by the first daunting premonitions of maturity. 'You'll be able to tell her all your news about Signor Galassi, and everything, when she comes in. About midnight, I expect!' added Phyllida with a small, sweet smile, and reached for the scissors.

(3)

They left the gondola at the Rialto, and wandered up into the glitter and blaze of the Mercerie, still alive and still doing business at eleven o'clock at night.

Everything was all right with Benvenuto. The whole episode had been as satisfying as wine to him, he had expressed himself joyously, had fought and been pursued, had rescued his little friend and seen the downfall of her enemies, and, into the bargain, had seven thousand unexpected lire in his pockets. About the origins of which, however, it was expedient that she should know nothing. He was very happy, he was entirely happy. He peered into shop windows beside her, and desired to make some gesture as large as his heart's satisfaction.

'What do you like best,' he asked, with a sweep of his free hand, 'among all these things? What would you like best to have?'

The busy night traffic of the Mercerie flowed noisily about them as she considered. There were so many ravishing things that it was difficult to make up one's mind, but she settled at last on a large oval brooch of painted shell in a coiled silver filigree setting, less exuberant than most of its kind. The painting, too, was no doggedly exact copy of a Canaletto or a Tiepolo, but an entirely modern and rapid sketch of the tottering little palaces on the Grand Canal. 'Look – that! Isn't it lovely? So economical, and so pretty. Don't you like it, too?' It had all the lucidity of Venice's colouring, made iridescent by the curve and texture of the shell, which was used in its design instead of being solidly painted over; and the more she looked at it, the more she liked it.

'Come along!' she said, taking Benvenuto determinedly by the arm. 'If I stand here looking at it much longer I shall really want it badly. I might even break the window and grab it. After all, I haven't been leading a very law-abiding life the last two days. Better take me away, before we get into trouble.'

Benvenuto drew her, instead, towards the shop doorway. 'Come with me, and we shall buy it,' he said, smiling down at her with a triumphant glitter of white teeth and shining eyes.

'Don't be silly, it costs over two thousand lire! I've got just twenty, and I don't suppose you've got very many more yourself.' But she was only laughing at him gently, having entirely failed to take the suggestion seriously; and she was really alarmed when he towed her towards the doorway still, in a teasing, smiling silence. She hung back in concern and distress. 'Oh, now, really! Don't be silly! *Please*, Benvenuto! I don't really want it. Please, if you don't behave I'm going to be angry!'

Inside the shop, as a small, alert man darted out of its recesses to accost them, she released herself from Benvenuto's hand, and said in a warning undertone: 'I won't take it, if you do! You can't afford it, and I'd much rather you kept your money, it would please me better than any present. Oh, *please* be sensible!'

He bought it, all the same; and when they were again outside, in the cool gay glitter of the streets, she had to let him pin it into the torn neck of her dress. It was even more charming at close quarters than through the glass of the window, but she couldn't help thinking rather of the large hole it had just made in Benvenuto's pocket, and there were tears in her eyes.

'You are angry?' asked Benvenuto reproachfully. 'You don't like it now?'

She looked up quickly. 'Of course I'm not *angry* – I do like it, I like it awfully, and it's sweet of you to give it to me. Only I – I didn't know you meant to buy anything, really, or I shouldn't have told you what I liked. It's such a lot of money.'

'Today,' said Benvenuto, fingering the almost five thousand lire which still reposed in his pocket, 'I can afford to be a little reckless, and you must not be anxious, for I have money enough. It is very fitting, you do not know how fitting, that I should give you a remembrance of today.' And he smiled down at her through his long lashes a sleek, bright, satisfied smile.

Mab's thumbs pricked again. She felt that she ought to ask him exactly what he meant by that, but then she thought, no, better let well alone; and she was growing sleepy, and it was really too much trouble. She moved on contentedly within the protecting circle of his arm, and stroked the silky surface of his gift with pleased, gentle finger-tips. And all she said, after all, was:

'It's lovely! I shall often wear it.'

'In England, too, you will wear it?'

'Yes, I shall.'

'To remind you of Benvenuto, who adores you?'

He said it with conviction, and she knew that it was true, if only for the few days that she remained here to trouble and delight him. But it was all right, neither he nor she would die of it.

'Yes,' she agreed serenely, and was shattered by a child's wide, candid yawn.

He was wonderfully sure-footed; his instincts always stopped him, accurately balanced, short of the step too far ahead, and the inconvenient question. When everything was so agreeable, and they were both enjoying it so much, why examine the potentialities ahead? There was plenty of time for them to develop, without letting them encroach upon tonight.

'Come,' said Benvenuto tenderly, 'I will take you home in the gondola, and you will have a long sleep. Tomorrow I will give you something better. Tomorrow I will give you Venice! Have you not earned it?'

A selection of bestsellers from Headline

FICTION

DANCING ON THE RAINBOW	Frances Brown	£4.99 ☐
NEVER PICK UP HITCH-HIKERS!	Ellis Peters	£4.50 ☐
THE WOMEN'S CLUB	Margaret Bard	£5.99 ☐
A WOMAN SCORNED	M. R. O'Donnell	£4.99 ☐
THE FALL OF HYPERION	Dan Simmons	£5.99 ☐
SIRO	David Ignatius	£4.99 ☐
DARKNESS, TELL US	Richard Laymon	£4.99 ☐
THE BOTTOM LINE	John Harman	£5.99 ☐

NON-FICTION

ROD STEWART	Tim Ewbank & Stafford Hildred	£4.99 ☐
JOHN MAJOR	Bruce Anderson	£6.99 ☐
WHITE HEAT	Marco Pierre White	£5.99 ☐

SCIENCE FICTION AND FANTASY

LENS OF THE WORLD	R. A. MacAvoy	£4.50 ☐
DREAM FINDER	Roger Taylor	£5.99 ☐
VENGEANCE FOR A LONELY MAN	Simon R. Green	£4.50 ☐

All Headline books are available at your local bookshop or newsagent, or can be ordered direct from the publisher. Just tick the titles you want and fill in the form below. Prices and availability subject to change without notice.

Headline Book Publishing PLC, Cash Sales Department, PO Box 11, Falmouth, Cornwall, TR10 9EN, England.

Please enclose a cheque or postal order to the value of the cover price and allow the following for postage and packing:
UK & BFPO: £1.00 for the first book, 50p for the second book and 30p for each additional book ordered up to a maximum charge of £3.00.
OVERSEAS & EIRE: £2.00 for the first book, £1.00 for the second book and 50p for each additional book.

Name ....

Address ....

....

....